Readers are gripped by
VANISH
Rated ★★★★★

'Engrossing'

'A terrifyingly great read'

'Excellently constructed and keeps you
enthralled'

'Brilliant. Nail biting. Fast moving'

'Difficult to put down'

'Exciting and compelling'

'A big page turner that had me holding my
breath and reading into the night'

'Totally absorbing from the start
to the very last page'

'Excellent – worthy of more than 5 stars'

www.penguin.co.uk

VANISH

When medical examiner Maura Isles looks down at the body
of a beautiful woman she gets the fright of her life.
The corpse opens its eyes...

'A horrifying tangle of rape, murder and blackmail'
Guardian

THE MEPHISTO CLUB

Can you really see evil when you look into someone's eyes?
Dr Maura Isles and detective Jane Rizzoli
encounter evil in its purest form.

'Gruesome, seductive and creepily credible'
The Times

KEEPING THE DEAD

A mummified corpse is brought before Dr Maura Isles for scanning.
She's been dead for centuries, or so the academics believe –
until the image of a very modern bullet is revealed...

'A seamless blend of good writing and pulse-racing tension'
Independent

THE KILLING PLACE

Dr Maura Isles has vanished, seemingly into thin air.
Detective Jane Rizzoli's search leads her to the snowbound
village of Kingdom Come, where the person who was watching
Maura now lies waiting for her.

'Bone chilling. Gerritsen plays on our fears'
Daily Mail

THE SILENT GIRL

A severed hand is found in a Chinatown alley in downtown Boston, reopening a horrifying murder-suicide case from nineteen years before. Detective Jane Rizzoli and Dr Maura Isles must track down and defeat an old evil, before it kills again . . .

'Suspense doesn't get smarter than this. Not just recommended but mandatory'
Lee Child

LAST TO DIE

Three children, orphaned by seemingly motiveless and extreme acts of violence, are placed in a boarding school for traumatized children. But Detective Jane Rizzoli and Dr Maura Isles soon discover that even this place of safety cannot shut out a gathering threat . . .

'Intelligent and unrelentingly realistic'
Sunday Express

DIE AGAIN

Six years ago a group of travellers set off on an African safari – but only one woman returned. Now it seems the 'safari killer' has resurfaced in Boston. Detective Jane Rizzoli has to go and visit the sole survivor in Africa, and see if she can convince her to face death once again . . .

'Gerritsen proves she is still at the top of her game . . . fantastically gripping'
Karin Slaughter

I KNOW A SECRET

A mysterious figure watches from the sidelines as Rizzoli and Isles race to find a killer. She has the answers they're looking for – but she has to stay quiet, if she wants to stay alive . . .

'Expect a white-knuckle ride to very dark places'
Paula Hawkins

LISTEN TO ME

Detective Jane Rizzoli and Forensic Pathologist Maura Isles are investigating the gruesome murder of a nurse, whilst also protecting a young student from a stalker. But immersed in their day jobs, will they lose sight of something sinister happening much closer to home?

'Absolutely first rate – readers will be thrilled and delighted by this new Rizzoli and Isles outing'
Shari Lapena

Tess Gerritsen's stand-alone thrillers are:

GIRL MISSING
Her stunning first thriller
The first body is a mystery. The next body
is a warning. The final body might be hers . . .

'Gerritsen is a better writer than such founders of the
school as Kathy Reichs and Patricia Cornwell'
Observer

HARVEST
How far would you go to save a life? A young surgical
resident is drawn into the deadly world of organ smuggling.

'Suspense as sharp as a scalpel's edge'
Tami Hoag

LIFE SUPPORT
A terrifying and deadly epidemic is about to be unleashed.

'If you like your crime medicine strong,
this will keep you gripped'
Mail on Sunday

THE BONE GARDEN
Boston 1830: A notorious serial killer preys on his victims,
flitting from graveyards and into maternity wards.
But no one knows who he is . . .

'Fascinating . . . gory . . .'
Mail on Sunday

PLAYING WITH FIRE
What if your child wanted you dead?

'I defy you to read the first chapter and not singe your
fingers reading all the rest'
David Baldacci

THE SHAPE OF NIGHT
Ava's isolated new house is full of long-held secrets,
but is the creeping sense of danger coming from within its walls,
or from somewhere else entirely?

'This will haunt you. Riveting!'
Shari Lapena

VANISH

Tess Gerritsen

PENGUIN BOOKS

TRANSWORLD PUBLISHERS
Penguin Random House, One Embassy Gardens,
8 Viaduct Gardens, London SW11 7BW
www.penguin.co.uk

Transworld is part of the Penguin Random House group of companies
whose addresses can be found at global.penguinrandomhouse.com

Penguin
Random House
UK

First published in Great Britain in 2005 by Bantam Press
an imprint of Transworld Publishers
Bantam edition published 2006
Bantam edition reissued 2010
Penguin paperback edition published 2023

A CIP catalogue record for this book is available from the British Library.

ISBN
9781804991312

Typeset in Sabon by Falcon Oast Graphic Art Ltd.
Printed and bound in Great Britain by Clays Ltd, Elcograf S.p.A.

The authorized representative in the EEA is Penguin Random House Ireland,
Morrison Chambers, 32 Nassau Street, Dublin D02 YH68.

Penguin Random House is committed to a sustainable future
for our business, our readers and our planet. This book is made
from Forest Stewardship Council® certified paper.

Once again, to Jacob.

VANISH

One

My name is Mila, and this is my journey.

There are so many places where I could begin the story. I could start in the town where I grew up, in Kryvicy, on the banks of the Servac River, in the district of Miadziel. I could begin when I was eight years old, on the day my mother died, or when I was twelve, and my father fell beneath the wheels of the neighbor's truck. But I think I should begin my story here, in the Mexican desert, so far from my home in Belarus. This is where I lost my innocence. This is where my dreams died.

It is a November day without clouds, and large black birds soar in a sky that is bluer than I have ever seen. I am sitting in a white van driven by two men who do not know my real name, nor do they seem to care. They just laugh and call me Red Sonja, the name they have used since they saw me step off the plane in Mexico City. Anja says it's because of my hair. *Red Sonja* is the name of a movie which I have never seen, but

Anja has seen it. She whispers to me that it's about a beautiful warrior woman who cuts down her enemies with a sword. Now I think the men are mocking me with this name because I am not beautiful; I am not a warrior. I am only seventeen, and I am scared because I do not know what happens next.

We are holding hands, Anja and me, as the van carries us, and five other girls, through a barren land of desert and scrub brush. The 'Mexican Package Tour' is what the woman in Minsk promised us, but we knew what it really meant: an escape. A chance. You take a plane to Mexico City, she told us, and there will be people to meet you at the airport, to help you across the border to a new life. 'What good is your life here?' she told us. 'There are no good jobs for girls, no apartments, no decent men. You have no parents to support you. And you, Mila – you speak English so well,' she told me. 'In America, you will fit in, just like *that*.' She snapped her fingers. 'Be brave! Take a chance. The employers will pay your way, so what are you both waiting for?'

Not for this, I think, as endless desert rolls past our windows. As Anja huddles close against me, all the girls on the van are quiet. We are all beginning to wonder the same thing. *What have I done?*

All morning, we have been driving. The two men in the front say nothing to us, but the man on the passenger side keeps turning to give us looks. His eyes always seek out Anja, and I do not like the way he stares at her. She doesn't notice it because she is dozing against my shoulder. The mouse, we always called her in school, because she is so shy. One glance from a boy will make her blush. We are the same age, but when I look at Anja's sleeping face, I see a child. And I think: I should not have let her come with me. I should have told her to stay in Kryvicy.

At last our van leaves the highway and bumps onto a dirt road. The other girls stir awake and stare out the windows at brown hills, where boulders lie scattered like old bones. In my hometown, the first snow has already fallen, but here, in this winterless land, there is only dust and blue sky and parched shrubs. We roll to a stop, and the two men look back at us.

The driver says in Russian: 'It's time to get out and walk. It's the only way across the border.'

They slide open the door and we climb out one by one, seven girls, blinking and stretching after the long ride. Despite the brilliant sunshine, it is chilly here, far cooler than I expected. Anja slips her hand into mine, and she is shivering.

'This way,' the driver orders, and he leads us off the dirt road, onto a trail that takes us up into the hills. We climb past boulders and thorny bushes that claw at our legs. Anja wears open-toed shoes and she has to pause often, to shake out the sharp stones. We are all thirsty, but the men allow us to stop only once to drink water. Then we keep moving, scrambling up the gravelly path like ungainly goats. We reach the crest and start sliding downward, toward a clump of trees. Only when we reach the bottom do we see there is a dry riverbed. Scattered on the bank are the discards of those who have crossed before us: plastic water bottles and a soiled diaper and an old shoe, the vinyl cracked from the sunlight. A remnant of blue tarp flutters from a branch. This way have so many dreamers come, and we are seven more, following in their footsteps to America. Suddenly my fears evaporate, because here, in this debris, is the evidence we are close.

The men wave us forward, and we start climbing up the opposite bank.

Anja tugs on my hand. 'Mila, I can't walk anymore,' she whispers.

'You have to.'

'But my foot is bleeding.'

I look down at her bruised toes, at the blood oozing from tender skin, and I call out to the men: 'My friend has cut her foot!'

The driver says, 'I don't care. Keep walking.'

'We can't go on. She needs a bandage.'

'Either you keep walking or we'll just leave you two behind.'

'At least give her time to change her shoes!'

The man turns. In that instant, he has transformed. The look on his face makes Anja shrink backward. The other girls stand frozen and wide-eyed, like scared sheep huddling together as he stalks toward me.

The blow is so swift I do not see it coming. All

at once, I am on my knees, and for a few seconds, everything is dark. Anja's screams seem far away. Then I register the pain, the throbbing in my jaw. I taste blood. I see it drip in bright spatters on the river stones.

'Get up. Come on, get up! We've wasted enough time.'

I stagger to my feet. Anja is staring at me with stricken eyes.

'Mila, just be good!' she whispers. 'We have to do what they tell us! My feet don't hurt anymore, really. I can walk.'

'You get the picture now?' the man says to me. He turns and glares at the other girls. 'You see what happens if you piss me off? If you talk back? Now walk!'

Suddenly the girls are scrambling across the riverbed. Anja grabs my hand and pulls me along. I am too dazed to resist, so I stumble after her, swallowing blood, scarcely seeing the trail ahead of me.

It is only a short distance farther. We climb up the opposite bank, wind our way through a stand of trees, and suddenly we are standing on a dirt road.

Two vans are parked there, waiting for us.

'Stand in a line,' our driver says. 'Come on, hurry up. They want to take a look at you.'

Though befuddled by this command, we form a line, seven tired girls with aching feet and dusty clothes.

Four men climb out of the vans and they greet

our driver in English. They are Americans. A heavyset man walks slowly up the row, eyeing us. He wears a baseball cap and he looks like a sunburned farmer inspecting his cows. He stops in front of me and frowns at my face. 'What happened to this one?'

'Oh, she talked back,' says our driver. 'It's just a bruise.'

'She's too scrawny, anyway. Who'd want her?'

Does he know I can understand English? Does he even care? I may be scrawny, I think, but you have a pig face.

His gaze has already moved on, to the other girls. 'Okay,' he says, and he breaks out in a grin. 'Let's see what they've got.'

Our driver looks at us. 'Take off your clothes,' he orders in Russian.

We stare back in shock. Until this moment, I have held on to a wisp of hope that the woman in Minsk told us the truth, that she has arranged jobs for us in America. That Anja will babysit three little girls, that I will sell dresses in a wedding shop. Even after the driver took our passports, even as we'd stumbled along that trail, I had thought: It can still turn out all right. It can still be true.

None of us moves. We still don't believe what he has asked us to do.

'Do you hear me?' our driver says. 'Do you all want to look like *her*?' He points to my swollen face, which still throbs from the blow. '*Do* it.'

One of the girls shakes her head and begins to

cry. This enrages him. His slap makes her head whip around and she staggers sideways. He hauls her up by the arm, grabs her blouse, and rips it open. Screaming, she tries to push him away. The second blow sends her sprawling. For good measure, he walks over and gives her a vicious kick in the ribs.

'Now,' he says, turning to look at the rest of us. 'Who wants to be next?'

One of the girls quickly fumbles at the buttons of her blouse. Now we are all complying, peeling off shirts, unzipping skirts and pants. Even Anja, shy little Anja, is obediently pulling off her top.

'Everything,' our driver orders. 'Take it all off. Why are you bitches so slow? You'll learn to be quick about it, soon enough.' He moves to a girl who stands with her arms crossed over her breasts. She has not removed her underwear. He grabs the waistband and she flinches as he tears it away.

The four Americans begin to circle us like wolves, their gazes roving across our bodies. Anja is shaking so hard I can hear her teeth chatter.

'I'll give this one a test drive.' One of the girls utters a sob as she is dragged from the line. The man does not even bother to hide the assault. He shoves the girl's face against one of the vans, unzips his pants, and thrusts himself into her. She shrieks.

The other men move in and make their choices. Suddenly Anja is wrenched away from me. I try to hold on to her, but the driver twists my hand from hers.

'No one wants *you*,' he says. He shoves me into the van and locks me inside.

Through the window, I see it all, hear it all. The men's laughter, the girls' struggles, their cries. I cannot bear to watch; neither can I turn away.

'Mila!' Anja screams. 'Mila, help me!'

I pound on the locked door, desperate to reach her. The man has shoved her to the ground and forced apart her thighs. She lies with her wrists pinned to the dirt, her eyes closed tight against the pain. I am screaming, too, my fists battering the window, but I cannot break through.

When the man finishes with her, he is streaked with her blood. He zips up his pants and declares loudly: 'Nice. Very nice.'

I stare at Anja. At first I think that she must be dead, because she does not move. The man doesn't even glance back at her, but reaches into a backpack for a water bottle. He takes a long drink. He does not see Anja come back to life.

Suddenly she rises to her feet. She begins to run.

As she flees into the desert, I press my hands against the window. *Hurry, Anja! Go. Go!*

'Hey!' one of the men yells. 'That one's running.'

Anja is still fleeing. She is barefoot, naked, and sharp rocks are surely cutting into her feet. But the open desert lies ahead, and she does not falter.

Don't look back. Keep running! Keep . . .

The gunshot freezes my blood.

Anja pitches forward and sprawls to the ground. But she is not yet conquered. She struggles back to her feet, staggers a few steps like a drunken woman, then falls to her knees. She is crawling now, every inch a fight, a triumph. She reaches out, as though to grab a helping hand that none of us can see.

A second gunshot rings out.

This time, when Anja falls, she does not rise again.

The van driver tucks the gun in his belt and looks at the girls. They are all crying, hugging themselves as they stare across the desert toward Anja's body.

'That's a waste,' says the man who raped her.

'Too much trouble to run them down,' the driver says. 'You still have six to choose from.'

They have tried out the merchandise; now the men begin to barter. When they have finished, they divide us up like livestock. Three girls in each van. I do not hear how much they pay for us; I only know that I am the bargain, the one thrown in as part of another deal.

As we drive away, I look back toward Anja's body. They have not bothered to bury her; she lies exposed to the sun and wind, and already hungry birds are circling in the sky. In a few weeks, there will be nothing left of her. She will vanish, just as I am about to vanish, into a land where no one knows my name. Into America.

We turn onto a highway. I see a sign: US 94.

Two

Dr. Maura Isles had not smelled fresh air all day. Since seven that morning she had been inhaling the scent of death, an aroma so familiar to her that she did not recoil as her knife sliced cold skin, as foul odors wafted up from exposed organs. The police officers who occasionally stood in the room to observe postmortems were not so stoic. Sometimes Maura caught a whiff of the Vicks ointment that they dabbed in their nostrils to mask the stench. Sometimes even Vicks was not enough, and she'd see them suddenly go wobbly and turn away, to gag over the sink. Cops were not accustomed, as she was, to the astringent bite of formalin, the sulfurous aroma of decaying membranes.

Today, there was an incongruous note of sweetness added to that bouquet of odors: the scent of coconut oil, emanating from the skin of Mrs. Gloria Leder, who now lay on the autopsy table. She was fifty years old, a divorcee with broad hips and heavy breasts and toenails painted a brilliant pink. Deep tan lines marked the edges of the bathing suit she had been wearing when she was found dead beside her apartment swimming pool. It had been a bikini – not the most flattering choice for a body sagging with middle age. When was the last time I had the chance to put on my bathing suit? Maura thought, and she felt an absurd flash of envy for Mrs. Gloria Leder, who'd spent the last moments of her life enjoying this summer day. It was almost August, and Maura had not yet visited the beach or sat by a swimming pool or even sunbathed in her own backyard.

'Rum and Coke,' said the young cop standing at the foot of the table. 'I think that's what she had in her glass. It was sitting next to her patio chair.'

This was the first time Maura had seen Officer Buchanan in her morgue. He made her nervous, the way he kept fussing with his paper mask and shifting from foot to foot. The boy looked way too young to be a cop. They were all starting to look too young.

'Did you retain the contents of that glass?' she asked Officer Buchanan.

'Uh . . . no, ma'am. I took a good whiff. She was definitely drinking a rum and Coke.'

'At nine A.M.?' Maura looked across the table at her assistant, Yoshima. As usual, he was silent, but she saw one dark eyebrow tilt up, as eloquent a comment as she would get from Yoshima.

'She didn't get down too much of it,' said *Officer Buchanan*. 'The glass was still pretty full.'

'Okay,' said Maura. 'Let's take a look at her back.'

Together, she and Yoshima log-rolled the corpse onto its side.

'There's a tattoo here on the hip,' noted Maura. 'Little blue butterfly.'

'Geez,' said Buchanan. 'A woman her age?'

Maura glanced up. 'You think fifty's ancient, do you?'

'I mean – well, that's my *mom's* age.'

Careful, boy. I'm only ten years younger.

She picked up the knife and began to cut. This was her fifth postmortem of the day, and she made swift work of it. With Dr. Costas on vacation, and a multivehicle accident the night before, the cold room had been crammed with body bags that morning. Even as she'd worked her way through the backlog, two more bodies had been delivered to the refrigerator. Those would have to wait until tomorrow. The morgue's clerical staff had already left for the evening, and Yoshima kept looking at the clock, obviously anxious to be on his way home.

She incised skin, gutted the thorax and abdomen. Removed dripping organs and placed them on the cutting board to be sectioned. Little by little, Gloria Leder revealed her secrets: a fatty liver, the telltale sign of a few too many rums and Cokes. A uterus knobby with fibroids.

And finally, when they opened the cranium, the reason for her death. Maura saw it as she lifted the brain in her gloved hands. 'Subarachnoid hemorrhage,' she said, and glanced up at Buchanan. He was looking far paler than when he had first walked into the room. 'This woman probably had a berry aneurysm – a weak spot in one of the arteries at the base of the brain. Hypertension would have exacerbated it.'

Buchanan swallowed, his gaze focused on the flap of loose skin that had been Gloria Leder's scalp, now peeled forward over the face. That's the part that usually horrified them, the point at which so many of them winced or turned away – when the face collapses like a tired rubber mask.

'So . . . you're saying it's a natural death?' he asked softly.

'Correct. There's nothing more you need to see here.'

The young man was already stripping off his gown as he retreated from the table. 'I think I need some fresh air . . .'

So do I, thought Maura. It's a summer night, my garden needs watering, and I have not been outside all day.

But an hour later she was still in the building, sitting at her desk reviewing lab slips and dictated reports. Though she had changed out of her scrub suit, the smell of the morgue still seemed to cling to her, a scent that no amount of soap and water could eradicate, because the memory itself was what lingered. She picked up the Dictaphone and began to record her report on Gloria Leder.

'Fifty-year-old white woman found slumped in a patio chair near her apartment swimming pool. She is a well-developed, well-nourished woman with no visible trauma. External exam reveals an old surgical scar on her abdomen, probably from an appendectomy. There is a small tattoo of a butterfly on her . . .' She paused, picturing the tattoo. Was it on the left or the right hip? God, I'm so tired, she thought. I can't remember. What a trivial detail. It made no difference to her conclusions, but she hated being inaccurate.

She rose from her chair and walked the deserted hallway to the stairwell, where her footfalls echoed on concrete steps. Pushing into the lab, she turned on the lights and saw that Yoshima had left the room in pristine condition as usual, the tables wiped down and gleaming, the floors mopped clean. She crossed to the cold room and pulled open the heavy locker door. Wisps of cold mist curled out. She took in a reflexive breath of air, as though about to plunge into foul water, and stepped into the locker.

Eight gurneys were occupied; most were awaiting pickup by funeral homes. Moving down the row, she checked the tags until she found Gloria Leder's. She unzipped the bag, slipped her hands under the corpse's buttocks and rolled her sideways just far enough to catch a glimpse of the tattoo.

28

It was on the left hip.

She closed the bag again and was just about to swing the door shut when she froze. Turning, she stared into the cold room.

Did I just hear something?

The fan came on, blowing icy air from the vents. Yes, that's all it was, she thought. The fan. Or the refrigerator compressor. Or water cycling in the pipes. It was time to go home. She was so tired, she was starting to imagine things.

Again she turned to leave.

Again she froze. Turning, she stared at the row of body bags. Her heart was thumping so hard now, all she could hear was the beat of her own pulse.

Something moved in here. I'm sure of it.

She unzipped the first bag and stared down at a man whose chest had been sutured closed. Already autopsied, she thought. Definitely dead.

Which one? Which one made the noise?

She yanked open the next bag, and confronted a bruised face, a shattered skull. *Dead.*

With shaking hands she unzipped the third bag. The plastic parted, and she saw the face of a pale young woman with black hair and cyanotic lips. Opening the bag all the way, she exposed a wet blouse, the fabric clinging to white flesh, the skin glistening with chilly droplets of water. She peeled open the blouse and saw full breasts, a slim waist. The torso was still intact, not yet incised by the pathologist's knife. The fingers and toes were purple, the arms marbled with blue.

She pressed her fingers to the woman's neck and felt icy skin. Bending close to the lips, she waited for the whisper of a breath, the faintest puff of air against her cheek.

The corpse opened its eyes.

Maura gasped and lurched backward. She collided with the gurney behind her, and almost fell as the wheels rolled away. She scrambled back to her feet and saw that the woman's eyes were still open, but unfocused. Blue-tinged lips formed soundless words.

Get her out of the refrigerator! Get her warm!

Maura shoved the gurney toward the door but it didn't budge; in her panic she'd forgotten to unlock the wheels. She stamped down on the release lever and pushed again. This time it rolled, rattling out of the cold room into the warmer loading area.

The woman's eyes had drifted shut again. Leaning close, Maura could feel no air moving past the lips. *Oh Jesus. I can't lose you now.*

She knew nothing about this stranger – not her name, nor her medical history. This woman could be teeming with viruses, yet she sealed her mouth over the woman's, and almost gagged at the taste of chilled flesh. She delivered three deep breaths, and pressed her fingers to the neck to check for a carotid pulse.

Am I imagining it? Is that my own pulse I feel, throbbing in my fingers?

She grabbed the wall phone and dialed 911.

'Emergency operator.'

'This is Dr. Isles in the medical examiner's office. I need an ambulance. There's a woman here, in respiratory arrest—'

'Excuse me, did you say the medical examiner's office?'

'Yes! I'm at the rear of the building, just inside the loading bay. We're on Albany Street, right across from the medical center!'

'I'm dispatching an ambulance now.'

Maura hung up. Once again, she quelled her disgust as she pressed her lips to the woman's. Three more quick breaths, then her fingers were back on the carotid.

A pulse. There was definitely a pulse!

Suddenly she heard a wheeze, a cough. The woman was moving air now, mucus rattling in her throat.

Stay with me. Breathe, lady. Breathe!

A loud whoop announced the arrival of the ambulance. She shoved open the rear doors and stood squinting against flashing lights as the vehicle backed up to the dock. Two EMTs jumped out, hauling their kits.

'She's in here!' Maura called.

'Still in respiratory arrest?'

'No, she's breathing now. And I can feel a pulse.'

The two men trotted into the building and halted, staring at the woman on the gurney. 'Jesus,' one of them murmured. 'Is that a *body* bag?'

'I found her in the cold room,' said Maura. 'By now, she's probably hypothermic.'

'Oh, man. If this isn't your worst nightmare.'

Out came the oxygen mask and IV lines. They slapped on EKG leads. On the monitor, a slow sinus rhythm blipped like a lazy cartoonist's pen. The woman had a heartbeat and she was breathing, yet she still looked dead.

Looping a tourniquet around one flaccid arm, the EMT asked: 'What's her story? How did she get here?'

'I don't know anything about her,' said Maura. 'I came down to check on another body in the cold room and I heard this one moving.'

'Does this, uh, happen very often here?'

'This is a first time for me.' And she hoped to God it was the last.

'How long has she been in your refrigerator?'

Maura glanced at the hanging clipboard, where the day's deliveries were recorded, and saw that a Jane Doe had arrived at the morgue around noon. *Eight hours ago. Eight hours zipped in a shroud. What if she'd ended up on my table? What if I had sliced into her chest?* Rummaging through the receiving in-basket, she found the envelope containing the woman's paperwork. 'Weymouth Fire and Rescue brought her in,' she said. 'An apparent drowning . . .'

'Whoa, Nelly!' The EMT had just stabbed an IV needle into a vein and the patient suddenly jerked to life, her torso bucking on the gurney. The IV site magically puffed blue as the punctured vein hemorrhaged into the skin.

'Shit, lost the site. Help me hold her down!'

'Man, this gal's gonna get up and walk away.'

'She's really fighting now. I can't get the IV started.'

'Then let's just get her on the stretcher and move her.'

'Where are you taking her?' Maura said.

'Right across the street. The ER. If you have any paperwork they'll want a copy.'

She nodded. 'I'll meet you there.'

A long line of patients stood waiting to register at the ER window, and the triage nurse behind the desk refused to meet Maura's attempts to catch her eye. On this busy night, it would take a severed limb and spurting blood to justify cutting to the front of the line, but Maura ignored the nasty looks of other patients and pushed straight to the window. She rapped on the glass.

'You'll have to wait your turn,' the triage nurse said.

'I'm Dr. Isles. I have a patient's transfer papers. The doctor will want them.'

'Which patient?'

'The woman they just brought in from across the street.'

'You mean that lady from the morgue?'

Maura paused, suddenly aware that the other patients in line could hear every word. 'Yes,' was all she said.

'Come on through, then. They want to talk to you. They're having trouble with her.'

The door lock buzzed open, and Maura pushed through, into the treatment area. She saw immediately what the triage nurse had meant by *trouble*. Jane Doe had not yet been moved into a treatment room, but was still lying in the hallway, her body now draped with a heating blanket. The two EMTs and a nurse struggled to control her.

'Tighten that strap!'

'Shit – her hand's out again—'

'Forget the oxygen mask. She doesn't need it.'

'Watch that IV! We're going to lose it!'

Maura lunged toward the stretcher and grabbed the patient's wrist before she could pull out the intravenous catheter. Long black hair lashed Maura's face as the woman tried to twist free. Only twenty minutes ago, this had been a blue-lipped corpse in a body bag. Now they could barely restrain her as life came roaring back into her limbs.

'Hold on. Hold on to that arm!'

The sound started deep in the woman's throat. It was the moan of a wounded animal. Then her head tilted back and her cry rose to an unearthly shriek. Not human, thought Maura, as the hairs stood up on the back of her neck. *My god, what have I brought back from the dead?*

'Listen to me. *Listen!*' Maura commanded. She grasped the woman's head in her hands and stared down at a face contorted in panic. 'I won't let anything happen to you. I promise. You have to let us help you.'

At the sound of Maura's voice, the woman went still. Blue eyes stared back, the pupils dilated to huge black pools.

One of the nurses quietly began to loop a restraint around the woman's hand.

No, thought Maura. Don't do that.

As the strap brushed the patient's wrist, she jerked as though scalded. Her arm flew and Maura stumbled backward, her cheek stinging from the blow.

'Assistance!' the nurse yelled. 'Can we get Dr. Cutler out here?'

Maura backed away, face throbbing, as a doctor and another nurse emerged from one of the treatment rooms. The commotion had drawn the attention of patients in the waiting room. Maura saw them eagerly peering through the glass partition, watching a scene that was better than any TV episode of *ER*.

'We know if she has any allergies?' the doctor asked.

'No medical history,' said the nurse.

'What's going on here? Why is she out of control?'

'We have no idea.'

'Okay. Okay, let's try five milligrams of Haldol IV.'

'IV's out!'

'Then give it IM. Just do it! And let's get some Valium in her, too, before she hurts herself.'

The woman gave another shriek as the needle pierced her skin.

'Do we know anything about this woman? Who is she?' The doctor suddenly noticed Maura standing a few feet away. 'Are you a relative?'

'I called the ambulance. I'm Dr. Isles.'

'Her physician?'

Before Maura could answer, one of the EMTs said: 'She's the medical examiner. This is the patient who woke up in the morgue.'

The doctor stared at Maura. 'You're kidding.'

'I found her moving in the cold room,' said Maura.

The doctor gave a disbelieving laugh. 'Who pronounced her dead?'

'Weymouth Fire and Rescue brought her in.'

He looked at the patient. 'Well, she's definitely alive now.'

'Dr. Cutler, room two's now empty,' a nurse called out. 'We can move her in there.'

Maura followed as they wheeled the stretcher down the hallway and into a treatment room. The woman's struggles had weakened, her strength giving way to the effects of Haldol and Valium. The nurses drew blood, reconnected EKG wires. The cardiac rhythm ticked across the monitor.

'Okay, Dr. Isles,' said the ER physician as he shone a penlight into the woman's eyes. 'Tell me more.'

Maura opened the envelope containing the photocopied paperwork that had accompanied the body. 'Let me just tell you what's in the transfer papers,' she said. 'At eight A.M.,

Weymouth Fire and Rescue responded to a call from the Sunrise Yacht Club, where boaters found the subject floating in Hingham Bay. When she was pulled from the water, she had no pulse or respirations. And no ID. A state police investigator was called to the scene, and he thought it was most likely accidental. She was transferred to our office at noon.'

'And no one at the ME's noticed that she was alive?'

'She arrived while we were swamped with other cases. There was that accident on I-95. And we were still backlogged from last night.'

'It's now nearly nine. And no one checked this woman?'

'The dead don't have emergencies.'

'So you just leave them in the refrigerator?'

'Until we can get to them.'

'What if you hadn't heard her moving tonight?' He turned to look at her. 'You mean she might have been left there until tomorrow morning?'

Maura felt her cheeks flush. 'Yes,' she admitted.

'Dr. Cutler, ICU has a bed available,' a nurse said. 'Is that where you want her?'

He nodded. 'We have no idea what drugs she might have taken, so I want her on a monitor.' He looked down at the patient, whose eyes were now closed. Her lips continued to move, as though in silent prayer. 'This poor woman's already died once. Let's not have it happen again.'

*　*　*

Maura could hear the phone ringing inside her house as she fumbled with her keys, trying to unlock the door. By the time she made it into the living room, the ringing had stopped. Whoever had called had not left a message. She cycled through the most recent numbers on caller ID, but did not recognize the last caller's name: ZOE FOSSEY. A wrong number?

I refuse to worry about it, she thought, and started toward the kitchen.

Now her cell phone was ringing. She dug it out of her purse, and saw from the digital display that the caller was her colleague, Dr. Abe Bristol.

'Hello, Abe?'

'Maura, you want to fill me in about what happened at the ER tonight?'

'You know about it?'

'I've gotten three calls already. The *Globe*, the *Herald*. And some local TV station.'

'What are these reporters saying?'

'They're all asking about the corpse who woke up. Said she just got admitted to the medical center. I had no idea what they were talking about.'

'Oh, Jesus. How did the press find out so soon?'

'So it's true?'

'I was going to call you—' She stopped. The phone was ringing in the living room. 'I've got another call coming in. Can I get back to you, Abe?'

38

'As long as you promise to fill me in.'

She ran into the living room and picked up the receiver. 'Dr. Isles.'

'This is Zoe Fossey, Channel Six News. Would you care to comment on—'

'It's almost ten o'clock,' cut in Maura. 'This is my home telephone. If you want to talk to me, you're going to have to call my office during business hours.'

'We understand that a woman woke up in the morgue tonight.'

'I'm not going to comment.'

'Sources tell us that both a state police investigator and a fire crew in Weymouth pronounced her dead. Did someone in your office make the same determination?'

'The ME's office was not involved in that determination.'

'But the woman was in your custody, right?'

'No one in our office made any pronouncement of death.'

'You're saying this was the fault of the Weymouth Fire Department and the state police? How can anyone make this kind of mistake? Isn't it pretty obvious when someone is still alive?'

Maura hung up.

Almost immediately the phone rang. A different number appeared on the caller ID screen.

She picked up the receiver. 'Dr. Isles.'

'This is Dave Rosen, Associated Press. I'm sorry to disturb you, but we're following up on a report about a young woman who was taken to the medical examiner's office and woke up in a body bag. Is this true?'

'How did you people find out about this? This is the second call I've gotten.'

'I suspect you're going to be getting a lot more calls.'

'And what have you been told about it?'

'That she was brought to the morgue this afternoon, by Weymouth Fire and Rescue. That you were the one who found her alive and called the ambulance. I've already spoken to the hospital, and they list her condition as serious but stable. All correct?'

'Yes, but—'

'Was she actually *in* the body bag when you found her? Was she zipped in there?'

'You're making it far too sensationalistic.'

'Does anyone in your office routinely check the bodies when they first come in? Just to be sure they're dead?'

'I'll have a statement for you in the morning. Good night.' She hung up. Before the phone could ring again, she unplugged it. It was the only way she'd get any sleep tonight. Staring down at the now-silent phone, she wondered: How the hell did the news get out so fast?

Then she thought of all the witnesses in the ER – the clerks, the nurses, the orderlies. The patients in the waiting room, watching through the glass partition. Any one of them could have picked up the phone. A single call, and the word would be out. Nothing spreads faster than

40

macabre gossip. Tomorrow, she thought, is going to be an ordeal and I'd better be ready for it.

She used her cell phone to call Abe. 'We have a problem,' she said.

'I figured.'

'Don't talk to the press. I'll come up with a statement. I've unplugged my home phone for the night. If you need to reach me, I'm on cell.'

'Are you prepared to deal with all this?'

'Who else is going to do it? I'm the one who found her.'

'You know this is going to be national news, Maura.'

'AP's already called me.'

'Oh, Christ. Have you talked to the Office of Public Safety? They'll be in charge of the investigation.'

'I guess they're next on my list to call.'

'Do you need any help preparing the statement?'

'I'll need some time to work on it. I'll be late coming in tomorrow. Just hold them off until I get into the office.'

'There's probably going to be a lawsuit.'

'We're blameless, Abe. We didn't do anything wrong.'

'It doesn't matter. Get ready for it.'

Three

'Do you solemnly swear that the testimony you are about to give to the court in the case now in hearing shall be the truth, the whole truth, and nothing but the truth, so help you God?'

'I do,' said Jane Rizzoli.

'Thank you. You may be seated.'

Jane felt all eyes in the courtroom watching her as she settled heavily into the witness-stand chair. They had stared at her from the moment she'd waddled into the courtroom, her ankles swollen, her belly bulging beneath the voluminous maternity dress. Now she shifted in the seat, trying to get comfortable, trying to project some semblance of authority, but the room was warm, and she could already feel perspiration beading on her forehead. A sweating, fidgeting, pregnant cop. Yes, quite an authority figure.

Gary Spurlock, the assistant DA for Suffolk County, rose to conduct the direct exam. Jane knew him to be a calm and methodical prosecutor, and she had no anxiety about this first round of questions. She kept her gaze on Spurlock, avoiding even a glance at the defendant, Billy Wayne Rollo, who slouched beside his female attorney and stared at Jane. She knew Rollo was trying to intimidate her with the evil eye. Rattle the cop, throw her off balance. He was like too many other assholes she'd known, and his stare was nothing new. Just the last resort of a loser.

'Could you tell the court your name and spell the last name, please?' Spurlock said.

'Detective Jane Rizzoli. R-I-Z-Z-O-L-I.'

'And your profession?'

'I'm a detective with the homicide unit, Boston Police Department.'

'Could you describe your education and background for us?'

She shifted again, her back starting to ache in the hard chair. 'I received my associate's degree in criminal justice from Massachusetts Bay Community College. After my training at Boston PD Academy, I was a beat patrolman in both the Back Bay and Dorchester.' She flinched as her baby gave a hard kick. *Settle down in there. Mama's on the stand.* Spurlock was still waiting for the rest of her answer. She continued. 'I worked as a detective in vice and narcotics for two years. Then, two and a half years ago, I transferred to the homicide unit, which is where I am currently assigned.'

'Thank you, Detective. Now I'd like to ask you about the events of February third of this year. In the course of your job, you visited a residence in Roxbury. Correct?'

'Yes, sir.'

'The address was 4280 Malcolm X Boulevard, correct?'

'Yes. It's an apartment building.'

'Tell us about that visit.'

'At approximately two thirty P.M., we – my partner, Detective Barry Frost, and I – arrived at that address to interview a tenant in apartment two-B.'

'In regards to what?'

'It was in regards to a homicide investigation. The subject in two-B was an acquaintance of the victim.'

'So he – or she – was not a suspect in that particular case?'

'No, sir. We did not consider her to be a suspect.'

'And what happened then?'

'We had just knocked on the door to two-B when we heard a woman screaming. It came from the apartment across the hall. In two-E.'

'Could you describe the screams?'

'I guess I would characterize them as screams of severe distress. Fear. And we heard several loud bangs, as though furniture was being over-turned. Or someone was being slammed against the floor.'

'Objection!' The defense attorney, a tall blond woman, rose to her feet. 'Pure speculation. She wasn't in the apartment to see that.'

'Sustained,' the judge said. 'Detective Rizzoli, please refrain from guessing about events you couldn't possibly see.'

Even if it wasn't just a frigging guess? Because that's exactly what was happening. Billy Wayne Rollo was slamming his girlfriend's head against the floor.

Jane swallowed her irritation and amended her statement. 'We heard a loud banging in the apartment.'

'And what did you do then?'

'Detective Frost and I immediately knocked on the door to two-E.'

'Did you identify yourselves as police officers?'

'Yes, sir.'

'And what happened—'

'That's a fucking lie,' said the defendant. 'They never said they were cops!'

Everyone looked at Billy Wayne Rollo; he was looking only at Jane.

'You will remain silent, Mr. Rollo,' the judge ordered.

'But she's a liar.'

'Counsel, either control your client or he will be ejected from this courtroom.'

'Shhh, Billy,' the defense attorney murmured. 'This is not helping.'

'All right,' the judge said. 'Mr. Spurlock, you may continue.'

The assistant DA nodded and turned back to Jane. 'What happened after you knocked on the door to two-E?'

'There was no answer. But we could still hear the screaming. The banging. We made the joint decision that a life was in danger, and that we needed to enter the apartment with or without consent.'

'And did you enter?'

'Yes, sir.'

'They kicked my fucking door down!' said Rollo.

'Silence, Mr. Rollo!' the judge snapped, and the defendant slouched back in his chair, his gaze burning on Jane.

Stare at me all you want, jerk. You think you scare me?

'Detective Rizzoli,' said Spurlock, 'what did you see inside that apartment?'

Jane turned her attention back to the assistant DA. 'We saw a man and a woman. The woman was lying on her back. Her face was severely bruised, and her lip was bleeding. The man was crouched over her. He had both his hands around her neck.'

'Is that man now sitting in this courtroom?'

'Yes, sir.'

'Please point him out.'

She pointed to Billy Wayne Rollo.

'What happened then?'

'Detective Frost and I pulled Mr. Rollo off the woman. She was still conscious. Mr. Rollo resisted us, and in the scuffle, Detective Frost received a heavy blow to the abdomen. Mr. Rollo then fled the apartment. I gave chase and followed him into the stairwell. There I was able to apprehend him.'

'By yourself?'

'Yes, sir.' She paused. Added, without any attempt at humor: 'After he fell down the stairs. He appeared to be quite intoxicated.'

'She fucking *pushed* me!' said Rollo.

The judge slammed down his gavel. 'I have heard *enough* out of you! Bailiff, please remove the defendant.'

'Your honor.' The defense attorney rose. 'I will keep him under control.'

'You haven't done a very good job of it so far, Ms. Quinlan.'

'He'll be quiet now.' She looked at her client. '*Won't* you?'

Rollo gave a resentful grunt.

Spurlock said: 'No further questions, your honor,' and sat down.

The judge looked at the defense attorney. 'Ms. Quinlan?'

Victoria Quinlan rose for the cross-examination. Jane had never before dealt with this particular attorney, and she was not sure what to expect. As Quinlan approached the witness stand, Jane thought: You're young, blond, and gorgeous. What are you doing defending this creep? The woman moved like a fashion model on a catwalk, long legs emphasized by a short skirt and pointy high heels. It made Jane's feet hurt just to look at those shoes. A woman like Quinlan had probably always been the center of attention, and she was milking it now as she strolled to the witness stand, clearly aware that every man sitting in that jury box was probably staring at her firm little ass.

'Good morning, Detective,' said Quinlan. Sweetly. Too sweetly. Any second now this blonde was going to sprout fangs.

'Good morning, ma'am,' said Jane, utterly neutral.

'You said that you are currently assigned to the homicide unit.'

'Yes, ma'am.'

'And what new cases are you actively investigating right now?'

'At the moment, I have no new cases. But I continue to follow up on—'

'Yet you are a Boston PD detective. And at this moment, are there no murder cases that require vigorous investigation?'

'I'm on maternity leave.'

'Oh. You're on *leave*. So you're not currently with the unit.'

'I'm performing administrative duties.'

'But let's be clear on this. You're not an *active* detective.' Quinlan smiled. 'At the moment.'

Jane felt her face flush. 'As I said, I'm on maternity leave. Even cops have babies,' she added with a note of sarcasm, and immediately regretted it. *Don't play her game. Keep your cool.* That was easier said than done in this oven of a courtroom. What was wrong with the air-conditioning anyway? Why didn't anyone else seem to be bothered by the heat?

'When is your baby due, Detective?'

Jane paused, wondering where this was going. 'My baby was due last week,' she finally said. 'It's late.'

'So back on February third, when you first encountered my client, Mr. Rollo, you were – what? About three months pregnant?'

'Objection,' said Spurlock. 'This is irrelevant.'

'Counsel,' the judge said to Quinlan, 'what is the point of your question?'

'It has to do with her earlier testimony, your honor. That Detective Rizzoli was somehow able to subdue and arrest my clearly able-bodied client in the stairwell all by herself.'

'And the state of her pregnancy has what, exactly, to do with this?'

'A three-months-pregnant woman would have a difficult time—'

'She's a police officer, Ms. Quinlan. Arresting people is her job.'

Way to go, Judge! You tell her.

Victoria Quinlan flushed at the setback. 'All right, your honor. I withdraw the question.' She turned, again, to Jane. Regarded her for a moment as she considered her next move. 'You said that you and your partner, Detective Frost, were both at the scene. That you and he made a joint decision to enter apartment two-B?'

'It wasn't apartment two-B, ma'am. It was apartment two-*E*.'

'Oh yes, of course. My mistake.'

Yeah, right. As if you aren't trying to trip me up.

'You say you knocked at the door and announced that you were police officers,' said Quinlan.

'Yes, ma'am.'

'And this interaction had nothing to do with why you were originally in that building.'

'No, ma'am. It was just a coincidence that we happened to be there. But when we determine that a citizen is in danger, it's our duty to intervene.'

'And that's why you knocked at apartment two-B.'

'Two-E.'

'And when no one answered, you burst through the door.'

'We felt a woman's life was in jeopardy, based on the screams we heard.'

'How did you know they were screams of distress? Couldn't they have been the sounds of, say, passionate lovemaking?'

Jane wanted to laugh at the question, but didn't. 'That was not what we heard.'

'And you know that for a fact? You can tell the difference?'

'A woman with a bloody lip is pretty good evidence.'

'The point is, you didn't know it *at the time*. You didn't give my client a chance to answer the door. You made a rush to judgment and just broke in.'

'We stopped a beating.'

'You're aware that the so-called victim has refused to press charges against Mr. Rollo? That they are still together as a loving couple?'

Jane's jaw squared. 'That's her decision.' *Dumb though it is.* 'What I saw that day, in apartment two-E, was clearly abuse. There was blood.'

'Like *my* blood doesn't count?' said Rollo. 'You pushed me down the stairs, lady! I still got the scar here, on my chin!'

'Silence, Mr. Rollo,' the judge ordered.

'Look! See where I hit the bottom step? I needed stitches!'

'Mr. Rollo!'

'*Did* you push my client down the stairs, Detective?' asked Quinlan.

'Objection,' said Spurlock.

'No, I did not,' said Jane. 'He was plenty drunk enough to fall down the stairs all by himself.'

'She's lying!' said the defendant.

The gavel banged down. '*Quiet, Mr. Rollo!*'

But Billy Wayne Rollo was just building up a head of outraged steam. 'She and her partner, they dragged me into the stairwell so no one would see what they were doing. You think *she* could arrest me all by herself? That little pregnant *girl*? What a crock of shit she's telling you!'

'Sergeant Givens, remove the defendant.'

'It's a case of police brutality!' Rollo yelled as

the bailiff hauled him to his feet. 'Hey, you people in the jury, are you stupid? Can't you see this is all made-up shit? These two cops kicked me down the fucking stairwell!'

The gavel slammed down. 'Let's take a recess. Please escort the jurors out.'

'Oh yeah! Let's take a *recess*!' Rollo laughed and shoved away the bailiff. 'Just when they're finally hearing the truth!'

'Get him out of here, Sergeant Givens.'

Givens grabbed Rollo's arm. Enraged, Rollo twisted around and charged, his head thudding into the bailiff's belly. They both slammed to the floor and began to grapple. Victoria Quinlan stared, openmouthed, as her client and the bailiff flopped around just inches from her high-heeled Manolo Blahniks.

Ah, Jesus. Someone's gotta take control of this mess.

Jane heaved herself out of the chair. Shoving aside the stunned Quinlan, Jane snatched up the bailiff's handcuffs, which he'd dropped on the floor in the confusion.

'Assistance!' yelled the judge, banging on his gavel. 'We need another bailiff in here!'

Sergeant Givens was lying on his back now, pinned beneath Rollo, who was just raising his right fist to deliver a blow. Jane grabbed Rollo's raised wrist and snapped on one of the cuffs.

'What the fuck?' Rollo said.

Jane rammed her foot into his back, twisted his arm behind him, and shoved him down against the bailiff. Another click, and the second cuff closed around Rollo's left wrist.

'Get off me, you fucking cow!' Rollo screamed. 'You're breaking my back!'

Sergeant Givens, trapped at the bottom of the pileup, looked like he was about to suffocate beneath the weight.

Jane took her foot off Rollo's back. Suddenly a gush of hot liquid flooded from between her legs, splashing down onto Rollo, onto Givens. She stumbled backward and looked down in shock at her soaked maternity dress. At the fluid dripping from her thighs onto the courtroom floor.

Rollo twisted onto his side and stared up at her. Suddenly he laughed. He couldn't stop laughing as he rolled onto his back. 'Hey,' he said. 'Look at that! The bitch just peed in her dress!'

Four

Maura was stopped at a traffic light in Brookline Village when Abe Bristol rang her on her cell phone. 'Did you watch TV this morning?' he asked.

'Don't tell me the story's already made the news.'

'Channel six. Reporter's name is Zoe Fossey. Did you speak to her?'

'Only briefly last night. What did she say?'

'In a nutshell? 'Woman found alive in body bag. Medical examiner blames the Weymouth Fire Department and state police for mis-diagnosing death.''

'Oh Jesus. I never said that.'

'I know you didn't. But now we've got a pissed-off fire chief down in Weymouth, and the state police aren't too happy either. Louise is already fielding calls from them.'

The traffic light turned green. As she drove through the intersection, she suddenly wished she could turn around and go home. Wished she could avoid the ordeal to come.

'Are you at the office?' she asked.

'I got in at seven. Thought you'd be here by now.'

'I'm in my car. I needed a few extra hours this morning to prepare that statement.'

'Well, I've gotta warn you, when you get here, you're going to get ambushed in the parking lot.'

'They're hanging around out there?'

'Reporters, TV vans. They're parked on Albany Street. Running back and forth between our building and the hospital.'

'How convenient for them. One-stop shopping for the press.'

'Have you heard anything more about the patient?'

'I called Dr. Cutler this morning. He said the patient's tox screen came back positive for barbiturates and alcohol. She must've been pretty loaded.'

'That probably explains why she took a tumble into the water. And with barbs on board, no wonder they had trouble finding her vital signs.'

'Why is this turning into such a feeding frenzy?'

'Because it's prime *National Enquirer* stuff. The dead rising from the grave. Plus, she's a young woman, isn't she?'

'I'd say she's in her twenties.'

'And attractive?'

'What difference does it make?'

'Come on.' Abe laughed. 'You *know* it makes a difference.'

Maura sighed. 'Yes,' she admitted. 'She's very attractive.'

'Yeah, well, there you go. Young, sexy, and almost sliced open alive.'

'She wasn't.'

'I'm just warning you, that's how the public's going to see it.'

'Can't I just call in sick today? Maybe catch the next flight to Bermuda?'

'And leave me with this mess? Don't you dare.'

When she turned onto Albany Street twenty minutes later, she spotted two TV vans parked near the front entrance of the ME's building. As Abe had warned her, reporters were poised to pounce. She stepped out of her air-conditioned Lexus, into a morning already thick with humidity, and half a dozen reporters scurried toward her.

'Dr. Isles!' a man called out. 'I'm from the *Boston Tribune*. Could I have a few words with you about Jane Doe?'

In response, Maura reached into her briefcase and pulled out copies of what she had composed that morning. It was a matter-of-fact summary of the night's events, and how she had responded. Briskly she handed out copies. 'This is my statement,' she said. 'I have nothing else to add.'

It did not stop the flood of questions.

'How can anyone make a mistake like this?'

'Do we know the woman's name yet?'

'We're told that Weymouth Fire Department

made the determination of death. Can you name names?'

Maura said, 'You'll have to talk to their spokesperson. I can't answer for them.'

Now a woman spoke up. 'You have to admit, Dr. Isles, that this is a clear case of incompetence on *someone's* part.'

Maura recognized that voice. She turned and saw a blond woman who'd pushed her way to the front of the pack. 'You're that reporter from channel six.'

'Zoe Fossey.' The woman started to smile, gratified to be recognized, but the look Maura gave her instantly froze that smile to stone.

'You misquoted me,' said Maura. 'I never said I blamed the fire department or the state police.'

'Someone must be at fault. If not them, then who? Are you responsible, Dr. Isles?'

'Absolutely not.'

'A woman was zipped into a body bag, still alive. She was trapped in the morgue refrigerator for eight hours. And it's nobody's fault?' Fossey paused. 'Don't you think someone should lose their job over this? Say, that state police investigator?'

'You're certainly quick to assign blame.'

'That mistake could have killed a woman.'

'But it didn't.'

'Isn't this a pretty basic error?' Fossey laughed. 'I mean, how hard can it be to tell that someone's not dead?'

'Harder than you'd think,' Maura shot back.

'So you're defending them.'

'I gave you my statement. I can't comment on the actions of anyone else.'

'Dr. Isles?' It was the man from the *Boston Tribune* again. 'You said that determining death isn't necessarily easy. I know there've been similar mistakes made in other morgues around the country. Could you educate us as to why it's sometimes difficult?' He spoke with quiet respect. Not a challenge, but a thoughtful question that deserved an answer.

She regarded the man for a moment. Saw intelligent eyes and windblown hair and a trim beard that made her think of a youthful college professor. Those dark good looks would surely inspire countless coed crushes. 'What's your name?' she said.

'Peter Lukas. I write a weekly column for the *Tribune*.'

'I'll talk to you, Mr. Lukas. And only you. Come inside.'

'Wait,' Fossey protested. 'Some of us have been waiting around out here a lot longer.'

Maura shot her a withering look. 'In this case, Ms. Fossey, it's not the early bird that gets the worm. It's the polite one.' She turned and walked into the building, the *Tribune* reporter right behind her.

Her secretary, Louise, was on the phone. Clapping her hand over the receiver, she whispered to Maura, a little desperately: 'It doesn't stop ringing. What do I tell them?'

Maura laid a copy of her statement on Louise's desk. 'Fax them this.'

'That's all you want me to do?'

'Head off any calls from the press. I've agreed to talk to Mr. Lukas here, but no one else. No more interviews.'

Louise's expression, as she regarded the reporter, was only too easy to read. *I see you chose a good-looking one.*

'We won't be long,' said Maura. She ushered Lukas into her office and closed the door. Pointed him to the chair.

'Thank you for talking to me,' he said.

'You were the only one out there who didn't irritate me.'

'That doesn't mean I'm not irritating.'

That got a small smile out of her. 'This is purely a self-defense strategy,' she said. 'Maybe if I talk to you, you'll become everyone else's go-to guy. They'll leave me alone and harass you.'

'I'm afraid it doesn't work that way. They'll still be chasing you.'

'There are so many bigger stories you could be writing about, Mr. Lukas. More important stories. Why this one?'

'Because this one strikes us on a visceral level. It addresses our worst fears. How many of us are terrified of being given up for dead when we aren't? Of being accidentally buried alive? Which, incidentally, *has* happened a few times in the past.'

She nodded. 'There have been some historically

59

documented cases. But those were prior to the days of embalming.'

'And waking up in morgues? That's not merely historical. I found out there've been several cases in recent years.'

She hesitated. 'It's happened.'

'More often than the public realizes.' He pulled out a notebook and flipped it open. 'In 1984, there was a case in New York. A man's lying on the autopsy table. The pathologist picks up the scalpel and is about to make the first incision when the corpse wakes up and grabs the doctor by the throat. The doctor keels over, dead of a heart attack.' Lukas glanced up. 'You've heard of that case?'

'You're focusing on the most sensationalistic example.'

'But it's true. Isn't it?'

She sighed. 'Yes. I know of that particular case.'

He flipped to another page in his notebook. 'Springfield, Ohio, 1989. A woman in a nursing home is declared dead and transferred to a funeral home. She's lying on the table, and the mortician is about to embalm her. Then the corpse starts talking.'

'You seem quite familiar with this subject.'

'Because it's fascinating.' He riffled through the pages in his notebook. 'Last night, I looked up case after case. A little girl in South Dakota who woke up in her open casket. A man in Des Moines whose chest was actually cut open. Only then does the pathologist suddenly realize the heart is *still beating*.' Lukas looked at her. 'These aren't urban legends. These are documented cases, and there are a number of them.'

'Look, I'm not saying it doesn't happen, because clearly it has. Corpses have woken up in morgues. Old graves have been dug up, and they've found claw marks inside the coffin lids. People are so terrified of the possibility that some casket makers sell coffins equipped with emergency transmitters to call for help. Just in case you're buried alive.'

'How reassuring.'

'So yes, it can happen. I'm sure you've heard the theory about Jesus. That the resurrection of Christ wasn't a true resurrection. It was merely a case of premature burial.'

'Why is it so hard to determine that someone is dead? Shouldn't it be obvious?'

'Sometimes it isn't. People who are chilled, through exposure or drowning in cold water, can look very dead. Our Jane Doe was found in cold water. And there are certain drugs that can mask vital signs and make it hard to see respirations or detect a pulse.'

'Romeo and Juliet. The potion that Juliet drank to make her look dead.'

'Yes. I don't know what the potion was, but that scenario was not impossible.'

'Which drugs can do it?'

'Barbiturates, for example. They can depress your respiration and make it hard to tell that a subject is breathing.'

61

'That's what turned up in Jane Doe's toxicology screen, isn't it? Phenobarbital.'

She frowned. 'Where did you hear that?'

'Sources. It's true, isn't it?'

'No comment.'

'Does she have a psychiatric history? Why would she take an overdose of phenobarb?'

'We don't even know the woman's name, much less her psychiatric history.'

He studied her for a moment, his gaze too penetrating for comfort. This interview is a mistake, she thought. Moments ago, Peter Lukas had impressed her as polite and serious, the type of journalist who would approach this story with respect. But the direction of his questioning made her uneasy. He had walked into this meeting fully prepared and well versed in the very details that she least wanted to dwell on; the very details that would rivet the public's attention.

'I understand the woman was pulled out of Hingham Bay yesterday morning,' he said. 'Weymouth Fire and Rescue were the first to respond.'

'That's correct.'

'Why wasn't the ME's office called to the scene?'

'We don't have the manpower to visit every death scene. Plus, this one was down in Weymouth, and there were no obvious indications of foul play.'

'And that was determined by the state police?'

'Their detective thought it was most likely accidental.'

'Or possibly a suicide attempt? Considering the results of her tox screen?'

She saw no point in denying what he already knew. 'She may have taken an overdose, yes.'

'A barbiturate overdose. And a body chilled by cold water. Two reasons to obscure a determination of death. Shouldn't that have been considered?'

'It's – yes, it's something one should consider.'

'But neither the state police detective nor the Weymouth Fire Department did. Which sounds like a mistake.'

'It can happen. That's all I can say.'

'Have you ever made that mistake, Dr. Isles? Declared someone dead who was still alive?'

She paused, thinking back to her internship years before. To a night on call during internal medicine rotation, when the ringing phone had awakened her from a deep sleep. The patient in bed 336A had just expired, a nurse told her. Could the intern come pronounce the woman dead? As Maura had made her way to the patient's room, she'd felt no anxiety, no crisis of confidence. In medical school, there was no special lesson on how to determine death; it was understood that you would recognize it when you saw it. That night, she had walked the hospital corridor thinking that she would make quick work of this task, then return to bed. The death was not unexpected; the patient had been in the terminal stages of cancer, and her chart was clearly labeled NO CODE. No resuscitation.

Stepping into room 336, she'd been startled to find the bed surrounded by tearful family members who'd gathered to say good-bye. Maura had an audience. This was not the calm communion with the deceased that she had expected. She was painfully aware of all the eyes watching her as she apologized for the intrusion, as she moved to the bedside. The patient lay on her back, her face at peace. Maura took out her stethoscope, slipped the diaphragm under the hospital gown, and laid it against the frail chest. As she'd bent over the body, she felt the family pressing in around her, felt the pressure of their smothering attention. She did not listen as long as she should have. The nurses had already determined the woman was dead; calling in the doctor to make a pronouncement was merely protocol. A note in a chart, an MD's signature, was all they really needed before a transfer to the morgue. Bent over the chest, listening to silence, Maura could not wait to escape the room. She'd straightened, her face appropriately sympathetic, and had focused her attention on the man she assumed to be the patient's husband. She'd been about to murmur: *I'm sorry but she's passed away*.

The whisper of a breath had stopped her.

Startled, she'd looked down, to see the patient's chest move. Had watched the woman take another breath, and then fall still. It was an agonal breathing pattern – not a miracle, just the brain's last electrical impulses, the final twitching of the diaphragm. Every family member in the room gave a gasp.

'Oh my god,' the husband said. 'She's not gone yet.'

'It . . . will be very soon,' was all Maura managed to say. She had walked out of the room, shaken by how close she'd come to making a mistake. Never again had she been so cavalier about a pronouncement of death.

She looked at the journalist. 'Everyone makes mistakes,' she said. 'Even something as basic as declaring death isn't as easy as you'd think.'

'So you're defending the fire crew? And the state police?'

'I'm saying that mistakes happen. That's all.' *And God knows, I've made a few of my own.* 'I can see how it might happen. The woman was found in cold water. She had barbiturates in her bloodstream. These factors could give the appearance of death. Under the circumstances, a mistake isn't so far-fetched. The personnel involved were simply trying to do their jobs, and I hope you'll be fair to them when you write your story.' She stood up, a signal that the interview was over.

'I always try to be fair,' he said.

'Not every journalist can make that claim.'

He, too, rose to his feet and stood gazing at her across the desk. 'Let me know if I've failed. After you read my column.'

She escorted him to the door. Watched as he walked past Louise's desk and out of the office.

Louise looked up from her keyboard. 'How did it go?'

'I don't know. Maybe I shouldn't have talked to him.'

'We'll find out soon enough,' said Louise, her eyes back on the computer screen. 'When his column comes out in the *Tribune* on Friday.'

Five

Jane could not tell if the news was good or bad.

Dr. Stephanie Tam bent forward, listening through the Doppler stethoscope, and her sleek black hair fell over her face so that Jane could not read her expression. Lying flat on her back, Jane watched as the Doppler head slid across her bulging belly. Dr. Tam had elegant hands, a surgeon's hands, and she guided the instrument with the same delicacy one might use to pluck a harp. Suddenly that hand paused, and Tam dipped her head lower, in concentration. Jane glanced at her husband, Gabriel, who was sitting right beside her, and she read the same anxiety in his eyes.

Is our baby all right?

At last Dr. Tam straightened and looked at Jane with a calm smile. 'Take a listen,' she said, and turned up the volume on the Doppler.

A rhythmic whoosh pulsed from the speaker, steady and vigorous.

'Those are strong fetal heart tones,' said Tam.

'Then my baby's okay?'

'Baby's doing fine so far.'

'So far? What does that mean?'

'Well, it can't stay in there much longer.' Tam bundled up the stethoscope and slipped it into its carrying case. 'Once you've ruptured your amniotic sac, labor usually starts on its own.'

'But nothing's happening. I'm not feeling any contractions.'

'Exactly. Your baby's refusing to cooperate. You've got a very stubborn kid in there, Jane.'

Gabriel sighed. 'Just like mom here. Wrestling down perps to the very last minute. Can you please tell my wife she's now *officially* on maternity leave?'

'You're definitely off the job now,' said Tam. 'I'm going to get you down to Ultrasound, so we can take a peek in there. Then I think it's time to induce labor.'

'It won't start on its own?' said Jane.

'Your water's broken. You've got an open channel for infection. It's been two hours, and still no contractions. Time to hurry junior along.' Tam moved briskly toward the door. 'They're going to get an IV in you. I'll check with Diagnostic Imaging, see if we can slip you in for a scan right now. Then we need to get that baby out of there, so you can finally be a mommy.'

'This is all happening so fast.'

Tam laughed. 'You've had nine months to think about it. It shouldn't be a *complete* surprise,' she said, and walked out of the room.

Jane stared up at the ceiling. 'I'm not sure I'm ready for this.'

Gabriel squeezed her hand. 'I've been ready for this a long time. It seems like forever.' He lifted her hospital gown and pressed his ear to her naked belly. 'Hello in there, kid!' he called out. 'Daddy's getting impatient, so stop fooling around.'

'Ouch. You did a bad job shaving this morning.'

'I'll do it again, just for you.' He straightened and his gaze met hers. 'I mean it, Jane,' he said. 'I've wanted this for a long time. My own little family.'

'But what if it's not everything you expected?'

'What do you think I expect?'

'You know. The perfect kid, the perfect wife.'

'Now, why would I want the perfect wife when I can have you?' he said and dodged away, laughing as she took a swing at him.

But I did manage to land the perfect husband, she thought, looking into his smiling eyes. I still don't know how I got so lucky. I don't know how a girl who grew up with the nickname Frog Face married a man who could turn every woman's head just by walking into the room.

He leaned toward her and said, softly: 'You still don't believe me, do you? I can say it a thousand times, and you'll never believe me. You're exactly what I want, Jane. You and the baby.' He gave her a kiss on the nose. 'Now. What am I supposed to bring back for you, Mom?'

'Oh, jeez. Don't call me that. It's so *not* sexy.'

'I think it's *very* sexy. In fact . . .'

Laughing, she slapped his hand. 'Go. Get yourself some lunch. And bring me back a hamburger and fries.'

'Against doctor's orders. No food.'

'She doesn't have to know about it.'

'Jane.'

'Okay, okay. Go home and get my hospital bag.'

He saluted her. 'At your command. This is exactly why I took the month off.'

'And can you try my parents again? They're still not answering the phone. Oh, and bring my laptop.'

He sighed and shook his head.

'What?' she said.

'You're about to have a baby, and you want me to bring your laptop?'

'I've got so much paperwork I need to clean up.'

'You're hopeless, Jane.'

She blew him a kiss. 'You knew that when you married me.'

'You know,' said Jane, looking at the wheelchair, 'I could just *walk* to Diagnostic Imaging, if you'll only tell me where it is.'

The volunteer shook her head and locked the brakes on the chair. 'Hospital rules, ma'am, no exceptions. Patients have to be transported in a wheelchair. We don't want you to slip and fall or something, do we?'

Jane looked at the wheelchair, then at the silver-haired volunteer who was going to be pushing it. Poor old lady, Jane thought, I should be the one pushing *her*. Reluctantly she climbed out of bed and settled into the chair as the volunteer transferred the IV bottle. This morning, Jane was wrestling with Billy Wayne Rollo; now she was getting carted around like the queen of Sheba. How embarrassing. As she was rolled down the hall, she could hear the woman wheezing, could smell the old-shoe odor of cigarettes on the woman's breath. What if her escort collapsed? What if she needed CPR? *Then am I allowed to get up, or is that against the rules, too?* She hunched deeper into the wheelchair, avoiding the gazes of everyone they passed in the hallway. Don't look at me, she thought. I feel guilty enough making poor old granny work so hard.

The volunteer backed Jane's wheelchair into the elevator, and parked her next to another patient. He was a gray-haired man, muttering to himself. Jane noticed the Posey restraint strapping the man's torso into the chair, and she thought: Jeez, they're really serious about these wheelchair rules. If you try to get out, they tie you down.

The old man glared at her. 'What the hell're you looking at, lady?'

'Nothing,' said Jane.

'Then stop looking.'

'Okay.'

The black orderly standing behind the old man gave a chuckle. 'Mr. Bodine talks like that

71

to everyone, ma'am. Don't let him bother you.'

Jane shrugged. 'I get a lot more abuse at work.' *Oh, and did I mention that bullets are involved?* She stared straight ahead, watching the floor numbers change, carefully avoiding any eye contact with Mr. Bodine.

'Too many people in this world don't keep to their own damn business,' the old man said. 'Just a bunch of busybodies. Won't stop staring.'

'Now Mr. Bodine,' the orderly said, 'no one's staring at you.'

'*She* was.'

No wonder they tied you up, you old coot, thought Jane.

The elevator opened on the ground floor, and the volunteer wheeled out Jane. As they rolled down the hall toward Diagnostic Imaging, she could feel the gazes of passersby. Able-bodied people walking on their own two feet, eyeing the big-bellied invalid with her little plastic hospital bracelet. She wondered: Is this what it's like for everyone who's confined to a wheelchair? Always the object of sympathetic glances?

Behind her, she heard a familiar cranky voice demand: 'What the hell you looking at, mister?'

Oh please, she thought. Don't let Mr. Bodine be headed to Diagnostic Imaging, too. But she could hear him grumbling behind her as they rolled down the hall and around the corner, into the reception area.

The volunteer parked Jane in the waiting room and left her there, sitting next to the old man.

Don't look at him, she thought. Don't even glance in his direction.

'What, you too stuck up to talk to me?' he said.

Pretend he's not there.

'Huh. So now you're pretending I'm not even here.'

She looked up, relieved, as a door opened and a woman technician in a blue scrub suit came into the waiting room. 'Jane Rizzoli?'

'That's me.'

'Dr. Tam will be down here in a few minutes. I'll bring you back to the room now.'

'What about me?' the old man whined.

'We're not quite ready for you, Mr. Bodine,' the woman said, as she swiveled Jane's wheelchair through the doorway. 'You just be patient.'

'But I gotta piss, goddammit.'

'Yes, I know, I know.'

'You don't know nothing.'

'Know enough not to waste my breath,' the woman muttered as she pushed Jane's chair down the hallway.

'I'm gonna wet your carpet!' he yelled.

'One of your favorite patients?' Jane asked.

'Oh, yeah.' The technician sighed. 'He's everyone's favorite.'

'You think he really has to pee?'

'All the time. Got a prostate as big as my fist, and won't let the surgeons touch it.'

The woman wheeled Jane into a procedure room and locked the wheelchair in place. 'Let me help you onto the table.'

'I can manage.'

'Honey, with a belly that big, you could use a hand up.' The woman grasped Jane's arm and pulled her out of the chair. She stood by as Jane climbed the footstool and settled onto the table.

'Now, you just relax here, okay?' she said, rehanging Jane's IV bottle. 'When Dr. Tam comes down, we'll get started on your sonogram.' The woman walked out, leaving Jane alone in the room. There was nothing to look at but imaging equipment. No windows, no posters on the walls, no magazines. Not even a boring issue of *Golf Digest*.

Jane settled back on the table and stared at the bare ceiling. Placing her hands on her bulging abdomen, she waited for the familiar jab of a tiny foot or elbow, but she felt nothing. Come on, baby, she thought. Talk to me. Tell me you're going to be okay.

Cold air wafted from the AC vent, and she shivered in the flimsy gown. She glanced at her watch and found herself gazing, instead, at the plastic band around her wrist. Patient's name: Rizzoli, Jane. Well, this patient is not particularly patient, she thought. Let's get on with it, people!

The skin on her abdomen suddenly prickled, and she felt her womb tighten. The muscles gently squeezed, held for a moment, then eased off. At last, a contraction.

She looked at the time. 11:50 A.M.

Six

By noon, the temperature had soared into the nineties, baking sidewalks into griddles, and a sulfurous summer haze hung over the city. Outside the medical examiner's building, no reporters still lingered in the parking lot; Maura was able to cross Albany Street unaccosted and walk into the medical center. She shared an elevator with half a dozen freshly minted interns, now on their first month's rotation, and she remembered the lesson she'd learned in medical school: *Don't get sick in July*. They're all so young, she thought, looking at smooth faces, at hair not yet streaked with gray. She seemed to be noticing that more often these days, about cops, about doctors. How young they all looked. And what do these interns see when they look at me? she wondered. Just a woman pushing middle age, wearing no uniform, no name tag with MD on my lapel. Perhaps they assumed she was a patient's relative, scarcely worth more than a glance. Once, she'd been like these interns, young and cocky in her white coat. Before she'd learned the lessons of defeat.

The elevator opened and she followed the interns into the medical unit. They breezed right past the nurses' station, untouchable in their white coats. It was Maura, in her civilian clothes, whom the ward clerk immediately stopped with a frown, a brisk question: 'Excuse me, are you looking for someone?'

'I'm here to visit a patient,' said Maura. 'She was admitted last night, through the ER. I understand she was transferred out of ICU this morning.'

'The patient's name?'

Maura hesitated. 'I believe she's still registered as Jane Doe. Dr. Cutler told me she's in room four-thirty-one.'

The ward clerk's gaze narrowed. 'I'm sorry. We've had calls from reporters all day. We can't answer any more questions about that patient.'

'I'm not a reporter. I'm Dr. Isles, from the medical examiner's office. I told Dr. Cutler I'd be coming by to check on the patient.'

'May I see some identification?'

Maura dug into her purse and placed her ID on the countertop. This is what I get for showing up without my lab coat, she thought. She could see the interns cruising down the hall, unimpeded, like a flock of strutting white geese.

'You could call Dr. Cutler,' Maura suggested. 'He knows who I am.'

'Well, I *suppose* it's okay,' said the ward clerk,

handing back the ID. 'There's been so much fuss over this patient, they had to send over a security guard.' As Maura headed up the hall, the clerk called out: 'He'll probably want to see your ID as well!'

Prepared to endure another round of questions, she kept her ID in hand as she walked to room 431, but she found no guard standing outside the closed door. Just as she was about to knock, she heard a thud inside the room, and the clang of falling metal.

At once, she pushed into the room and found a confusing tableau. A doctor stood at the bed-side, reaching up toward the IV bottle. Opposite him, a security guard was leaning over the patient, trying to restrain her wrists. A bedside stand had just toppled, and the floor was slick with spilled water.

'Do you need help?' called Maura.

The doctor glanced over his shoulder at her, and she caught a glimpse of blue eyes, blond hair cut short as a brush. 'No, we're fine. We've got her,' he said.

'Let me tie that restraint,' she offered, and moved to the guard's side of the bed. Just as she reached for the loose wrist strap, she saw the woman's hand snap free. Heard the guard give a grunt of alarm.

The explosion made Maura flinch. Warmth splashed her face, and the guard suddenly staggered sideways, against her. She stumbled under his weight, landing on her back beneath him. Cold water soaked into her blouse from the wet floor, and from above seeped the liquid heat of blood. She tried to shove aside the body now weighing down on her, but he was heavy, so heavy he was crushing the breath from her lungs.

His body began to shake, seized by agonal twitches. Fresh heat splashed her face, her mouth, and she gagged at the taste. *I'm drowning in it.* With a cry, she pushed against him, and the body, slippery with blood, slid off her.

She scrambled to her feet, and focused on the woman, who was now free of all her restraints. Only then did she see what the woman was gripping in both hands.

A gun. She has the guard's gun.

The doctor had vanished. Maura was alone with Jane Doe, and as they stared at each other, every detail of the woman's face stood out with terrible clarity. The tangled black hair, the wild-eyed gaze. The inexorable tightening of the tendons in her arm as she slowly squeezed the grip.

Dear god, she's going to pull the trigger.

'Please,' whispered Maura. 'I only want to help you.'

The sound of running footsteps made the woman's attention jerk sideways. The door flew open and a nurse stared, openmouthed, at the carnage in the room.

Suddenly Jane Doe sprang out of the bed. It happened so fast that Maura had no time to react. She snapped rigid as the woman grabbed

78

her arm, as the gun barrel bit into her neck. Heart slamming against her ribs, Maura let herself be shoved to the door, cold steel pressed against her flesh. The nurse backed away, too terrified to say a word. Maura was forced out of the room, into the hallway. Where was security? Was anyone calling for help? They kept moving, toward the nurses' station, the woman's sweating body pressed close, her panicked breaths roaring in Maura's ear.

'Watch out! Get out of the way, she's got a gun!' Maura heard, and she glimpsed the group of interns she'd seen only moments earlier. Not so cocky now in their white coats, they were backing off, wide-eyed. So many witnesses; so many useless people.

Someone help me, goddammit!

Jane Doe and her hostage now moved into full view of the nurses' station, and the stunned women behind the counter watched their progress, silent as a group of wax figurines. The phone rang, unanswered.

The elevator was straight ahead.

The woman punched the down button. The door slid open, and the woman gave Maura a shove into the elevator, stepped in behind her, and pressed ONE.

Four floors. *Will I still be alive when that door opens again?*

The woman backed away to the opposite wall. Maura stared back, unflinching. *Force her to see who I am. Make her look me in the eye when she pulls the trigger.* The elevator was chilly, and Jane Doe was naked under the flimsy hospital gown, but sweat glistened on her face, and her hands trembled around the grip.

'Why are you doing this?' Maura asked. 'I never hurt you! Last night, I tried to help you. I'm the one who *saved* you.'

The woman said nothing. Uttered not a word, not a sound. All Maura heard was her breaths, harsh and rapid with fear.

The elevator bell rang, and the woman's gaze shot to the door. Frantically Maura tried to remember the layout of the hospital lobby. She recalled an information kiosk near the front door, staffed by a silver-haired volunteer. A gift shop. A bank of telephones.

The door opened. The woman grabbed Maura's arm and shoved her out of the elevator first. Once again, the gun was at Maura's jugular. Her throat was dry as ash as she emerged into the lobby. She glanced left, then right, but saw no people, no witnesses. Then she spotted the lone security guard, cowering behind the information kiosk. One look at his white hair, and Maura's heart sank. This was no rescuer; he was just a scared old guy in a uniform. A guy who was just as likely to shoot the hostage.

Outside, a siren howled, like an approaching banshee.

Maura's head was snapped back as the woman grabbed her hair, yanking her so close she could feel hot breath against the back of her neck, could smell the woman's sharp scent of fear. They moved toward the lobby exit, and Maura caught a panicked glimpse of the elderly guard, quaking behind the desk. Saw silver balloons bobbing in the gift shop window, and a telephone receiver, dangling by its cord. Then she was forced out the door, straight into the heat of afternoon.

A Boston PD cruiser screeched to a stop at the curb, and two cops scrambled out, weapons drawn. They froze, their gazes on Maura, who now stood blocking their line of fire.

Another siren screamed closer.

The woman's breaths were now desperate gasps as she confronted her rapidly narrowing options. No way forward; she yanked Maura backward, dragging her once again into the building, retreating into the lobby.

'Please,' Maura whispered as she was tugged toward the hallway. 'There's no way out! Just put it down. Put the gun down, and we'll meet them together, okay? We'll walk over to them, and they won't hurt you . . .'

She saw the two cops edge forward step by step, matching their quarry's pace the whole way. Maura still blocked their line of fire, and they could do nothing but watch, helpless, as the woman retreated up the hall pulling her hostage with her. Maura heard a gasp, and out of the corner of her eye, she spotted shocked bystanders frozen in place.

'Back away, people!' one of the cops yelled. 'Everyone get out of the way!'

This is where it ends, thought Maura. I'm cornered with a madwoman who can't be talked into surrender. She could hear the woman's breathing accelerating to frantic whimpers, could feel the fear running through the woman's arm, like a current through high-voltage wires. She felt herself being dragged inexorably toward a bloody conclusion, and she could almost see it through the eyes of the cops who were now inching forward. The blast of the woman's gun, the gore exploding from the hostage's head. The inevitable hail of bullets that would finally end it. Until then, the police were stalemated. And Jane Doe, trapped in the jaws of panic, was just as helpless and unable to change the course of events.

I'm the only one who can change things. Now is the time to do it.

Maura took a breath, released it. As the air whooshed from her lungs she let her muscles go slack. Her legs collapsed, and she sagged to the floor.

The woman gave a grunt of surprise, struggling to support Maura. But a limp body is heavy, and already her hostage was sliding to the ground, her human shield collapsing. Suddenly Maura was free, rolling sideways. She wrapped her arms around her head and curled into a ball, waiting for the blast of gunfire. But all she heard was running footsteps and shouts.

'Shit. I can't get a clean shot!'

'Everyone, move the fuck *out* of the way!'

A hand grabbed her, shook her. 'Lady? Are you okay? Are you *okay*?'

Trembling, she finally looked up into the face of the cop. She heard radios crackle, and sirens keened like women grieving the dead.

'Come on, you need to move away.' The cop grabbed her arm and pulled her to her feet. She was shaking so violently she could barely stand, so he slung his arm around her waist and guided her toward the exit. 'All of you!' he yelled at the bystanders. 'Get out of the building *now*.'

Maura glanced back. Jane Doe was nowhere to be seen.

'Can you walk?' the cop asked.

Unable to say a word, she merely nodded.

'Then go! We need everyone to evacuate. You don't want to be in here.'

Not when it's about to get bloody.

She took a few steps forward. Glanced back one last time, and saw that the cop was already moving down the hallway. A sign pointed to the wing where Jane Doe was about to make her last stand.

Diagnostic Imaging.

Jane Rizzoli startled awake and blinked, momentarily confused, at the ceiling. She had not expected to doze off, but the exam table was surprisingly comfortable, and she was tired; she had not been sleeping well for the past few nights. She looked at the clock on the wall and realized that she'd been left alone for over half an hour. How much longer was she supposed to wait? She let another five minutes go by, her irritation mounting.

Okay, I've had it. I'm going to find out what's taking so long. And I'm not going to wait for the wheelchair.

She climbed off the table and her bare feet slapped onto the cold floor. She took two steps, and realized that her arm was still tethered by the IV to a plastic bag of saline. She moved the bag to a rolling IV pole and wheeled it to the door. Looking into the hallway, she saw no one. Not a nurse or an orderly or an X-ray tech.

Well, *this* was reassuring. They'd forgotten all about her.

She headed down the windowless hall, pushing her IV pole, the wheels shimmying as they rolled over linoleum. She passed one open doorway, then another, and saw vacant procedure tables, deserted rooms. Where had everyone gone? In the short time she'd been sleeping, they had all disappeared.

Has it really been only half an hour?

She halted in that empty hallway, gripped by the sudden, *Twilight Zone* thought that while she'd been asleep, everyone else in the world had vanished. She glanced up and down the hallway, trying to remember the route back to the waiting area. She had not been paying attention when the technician had wheeled her into the procedure room. Opening a door, she saw an office. Opened another door and found a file room.

No people.

She began to pad faster through the warren of hallways, the IV pole clattering beside her. What kind of hospital was this, anyway, leaving a poor pregnant woman all alone? She was going to complain, damn right, she was going to complain. She could be in labor! She could be dying! Instead, she was royally pissed off, and that was *not* the mood you wanted a pregnant woman to be in. Not *this* pregnant woman.

At last she spotted the exit sign, and with choice words already on her lips, she yanked open the door. At her first glimpse into the waiting room, she did not immediately understand the situation. Mr. Bodine was still strapped to his wheelchair and parked in the corner. The ultrasound technician and the receptionist were huddled together on one of the couches. On the other couch, Dr. Tam sat next to the black orderly. What was this, a tea party? While she'd been forgotten in the back room, why had her doctor been lounging out here on the couch?

Then she spotted the medical chart lying on the floor, and she saw the toppled mug, the spilled coffee splattered across the rug. And she realized that Dr. Tam was not lounging; her back was rigid, the muscles of her face tight with fear. Her eyes were not focused on Jane, but on something else.

That's when Jane understood. *Someone is standing right behind me.*

Seven

Maura sat in the mobile operations command trailer, surrounded by telephones, TVs, and laptop computers. The air-conditioning was not working, and the trailer had to be well over ninety degrees inside. Officer Emerton, who was monitoring radio chatter, fanned himself as he gulped from a bottle of water. But Captain Hayder, Boston PD's special ops commander, looked perfectly cool as he studied the CAD diagrams now displayed on the computer monitor. Beside him sat the hospital's facilities manager, pointing out the relevant features on the blueprints.

'The area where she's now holed up is Diagnostic Imaging,' said the manager. 'That used to be the hospital's old X-ray wing, before we moved it into the new addition. I'm afraid that's going to present a big problem for you, Captain.'

'What problem?' said Hayder.

'There's lead shielding in these outside walls,

and there are no exterior windows or doors in that wing. You're not going to be able to blast your way in from the outside. Or toss in a tear gas canister.'

'And the only way into Diagnostic Imaging is through this interior hallway door?'

'Correct.' The manager looked at Hayder. 'I take it she's locked that door?'

Hayder nodded. 'Which means she's trapped herself in there. We've pulled our men back down the hall, so they're not in the direct line of fire if she decides to make a run.'

'She's in a dead end. The only way out is going to be through your men. For the moment, you've got her locked up tight. But conversely, you are going to have a hard time getting *in*.'

'So we're at an impasse.'

The manager clicked the mouse, zooming in on a section of the blueprint. 'Now, there *is* one possibility here, depending on where in that particular wing she's chosen to hole up. The lead shielding is built into all these diagnostic areas. But here in the waiting room, the walls aren't shielded.'

'What building materials are we talking about there?'

'Plaster. Drywall. You could easily drill through this ceiling from the floor above.' The facilities manager looked at Hayder.

'But all she has to do then is pull back into the lead-shielded area, and she's untouchable.'

'Excuse me,' cut in Maura.

Hayder turned to her, blue eyes sharp with irritation. 'Yes?' he snapped.

'Can I leave now, Captain Hayder? There's nothing else I can tell you.'

'Not yet.'

'How much longer?'

'You'll have to wait here until our hostage negotiator can interview you. He wanted all witnesses retained.'

'I'll be happy to talk to him, but there's no reason I have to sit in here. My office is right across the street. You know where to find me.'

'That's not close enough, Dr. Isles. We need to keep you sequestered.' Already, Hayder was turning his attention back to the CAD display, her protest of no concern to him. 'Things are moving fast, and we can't waste time tracking down witnesses who wander off.'

'I won't wander off. And I'm not the only witness. There were nurses taking care of her.'

'We've sequestered them as well. We're talking to all of you.'

'And there was that doctor, in her room. He was right there when it happened.'

'Captain Hayder?' said Emerton, turning from the radio. 'First four floors are now evacuated. They can't move the critically ill patients from the upper floors, but we've got all nonessentials out of the building.'

'Our perimeters?'

'The inner is now established. They've got the barricades up in the hallway. We're still awaiting more personnel to tighten the outer perimeter.'

The TV above Hayder's head was tuned to a local Boston station, with the sound turned off. It was a live news broadcast, the images startlingly familiar. That's Albany Street, Maura thought. And there's the command trailer where, at this moment, I'm being held prisoner. While the city of Boston was watching the drama play out on their TV screens, she was trapped at the center of the crisis.

The sudden rocking of the trailer made her turn toward the door, and she saw a man step in. Another cop, she thought, noting the weapon holstered at his hip, but this man was shorter and far less imposing than Hayder. Sweat had shellacked sparse strands of brown hair to his bright red scalp.

'Christ, it's even hotter in here,' the man said. 'Isn't your AC on?'

'It's on,' said Emerton. 'But it's not worth shit. We didn't have time to get it serviced. It's hell on the electronics.'

'Not to mention the people,' the man said, his gaze settling on Maura. He held out his hand to her. 'You're Dr. Isles, right? I'm Lieutenant Leroy Stillman. They've called me in to try to calm things down. See if we can resolve this without any violence.'

'You're the hostage negotiator.'

He gave a modest shrug. 'That's what they call me.'

They shook hands. Perhaps it was his

unassuming appearance – the hang-dog face, the balding head – that put her at ease. Unlike Hayder, who seemed to be driven by pure testosterone, this man regarded her with a quiet and patient smile. As if he had all the time in the world to talk to her. He looked at Hayder. 'This trailer is unbearable. She shouldn't have to sit in here.'

'You asked us to retain the witnesses.'

'Yes, but not roast them alive.' He opened the door. 'Just about anywhere else is going to be more comfortable than in here.'

They stepped out, and Maura took in deep breaths, grateful to be out of that stifling box. Here, at least, there was a breeze. During the time she'd been sequestered, Albany Street had transformed into a sea of police vehicles. The driveway to the medical examiner's building across the street was now hemmed in, and she didn't know how she was going to get her car out of that parking lot. In the distance, beyond the police barricades, she saw satellite dishes, like blossoms perched on tall stalks above the news vans. She wondered if the TV crews were just as hot and miserable, sitting inside their vehicles, as she had been inside the command trailer. She hoped so.

'Thank you for waiting,' said Stillman.

'I was hardly given a choice.'

'I know it's an inconvenience, but we have to hold on to witnesses until we can debrief them. Now the situation's contained, and I need intelligence. We don't know her motives. We don't

90

know how many people might be in there with her. I need to know who we're dealing with, so I can choose the right approach when she starts talking to us.'

'She hasn't yet?'

'No. We've isolated the three phone lines into the hospital wing where she's barricaded, so we control all her outgoing communications. We've tried calling in half a dozen times, but she keeps hanging up on us. Eventually, though, she's going to want to communicate. They almost always do.'

'You seem to think she's like every other hostage taker.'

'People who do this tend to behave in similar ways.'

'And how many hostage takers are women?'

'It's unusual, I have to admit.'

'Have you ever dealt with a female hostage taker?'

He hesitated. 'The truth is,' he said, 'this is a first for me. A first for all of us. We're confronting the rare exception here. Women just don't take hostages.'

'This one did.'

He nodded. 'And until I know more, I have to approach it the way I would any other hostage crisis. Before I negotiate with her, I need to know as much about her as possible. Who she is, and why she's doing this.'

Maura shook her head. 'I don't know that I can help you with that.'

'You're the last person who had any contact with her. Tell me everything you can remember. Every word she spoke, every twitch.'

'I was alone with her for such a short time. Only a few minutes.'

'Did you two talk?'

'I tried to.'

'What did you say to her?'

Maura felt her palms go slick again as she remembered that ride in the elevator. How the woman's hand had trembled as she gripped the weapon. 'I tried to calm her down, tried to reason with her. I told her I only wanted to help.'

'How did she respond?'

'She didn't say anything. She was completely silent. That was the most frightening part.' She looked at Stillman. 'Her absolute silence.'

He frowned. 'Did she react to your words in any way? Are you sure she could hear you?'

'She's not deaf. She reacted to sounds. I know she heard the police sirens.'

'Yet she didn't say a single word?' He shook his head. 'This is bizarre. Are we dealing with a language barrier? This will make it tough to negotiate.'

'She didn't strike me as the negotiating type anyway.'

'Start from the beginning, Dr. Isles. Everything she did, everything you did.'

'I've gone over all this with Captain Hayder. Asking me the same questions again and again isn't going to get you any more answers.'

92

'I know you're repeating yourself. But something you remember could be the vital detail. The one thing I can use.'

'She was pointing a gun at my head. It was hard to focus on anything else but staying alive.'

'You were with her. You know her most recent state of mind. Do you have any idea why she took these actions? Whether she's likely to harm any hostages she's holding?'

'She's already killed one man. Shouldn't that tell you something?'

'But we've heard no gunshots since then, so we've gotten past the critical first thirty minutes, which is the most dangerous period. The time when the shooter's still scared and most likely to kill a captive. It's been almost an hour now, and she's made no other moves. Hurt no one else, as far as we know.'

'Then what is she doing in there?'

'We have no idea. We're still scrambling for background information. The homicide unit is checking into how she ended up at the morgue, and we've lifted what we think are her fingerprints from the hospital room. As long as no one's getting hurt, time is our friend. The longer this goes on, the more information we'll have on her. And the more likely we'll settle it without bloodshed, without heroics.' He glanced toward the hospital. 'See those cops over there? They're probably champing at the bit to rush the building. If it comes to that, then I've failed. My rule of thumb for hostage incidents is simple: Slow things down. We've got her contained in a wing with no windows, no exits, so she can't escape. She can't go mobile. So we let her sit and think about her situation. And she'll realize that she's got no other choice but to surrender.'

'If she's rational enough to understand that.'

He regarded her for a moment. A look that gently probed the significance of what she just said. 'Do you think she's rational?'

'I think she's terrified,' Maura said. 'When we were alone in that elevator, I saw the look in her eyes. The panic.'

'Is that why she fired the gun?'

'She must have felt threatened. There were three of us crowding around her bed, trying to restrain her.'

'Three of you? The nurse I spoke to said that when she stepped into the room, she saw only you and the guard.'

'There was a doctor as well. A young man, blond.'

'The nurse didn't see him.'

'Oh, he ran. After that gun went off, he was out of there like a rabbit.' She paused, still bitter about the abandonment. 'I was the one trapped in the room.'

'Why do you think the patient shot only the guard? If there were three of you standing around the bed?'

'He was bending toward her. He was closest.'

'Or was it his uniform?'

She frowned. 'What do you mean?'

'Think about it. A uniform is a symbol of authority. She could have thought he was a policeman. It makes me wonder if she has a criminal record.'

'A lot of people are afraid of the police. You don't have to be a criminal.'

'Why didn't she shoot the doctor?'

'I told you, he ran. He was out of there.'

'She didn't shoot you, either.'

'Because she needed a hostage. I was the closest warm body.'

'Do you think she would have killed you? Given the chance?'

Maura met his gaze. 'I think that woman will do anything to stay alive.'

The trailer door suddenly swung open. Captain Hayder stuck his head out and said to Stillman: 'You'd better come in and listen to this, Leroy.'

'What is it?'

'It just aired on the radio.'

Maura followed Stillman back into the trailer, which had grown even more stifling in just the short time they had been standing outside.

'Replay the broadcast,' Hayder said to Emerton.

Over the speaker came a man's excited voice. '. . . you're listening to KBUR, and this is Rob Roy, your host on this very weird afternoon. We've got a *bee-zarre* situation here, folks. There's a lady caller on the line right now who claims she's the one holding our local SWAT

95

team at bay over at the medical center. Now, I didn't believe her at first, but our producer's been talking to her. We think she's the real deal . . .'

'What the hell is this?' said Stillman. 'It's got to be a hoax. We have those phone lines isolated.'

'Just listen,' said Hayder.

'. . . so hello, miss?' said the DJ. 'Talk to us. Tell us your name.'

A woman's throaty voice answered: 'My name is not important.'

'Okay. Well, why the heck are you doing this?'

'The die is cast. This is all I wish to say.'

'What's that supposed to mean?'

'Tell them. Say it. The die is cast.'

'Okay, okay. Whatever it means, the whole city of Boston's just heard it. Folks, if you're listening, the die is cast. This is Rob Roy at KBUR, and we're on the phone with the lady who's causing all that ruckus over at the—'

'You tell the police to stay away,' the woman said. 'I have six people here in this room. I have enough bullets for everyone.'

'Whoa, ma'am! You want to calm down there. There's no reason to hurt anybody.'

Stillman's face had flushed an angry red. He turned to Hayder. 'How did this happen? I thought we isolated those phone lines.'

'We did. She used a cell phone to call out.'

'Whose cell phone?'

'The number's listed to a Stephanie Tam.'

'Do we know who that is?'

'. . . oops! Folks, I'm in trouble,' said Rob Roy.

'My producer just told me that I have been ordered by Boston's finest to cease and desist talking to this caller. The police are going to shut us down, friends, and I'm going to have to cut this conversation short. Are you still there, ma'am? Hello?' A pause. 'It looks like we lost our caller. Well, I hope she calms down. Lady, if you're still listening to me, please don't hurt anyone. We can get you help, okay? And to all my listeners out there, you heard it on KBUR. "The die is cast . . ."'

Emerton stopped the recording. 'That's it,' he said. 'That's what we caught on tape. We shut down that call right there, as soon as we heard who the DJ was talking to. But that much of the conversation got on the air.'

Stillman looked stunned. He stared at the now-silent audio equipment.

'What the hell is she doing, Leroy?' asked Hayder. 'Was that just a cry for attention? Is she trying to get public sympathy?'

'I don't know. It was weird.'

'Why isn't she talking to *us*? Why call a radio station? We're the ones trying to call her, and she keeps hanging up on us!'

'She has an accent.' Stillman looked at Hayder. 'She's definitely not American.'

'And what was that thing she said? *The die is cast.* What's that supposed to mean? The game's in play?'

'It's a quote from Julius Caesar,' said Maura.

They all looked at her. 'What?'

'It's what Caesar said as he stood on the edge of the Rubicon. If he crossed the river, it meant he was declaring civil war on Rome. He knew, if he made that move, there'd be no turning back.'

'What does Julius Caesar have to do with any of this?' said Hayder.

'I'm just telling you where the phrase comes from. When Caesar ordered his troops to cross the river, he knew he'd passed the point of no return. It was a gamble, but he was a gambler, and he liked to play dice. When he made his choice, he said, "The die is cast."' She paused. 'And he marched into history.'

'So that's what it means to cross the Rubicon,' said Stillman.

Maura nodded. 'Our hostage taker has made a choice. She's just told us there's no turning back.'

Emerton called out: 'We've got the info on that cell phone. Stephanie Tam is one of the doctors at the medical center. Department of OB-Gyn. She's not answering her beeper, and the last time anyone saw her, she was headed down to Diagnostic Imaging to see her patient. The hospital's going through their personnel roster, trying to identify everyone on staff who's still unaccounted for.'

'It seems we now have the name of at least one of the hostages,' said Stillman.

'What about that cell phone? We tried calling it, but she hangs up on us. Do we let it stay operative?'

'If we cut off service, we could make her angry.

For the moment, allow her to keep the link. We'll just monitor her calls.' Stillman paused and took out a handkerchief to wipe the sweat from his forehead. 'At least she's now communicating – just not with us.'

It's already stifling in here, thought Maura, looking at Stillman's flushed face. And the day's about to get much hotter. She felt herself swaying and realized she could not bear to stay in this trailer a moment longer. 'I need to get some fresh air,' she said. 'Can I leave?'

Stillman gave her a distracted glance. 'Yes. Yes, go ahead. Wait – do we have your contact information?'

'Captain Hayder has my home and cell phone number. You can reach me twenty-four hours a day.'

She stepped outside and paused, blinking in the midday sunshine. Taking in, through dazed eyes, the chaos on Albany Street. This was the same street she traveled to work every day, the same view she saw every morning as she approached the driveway of the medical examiner's building. It had been transformed into a snarl of vehicles and a regiment of Special Operations Division cops in black uniforms. Everyone was waiting for the next move of the woman who had lit the fuse on this crisis. A woman whose identity was still a mystery to them all.

She started toward her building, weaving past parked cruisers, and ducked beneath a strand of police tape. Only as she straightened again did she spot the familiar figure walking toward her. In the two years she'd known Gabriel Dean, she had never seen him agitated, had seldom seen him display any strong emotions. But the man she now saw was wearing an expression of unalloyed panic.

'Have you heard any names yet?' he asked.

She shook her head, bewildered. 'Names?'

'The hostages. Who's in the building?'

'I've only heard them mention one name so far. A doctor.'

'*Who?*'

She paused, startled by his sharp query. 'A Dr. Tam. Her cell phone was used to call a radio station.'

He turned and stared at the hospital. 'Oh, Jesus.'

'What's the matter?'

'I can't find Jane. She wasn't evacuated with the other patients on her floor.'

'When did she go into the hospital?'

'This morning, after her water broke.' He looked at Maura.

'Dr. Tam was the one who admitted her.'

Maura stared at him, suddenly remembering what she'd just heard in the command trailer. That Dr. Tam had been headed down to Diagnostic Imaging to see her patient.

Jane. The doctor was going down to see Jane.

'I think you'd better come with me,' said Maura.

Eight

I come to the hospital to have a baby. Instead I'm about to get my head blown off.

Jane sat on the couch, wedged between Dr. Tam on her right and the black orderly on her left. She could feel him trembling beside her, his skin cold and clammy in the air-conditioned room. Dr. Tam sat perfectly still, her face a stone mask. On the other couch, the receptionist sat hugging herself, and beside her, the woman technician was quietly crying. No one dared say a word; the only sound came from the waiting-room television, which had been playing continuously. Jane looked around at the name tags on the uniforms. Mac. Domenica. Glenna. Dr. Tam. She glanced down at the patient wristband she was wearing. RIZZOLI, JANE. All of us are neatly labeled for the morgue. No ID problems here, folks. She thought of Bostonions opening their *Tribune* tomorrow morning and seeing these same names printed in stark black and white on the front page. VICTIMS KILLED IN

HOSPITAL SIEGE. She thought of those readers skimming right past the name 'Rizzoli, Jane,' and then turning their attention straight to the sports page.

Is this how it ends? Something as stupid as being in the wrong place at the wrong time? Hey wait, she wanted to shout. I'm pregnant! In the movies, nobody shoots the pregnant hostage!

But this wasn't the movies, and she couldn't predict what the crazy lady with the gun would do. That's what Jane had dubbed her. The Crazy Lady. What else could you call a woman who stalks back and forth, waving a gun? Only occasionally did the woman stop to look at the TV, which was tuned to channel six. Live coverage of the medical center hostage situation. Look Ma, I'm on television, thought Jane. I'm one of the lucky hostages trapped in that building. It's kind of like the reality show Survivor but with bullets.

And real blood.

She noticed that the Crazy Lady was wearing a patient wristband like Jane's. Escapee from the psych unit? Just try to make *her* sit obediently in a wheelchair. The woman was barefoot, her shapely ass peeking out from the backless hospital gown. She had long legs, muscular thighs, and a luxuriant mane of jet black hair. Dress her up in a sexy leather outfit, and she'd look like Xena the Warrior Princess.

'I gotta pee,' Mr. Bodine said.

The Crazy Lady didn't even glance at him.

'Hey! Is anyone listening to me? I said I gotta *pee*!'

Oh jeez, just do it, old man, thought Rizzoli. Pee in your wheelchair. Don't tick off someone who's holding a gun.

On the TV, a blond reporter appeared. Zoe Fossey, reporting from Albany Street. 'We have no word yet on how many hostages are trapped inside the hospital wing. Police have cordoned off the building. So far there is one known fatality, a security guard who was shot to death while trying to restrain the patient . . .'

The Crazy Lady halted, her gaze riveted on the screen. One of her bare feet landed on the manila folder that was lying on the floor. Only then did Jane notice the name on that chart, written in black felt ink.

Rizzoli, Jane.

The news report ended, and Crazy Lady resumed her pacing, her bare feet slapping across the folder. It was Jane's outpatient chart, which Dr. Tam had probably been carrying when she'd walked into Diagnostic Imaging. Now it was right at the Crazy Lady's feet. All she had to do was bend down and flip open the cover and read the first page, where the patient information was listed. Name, birth date, marital status, Social Security number.

And occupation. *Detective, Homicide. Boston Police Department.*

This woman is now under siege by the Boston

PD SWAT team, thought Jane. When she finds out that I'm a cop, too . . .

She didn't want to complete the thought; she knew where it would lead. She looked down once again at her arm, at the hospital ID band printed with the name: RIZZOLI, JANE. If she could just get this thing off, she could jam it between the cushions, and the Crazy Lady wouldn't be able to match her to the chart. That was the thing to do, get rid of this dangerous ID band. Then she'd be just another pregnant lady in the hospital. Not a cop, not a threat.

She slipped a finger under the wristband and tugged, but it didn't give way. She pulled harder, but could not break it. What the hell was it made of, anyway? Titanium? But of course it had to be sturdy. You didn't want confused old guys like Mr. Bodine yanking off their IDs and wandering the halls, anonymous. She strained harder against the plastic, her teeth gritting together, the muscles quietly straining. I'll have to chew it off, she thought. When the Crazy Lady isn't looking, I could—

She froze. Realized the woman was standing right in front of her, a bare foot planted once again on Jane's medical chart. Slowly Jane's gaze lifted to the woman's face. Up till then she had avoided looking directly at her captor, afraid to draw any attention to herself. Now, to her horror, she saw that the woman was focused on her – only on her – and she felt like the herd's lone gazelle singled out for slaughter. The woman even *looked* like a feline, long-limbed and graceful, her black hair glossy as a panther's. Her blue eyes were as intense as searchlights, and Jane was now caught in the beam.

'This is what they do,' the woman said, eyeing Jane's wristband. 'They put labels on you. Like in concentration camp.' She showed her own wristband, printed with DOE, JANE. There was an original name for you, thought Jane, and she almost wanted to laugh. I'm being held hostage by Jane Doe. It's down to Jane vs. Jane. The real one versus the fake one. Didn't the hospital know who this woman was when they admitted her? Judging by the few words she'd spoken, it was clear she was not American. Eastern European. Russian, maybe.

The woman ripped off her own wristband and tossed it aside. Then she grabbed Jane's wrist and gave her ID band a sharp yank as well. It snapped apart.

'There. No more labels,' the woman said. She glanced at Jane's wristband. 'Rizzoli. This is Italian.'

'Yes.' Jane kept her gaze on the woman's face, afraid to even glance downward, to draw her attention to the manila folder lying beneath her bare foot. The woman took her steady eye contact as a sign of connection between them. Up till now, Crazy Lady had scarcely said a word to any of them. Now she was talking. This is good, thought Jane. An attempt at conversation. Try to connect with her, establish a relationship. Be her friend. She wouldn't kill a friend, would she?

The woman was looking at Jane's pregnant belly.

'I'm having my first baby,' said Jane.

The woman looked up at the clock on the wall. She was waiting for something. Counting the minutes as they ticked by.

Jane decided to dip her toe further into conversational waters. 'What – what is your name?' she ventured.

'Why?'

'I just wanted to know.' *So I can stop calling you the Crazy Lady.*

'It makes no difference. I am dead already.' The woman looked at her. 'So are you.'

Jane stared into those burning eyes, and for one frightening moment she thought: What if it's true? What if we *are* already dead, and this is just a version of hell?

'Please,' the receptionist murmured. 'Please let us go. You don't need us. Just let us open the door and walk out.'

The woman began to pace again, her bare feet intermittently treading across the fallen chart. 'You think they will let you live? After you have been with me? Everyone who is with me dies.'

'What's she talking about?' Dr. Tam whispered.

She's paranoid, thought Jane. Having delusions of persecution.

The woman suddenly came to a stop and stared down at the manila folder near her feet.

Don't open it. Please don't open it.

The woman picked it up, eyeing the name on the cover.

Distract her, now!

'Excuse me,' she said. 'I really – I really need to use the bathroom. Being pregnant and all.' She pointed to the waiting room toilet. 'Please, can I go?'

The woman dropped the chart down on the coffee table where it landed just out of Jane's reach. 'You do not lock the door.'

'No. I promise.'

'Go.'

Dr. Tam touched Jane's hand. 'Do you need help? Do you want me to go with you?'

'No. I'm okay,' said Jane and she rose on unsteady legs. Wanted desperately to sweep up the medical chart as she moved past the coffee table, but the Crazy Lady was watching her the whole time. She walked to the restroom, turned on the light, and closed the door. Felt sudden relief to be alone, and not staring at a gun.

I could lock the door anyway. I could just stay in here and wait it out until it's over.

But she thought of Dr. Tam and the orderly and Glenna and Domenica clinging to one another on the couch. If I piss off Crazy Lady, they'll be the ones to suffer. I'd be a coward, hiding behind a locked door.

She used the toilet and washed her hands. Scooped water into her mouth, because she did not know when she'd next get a chance to drink.

Wiping her wet chin, she scanned the small restroom, searching for something she could use as a weapon, but all she saw were paper towels and a soap dispenser and a stainless steel trash can.

The door suddenly swung open. She turned to see her captor staring at her. *She doesn't trust me. Of course she doesn't trust me.*

'I'm finished,' said Jane. 'I'm coming out now.' She left the restroom and crossed back to the couch. Saw that the medical chart was still lying on the coffee table.

'Now we sit and wait,' the woman said, and she settled into a chair, the gun on her lap.

'What are we waiting for?' Jane asked.

The woman stared at her. Said, calmly: 'The end.'

A shudder went through Jane. At the same time, she felt something else: a tightening in her abdomen, like a hand slowly squeezing into a fist. She held her breath as the contraction turned painful, as sweat beaded on her forehead. Five seconds. Ten. Slowly it eased off, and she leaned back against the couch, breathing deeply.

Dr. Tam frowned at her. 'What's wrong?'

Jane swallowed. 'I think I'm in labor.'

'We've got a cop in there?' said Captain Hayder.

'You can't let this leak out,' said Gabriel. 'I don't want *anyone* to know what her job is. If the hostage taker finds out she's holding a cop . . .' Gabriel took a deep breath, and said quietly: 'It can't get out to the media. That's all.'

Leroy Stillman nodded. 'We won't let it. After what happened to that security guard . . .' He stopped. 'We need to keep this under wraps.'

Hayder said, 'Having a cop in there could work to our advantage.'

'Excuse me?' said Maura, startled that Hayder would make such a statement in Gabriel's presence.

'Detective Rizzoli's got a good head on her shoulders. And she can handle a weapon. She could make a difference in how this goes down.'

'She's also nine months pregnant and due to deliver any minute. What, exactly, do you expect her to do?'

'I'm just saying she's got a cop's instincts. That's good.'

'Right now,' said Gabriel, 'the only instinct I want my wife to follow is the one for self-preservation. I want her alive and safe. So don't count on her to be heroic. Just get her the hell out of there.'

Stillman said, 'We won't do anything to endanger your wife, Agent Dean. I promise you that.'

'Who is this hostage taker?'

'We're still trying to ID her.'

'What does she want?'

Hayder cut in: 'Maybe Agent Dean and Dr. Isles should step out of the trailer and let us get back to work.'

'No, it's okay,' said Stillman. 'He needs to know. Of course he needs to know.' He looked at

Gabriel. 'We're going slow on this, giving her a chance to calm down and start talking. As long as no one's getting hurt, we have time.'

Gabriel nodded. 'That's the way it should be handled. No bullets, no assault. Just keep them all alive.'

Emerton called out: 'Captain, we've got the list. Names of personnel and patients still unaccounted for.'

Stillman snatched up the page as it came off the printer and scanned down the names.

'Is she on it?' Gabriel asked.

After a pause, Stillman nodded. 'I'm afraid she is.' He handed the list to Hayder. 'Six names. That's what the hostage taker said on the radio. That she's holding six people.' He neglected to add what else the woman had said. *And I have enough bullets for them all.*

'Who's seen that list?' said Gabriel.

'Hospital administrator,' said Hayder. 'Plus whoever helped him compile it.'

'Before it goes any further, take my wife off it.'

'These are just names. No one knows—'

'Any reporter could find out in ten seconds that Jane's a cop.'

Maura said, 'He's right. All the crime beat reporters in Boston know her name.'

'Scratch her name off the list, Mark,' said Stillman. 'Before anyone else sees it.'

'What about our entry team? If they go in, they'll need to know who's inside. How many people they're rescuing.'

'If you do your jobs right,' said Gabriel, 'there'll be no need for *any* entry team. Just talk that woman out of there.'

'Well, we're not having much luck on the talking part, are we?' Hayder looked at Stillman. 'Your girl refuses to even say hello.'

'It's only been three hours,' said Stillman. 'We need to give her time.'

'And after six hours? Twelve?' Hayder looked at Gabriel.

'Your wife is due to give birth any minute.'

'You think I'm not considering that?' Gabriel shot back. 'It's not just my wife, it's also my child in there. Dr. Tam may be with them, but if something goes wrong with the birth, there's no equipment, no operating room. So yes, I want this over as quickly as possible. But not if there's a chance you'll turn this into a bloodbath.'

'*She's* the one who set this off. The one who chooses what happens next.'

'Then don't force her hand. You've got a negotiator here, Captain Hayder. *Use* him. And keep your SWAT team the hell away from my wife.' Gabriel turned and walked out of the trailer.

Outside, Maura caught up with him on the sidewalk. She had to call his name twice before he finally stopped and turned to face her.

'If they screw up,' he said, 'if they go charging in there too soon—'

'You heard what Stillman said. He wants to go slow on this, just like you.'

Gabriel stared at a trio of cops in SWAT uniforms, huddled near the lobby entrance. 'Look at them. They're pumped up, hoping for action. I know what it's like, because I've been there. I've felt it myself. You get tired of standing around, endlessly negotiating. They just want to get on with it, because that's what they're trained to do. They can't wait to pull that trigger.'

'Stillman thinks he can talk her out.'

He looked at her. 'You were with the woman. Will she listen?'

'I don't know. The truth is, we know almost nothing about her.'

'I heard she was pulled out of the water. Brought to the morgue by a fire and rescue crew.'

Maura nodded. 'It was an apparent drowning. She was found in Hingham Bay.'

'Who found her?'

'Some guys at a yacht club down in Weymouth. Boston PD's already got a team from homicide working the case.'

'But they don't know about Jane.'

'Not yet.' It will make a difference to them, thought Maura. One of their own is a hostage. When another cop's life is on the line, it always made a difference.

'Which yacht club?' Gabriel asked.

Nine

Mila

There are bars on the windows. This morning, frost is etched like a crystal spiderweb in the glass. Outside are trees, so many of them that I do not know what lies beyond. All I know is this room and this house, which has become our only universe since the night the van brought us here. Sun sparkles on the frost outside our window. It is beautiful in those woods, and I imagine walking among the trees. The crackling leaves, the ice glistening on branches. A cool, pure paradise.

In this house, it is hell.

I see its reflection in the faces of the other girls, who now lie sleeping on dirty cots. I hear the torment in their restless moans, their whimpers. Six of us share this room. Olena has been here the longest, and on her cheek is an ugly bruise, a souvenir left by a client who liked to play rough. Even so, Olena sometimes still fights back. She is the only one among us who does, the only one they cannot quite control, despite their calming drugs and injections. Despite their beatings.

I hear a car roll into the driveway, and I wait with dread for the buzzing of the doorbell. It is like a jolt from a live wire. The girls all startle awake at the sound and they sit up, hugging their blankets to their chests. We know what happens next. We hear the key in the lock, and our door swings open.

The Mother stands in the doorway like a fat cook, ruthlessly choosing which lamb to slaughter. As always, she is cold-blooded about it, her pockmarked face showing no emotion as she scans her flock. Her gaze moves past the girls huddled on their cots and then shifts to the window, where I am standing.

'You,' she says in Russian. 'They want someone new.'

I glance at the other girls. All I see in their eyes is relief that this time they are not the chosen sacrifice.

'What are you waiting for?' the Mother says.

My hands have gone cold; already I feel nausea twisting my stomach. 'I – I am not feeling well. And I'm still sore down there . . .'

'Your first week, and already you're sore?' The Mother snorts. 'Get used to it.'

The other girls are all staring at the floor, or at their hands, avoiding my gaze. Only Olena looks at me, and in her eyes I see pity.

Meekly I follow the Mother out of the room. I

already know that to resist is to be punished, and I still have the bruises from the last time I protested. The Mother points to the room at the end of the hall.

'There's a dress on the bed. Put it on.'

I walk into the room and she shuts the door behind me. The window looks out over the driveway, where a blue car is parked. Bars cover the windows here as well. I look at the large brass bed, and what I see is not a piece of furniture, but the device of my torture. I pick up the dress. It is white, like a doll's frock, with ruffles around the hem. At once I understand what this signifies, and my nausea tightens to a knot of fear. When they ask you to play a child, Olena warned me, it means they want you to be scared. They want you to scream. They enjoy it if you bleed.

I do not want to put on the dress, but I'm afraid not to. By the time I hear footsteps approaching the room, I am wearing the dress, and steeling myself for what comes next. The door opens, and two men step in. They look me over for a moment, and I'm hoping that they are disappointed, that they think I am too thin or too plain, and they'll turn around and walk out. But then they shut the door and come toward me, like stalking wolves.

You must learn to float away. That's what Olena taught me, to float above the pain. This I try to do as the men rip off the doll's dress, as their rough hands close around my wrists, as

115

they force me to yield. My pain is what they have paid for, and they are not satisfied until I am screaming, until sweat and tears streak my face. *Oh Anja, how lucky you are to be dead!*

When it is over, and I hobble back to the locked room, Olena sits down beside me on my cot, and strokes my hair. 'Now you need to eat,' she says.

I shake my head. 'I only want to die.'

'If you die, then they win. We can't let them win.'

'They've already won.' I turn on my side and hug my knees to my chest, curling into a tight ball that nothing can penetrate. 'They've already won . . .'

'Mila, look at me. Do you think I've given up? Do you think I'm already dead?'

I wipe tears from my face. 'I'm not as strong as you are.'

'It's not strength, Mila. It's hate. That's what keeps you alive.' She bends close, and her long hair is a waterfall of black silk. What I see in her eyes scares me. A fire burns there; she is not quite sane. This is how Olena survives, on drugs and madness.

The door opens again, and we all shrink as the Mother glances around the room. She points to one of the girls. 'You, Katya. This one's yours.'

Katya just stares back, unmoving.

With two paces, the Mother crosses toward her and slaps her across the ear. 'Go,' she orders, and Katya stumbles out of the room. The Mother locks the door.

'Remember, Mila,' Olena whispers. 'Remember what keeps you alive.'

I look into her eyes and see it. *Hate*.

Ten

'We can't let this information get out,' said Gabriel. 'It could kill her.'

Homicide detective Barry Frost reacted with a stunned gaze. They were standing in the parking lot of the Sunrise Yacht Club. Not a breeze stirred, and out on Hingham Bay, sailboats drifted, dead in the water. Under the glare of the afternoon sun, sweat pasted wispy strands of hair to Frost's pale forehead. In a room full of people, Barry Frost was the one you'd most likely overlook, the man who'd quietly recede into a corner where he'd stand smiling and unnoticed. His bland temperament had helped him weather his occasionally stormy partnership with Jane, a partnership that, over the past two and a half years, had grown strong roots in trust. Now the two men who cared about her, Jane's husband and Jane's partner, faced each other with shared apprehension.

'No one told us she was in there,' murmured Frost. 'We had no idea.'

'We can't let the media find out.'

Frost huffed out a shocked breath. 'That would be a disaster.'

'Tell me who Jane Doe is. Tell me everything you know.'

'Believe me, we'll pull out all the stops on this. You have to trust us.'

'I can't sit on the sidelines. I need to know everything.'

'You can't be objective. She's your wife.'

'Exactly. She's my *wife*.' A note of panic had slipped into Gabriel's voice. He paused to rein in his agitation and said quietly:

'What would you do? If it was Alice trapped in there?'

Frost regarded him for a moment. At last he nodded. 'Come inside. We're talking to the commodore. He pulled her out of the water.'

They stepped from glaring sunshine into the cool gloom of the yacht club. Inside, it smelled like every seaside bar that Gabriel had ever walked into, the scent of ocean air mingled with citrus and booze. It was a rickety building, perched on a wooden pier overlooking Hingham Bay. Two portable air-conditioning units rattled in the windows, muffling the clink of glasses and the low hum of conversation. The floors creaked as they headed toward the lounge.

Gabriel recognized the two Boston PD detectives standing at the bar, talking with a bald man. Both Darren Crowe and Thomas Moore were Jane's colleagues from the homicide unit;

both of them greeted Gabriel with looks of surprise.

'Hey,' Crowe said. 'I didn't know the FBI was coming in on this.'

'FBI?' said the bald man. 'Wow, this must be getting pretty serious.' He stuck out his hand to Gabriel. 'Skip Boynton. I'm the commodore, Sunrise Yacht Club.'

'Agent Gabriel Dean,' said Gabriel, shaking the man's hand. Trying, as best he could, to play it official. But he could feel Thomas Moore's puzzled gaze. Moore could see that something was not right here.

'Yeah, I was just telling these detectives how we found her. Quite a shock, lemme tell you, seeing a body in the water.' He paused. 'Say, you want a drink, Agent Dean? It's on the club.'

'No, thank you.'

'Oh, right. On duty, huh?' Skip gave a sympathetic laugh. 'You guys really play it by the book, don't you? No one'll take a drink. Well, hell, I will.' He slipped behind the bar and dropped ice cubes in a glass. Splashed vodka on top. Gabriel heard ice clinking in other glasses, and he gazed around the room at the dozen club members sitting in the lounge, almost all of them men. Did any of them actually sail boats? Gabriel wondered. Or did they just come here to drink?

Skip slipped out from behind the counter, his vodka in hand. 'It's not the kind of thing that happens every day,' he said. 'I'm still kind of rattled about it.'

'You were telling us how you spotted the body,' said Moore.

'Oh. Yeah. About eight A.M. I came in early to change out my spinnaker. We have a regatta coming up in two weeks, and I'm gonna fly a new one. Got a logo on it. A green dragon, really striking. So anyway, I'm walking out to the dock, carrying my new spinnaker, and I see what looks like a mannequin floating out in the water, kinda snagged up on one of the rocks. I get in my rowboat to take a closer look and hell, if it ain't a woman. Damn nice-looking one, too. So I yelled for some of the other guys, and three of us pulled her out. Then we called nine one one.' He took a gulp of his vodka and drew a breath. 'Never occurred to us she was still alive. I mean, hell. That gal sure looked dead to us.'

'Must have looked dead to Fire and Rescue, too,' said Crowe.

Skip laughed. 'And they're supposed to be the professionals. If they can't tell, who can?'

'Show us,' said Gabriel. 'Where you found her.'

They all walked out the lounge door, onto the pier. The water magnified the sun's glare, and Gabriel had to squint against the brilliant reflection to see the rocks that Skip now pointed out.

'See that shoal over there? We have it marked off with buoys, 'cause it's a navigation hazard. At high tide, it's only a few inches deep there, so you don't even see it. Real easy to run aground.'

121

'What time was high tide yesterday?' asked Gabriel.

'I don't know. Ten A.M., I think.'

'Was that shoal exposed?'

'Yeah. If I hadn't spotted her then, a few hours later, she might have drifted out to sea.'

The men stood in silence for a moment, squinting off over Hingham Bay. A motor cruiser rumbled by, churning up a wake that made the boats rock on their moorings and set halyards clanging on masts.

'Had you ever seen the woman before?' Moore asked.

'Nope.'

'You're sure?'

'A gal who looks like that? I'd sure as hell remember.'

'And no one in the club recognized her?'

Skip laughed. 'No one who'll admit to it.'

Gabriel looked at him. 'Why wouldn't they?'

'Well, you know.'

'Why don't you tell me?'

'These guys in the club . . .' Skip gave a nervous laugh. 'I mean, you see all these boats moored out here? Who do you think sails them? It's not the wives. It's the men who lust after boats, not the women. And it's the men who hang around here. A boat's your home away from home.' Skip paused. 'In every respect.'

'You think she was someone's girlfriend?' said Crowe.

'Hell, I don't know. It's just that the possibility

occurred to me. You know, bring a chickie here late at night. Fool around on your boat, get a little drunk, a little high. It's easy to fall overboard.'

'Or get pushed.'

'Now wait a minute.' Skip looked alarmed. 'Don't you go jumping to *that* conclusion. These are good guys in the club. Good guys.'

Who might be banging chickies on their boats, thought Gabriel.

'I'm sorry I even mentioned the possibility,' said Skip. 'It's not like people don't get drunk and fall off boats all the time. Could've been any boat, not just one of ours.' He pointed out to Hingham Bay, where a cabin cruiser was gliding across the blindingly bright water. 'See all the traffic out there? She could've tripped off some motorboat that night. Drifted in on the tide.'

'Nevertheless,' said Moore, 'we'll need a list of all your members.'

'Is that really necessary?'

'Yes, Mr. Boynton,' said Moore with quiet but unmistakable authority. 'It is.'

Skip gulped down the rest of his vodka. The heat had flushed his scalp bright red, and he swiped away sweat. 'This is going to go over *real* well with the members. Here we do our civic duty and pull a woman out of the water. Now we're all suspects?'

Gabriel turned his gaze up the shoreline to the boat ramp, where a truck was now backing up to launch a motorboat into the water. Three other vehicles towing boats were lined up in the parking area, waiting their turns. 'What's your nighttime security like, Mr. Boynton?' he asked.

'Security?' Skip shrugged. 'We lock the club doors at midnight.'

'And the pier? The boats? There's no security guard?'

'We haven't had any break-ins. The boats are all locked. Plus, it's quiet out here. If you get any closer to the city, you'll find people hanging around the waterfront all night. This is a special little club. A place to get away from it all.'

A place where you could drive down to the boat ramp at night, thought Gabriel. You could back right down to the water, and no one would see you open your trunk. No one would see you pull out a body and toss it into Hingham Bay. If the tide was right, that body would drift out past the islands just offshore, straight into Massachusetts Bay.

But not if the tide was coming in.

His cell phone rang. He moved away from the others and walked down the pier a few paces before he answered the call.

It was Maura. 'I think you might want to get back here,' she said. 'We're about to do the autopsy.'

'Which autopsy?'

'On the hospital security guard.'

'The cause of death is clear, isn't it?'

'Another question has come up.'

'What?'

'We don't know who this man is.'

'Can't someone at the hospital ID him? He was their employee.'

'That's the problem,' said Maura. 'He wasn't.'

They had not yet undressed the corpse.

Gabriel was no stranger to the horrors of the autopsy room, and the sight of this victim, in the scope of his experience, was not particularly shocking. He saw only a single entry wound that tunneled into the left cheek; otherwise the features were intact. The man was in his thirties, with neatly clipped dark hair and a muscular jaw. His brown eyes, exposed to air by partially open lids, were already clouded. A name tag with PERRIN was clipped to the breast pocket of the uniform. Staring at the table, what disturbed Gabriel most was not the gore or the sightless eyes; it was the knowledge that the same weapon that had ended this man's life was now threatening Jane's.

'We waited for you,' said Dr. Abe Bristol. 'Maura thought you'd want to watch this from the beginning.'

Gabriel looked at Maura, who was gowned and masked, but standing at the foot of the table, and not at her usual place at the corpse's right side. Every other time he'd entered this lab, she had been the one in command, the one holding the knife. He was not accustomed to seeing her cede control in the room where she usually reigned. 'You're not doing this postmortem?' he asked.

'I can't. I'm a witness to this man's death,' said Maura. 'Abe has to do this one.'

'And you still have no idea who he is?'

She shook her head. 'There's no hospital employee with the name Perrin. And the chief of security came to view the body. He didn't recognize this man.'

'Fingerprints?'

'We've sent his prints to AFIS. Nothing's back on him so far. Or on the shooter's fingerprints, either.'

'So we've got a John Doe and a Jane Doe?' Gabriel stared at the corpse. 'Who the hell are these people?'

'Let's get him undressed,' Abe said to Yoshima.

The two men removed the corpse's shoes and socks, unbuckled the belt, and peeled off the trousers, laying the items of clothing on a clean sheet. With gloved hands Abe searched the pants pockets but found them empty. No comb, no wallet, no keys. 'Not even any loose change,' he noted.

'You'd think there'd be at least a spare dime or two,' said Yoshima.

'These pockets are clean.' Abe looked up. 'Brand-new uniform?'

They turned their attention to the shirt. The fabric was now stiff with dried blood, and they had to peel it away from the chest, revealing muscular pectorals and a thick mat of dark hair. And scars. Thick as twisted rope, one scar slanted up beneath the right nipple; the other slashed diagonally from abdomen to left hip bone.

'Those aren't surgical scars,' said Maura, frowning from her position at the foot of the table.

'I'd say this guy's been in a pretty nasty fight,' said Abe. 'These look like old knife wounds.'

'You want to cut off these sleeves?' said Yoshima.

'No, we can work them off. Let's just roll him.'

They tipped the corpse onto its left side to pull the sleeve free. Yoshima, facing the corpse's back, suddenly said: 'Whoa. You should see this.'

The tattoo covered the entire left shoulder blade. Maura leaned over to take a look and seemed to recoil from the image, as though it were alive, its venomous stinger poised to strike. The carapace was a brilliant blue. Twin pincers stretched toward the man's neck. Encircled by the coiled tail was the number 13.

'A scorpion,' said Maura softly.

'That's a pretty impressive meat tag,' Yoshima said.

Maura frowned at him. 'What?'

'It's what we called them in the army. I saw some real works of art when I was working in the morgue unit. Cobras, tarantulas. One guy had his girlfriend's name tattooed on . . .' Yoshima paused. 'You wouldn't get a needle anywhere near *mine*.'

They pulled off the other sleeve and returned the now-nude corpse to its back. Though still a young man, his flesh had already amassed a record of trauma. The scars, the tattoo. And now the final insult: the bullet wound in the left cheek.

Abe moved the magnifier over the wound. 'I see a sear zone here.' He glanced at Maura. 'They were in close contact?'

'He was leaning over her bed, trying to restrain her when she fired.'

'Can we see those skull X-rays?'

Yoshima pulled films out of an envelope and clipped them onto the light box. There were two views, an anteroposteral and a lateral. Abe maneuvered his heavy girth around the table to get a closer view of the spectral shadows cast by cranium and facial bones. For a moment he said nothing. Then he looked at Maura.

'How many shots did you say she fired?' he asked.

'One.'

'You want to take a look at this?'

Maura crossed to the light box. 'I don't understand,' she murmured. 'I was there when it happened.'

'There are definitely two bullets here.'

'I *know* that gun fired only once.'

Abe crossed back to the table and stared down at the corpse's head. At the bullet hole, with its oval halo of blackened sear zone.

'There's only one entrance wound. If the gun fired twice in rapid succession, that would explain a single wound.'

'That's not what I heard, Abe.'

'In all the confusion, you might have missed the fact there were two shots.'

Her gaze was still on the X-rays. Gabriel had never seen Maura look so unsure of herself. At that moment, she was clearly struggling to reconcile what she remembered with the undeniable evidence now glowing on the light box.

'Describe what happened in that room, Maura,' Gabriel said.

'There were three of us, trying to restrain her,' she said. 'I didn't see her grab the guard's gun. I was focused on the wrist restraint, trying to get it tied. I had just reached for the strap when the gun went off.'

'And the other witness?'

'He was a doctor.'

'What does he remember? One gunshot or two?'

She turned, her gaze meeting Gabriel's. 'The police never spoke to him.'

'Why not?'

'Because no one knows who he was.' For the first time, he heard the note of apprehension in her voice. 'I'm the only one who seems to remember him.'

Yoshima turned toward the phone. 'I'll call Ballistics,' he said. 'They'll know how many cartridges were left at the scene.'

'Let's get started,' said Abe, and he picked up a knife from the instrument tray. There was so little they knew about this victim. Not his real name or his history or how he came to arrive at the time and place of his death. But when this postmortem was over, they would know him more intimately than anyone had before.

With the first cut, Abe made his acquaintance.

His blade sliced through skin and muscle, scraping across ribs as he made the Y incision, his cuts angling from the shoulders to join at the xiphoid notch, followed by a single slice down the abdomen, with only a blip of a detour around the umbilicus. Unlike Maura's deft and elegant dissections, Abe worked with brutal efficiency, his huge hands moving like a butcher's, the fingers too fat to be graceful. He peeled back flesh from bone, then reached for the heavy-duty garden pruners. With each squeeze, he snapped through a rib. A man could spend years developing his physique, as this victim surely had, straining against pulleys and barbells. But all bodies, muscular or not, yield to a knife and a pruner.

Abe cut through the last rib and lifted off the triangle containing the sternum. Deprived of its bony shield, the heart and lungs now lay exposed to his blade, and he reached in to resect them, his arm sinking deep into the chest cavity.

'Dr. Bristol?' said Yoshima, hanging up the phone. 'I just spoke to Ballistics. They said that CSU only turned in one cartridge.'

Abe straightened, his gloves streaked with blood. 'They didn't find the second one?'

'That's all they received in the lab. Just one.'

'That's what I heard, Abe,' said Maura. 'One gunshot.'

Gabriel crossed to the light box. He stared at the films with a growing sense of dismay. One shot, two bullets, he thought. This may change everything. He turned and looked at Abe. 'I need to look at those bullets.'

'Anything in particular you're expecting to find?'

'I think I know why there are two of them.'

Abe nodded. 'Let me finish here first.' Swiftly his blade sliced through vessels and ligaments. He lifted out the heart and lungs, to be weighed and inspected later, then moved on to the abdomen. All looked normal. These were the healthy organs of a man whose body would have served him well for decades to come.

He moved, at last, to the head.

Gabriel watched, unflinching, as Abe sliced through the scalp and peeled it forward, collapsing the face, exposing cranium.

Yoshima turned on the saw.

Even then, Gabriel remained focused, through the whine of the saw, the grinding of bone, moving even closer to catch his first glimpse of the cavity. Yoshima pried off the skullcap and blood trickled out. Abe reached in with the scalpel to free the brain. As he pulled it from the cranial cavity, Gabriel was right beside him, holding a basin to catch the first bullet that tumbled out.

He took one glance at it under the magnifying lens, then said: 'I need to see the other one.'

'What are you thinking, Agent Dean?'

'Just find the other bullet.' His brusque

demand took everyone by surprise, and he saw Abe and Maura exchange startled glances. He was out of patience; he needed to know.

Abe set the resected brain on the cutting board. Studying the X-rays, he pinpointed the second bullet's location, and with the first slice, he found it, buried within a pocket of hemorrhaged tissue.

'What are you looking for?' Abe asked, as Gabriel rotated the two bullets beneath the magnifying lens.

'Same caliber. Both about eighty grams . . .'

'They should be the same. They were fired from the same weapon.'

'But these are not identical.'

'What?'

'Look at how the second bullet sits on its base. It's subtle, but you can see it.'

Abe leaned forward, frowning through the lens. 'It's a little off-kilter.'

'Exactly. It's at an angle.'

'The impact could have deformed it.'

'No, it was manufactured this way. At a nine-degree cant, to send it in a slightly different trajectory from the first. Two missiles, designed for controlled dispersion.'

'There was only one cartridge.'

'And only one entrance wound.'

Maura was frowning at the skull X-rays hanging on the light box. At the two bullets, glowing brightly against the fainter glow of cranium. 'A duplex round,' she said.

'That's why you only heard one shot fired,' said Gabriel. 'Because there *was* only one shot.'

Maura was silent for a moment, her gaze on the skull films. Dramatic as they were, the X-rays did not reveal the track of devastation those two bullets had left in soft tissue. Ruptured vessels, mangled gray matter. A lifetime's worth of memories atomized.

'Duplex rounds are designed to inflict maximum damage,' she said.

'That's their selling point.'

'Why would a security guard arm himself with bullets like these?'

'I think we've already established this man was not a hospital employee. He walked in with a fake uniform, a fake name tag, armed with bullets designed not just to maim, but to kill. There's only one good explanation I can come up with.'

Maura said, softly: 'The woman was meant to die.'

For a moment no one spoke.

It was the voice of Maura's secretary that suddenly broke the silence. 'Dr. Isles?' she said, over the intercom.

'Yes, Louise?'

'I'm sorry to bother you, but I thought you and Agent Dean should know . . .'

'What is it?'

'Something's happening across the street.'

Eleven

They ran outside, into heat so thick that Gabriel felt as though he'd just plunged into a hot bath. Albany Street was in chaos. The officer manning the police line was shouting, 'Stay back! Stay back!' while reporters pressed forward, a determined amoeba threatening to ooze through the barriers. Sweating Tactical Ops officers were scrambling to tighten the perimeter, and one of them glanced back, toward the crowd. Gabriel saw the look of confusion on his face.

That officer doesn't know what's going on, either.

He turned to a woman standing a few feet away. 'What happened?'

She shook her head. 'I don't know. The cops just went crazy and started toward the building.'

'Was there gunfire? Did you hear shots?'

'I didn't hear anything. I was just walking to the clinic when I heard them all start yelling.'

'It's nuts out here,' said Abe. 'No one knows anything.'

Gabriel ran toward the command and control trailer, but a knot of reporters blocked his way. In frustration, he grabbed a TV cameraman's arm and pulled him around. 'What happened?'

'Hey, man. Ease off.'

'Just tell me what happened!'

'They had a breach. Walked right through their goddamn perimeter.'

'The shooter *escaped*?'

'No. Someone got in.'

Gabriel stared at him. 'Who?'

'No one knows who he is.'

Half the ME's staff was gathered in the conference room, watching the TV. The set was tuned to the local news; on the screen was a blond reporter named Zoe Fossey, standing right in front of the police barrier. In the background cops milled among parked vehicles and voices were yelling in confusion. Gabriel glanced out the window at Albany Street, and saw the same scene they were now watching on TV.

'. . . extraordinary development, clearly something no one expected. The man walked right through this perimeter behind me, just strolled into that controlled area, completely nonchalant, as though he belonged there. That may have been what caught the police off guard. Plus, the man was heavily armed and wearing a black uniform very much like those you see behind me. It would have been easy to mistake him as one of these Tactical Operations officers . . .'

Abe Bristol gave a *can-you-believe-this?* snort. 'Guy walked right in off the street, and they let him through!'

'. . . we're told there is also an inner police perimeter. But it's inside the lobby, which we can't see from here. We haven't heard yet if this man penetrated the second perimeter. But when you see how easily he walked right through the outer line, you can imagine he must have caught the police inside the building by surprise as well. I'm sure they were focused on containing the hostage taker. They probably didn't expect a gunman to walk *in.*'

'They should have known,' said Gabriel, staring in disbelief at the TV. 'They should have expected this.'

'. . . it's been twenty minutes now, and the man has not reemerged. There was initial speculation that he's some self-styled Rambo, trying to single-handedly launch a rescue operation. Needless to say, the consequences could be disastrous. But so far, we've heard no gunfire, and we've seen no indication that his entry into the building has touched off any violence.'

The anchorman cut in: 'Zoe, we're going to run that footage again, so that the viewers who've just joined us can see the startling development. It took place about twenty minutes ago. Our cameras caught it live as it happened . . .'

Zoe Fossey's image was replaced by a video clip. It was a longshot view up Albany Street, almost the same view they could see out the conference room window. At first, Gabriel did not even know what he was supposed to focus on. Then an arrow appeared on screen, a helpful graphic added by the TV station, pointing to a dark figure moving along the lower edge. The man walked purposefully past police cars, past the command post trailer. None of the cops standing nearby tried to stop the intruder, though one did glance uncertainly in his direction.

'Here we've magnified the image for a better look at this fellow,' the anchorman said. The view zoomed in and froze, the intruder's back now filling the screen. 'He seems to be carrying a rifle, as well as some sort of backpack. Those dark clothes do blend in with all the other cops standing around, which is why our cameraman at the time didn't realize what he was seeing. At first glance, you'd assume this is a Tactical Operations uniform he's wearing. But on closer inspection, you can see there is no insignia on the back to indicate he's part of the team.'

The video clip rolled forward a few frames and again froze, this time on the man's face, as he turned to glance over his shoulder. He had receding dark hair and a narrow, almost gaunt face. An unlikely Rambo. That one long-distance frame was the only glimpse the camera caught of his features. In the next frame, his back was once again to the camera. The video clip continued, tracking the man's progress toward the building, until he vanished through the lobby doors.

Zoe Fossey was back onscreen, microphone in

hand. 'We've tried to get some official statement about just what happened here, but no one's talking, Dave.'

'You think the police might be just the slightest bit embarrassed?'

'To put it mildly. Adding to their embarrassment, I hear the FBI has just stepped in.'

'A not-so-subtle hint that things could be better managed?'

'Well, things are pretty chaotic out here right now.'

'Any confirmation yet on the number of hostages being held?'

'The hostage taker claimed, during her call to the radio station, that she was holding six people. I've since heard from sources that the number is probably correct. Three hospital employees, a doctor, and two patients. We're trying to get their names now . . .'

Gabriel went rigid in his chair, staring in rage at the TV. At the woman who was so eager to reveal Jane's identity. Who could unwittingly condemn her to death.

'. . . as you can see, over my shoulder, there's a lot of yelling going on. A lot of rising tempers in this heat. Another station's cameraman just got shoved to the ground when he tried to get too close to the perimeter. One unauthorized person has already slipped through, and the police aren't about to let it happen again. But it's like shutting the barn door after the horse gets out. Or, in this case, gets *in*.'

'Any idea who this Rambo is?'

'As I said, no one's talking. But we've heard reports that the police are checking out an illegally parked car about two blocks away from here.'

'They think it's Rambo's car?'

'Apparently. A witness saw this man leaving the car. I guess even Rambo needs transportation.'

'But what's his motive?'

'You have to consider two possibilities. One, that the man's trying to be a hero. Maybe he knows one of the hostages, and he's launching his own rescue operation.'

'And the second possibility?'

'The second possibility is scary. That this man is a reinforcement. He's come to join the hostage taker.'

Gabriel rocked back in his chair, stunned by what had suddenly become obvious to him. 'That's what it meant,' he said softly. '*The die is cast.*'

Abe swiveled around to face him. 'It meant something?'

Gabriel shot to his feet. 'I need to see Captain Hayder.'

'It's an activation code,' said Gabriel. 'Jane Doe called that radio station to broadcast the phrase. To get it out to the public.'

'An activation code for what?' asked Hayder.

'A call to arms. Reinforcements.'

Hayder snorted. 'Why didn't she just say, *Help me out here, guys?* Why use a code?'

'You weren't prepared, were you? None of you were.' Gabriel looked at Stillman, whose face was gleaming with sweat in that oven of a trailer. 'That man walked right through your perimeter, carrying in a knapsack with god-knows-what weapons. You weren't ready for him because you never expected a gunman to walk *into* the building.'

'We know it's always a possibility,' said Stillman. 'That's the reason we set up perimeters.'

'Then how did this man get through?'

'Because he knew exactly how to do it. His clothing, his gear. This was well thought out, Agent Dean. That man was ready.'

'And Boston PD wasn't. That's why they used a code. To take you by surprise.'

Hayder stared in frustration out the open doorway of the command trailer. Though they'd brought in two oscillating fans, and the street had now fallen into the shadow of late afternoon, it was still unbearably hot in the vehicle. Outside, on Albany Street, cops stood red-faced and sweating, and reporters were retreating back into their air-conditioned news vans. Everyone was waiting for something to happen. The calm before the next storm.

'It does start to make sense,' said Stillman. The negotiator had been listening to Gabriel's points with a deepening frown. 'Consider the sequence

140

of events. Jane Doe refuses to negotiate with me. She won't even talk to me. That's because she's not ready – she needs her back covered, first. She needs to strengthen her position. She calls the radio station and they broadcast the activation code. Five hours later, that man with the knapsack arrives. He shows up because he was summoned.'

'And he blithely walks into a suicide mission?' said Hayder. 'Does anyone have friends who are *that* loyal?'

'A marine will lay down his life for his company,' said Gabriel.

'*Band of brothers?* Yeah, sure.'

'I take it you've never served.'

Hayder flushed an even deeper red in the heat. 'Are you saying this is some sort of military operation? Then what's the next step? If this is so logical, tell us what's next on their agenda.'

'Negotiations,' said Gabriel. 'The takers have now cemented their position. I think you're going to be hearing from them soon.'

A new voice cut in, 'Reasonable prediction, Agent Dean. You're probably right.'

They all turned to look at the stocky man who had just stepped into the trailer. As usual, Agent John Barsanti wore a silk tie and a button-down shirt; as usual, his clothes did not fit well. He responded to Gabriel's look of surprised recognition with a sober nod of greeting. 'I'm sorry about Jane,' he said. 'They told me you were involved in this mess.'

141

'No one told me you were, John.'

'We're just monitoring developments. Ready to assist if we need to.'

'Why send someone all the way from Washington? Why not use the Boston field office?'

'Because this will likely go into negotiations. It made sense to send someone with experience.'

The two men regarded each other for a moment in silence. Experience, thought Gabriel, couldn't be the only reason John Barsanti had turned up. The FBI would not normally send a man straight from the deputy director's office to supervise a local hostage negotiation.

'Then who's in charge of the deal making?' Gabriel asked. 'The FBI? Or Boston PD?'

'Captain Hayder!' called Emerton. 'We've got a call coming in from the hospital! It's on one of their lines!'

'They're ready to negotiate,' said Gabriel. Just as he'd predicted.

Stillman and Barsanti looked at each other. 'You take it, Lieutenant,' said Barsanti. Stillman nodded, and crossed to the phone.

'I've got you on speaker,' said Emerton.

Stillman took a deep breath, then pressed the connect button.

'Hello,' he said calmly. 'This is Leroy Stillman.'

A man answered, just as calm. A reedy voice, with a hint of a southern drawl. 'You're a policeman?'

'Yes. I'm Lieutenant Stillman, Boston PD. Who am I speaking to?'

142

'You already know my name.'

'I'm afraid I don't.'

'Why don't you ask the FBI guy. There is an FBI guy, isn't there? Standing in that trailer with you?'

Stillman glanced over at Barsanti with a look of *how the hell does he know*? 'I'm sorry, sir,' said Stillman. 'I really don't know your name, and I'd like to know who I'm speaking to.'

'Joe.'

'Right. Joe.' Stillman released a breath. So far, so good. At least they had a name.

'How many people are in that trailer with you, Leroy?'

'Let's talk about you, Joe—'

'The FBI is there, though. Am I right?'

Stillman said nothing.

Joe laughed. 'I knew they'd show up. FBI, CIA, Defense Intelligence, Pentagon. Yeah, they all know who I am.'

Gabriel could read the expression on Stillman's face. *We're dealing with a man who clearly has delusions of persecution.*

'Joe,' said Stillman, 'there's no reason to draw this out any longer. Why don't we talk about ending it quietly?'

'We want a TV camera in here. A live feed to the media. We have a statement to make, and a videotape to show you.'

'Slow down. Let's get to know each other first.'

'I don't want to know you. Send in a TV camera.'

'That's going to present a problem. I need to clear this through a higher level.'

'They're standing right there, aren't they? Why don't you turn around and ask them, Leroy? Ask that *higher level* to get the ball rolling.'

Stillman paused. Joe understood exactly what was going on. He finally said, 'We can't authorize a live media feed.'

'No matter what I offer you in exchange?'

'What would that be?'

'Two hostages. We send them out as a sign of good faith. You send in a cameraman and a reporter, and we all go on live TV. Once our message gets out, then we send out two more hostages. That's four people we're giving you, Leroy. Four lives for ten minutes of TV airtime. I promise you a show that'll knock your socks off.'

'What's the point of this, Joe?'

'The point is, no one will listen to us. No one believes us. We're tired of running, and we want our lives back. This is the only way left. The only way people in this country will know we're telling the truth.'

Hayder swept a finger across his throat, a signal to interrupt the conversation.

'Hold on, Joe,' said Stillman, cupping his hand over the receiver. He looked at Hayder.

'Do you think he'll even know whether it's a live TV feed?' asked Hayder. 'If we could make him believe it's actually going on the air—'

'This man is not stupid,' cut in Gabriel. 'Don't even think of playing games with him. You cross him, you'll make him angry.'

'Agent Dean, maybe you could step outside?'

'They want media attention, that's all! Let them have their say. Let them rant to the public, if that's what it takes to end this!'

Joe's voice said, over the speaker: 'Do you want to deal or not, Leroy? Because we can do it the hard way, too. Instead of live hostages, we can send out dead ones. You have ten seconds to make up your mind.'

Stillman said, 'I'm listening, Joe. The problem is, a live feed isn't something I can just pull off. I need the cooperation of a TV station. How about we make it a taped statement? We deliver a camcorder to you. You say whatever you want, take as long as you need to—'

'And then you bury the tape, right? It'll never see the light of day.'

'That's my offer, Joe.'

'We both know you can do better. So does everyone else standing in that command trailer with you.'

'Live TV is out of the question.'

'Then we have nothing more to say to you. Good-bye.'

'Wait—'

'Yes?'

'You're serious? About releasing hostages?'

'If you keep up your end of the bargain. We want a cameraman and a reporter to witness what happens here. A *real* reporter, not some cop with a fake press pass.'

'Do it,' said Gabriel. 'This may be the way to end it.'

Stillman covered the receiver. 'Live TV is not on the table, Agent Dean. It never is.'

'Goddamn it, if this is what it takes, *give* it to them!'

'Leroy?' It was Joe talking again. 'Are you still there?'

Stillman took a breath. He said: 'Joe, you have to understand. It's going to take time. We'd have to find a reporter who's willing to do this. Someone willing to risk his life—'

'There's only one reporter we'll talk to.'

'Wait. You didn't specify anyone.'

'He knows the background. He's done his homework.'

'We can't guarantee that this reporter will—'

'Peter Lukas, *Boston Tribune*. Call him.'

'Joe—'

There was a click, then the dial tone. Stillman looked at Hayder. 'We're not sending in any civilians. It will just give them more hostages.'

'He said he'd release two people first,' said Gabriel.

'You believe that?'

'One of them might be my wife.'

'How do we know this reporter will even agree to it?'

'For what could be the biggest story of his life? A journalist just might do it.'

Barsanti said, 'I think there's another question here that no one's answered. Who the hell is Peter Lukas? A *Boston Tribune* reporter? Why ask for him in particular?'

'Let's call him,' said Stillman. 'Maybe he knows.'

Twelve

You're still alive. You have to be alive. I would know it, feel it, if you weren't.

Wouldn't I?

Gabriel slumped on the couch in Maura's office, his head resting in his hands, trying to think of what else he could do, but fear kept clouding any logic. As a marine, he had never lost his cool under fire. Now he could not even focus, could not shut out the image that had haunted him since the autopsy, of a different body lying on the table.

Did I ever tell you how much I love you?

He did not hear the door open. Only when Maura sat down in the chair across from him, and set two mugs on the coffee table, did he finally raise his head. She's always composed, always in control, he thought, looking at Maura. So unlike his brash and temperamental wife. Two such different women, yet somehow they had forged a friendship that he did not quite understand.

Maura pointed to the coffee. 'You like it black, right?'

'Yes. Thanks.' He took a sip, then set it down again, because he had not really wanted it.

'Did you eat any lunch?' she asked.

He rubbed his face. 'I'm not hungry.'

'You look exhausted. I'll get you a blanket, if you'd like to rest here for a while.'

'There's no way I can sleep. Not until she's out of there.'

'Did you reach her parents?'

'Oh god.' He shook his head. 'That was an ordeal. The hardest part was convincing them they had to keep it a secret. They can't show up here, they can't call their friends. I almost wonder if I should have kept it from them.'

'The Rizzolis would want to know.'

'But they're not good at keeping secrets. And if this one gets out, it could kill their daughter.'

They sat for a moment in silence. The only sound was the hiss of cool air blowing from the AC vent. On the wall behind the desk were elegantly framed floral prints. The office reflected the woman: neat, precise, cerebral.

She said, quietly: 'Jane's a survivor. We both know that. She'll do whatever it takes to stay alive.'

'I just want her to stay out of the line of fire.'

'She's not stupid.'

'The problem is, she's a cop.'

'Isn't that a good thing?'

'How many cops get killed trying to be heroes?'

'She's pregnant. She won't take any chances.'

'No?' He looked at her. 'Do you know how she ended up in the hospital this morning? She was testifying in court when the defendant got out of control. And my wife – my *brilliant* wife – jumped into the fight to subdue him. That's when her water broke.'

Maura looked appropriately shocked. 'She really did that?'

'That's exactly what you'd expect Jane to do.'

'I guess you're right,' Maura said with a shake of the head. 'That's the Jane we both know and love.'

'For once, just this once, I want her to play the coward. I want her to forget she's a cop.' He laughed. 'As if she'd ever listen to *me*.'

Maura couldn't help smiling as well. 'Does she ever?'

He looked at her. 'You know how we met, don't you?'

'Stony Brook Reservation, wasn't it?'

'That death scene. It took us about thirty seconds to get into our first argument. About five minutes before she ordered me off her turf.'

'Not a very promising start.'

'And a few days later, she pulls her gun on me.' At Maura's startled look, he added: 'Oh, it was justified.'

'I'm surprised that didn't scare you off.'

'She can be a scary woman.'

'And you may be the only man she doesn't terrify.'

'But that's what I liked about her,' said Gabriel. 'When you look at Jane, what you see is honest, and brave. I grew up in a family where nobody said what they really thought. Mom hated Dad, Dad hated Mom. But everything was just fine, right up till the day they died. I thought that was how most people went through life, by telling lies. But Jane doesn't. She's not afraid to say exactly what she thinks, no matter how much trouble it lands her in.' He paused. Added, quietly: 'That's what worries me.'

'That she'll say something she shouldn't.'

'You give Jane a shove, and she'll shove right back. I'm hoping that for once, she'll stay quiet. Just play the scared pregnant lady in the corner. It may be the one thing that saves her.'

His cell phone rang. At once he reached for it, and the number he saw on the display made his pulse kick into a gallop. 'Gabriel Dean,' he answered.

'Where are you right now?' said Detective Thomas Moore.

'I'm sitting in Dr. Isles's office.'

'I'll meet you there.'

'Wait, Moore. What is it?'

'We know who Joe is. His full name is Joseph Roke, age thirty-nine. Last known address Purcellville, Virginia.'

'How did you ID him?'

'He abandoned his car about two blocks from the hospital. We have a witness who saw an armed man leave the car, and she confirms he's the man on the TV videotape. His fingerprints are all over the steering wheel.'

'Wait. Joseph Roke's prints are on file?'

'Military records. Look, I'll come right over.'

'What else do you know?' said Gabriel. He'd heard the urgency in Moore's voice, and knew there was something the detective had not yet told him. 'Just tell me.'

'There's a warrant for his arrest.'

'What charges?'

'It was . . . a homicide. A shooting.'

'Who was the victim?'

'I'll be there in twenty minutes. We can talk about it when I get there.'

'Who was the victim?' Gabriel repeated.

Moore sighed. 'A cop. Two months ago, Joseph Roke killed a cop.'

'It started off as a routine traffic stop,' said Moore. 'The event was automatically recorded by the video camera mounted in the police officer's cruiser. New Haven PD didn't attach the entire video, but here's the first of the freeze-frame images they emailed me.' Moore clicked the mouse, and a photo appeared on his laptop computer. It showed the back of the New Haven police officer, caught in midstride as he walked toward a vehicle parked in front of his cruiser. The other car's rear license plate was visible.

'It's a Virginia plate,' said Moore. 'You can see it more clearly with image enhancement. It's the same car we found this afternoon, parked illegally on Harrison Street a few blocks from the medical center.' He looked at Gabriel. 'Joseph Roke is the registered owner.'

'You said he was from Virginia.'

'Yes.'

'What was he doing in Connecticut two months ago?'

'We don't know. Nor do we know what he's now doing in Boston. All I've got on him is the rather sketchy biographical profile that New Haven PD has put together.' He pointed to his laptop. 'And this. A shooting caught on camera. But that's not the only thing you see in these photos.'

Gabriel focused on Roke's vehicle. On the view through the rear window. 'There's a passenger,' he said. 'Roke has someone sitting beside him.'

Moore nodded. 'With image enhancement, you can clearly see this passenger has long dark hair.'

'It's her,' said Maura, staring at the screen. 'It's Jane Doe.'

'Which means they were together in New Haven two months ago.'

'Show us the rest,' said Gabriel.

'Let me go to the last image—'

'I want to see them all.'

Moore paused, his hand on the mouse. He looked at Gabriel. 'You don't really need to,' he said quietly.

'Maybe I do. Show me the whole sequence.'

After a hesitation, Moore clicked the mouse,

153

advancing to the next photo. The police officer was now standing at Roke's window, looking in at the man who, in the next few seconds, would end his life. The cop's hand was resting on his weapon. Merely a cautionary stance? Or did he already have an inkling that he was looking into the face of his killer?

Again, Moore hesitated before advancing to the next image. He had already seen these; he knew what horrors lay ahead. He clicked the mouse.

The image was an instant in time, captured in all its gruesome detail. The police officer was still standing, and his weapon was out of its holster. His head was snapped back by the bullet's impact, his face caught in mid-disintegration, flesh exploding in a bloody mist.

A fourth and final photo finished the sequence. The officer's body was now lying on the road beside the shooter's car. It was just the postscript, yet this was the image that made Gabriel suddenly lean forward. He stared at the car's rear window. At a silhouette that had not been visible in the three earlier images.

Maura saw it, too. 'There's someone in Roke's backseat,' she said.

'That's what I wanted you both to see,' said Moore. 'A third person was in Roke's car. Hiding, maybe, or sleeping in the backseat. You can't tell if it's a man or a woman. All you can see is this head with short hair, popping up right after the shooting.' He looked at Gabriel.

'There's a third associate we haven't seen or heard yet. Someone who was with them in New Haven. That activation code may have been meant for more than one person.'

Gabriel's gaze was still riveted on the screen. On that mysterious silhouette. 'You said he had a military record.'

'That's how we matched his prints. He served in the army, 1990 to '92.'

'Which unit?' When Moore did not immediately answer, Gabriel looked at him. 'What was he trained to do?'

'EOD. Explosive ordnance disposal.'

'Bombs?' said Maura. She looked, startled, at Moore. 'If he knows how to disarm them, then he probably knows how to build them.'

'You said he only served two years,' said Gabriel. His own voice struck him as eerily calm. A cold-blooded stranger's.

'He had . . . problems overseas, when he got to Kuwait,' said Moore. 'He received a dishonorable discharge.'

'Why?'

'Refusing to obey orders. Striking an officer. Repeated conflicts with other men in his unit. There was some concern that he was emotionally unstable. That he might be suffering from paranoia.'

Moore's words had felt like blow after pummeling blow, pounding the breath from Gabriel's lungs. 'Jesus,' he murmured. 'This changes everything.'

'What do you mean?' asked Maura.

He looked at her. 'We can't waste any more time. We've got to get her out *now*.'

'What about negotiations? What about going slow?'

'It doesn't apply here. Not only is this man unstable, he's already killed a cop.'

'He doesn't know Jane's a cop,' said Moore. 'And we're not going to let him find out. Look, the same principles apply here. The longer a hostage crisis goes on, the better it usually comes out. Negotiation works.'

Gabriel pointed to the laptop. 'How the hell do you negotiate with someone who does *that*?'

'It can be done. It has to be done.'

'It's not *your* wife in there!' He saw Maura's startled gaze, and he turned away, struggling for composure.

It was Moore who spoke next, his voice quiet. Gentle. 'What you're feeling now – what you're going through – I've been there, you know. I know exactly what you're dealing with. Two years ago, my wife, Catherine, was abducted, by a man you may remember. Warren Hoyt.'

The Surgeon. Of course, Gabriel remembered him. The man who late at night would slip into homes where women slept, awakening to find a monster in their bedrooms. It was the aftermath of Hoyt's crimes that had first brought Gabriel to Boston a year ago. The Surgeon, he suddenly realized, was the common thread that bound them all together. Moore and Gabriel, Jane and

Maura. They had all, in one way or another, been touched by the same evil.

'I knew Hoyt was holding her,' said Moore. 'And there was nothing I could do about it. No way I could think of to save her. If I could have exchanged my life for hers, I would have done it in a heartbeat. But all I could do was watch the hours go by. The worst part of it was, I *knew* what he was doing to her. I'd watched the autopsies on his other victims. I saw every cut he ever made with his scalpel. So yes, I know exactly what you're feeling. And believe me, I'm going to do whatever it takes to get Jane out of there alive. Not just because she's my colleague, or because you're married to her. It's because I owe her my happiness. She's the one who found Catherine. Jane's the one who saved her life.'

At last Gabriel looked at him. 'How do we negotiate with these people?'

'We need to find out exactly what they want. They know they're trapped. They have no choice but to talk to us, so we keep talking to them. You've dealt with other hostage situations, so you know the negotiator's playbook. The rules haven't changed, just because you're on the other side of it now. You have to take your wife, your emotions, out of this equation.'

'Could you?'

Moore's silence answered the question. Of course he couldn't.

And neither can I.

Thirteen

Mila

Tonight we are going to a party.

The Mother tells us that important people will be there, so we must look our prettiest, and she has given us new clothes for the occasion. I am wearing a black velvet dress with a skirt so tight that I can scarcely walk, and I must pull the hem all the way up to my hips just so I can climb into the van. The other girls slide in beside me in a rustle of silk and satin, and I smell their clashing bouquet of perfumes. We have spent hours with our makeup creams and lipsticks and mascara brushes, and now we sit like masked dolls about to perform in a Kabuki play. Nothing you see is real. Not the eyelashes or the red lips or the blushing cheeks. The van is cold, and we shiver against each other, waiting for Olena to join us.

The American driver yells out the window that we must leave now, or we'll be late. At last the Mother comes out of the house, tugging Olena after her. Olena angrily shakes off the Mother's hand and proceeds to walk the rest of the way on her own. She is wearing a long, green silk dress with a high Chinese collar and a side slit that reaches all the way to her thigh. Her black hair swings straight and sleek to her shoulders. I have never seen anyone so beautiful, and I stare at her as she crosses to the van. The drugs have calmed her down as usual, have turned her docile, but they have also made her unsteady, and she sways in her high heels.

'Get in, get in,' the driver orders.

The Mother has to help Olena into the van. Olena slides onto the seat in front of mine and promptly slumps against the window. The Mother slides the door shut and climbs in beside the driver.

'It's about time,' he says, and we pull away from the house.

I know why we are going to this party; I know what is expected of us. Still, this feels like an escape because it is the first time in weeks that we have been allowed out of the house, and I eagerly press my face to the window as we turn onto a paved road. I see the sign: DEERFIELD ROAD.

For a long time, we drive.

I watch the road signs, reading the names of the towns we are passing through. RESTON and ARLINGTON and WOODBRIDGE. I look at people in other cars, and I wonder if any of them can see the silent plea in my face. If any of them cared. A woman driver in the next lane glances at me, and for an instant our eyes meet. Then she turns her attention back to the road. What did she see, really? Just a redheaded girl in a black dress, going out for a good time. People see what they expect to see. It never occurs to them that terrible things can look pretty.

I begin to catch glimpses of water, a wide ribbon of it, in the distance. When the van finally stops, we are parked at a dock, where a large motor yacht is moored. I did not expect tonight's party to be on a boat. The other girls are craning their necks to see it, curious about what this enormous yacht looks like inside. And a little afraid, too.

The Mother slides open the van door. 'These are important men. You will all smile and be happy. Do you understand?'

'Yes, Mother,' we murmur.

'Get out.'

As we scramble from the van, I hear Olena say, in a slurred voice, 'Fuck yourself, Mother,' but no one else hears her.

Tottering on high heels, shivering in our dresses, we walk single file up the ramp and onto the boat. On the deck, a man stands waiting for us. Just by the way the Mother hurries forward to greet him, I know this man is important. He gives us a cursory glance, and nods in approval. Says in English, to the Mother: 'Take them inside and get a few drinks in them. I want them in the mood when our guests arrive.'

'Yes, Mr. Desmond.'

160

The man's gaze pauses on Olena, who is swaying unsteadily near the railing. 'Is that one going
to cause us trouble again?'

'She took the pills. She'll be quiet.'

'Well, she'd better be. I don't want her acting
up tonight.'

'Go,' the Mother directs us. 'Inside.'

We step through the doorway into the cabin,
and I am dazzled by my first glimpse. A crystal
chandelier sparkles over our heads. I see dark
wood paneling, couches of cream-colored suede.
A bartender pops open a bottle, and a waiter in
a white jacket brings us flutes of champagne.

'Drink,' the Mother says. 'Find a place to sit
and be happy.'

We each take a flute and spread out around the
cabin. Olena sits on the couch beside me, sipping
champagne, crossing her long legs so that the top
of her thigh peeks out through the slit.

'I'm watching you,' the Mother warns Olena
in Russian.

Olena shrugs. 'So does everyone else.'

The bartender announces: 'They're here.'

The Mother gives Olena one last threatening
look, then retreats through a doorway.

'See how she has to hide her fat face?' Olena
says. 'No one wants to look at *her*.'

'Shh,' I whisper. 'Don't get us into trouble.'

'In case you haven't noticed, my darling little
Mila, we are already in trouble.'

We hear laughter, and hearty greetings
between colleagues. Americans. The cabin door

opens and all the girls snap straight and smile as four men walk in. One is the host, Mr. Desmond, who met us on the deck. His three guests are all men, all nicely dressed in suits and ties. Two of them are young and fit, men who walk with the confident grace of athletes. But the third man is older, as old as my grandfather and far heavier, with wire-rimmed glasses and graying hair that is giving way to inevitable baldness. The guests gaze around the room, inspecting us with clear interest.

'I see you've brought in a few new ones,' the older man says.

'You should come by the house again, Carl. See what we have.' Mr. Desmond gestures toward the bar. 'Something to drink, gentlemen?'

'Scotch would be good,' says the older man.

'And what about you, Phil? Richard?'

'Same for me.'

'That champagne will do nicely.'

The boat's engines are now rumbling. I look out the window and see that we are moving, heading out into the river. At first the men do not join us. Instead they linger near the bar, sipping their drinks, talking only to one another. Olena and I understand English, but the other girls know only a little, and their mechanical smiles soon fade to looks of boredom. The men discuss business. I hear them talk about contracts and bids and road conditions and casualties. Who is vying for which contract and for how much. This is the real reason for the party; business first, then fun. They finish their drinks, and the bartender pours another round. A few final pleasantries before they fuck the whores. I see the glint of wedding rings on the hands of the three guests, and I picture these men making love to their wives in big beds with clean sheets. Wives who have no idea what their husbands do, in other beds, to girls like me.

Even now, the men glance our way, and my hands begin to sweat, anticipating the evening's ordeal. The older one keeps looking toward Olena.

She smiles at him, but under her breath she says to me in Russian: 'What a pig. I wonder if he oinks when he comes.'

'He can hear you,' I whisper.

'He can't understand a word.'

'You don't know that.'

'Look, he's smiling. He thinks I'm telling you how handsome he is.'

The man sets his empty glass on the bar and crosses toward us. I think he wishes to be with Olena, so I stand up to make room for him on the couch. But it is my wrist he reaches for, and he stops me from leaving.

'Hello,' he says. 'Do you speak English?'

I nod; my throat has gone too dry to answer. I can only gaze at him in dismay. Olena rises from the couch, flashes me a sympathetic look, and wanders away.

'How old are you?' he asks.

'I am . . . I am seventeen.'

'You look much younger.' He sounds disappointed.

'Hey Carl,' Mr. Desmond calls out. 'Why don't you take her for a little stroll?'

Already, the other two guests have chosen their companions. One of them is now leading Katya away, down the corridor.

'Any stateroom will do,' our host adds.

Carl stares at me. Then his hand tightens around my wrist, and he leads me down the corridor. He pulls me into a handsome stateroom, paneled with gleaming wood. I back away, my heart hammering as he locks the door. When he turns back to me, I see that his pants are already bulging.

'You know what to do.'

But I don't; I have no idea what he expects, so I am shocked by the sudden blow. His slap sends me to my knees and I huddle at his feet, bewildered.

'Don't you listen? You stupid slut.'

I nod, dropping my head and staring at the floor. Suddenly I understand what the game is, what he craves. 'I've been very bad,' I whisper.

'You need to be punished.'

Oh god. Let this be over soon.

'*Say it!*' he snaps.

'I need to be punished.'

'Take off your clothes.'

Shaking now, terrified of being hit again, I obey. I unzip my dress, pull off my stockings, my underwear. I keep my gaze lowered; a good girl must be respectful. I am completely silent as I stretch out on the bed, as I open myself to him. No resistance, just subservience.

As he undresses, he stares at me, savoring his view of compliant flesh. I swallow my disgust when he climbs on top of me, his breath sharp with scotch. I close my eyes and concentrate on the growl of the engines, on the slap of water against the hull. I float above my body, feeling nothing as he thrusts into me. As he grunts and comes.

When he is finished, he does not even wait for me to dress. He simply rises, puts on his clothes, and walks out of the stateroom. Slowly, I sit up. The boat's engines have quieted to a low purr. Looking out the window, I see that we are returning to land. The party is over.

By the time I finally creep from the stateroom, the boat is once again docked, and the guests have left. Mr. Desmond is at the bar sipping the last of the champagne, and the Mother is gathering together her girls.

'What did he say to you?' she asks me.

I shrug. I can feel Desmond's eyes studying me, and I am afraid of saying the wrong thing.

'Why did he choose you? Did he say?'

'He only wanted to know how old I was.'

'That's all?'

'It's all he cared about.'

The Mother turns to Mr. Desmond, who has been watching us both with interest. 'You see? I told you,' she says to him. 'He always goes for the youngest one in the room. Doesn't care what they look like. But he wants them young.'

Mr. Desmond thinks about this for a moment. He nods. 'I guess we'll just have to keep him happy.'

Olena wakes up to find me standing at the window, staring out through the bars. I have lifted the sash and cold air pours in, but I do not care. I want only to breathe in fresh air. I want to cleanse the evening's poison from my lungs, my soul.

'It's too cold,' Olena says. 'Close the window.'

'I am suffocating.'

'Well, it's freezing in here.' She crosses to the window and pulls it shut. 'I can't sleep.'

'Neither can I,' I whisper.

By the glow of moonlight that shines through the grimy window, she studies me. Behind us, one of the girls whimpers in her sleep. We listen to the sound of their breathing in the darkness, and suddenly there is not enough air left in the room for me. I am fighting to breathe. I push at the window, trying to raise it again, but Olena holds it shut.

'Stop it, Mila.'

'I'm dying!'

'You're hysterical.'

'Please open it. Open it!' I'm sobbing now, clawing at the window.

'You want to wake up the Mother? You want to get us in trouble?'

My hands have cramped into painful claws, and I cannot even clutch the sash. Olena grabs my wrists.

'Listen,' she says. 'You want air? I'll get you some air. But you have to be quiet. The others can't know about it.' I am too panicked to care what she's saying. She grabs my face in her hands, forces me to look at her. 'You did not see this,' she whispers. Then she pulls something from her pocket, something that gleams faintly in the darkness.

A key.

'How did you—'

'Shhh.' She snatches the blanket from her cot and pulls me past the other girls, to the door. There she pauses to glance back at them, to confirm they are all asleep, then slips the key into the lock. The door swings open and she pulls me through, into the hallway.

I am stunned. Suddenly I've forgotten that I am suffocating, because we are out of our prison; we are free. I turn toward the stairs to flee, but she yanks me back sharply.

'Not that way,' she says. 'We can't get out. There's no key to the front door. Only the Mother can open it.'

'Then where?'

'I'll show you.'

She pulls me down the hallway. I can see almost nothing. I put my trust entirely in her hands, letting her lead me through a doorway. Moonlight glows through the window, and she glides like a pale ghost across the bedroom, picks up a chair, and quietly sets it down in the center of the room.

'What are you doing?'

She doesn't answer, but climbs onto the chair and reaches toward the ceiling. A trap door creaks open above her head, and a ladder unfolds downward.

'Where does it go?' I ask.

'You wanted fresh air, didn't you? Let's go find some,' she says, and climbs the ladder.

I follow her up the rungs and scramble through the trap door, into an attic. Through a single window, moonlight shines in, and I see the shadows of boxes and old furniture. The air is stale up here; it is not fresh at all. She opens the window and climbs through. Suddenly it strikes me: this window has no bars. When I poke my head out, I understand why. The ground is too far below us. There is no escape here; to jump would be suicide.

'Well?' says Olena. 'Aren't you going to come out, too?'

I turn my head and see that she is sitting on the roof, lighting a cigarette. I look down again at the ground, so far away, and my hands go clammy at the thought of climbing out onto the ledge.

'Don't be such a scared rabbit,' says Olena. 'It's nothing. The worst that can happen is you fall and break your neck.'

Her cigarette glows, and I smell the smoke as

she casually exhales a breath. She is not nervous at all. At that moment, I want to be exactly like her. I want to be fearless.

I climb out the window, inch my way along the ledge, and with a heavy sigh of relief, settle down beside her on the roof. She shakes out the blanket and throws it over our shoulders so that we sit snug together, under a warm mantle of wool.

'It's my secret,' she said. 'You're the only one I trust to keep it.'

'Why me?'

'Katya would sell me out for a box of chocolates. And that Nadia is too stupid to keep her mouth shut. But you're different.' She looks at me, a gaze that is thoughtful. Almost tender. 'You may be a scared rabbit. But you're not stupid, and you're not a traitor.'

Her praise makes the heat rise in my face, and the pleasure is a rush better than any drug. Better than love. Suddenly, recklessly, I think: I would do anything for you, Olena. I move closer to her, seeking her warmth. I have known only punishment from men's bodies. But Olena's offers comfort, and soft curves, and hair that brushes like satin against my face. I watch the glow of her cigarette, and how elegantly she flicks off ash.

'Want a puff?' she asks, offering it to me.

'I don't smoke.'

'Heh. It's not good for you anyway,' she says and takes another drag. 'Not good for me either, but I'm not going to waste them.'

'Where did you get it?'

169

'The boat. Took a whole pack of them, and no one noticed.'

'You stole them?'

She laughs. 'I steal a lot of things. How do you think I got the key? The Mother thinks she lost it, the dumb cow.' Olena takes another puff, and her face briefly glows orange. 'It's what I used to do in Moscow. I was good at it. If you speak English, they'll let you into any hotel where you can turn a few tricks. Pick a few pockets.' She blew out a lung full of smoke. 'That's why I can't go home. They know me there.'

'Don't you want to?'

She shrugs and taps off an ash. 'There's nothing there for me. That's why I left.'

I stare up at the sky. The stars are like angry pinpricks of light. 'There's nothing here, either. I didn't know it would be like this.'

'You're thinking of running, aren't you, Mila?'

'Aren't you?'

'And what would you go home to? You think your family wants you back? After they find out what you've been doing here?'

'There's only my grandmother.'

'And what would you do in Kryvicy, if all your dreams were to come true? Would you be rich, marry a nice man?'

'I have no dreams,' I whisper.

'It's better that way.' Olena gives a bitter laugh. 'Then you can't be disappointed.'

'But anything, anywhere, is better than here.'

'You think so?' She looks at me. 'I knew a girl

who ran. We were at a party, like the one tonight. At Mr. Desmond's house. She climbed out a window and got away. Which was just the first of her problems.'

'Why?'

'What do you eat out there? Where do you live? If you have no papers, there is no way to survive but to turn tricks, and you might as well do it here. So she finally went to the police, and you know what happened? They deported her, back to Belarus.' Olena blew out a cloud of smoke and looked at me. 'Don't ever trust the police. They're not your friends.'

'But she got away. She went home.'

'You know what happens if you run away and make it back home? They'll find you there. They find your family, too. And when they do, you're all better off dead.' Olena stubbed out her cigarette. 'Here it may be hell. But at least they don't skin you alive, the way they did to her.'

I am shaking, and not from the cold. I'm thinking of Anja again. Always, I think of poor Anja, who tried to run. I wonder if her body still lies in the desert. If her flesh has rotted away.

'Then there's no choice,' I whisper. 'There's no choice at all.'

'Sure there is. You play along with them. Fuck a few men every day, give them what they want. In a few months, a year, the Mother gets her next shipment of girls, and you're just used merchandise. That's when they let you go. That's when you're free. But if you try to run first, then they have to make an example of you.' She looks at me. I am startled when she suddenly reaches out and touches my face, her hand lingering on my cheek. Her fingers trail heat across my skin. 'Stay alive, Mila,' she says. 'This won't last forever.'

Fourteen

Even by the lofty standards of Beacon Hill, the house was impressive, the largest on a street of distinguished residences which had housed generations of Boston Brahmins. It was Gabriel's first visit to this home, and under different circumstances, he might have paused on the cobblestoned walkway to admire, in the fading daylight, the carved lintels and the decorative ironwork and the fanciful brass knocker on the front door. Today, though, his mind was not on architecture, and he did not linger on the sidewalk, but hurried up the steps and rang the doorbell.

It was answered by a young woman wearing tortoiseshell glasses and a look of cool assessment. The latest keeper of the gate, he thought. He hadn't met this particular assistant before, but she fit the mold for a typical Conway hire: brainy, efficient – probably Harvard. *Conway's eggheads* they were called on the Hill, the cadre of young men and women known for their brilliance as well as their absolute loyalty to the senator.

'I'm Gabriel Dean,' he said. 'Senator Conway's expecting me.'

'They're waiting for you in his office, Agent Dean.'

They?

'Follow me.' She turned and led him briskly up the hallway, her low and unfashionably practical heels clicking across dark oak as they passed a series of portraits on the wall: a stern patriarch posed at his writing desk. A man garbed in the powdered wig and black robes of a judge. A third, standing before a draped curtain of green velvet. In this hallway, Conway's distinguished lineage was comfortably on display, a lineage that he purposefully avoided flaunting in his townhouse in Georgetown, where blue blood was a political liability.

The woman discreetly knocked at a door, then poked her head into the room. 'Agent Dean is here.'

'Thank you, Jillian.'

Gabriel stepped into the room, and the door closed quietly behind him. At once the senator stepped out from behind a massive cherrywood desk to greet him. Though already in his sixties, the silver-haired Conway still moved with the power and agility of a marine, and when they shook hands, it was the robust greeting between men who have both known combat, and respect each other for it.

'How are you holding up?' Conway asked quietly.

It was the gentlest of queries, and it brought an unexpected flash of tears to Gabriel's eyes. He cleared his throat. 'The truth is,' he admitted, 'I'm trying hard not to lose it.'

'I understand she went into the hospital this morning.'

'The baby was actually due last week. Her water broke this morning, and . . .' He paused, flushing. The conversation of old soldiers seldom strayed into the intimate details of their wives' anatomy.

'So we've got to get her out of there. As soon as possible.'

'Yes, sir.' *Not just soon. Alive.* 'I'm hoping you can tell me what's really going on here. Because Boston PD has no idea.'

'You've done me enough favors over the years, Agent Dean. I'll do whatever it takes, I promise.' He turned, gesturing toward the intimate grouping of furniture that faced a massive brick fireplace. 'Maybe Mr. Silver here can help.'

For the first time, Gabriel focused on the man who'd sat so silently in the leather armchair that he might easily have been overlooked. The man stood, and Gabriel saw that he was uncommonly tall, with receding dark hair and mild eyes that peered through professorial spectacles.

'I don't believe you two have met,' said Conway. 'This is David Silver, Deputy Director

175

of National Intelligence. He just flew up from Washington.'

This is a surprise, thought Gabriel as he shook David Silver's hand. The Director of National Intelligence was a lofty Cabinet-level post with authority over every intelligence agency in the country, from the Federal Bureau of Investigation to Defense Intelligence to the Central Intelligence Agency. And David Silver was the DNI's second in command.

'As soon as we got word of the situation,' said Silver, 'Director Wynne asked me to fly up here. The White House doesn't think this is your usual sort of hostage crisis.'

'Whatever *usual* means these days,' added Conway.

'We already have a direct line to the police commissioner's office,' said Silver. 'We're keeping close tabs on Boston PD's investigation. But Senator Conway tells me you have additional information that could affect how we approach this.'

Conway pointed toward the couch. 'Let's all sit down. We have a lot to talk about.'

'You said you don't believe this is your standard hostage crisis,' said Gabriel as he settled onto the couch. 'I don't either. And not just because my wife is involved.'

'What strikes you as different?'

'Aside from the fact the first hostage taker was female? That she had an armed compatriot who walked in to join her? Aside from the fact she

176

broadcast what seemed to be an activation code?'

'All the things that got Director Wynne concerned,' said Silver. 'Plus, there's an additional detail that worries us. I have to admit, I didn't pick up on the significance myself when I first heard the recording.'

'Which recording?'

'The call she made to that radio station. We asked a Defense linguist to analyze her speech. Her grammar was perfect – almost too perfect. No contractions, no slang. The woman is clearly not American, but foreign born.'

'The Boston PD negotiator made the same conclusion.'

'Now this is the part that worries us. If you listen carefully to what she said – in particular, to that phrase she used, "the die is cast" – you can hear the accent. It's definitely there. Russian maybe, or Ukrainian, or some other Eastern European language. It's impossible to distinguish her precise origins, but the accent is Slavic.'

'That's what's got the White House worried,' said Conway.

Gabriel frowned. 'They're thinking terrorism?'

'Specifically, Chechen,' said Silver. 'We don't know who this woman is, or how she got into the country. We know that Chechens often use female compatriots in their attacks. In the Moscow theater siege, several women were wired with explosives. Then there were those two jetliners that went down in southern Russia a few years ago, after taking off from Moscow. We believe both were brought down by female passengers wearing bombs. The point is, these particular terrorists routinely use women in their attacks. That's what our director of National Intelligence is most afraid of. That we're dealing with people who have no real interest in negotiation. They may be fully prepared to die, and spectacularly.'

'Chechnya's quarrel is with Moscow. Not us.'

'The war on terror is global. This is precisely why the DNI's office was created – to make sure 9/11 never happens again. Our job is to make all our intelligence agencies work together, and not at cross purposes, the way they sometimes did. No more rivalries, no more spy versus spy. We're all in this together. And we all agree that Boston Harbor's a tempting target for terrorists. They could go after fuel depots or a tanker. One motorboat loaded with explosives could cause a catastrophe.' He paused. 'That female hostage taker was found in the water, wasn't she?'

Conway said: 'You look dubious, Agent Dean. What's bothering you?'

'We're talking about a woman who was forced into this situation by accident. You're aware she was brought to the morgue as a drowning victim? Admitted to the hospital after she woke up?'

'Yes,' said Silver. 'It's a bizarre story.'

'She was a lone woman—'

'She's no longer alone. She now has a partner.'

'This hardly sounds like a planned terrorist operation.'

'We're not saying this hostage taking was planned. The timing was forced on them. Maybe it started as an accident. Maybe she fell overboard while being smuggled into the country. Woke up in the hospital, realized she was going to be questioned by authorities, and she panicked. She could be one arm of the octopus, part of a much larger operation. An operation that's now been prematurely exposed.'

'Joseph Roke isn't Russian, he's American.'

'Yes, we know a bit about Mr. Roke from his service record,' said Silver.

'He's hardly your typical Chechen sympathizer.'

'Did you know that Mr. Roke had explosives training in the army?'

'So have a lot of other soldiers who didn't wind up as terrorists.'

'Mr. Roke also has a history of antisocial behavior. Disciplinary problems. Are you aware of that?'

'I know he was given a dishonorable discharge.'

'For striking an officer, Agent Dean. For repeatedly disobeying orders. There was even some question about a serious emotional disorder. One army psychiatrist considered a diagnosis of paranoid schizophrenia.'

'Was he treated for that?'

'Roke refused any and all medications. After

179

he left the army, he essentially went into seclusion. We're talking about a guy just like the Unabomber, who withdrew from society and nursed oddball grudges. With Roke, it was all about government conspiracies, delusions of persecution. This is a very bitter man who believes his government has misused him. He's written so many letters to the FBI about his theories that they have a special file on him.' Silver reached for a folder on the coffee table and handed it to Gabriel. 'A sample of his writing. It's a letter he sent to them in June, 2004.'

Gabriel opened the folder and read the letter.

. . . I've provided you with case after case of documented heart attacks that were secretly induced by PRC-25 mixed with burning tobacco. The combination, as our Defense Department well knows, results in a deadly nerve gas. Scores of veterans have been murdered this way, so the Veterans Administration can save millions of dollars in health care costs. Is there no one at the FBI who cares?

'That's just one of dozens of nutty letters he wrote to the Bureau, to his Congressmen, to newspapers and TV stations. The *Washington Post* got so much of his paranoid crap, they just toss out anything with his name on it. As you can see from that sample, the man is intelligent. He is verbal. And he's utterly convinced that the government is evil.'

'Why isn't he under psychiatric care?'

'He doesn't believe he's crazy. Even though

everyone else can see he's clearly around the bend.'

'Terrorists wouldn't recruit a psychotic.'

'They might if he's useful.'

'You can't control them. You can't predict what they'll do.'

'But you *can* incite them to violence. You can reinforce their beliefs that their own government is against them. And you can use their skills. Roke may be paranoid, but he also knows his explosives. This is an embittered loner with military training. The perfect terrorist recruit, Agent Dean. Until we have evidence to the contrary, we have to assume that this situation has national security implications. We don't think Boston PD is up to handling this on their own.'

'So that's why John Barsanti is here.'

'Who?' Silver looked bewildered.

'Agent Barsanti from the FBI's deputy director's office. The Bureau doesn't normally send someone straight from Washington when there's a local field office to call on.'

'I wasn't aware the FBI had stepped in,' said Silver. An admission that startled Gabriel. The DNI's office wielded authority over the FBI; Silver should certainly have known about Barsanti's involvement.

'The FBI won't be handling the rescue,' said Silver. 'We've authorized a special antiterrorist unit from the Strategic Support Branch to come in.'

Gabriel stared at him. 'You're bringing in a team from the Pentagon? A military operation on US soil?'

Senator Conway interjected: 'I know it sounds illegal, Agent Dean. But there's a recent directive called JCS Conplan 0300-97. It authorizes the Pentagon to employ antiterrorist military units within our borders when the situation calls for it. It's so new, most of the public doesn't even know about it.'

'And you think this is a *good* idea?'

'Frankly?' The senator sighed. 'It scares the hell out of me. But the directive is on the books. The military *can* come in.'

'For good reason,' said Silver. 'In case you haven't noticed, our country is under attack. This is our chance to take out this nest before it can launch a strike. Before more people are endangered. In the larger scheme of things, this could prove to be a lucky accident.'

'Lucky?'

Too late, Silver registered his own insensitivity. He held up his hand in apology. 'I'm sorry, that was a terrible thing for me to say. I'm so focused on my mission, I sometimes get a case of tunnel vision.'

'It may also be limiting your view of the situation.'

'What do you mean?'

'You look at this siege and automatically you think terrorism.'

'I have to consider it. *They* forced us to adopt this attitude. Remember that.'

'To the exclusion of all other possibilities?'

'Of course not. It's perfectly possible we're just dealing with a pair of crazies. Two people who are trying to avoid capture after shooting that police officer in New Haven. We've considered that explanation.'

'Yet you focus only on terrorism.'

'Mr. Wynne wouldn't have it any other way. As director of National Intelligence, he takes his job seriously.'

Conway had been watching Gabriel, reading his reactions. 'I can see you're having problems with this terrorism angle.'

'I think it's too simple,' said Gabriel.

'And what's your explanation? What are these people after?' asked Silver. He had settled back in his chair, long legs crossed, hands relaxed on the armrests. Not a sign of tension in his lanky frame. He's not really interested in my opinion, thought Gabriel; he's already made up his mind.

'I don't have an answer yet,' said Gabriel. 'What I do have are a number of puzzling details that I can't explain. That's why I called Senator Conway.'

'What details?'

'I just attended the postmortem on that hospital guard. The man our Jane Doe shot to death. It turns out he wasn't a hospital employee at all. We don't know who he was.'

'They ran fingerprints on him?'

183

'He doesn't turn up on AFIS.'

'So he has no criminal record.'

'No. His fingerprints don't turn up on *any* databases we've checked.'

'Not everyone has fingerprints on file.'

'This man walked into that hospital carrying a weapon loaded with duplex rounds.'

'That's a surprise,' said Conway.

'What's a duplex round?' said Silver. 'I'm just a lawyer so you'll have to explain it to me. I'm afraid I'm illiterate when it comes to guns.'

'It's ammunition in which more than one bullet is loaded into a single cartridge case,' said Conway. 'Designed for greater lethality.'

'I just spoke to Boston PD's ballistics lab,' said Gabriel. 'They recovered a cartridge from the hospital room. It's an M-198.'

Conway stared at him. 'US Army military issue. That's not what you'd expect a security guard to carry.'

'A *fake* hospital guard.' Gabriel reached into his breast pocket and pulled out a folded piece of paper. He smoothed it flat on the coffee table. 'And here's the next detail that concerns me.'

'What's this?' asked Silver.

'This is the sketch I made at the postmortem. It's a tattoo on the dead man's back.'

Silver rotated the paper to face him. 'A scorpion?'

'Yes.'

'So are you going to explain to me why this is significant? Because I'm willing to bet there are more than a few men walking around with scorpion tattoos.'

Conway reached for the sketch. 'You said this was on his back? And we don't have *any* ID on this dead man?'

'Nothing came back on his fingerprints.'

'I'm surprised he doesn't have prints on file.'

'Why?' asked Silver.

Gabriel looked at him. 'Because there's a good chance this man is military.'

'You can tell that just by looking at his tattoo?'

'It's not just any tattoo.'

'What's so special about this one?'

'It's not on his arm, it's on his back. In the marines, we call them 'torso meat tags' because they're useful for identifying your corpse. In a blast, there's a good chance you'd lose your extremities. So a lot of soldiers choose to get their tattoos on their chest or back.'

Silver grimaced. 'A morbid reason.'

'But practical.'

'And the scorpion? Is that supposed to be significant?'

'It's the number thirteen that catches my eye,' said Gabriel. 'You see it here, circled by the stinger. I think it refers to the Fighting Thirteenth.'

'That's a military unit?'

'Marine Expeditionary. Special ops capable.'

'You're saying this dead man was an ex-marine?'

'You're never an *ex*-marine,' Conway pointed out.

'Oh. Of course,' Silver corrected himself. 'He's a *dead* marine.'

'And that leads us to the detail that bothers me most,' said Gabriel. 'The fact his fingerprints aren't in any database. This man has no military record.'

'Then maybe you're wrong about the significance of this tattoo. And the duplex ammo.'

'Or I'm right. And his fingerprints were specifically purged from the system to make him invisible to law enforcement.'

There was a long silence.

Silver's eyes suddenly widened as he realized what Gabriel was implying. 'Are you saying one of *our* intelligence agencies purged his prints?'

'To conceal any black ops missions within our borders.'

'Whom are you accusing? CIA? Military Intelligence? If he was one of ours, I sure wasn't told about it.'

'Whoever this man was, whoever he was working for, it's now obvious he and his associate showed up in that hospital room for only one reason.' Gabriel looked at Conway. 'You're on the Senate Intelligence Committee. You have sources.'

'But I'm totally out of the loop on this one,' said Conway, shaking his head. 'If one of our agencies ordered a hit on that woman, that's a serious scandal. An assassination on US soil?'

'But this hit went very wrong,' said Gabriel.

'Before they could finish it, Dr. Isles walked in on them. Not only did the target survive the hit, she took hostages. Now this is a huge media event. A black ops screwup that's going to end up on the front pages. The facts are going to come out anyway, so if you know, you might as well tell me. Who is this woman, and why does our country want her dead?'

'This is pure speculation,' said Silver. 'You're following a pretty thin thread, Agent Dean. Extrapolating from a tattoo and a bullet to a government-sponsored assassination.'

'These people have my wife,' Gabriel said quietly. 'I'm willing to follow any thread, however thin. I need to know how to make this end without someone getting killed. That's all I want. That no one gets killed.'

Silver nodded. 'It's what we all want.'

Fifteen

Darkness had fallen by the time Maura turned onto the quiet Brookline street where she lived. She drove past familiar houses, familiar gardens. Saw the same redheaded boy heaving his basketball at the hoop over his garage. Missing it, as usual. Everything looked as it had yesterday, just another hot summer's evening in suburbia. But tonight is different, she thought. Tonight, she wouldn't be lingering over her glass of chilled wine or her latest issue of *Vanity Fair*. How could she enjoy her usual pleasures, knowing what Jane was enduring at that moment?

If Jane was still alive.

Maura pulled into her garage and walked into the house, grateful for the cool breath of central air-conditioning. She would not be staying long; she'd come home only to grab a quick supper, to shower, and change clothes. For even this brief respite, she felt guilty. I'll bring back sandwiches for Gabriel, she thought. She doubted the thought of food had even crossed his mind.

She had just stepped out of the shower when she heard her doorbell ring. Pulling on a robe, she hurried to answer it.

Peter Lukas stood on her front porch. Only that morning, they had spoken, but judging by his wrinkled shirt and the tense lines around his eyes, the hours since then had taken a toll. 'I'm sorry to just show up here,' he said. 'I did try to call you a few minutes ago.'

'I didn't hear the phone. I was in the shower.'

His gaze dropped, just for an instant, to her bathrobe. Then he looked past her, focusing on a spot over her shoulder, as though he was uncomfortable staring directly at an undressed woman. 'Can we talk? I need your advice.'

'Advice?'

'About what the police are asking me to do.'

'You've spoken to Captain Hayder?'

'And that FBI guy. Agent Barsanti.'

'Then you already know what the hostage takers want.'

Lukas nodded. 'That's why I'm here. I need to know what you think about this whole crazy setup.'

'You're actually considering it?'

'I need to know what you'd do, Dr. Isles. I trust your judgment.' His gaze finally met hers and she felt the heat rise in her face, found herself tugging her robe tighter.

'Come inside,' she finally said. 'Let me get dressed, and we'll talk about it.'

As he waited in the living room, she hunted in

her closet for clean slacks and a blouse. Pausing before the mirror, she winced at the reflection of smeared eye makeup, tangled hair. He's only a reporter, she thought. This isn't a date. It doesn't matter what the hell you look like.

When she finally walked back into the living room, she found him standing at the window, gazing out at the dark street. 'It's gone national, you know,' he said, turning to look at her. 'Right this minute, they're watching it in LA.'

'Is that why you're thinking of doing this? A chance at fame? The fact you could get your name in the headlines?'

'Oh yeah, I can see it now: "Reporter gets bullet in brain." I'm really crazy about *that* headline.'

'So you do realize this is not a particularly wise move.'

'I haven't decided.'

'If you want my advice—'

'I want more than just your advice. I need information.'

'What can I tell you?'

'You could start by telling me what the FBI is doing here.'

'You said you spoke to Agent Barsanti. Didn't you ask him?'

'I've heard there's an Agent Dean involved as well. Barsanti wouldn't tell me a thing about him. Why would the Bureau send two men all the way from Washington, for a crisis that would normally be handled by Boston PD?'

His question alarmed her. If he already knew about Gabriel, it would not take long for him to learn that Jane was a hostage.

'I don't know,' she lied, and found it hard to meet his gaze. He was watching her so intently that she finally had to turn away and sit down on the couch.

'If there's something I should know,' he said, 'I hope you'd tell me. I'd like to know ahead of time what I'm walking into.'

'By now, you probably know as much as I do.'

He sat down in the chair facing her, his gaze so direct she felt like a pinned butterfly. 'What do these people want?'

'What did Barsanti tell you?'

'He told me about their offer. That they promised to release two hostages. Then I walk in with a TV cameraman, talk to this guy, and two more hostages will be released. That's the deal. What happens after that is anyone's guess.'

This man could save Jane's life, she thought. If he walked in there, Jane might be one of the two hostages who walks out. *I would do it. But I can't ask this man to risk his life, even for Jane.*

'It's not every day a man gets the chance to play hero,' he said. 'It *is* an opportunity of sorts. A lot of journalists would jump at it.'

She laughed. 'Very tempting. Book deal, TV movie of the week. Risk your life for a little fame and fortune?'

'Hey, I've got a rusty old Toyota parked out there right now, and a mortgage with twenty-nine years left to go, so fame and fortune doesn't sound too bad.'

'If you live long enough to enjoy it.'

'That's why I'm talking to you. You were with the shooter. You know what kind of people we're dealing with. Are they rational? Are they going to keep their side of the bargain? Will they let me walk out of there after the interview's over?'

'I can't predict that.'

'That's not a very helpful answer.'

'I refuse to be responsible for what happens to you. I can't predict what they'll do. I don't even know what they want.'

He sighed. 'I was afraid you'd say that.'

'Now I have a question for you. I assume you know the answer.'

'Your question is?'

'Of all the journalists they could have asked for, why did they choose you?'

'I have no idea.'

'You must have had some contact with them before.'

It was his hesitation that caught her attention. She leaned toward him. 'You've heard from them.'

'You have to understand, reporters hear from a lot of crazy people. Every week, I get at least a few bizarre letters or phone calls about secret government conspiracies. If it's not the evil oil companies, then it's black helicopters or UN plots. Most of the time I just ignore them. That's why I didn't really think much of it. It was just another screwy phone call.'

'When?'

'A few days ago. One of my colleagues just reminded me of it, because he was the one who answered the phone. Frankly, when the call came in, I was too busy to pay much attention. It was late, and I was about to hit a deadline, and the last thing I wanted to do was talk to some nutty guy.'

'The call was from a man?'

'Yeah. It came into the *Tribune* newsroom. The man asked if I'd looked at the package he sent me. I didn't know what he was talking about. He said he'd mailed me something a few weeks before, which I never got. So he told me a woman would drop off another package at the front desk that night. That as soon as it arrived, I should go down to the lobby immediately and pick it up, because it was extremely sensitive.'

'Did you ever get that second package?'

'No. The guard at the front desk said no woman ever showed up that night. I went home and forgot all about it. Until now.' He paused. 'I'm wondering if that was Joe who called me.'

'Why choose you?'

'I have no idea.'

'These people seem to know you.'

'Maybe they've read my column. Maybe they're fans.' At Maura's silence, he gave a self-deprecating laugh. 'Fat chance, huh?'

'Have you ever appeared on television?' she asked, thinking: He has the face, the dark good looks for it.

'Never.'

'And you're only published in the *Boston Tribune*?'

'*Only?* Nice put-down, Dr. Isles.'

'I didn't mean it that way.'

'I've been a reporter since I was twenty-two. Started off freelancing for the *Boston Phoenix* and *Boston Magazine*. It was fun for a while, but freelancing is no way to pay the bills, so I was happy to land a spot at the *Tribune*. Started off on the city beat, spent a few years in DC as their Washington correspondent. Then came back to Boston when they offered me a weekly column. So yeah, I've been at this reporting gig for a while. I'm not making a fortune, but obviously I've got some fans. Since Joseph Roke seems to know who I am.' He paused. 'At least I *hope* he's a fan. And not some pissed-off reader.'

'Even if he is a fan, this is a dangerous situation you're walking into.'

'I know.'

'You understand the setup?'

'A cameraman and me. It'll be a live feed to some local TV station. I assume the hostage takers have some way of monitoring that we're actually on the air. I also assume they won't object to the standard five-second delay, just in case . . .' He stopped.

In case something goes terribly wrong.

Lukas took a deep breath. 'What would you do, Dr. Isles? In my place?'

'I'm not a journalist.'

194

'So you'd refuse.'

'A normal person doesn't willingly walk into a hostage situation.'

'Meaning, journalists aren't normal people?'

'Just think hard about it.'

'I'll tell you what I'm thinking. That four hostages could walk out of there alive if I do this. For once, something *I* do will be worth writing about.'

'And you're willing to risk your life?'

'I'm willing to take the chance,' he said. Then added with quiet honesty: 'But I'm scared as hell of it, too.' His frankness was disarming; few men were brave enough to admit they were afraid. 'Captain Hayder wants my answer by nine P.M.'

'What are you going to do?'

'The cameraman's already agreed to go in. That makes me feel like a coward if I don't do it. Especially if four hostages could be saved. I keep thinking of all those reporters in Baghdad right now, and what they face every day. This should be a cakewalk in comparison. I go in, talk to the wackos, let them tell me their story, and then I walk out. Maybe that's all they want – a chance to vent, to have people listen to them. I could end the whole crisis by doing this.'

'You want to be a savior.'

'No! No, I'm just . . .' He laughed. 'Trying to justify taking this crazy chance.'

'You called it that. I didn't.'

'The truth is, I'm no hero. I never saw the point of risking my life if I didn't have to. But I'm as baffled about this as you are. I want to know why they chose me.' He glanced at his watch. 'It's almost nine. I guess I'd better call Barsanti.' Rising to his feet, he turned toward the door. Suddenly paused and glanced back.

Maura's phone was ringing.

She picked it up to hear Abe Bristol say: 'Are you watching TV?' he asked.

'Why?'

'Turn it on, channel six. It's not good.'

As Lukas watched, she crossed to the TV, her heart suddenly pounding. *What has happened? What's gone wrong?* She clicked on the remote, and the face of Zoe Fossey at once filled the screen.

'. . . official spokesman has refused comment, but we have confirmed that one of the hostages is a Boston police officer. Detective Jane Rizzoli made national headlines just last month, during the investigation of a kidnapped housewife in Natick. We have no word yet as to the condition of any of the hostages, or how Detective Rizzoli happened to be among them . . .'

'My god,' murmured Lukas, standing right beside her. She had not been aware that he had moved so close to her. 'There's a *cop* trapped in there?'

Maura looked at him. 'She could very well be a dead cop.'

Sixteen

That's it. I'm going to die.

Jane sat frozen on the couch, waiting for the gun's blast as Joe turned from the TV to stare at her. But it was the woman who advanced on Jane, her steps slow and excruciatingly deliberate. *Olena* was the name Joe had called his partner. At least now I know the names of my murderers, thought Jane. She felt the orderly lean away from her, as though to avoid getting splattered with her blood. Jane's gaze remained fixed on Olena's face; she dared not look at the gun. She did not want to see that barrel rising toward her head, did not want to watch the hand tighten around the grip. Better that I can't see the bullet coming, she thought. Better that I look this woman in the eye, that I force her to see the human being she's about to blow away. She could read no emotions there; they were a doll's eyes. Blue glass. Olena was now dressed in clothes that she had scrounged from a locker room: scrub pants and a doctor's lab coat. A killer disguised in healer's garb.

'This is true?' Olena asked softly.

Jane felt her womb tighten, and she bit her lip at the mounting pain of the new contraction. My poor baby, she thought. You will never take your first breath. She felt Dr. Tam reach out and grasp her hand, offering silent comfort.

'The TV, it tells the truth? You are police?'

Jane swallowed. 'Yes,' she whispered.

'They said you're a detective,' Joe cut in. 'Are you?'

Gripped by the contraction, Jane rocked forward, her vision darkening. 'Yes,' she groaned. 'Yes, goddamm it! I'm with – with the homicide unit . . .'

Olena glanced down at the hospital ID bracelet that she'd earlier torn from Jane's wrist. It was still on the floor near the couch. She picked it up and handed it to Joe.

'Rizzoli, Jane,' he read.

The worst of the contraction was over now. She released a sharp breath and sank back against the couch, her hospital gown drenched in sweat. Too exhausted to fight back, even to save her own life. How could she fight back? *I cannot even get up off this soft couch without a helping hand.* Defeated, she watched as Joe picked up her medical chart and flipped open the manila cover.

'Rizzoli, Jane,' he read aloud. 'Married, address on Claremont Street. Occupation: Detective, Homicide Unit. Boston PD.' He looked at her with dark eyes so penetrating that she wanted to shrink from them. Unlike Olena, this man was utterly calm and in control. That's what scared Jane most – that he seemed to know exactly what he was doing. 'A homicide detective. And you just *happen* to be here?'

'Must be my lucky day,' she muttered.

'What?'

'Nothing.'

'Answer me. How did you just happen to be here?'

Jane's chin snapped up. 'In case you didn't notice, I'm having a baby.'

Dr. Tam said, 'I'm her obstetrician. I admitted her this morning.'

'The timing, that's what I don't like,' said Joe. 'This is all wrong.'

Jane flinched as Joe grabbed her hospital gown and yanked it up. For a moment he stared down at Jane's swollen abdomen, her heavy breasts, now bared for everyone in the room to see. Without a word, he let the gown fall back over Jane's torso.

'Are you satisfied, asshole?' Jane blurted, cheeks burning from the humiliation. 'What did you expect, a fat suit?' The instant the words were out of her mouth, she knew it was a stupid thing to say. First rule of hostage survival: *Never piss off the guy holding the gun*. But by wrenching aside her gown, he had assaulted her, exposed her, and she was now trembling with rage. 'You think I *want* to be trapped in here with you two whack jobs?'

She felt Dr. Tam's hand tighten around her wrist in a silent plea to shut up. Jane shook off the hand and kept her fury focused on their captors.

'Yes, I'm a cop. And guess what? You two are royally screwed. You kill me, and you know what happens, don't you? You know what my buddies do to cop killers?'

Joe and Olena looked at each other. Were they making a decision? Coming to an agreement about whether she lived or died?

'A mistake,' said Joe. 'That's all you are, Detective. You're in the wrong fucking place at the wrong fucking time.'

You said it, asshole.

She was startled when Joe suddenly laughed. He paced to the other end of the room, shaking his head. When he turned back to face her, she saw that his weapon was now pointed at the floor. Not at her.

'So are you a good cop?' he asked.

'What?'

'On TV, they said you worked a case with a missing housewife.'

'A pregnant woman. She was kidnapped.'

'How did it end?'

'She's alive. The perp's dead.'

'So you're good.'

'I did my job.'

Another look passed between Olena and Joe.

He came toward Jane, until he was standing right in front of her. 'What if I was to tell you about a crime? What if I told you that justice wasn't served? That it can never be served?'

'Why can't it be?'

He reached for a chair, pulled it in front of her, and sat down. Their gazes were now level. Dark eyes met hers with unwavering focus. 'Because it was committed by our own government.'

Oops. Cuckoo alert.

'Do you have proof?' Jane asked, managing to keep her voice neutral.

'We have a witness,' he said, and pointed to Olena. 'She saw it happen.'

'Witness reports aren't necessarily sufficient.' *Especially when the witness is crazy.*

'Are you aware of all the criminal acts our government is guilty of? The crimes they commit every day? The assassinations, kidnappings? Poisoning their own citizens, in the name of profits? It's big business that runs this country, and we're all expendable. Take soft drinks, for example.'

'Excuse me?'

'Diet soft drinks. The US government bought 'em by the container load for its troops in the Gulf. I was there, and I saw cans and cans, sitting in the heat. What do you think happens to the chemicals in diet drinks when they're exposed to heat? They turn toxic. They turn to poison. That's why thousands of Gulf War vets came home sick. Oh yeah, our government knows about it, but we never will. The soda pop industry's too big, and they know just whom to bribe.'

201

'So . . . this is all about soda pop?'

'No. *This* is much worse.' He leaned closer. 'And this time we've finally got them, Detective. We have a witness and we have the proof. And we have the country's attention. That's why we've got them scared. That's why they want us dead. What would you do, Detective?'

'About what? I still don't understand.'

'If you knew about a crime committed by people in our government. And you knew it had gone unpunished. What would you do?'

'That's easy. I'd do my job. The same as always.'

'You'd see that justice is served?'

'Yes.'

'No matter who stood in your way?'

'Who would try to stop me?'

'You don't know these people. You don't know what they're capable of.'

She tensed as another contraction squeezed its fist around her womb. She felt Dr. Tam take her hand again, and Jane held on tight. Suddenly everything went out of focus as the pain roared in, pain that made her rock forward, groaning. Oh god, what had they taught her in Lamaze class? She'd forgotten it all.

'Cleansing breath,' murmured Dr. Tam. 'Find your focus.'

That was it. Now she remembered. *Take a breath. Focus on one spot.* These crazy people weren't going to kill her in the next sixty seconds.

She just had to get past this pain. *Breathe and focus. Breathe and focus . . .*

Olena moved close, and suddenly her face loomed right in front of Jane's. 'Look at me,' Olena said. She pointed to her own eyes. 'Look here, right at me. Until it is over.'

I can't believe it. A crazy woman wants to be my labor coach.

Jane began to pant, her breath quickening as the pain mounted. Olena was right in front of her, her gaze fixed on hers. Cool blue water. That's what those eyes reminded Jane of. Water. Clear and calm. A pond with no ripples.

'Good,' the woman murmured. 'You did good.'

Jane exhaled a sigh of relief and sprawled back against the cushions. Sweat trickled down her cheek. Another five blessed minutes to recover. She thought of all the women through millennia who had endured childbirth, thought of her own mother who, thirty-four years ago, had labored through a hot summer's night to bring Jane into the world. *I did not appreciate what you went through. Now I understand. This is the price women have paid for every child ever born.*

'Whom do you trust, Detective Rizzoli?'

Joe was talking to her again. She raised her head, still too dazed to understand what he wanted from her.

'There must be someone you trust,' he said. 'Someone you work with. Another cop. Maybe your partner.'

She gave a weary shake of her head. 'I don't know what you're getting at.'

'What if I held this gun to your head?'

She froze as he suddenly raised his weapon and pressed it to her temple. She heard the receptionist give a gasp. Felt her fellow hostages on the couch shrink away from the victim between them.

'Now tell me,' Joe said coldly. Reasonably. 'Is there anyone who'd take this bullet for you?'

'Why are you doing this?' she whispered.

'I'm just asking. Who would take this bullet for you? Who would you trust with your life?'

She stared at the hand holding the gun, and she thought: It's a test. And I don't know the answer. I don't know what he wants to hear.

'Tell me, Detective. Isn't there someone you completely believe in?'

'Gabriel . . .' She swallowed. 'My husband. I trust my husband.'

'I'm not talking about family. I'm talking about someone with a badge, like you. Someone clean. Someone who'll do his duty.'

'Why are you asking me this?'

'Answer the question!'

'I told you. I gave you an answer.'

'You said your husband.'

'Yes!'

'Is he a cop?'

'No, he's . . .' She stopped.

'What is he?'

She straightened. Looked past the gun, and

focused instead on the eyes of the man holding it. 'He's FBI,' she said.

Joe stared at her for a moment. Then he looked at his partner. 'This changes everything,' he said.

Seventeen

Mila

There is a new girl in our house.

This morning, a van pulled up in the driveway, and the men carried her up to our room. All day she has been lying on Olena's cot, sleeping off the drugs they gave her for the journey. We all watch her, staring down at a face so pale that it does not look like living flesh, but translucent marble. Her breaths come in soft little puffs, a strand of her blond hair fluttering every time she exhales. Her hands are small – a doll's hands, I think, looking at the little fist, at the thumb pressed against her lips. Even when the Mother unlocks the door and steps into the room, the girl does not stir.

'Wake her,' the Mother orders.

'How old is she?' Olena asks.

'Just get her up.'

'She's only a child. What is she, twelve? Thirteen?'

'Old enough to work.' The Mother crosses to the cot and gives the girl a shake. 'Come on,' she snaps, yanking off the blanket. 'You've slept too long.'

The girl stirs and rolls onto her back. That's when I see the bruises on her arm. She opens her eyes, sees us staring at her, and her frail body instantly stiffens in alarm.

'Don't make him wait,' the Mother says.

We hear the car approaching the house. Darkness has fallen, and when I look out the window, I see headlights winking through the trees. Tires crackle over gravel as the car pulls into the driveway. The first client of the evening, I think with dread, but the Mother does not even look at us. She grabs the new girl's hand and pulls her to her feet. The girl stumbles, sleepy-eyed, out of the room.

'How did they get a girl that young?' whispers Katya.

We hear the door buzzer. It is a sound we have learned to shrink from, the sound of our tormentors' arrival. We all fall still, listening to the voices downstairs. The Mother greets a client in English. The man says little; we hear only a few words from him. Then there are his heavy footsteps on the stairs, and we back away from the door. He walks right past our room and continues down the hall.

Downstairs, the girl raises her voice in protest. We hear a slap, a sob. Then footsteps thump up the stairs again as the Mother drags the girl to the client's room. The door slams shut, and the Mother walks away, leaving the girl with the man.

'The bitch,' Olena mutters. 'She'll burn in hell.'

But tonight, at least I will not suffer. I feel guilty as soon as that thought crosses my mind. Still, the thought is there. *Better her than me.* I go to the window and stare out at the night, at darkness that cannot see my shame. Katya pulls a blanket over her head. All of us are trying not to listen, but even through closed doors, we can hear the girl's screams, and we can imagine what he is doing to her, because the same has been done to us. Only the faces of the men vary; the pain they inflict does not.

When it is over, when the cries finally cease, we hear the man walk down the stairs, and out of the house. I release a deep breath. No more, I think. Please, let there be no more clients tonight.

The Mother comes back up the stairs to retrieve the girl, and there is a long, strange silence. Suddenly she is running past our door and down the stairs again. We hear her talking to someone on her cell phone. Quiet, urgent words. I look at Olena, wondering if she understands what is going on. But Olena does not return my glance. She hunches on her cot, her hands turned to fists in her lap. Outside, something flutters past the window, like a white moth, twirling on the wind.

It is starting to snow.

*   *   *

The girl did not work out. She scratched the client's face, and he was angry. A girl like that is bad for business, so she is being sent back to Ukraine. That is what the Mother told us last night, when the girl did not come back to the room.

That, at least, is the story.

'Maybe it's true,' I say, and my breath is a puff of steam in the darkness. Olena and I are once again sitting on the roof. Tonight it sparkles like a frosted cake under the moonlight. Last night it snowed, barely a centimeter, but enough to make me think of home, where there has surely been snow on the ground for weeks. I am glad to see the stars again, to be sharing this sky with Olena. We have brought both our blankets outside, and we sit with our bodies pressed together.

'You're stupid if you really believe that,' says Olena. She lights a cigarette, the last one from the party on the boat, and she savors it, looking up at the sky as she inhales the smoke, as though offering thanks to heaven for the blessings of tobacco.

'Why don't you believe it?'

She laughs. 'Maybe they sell you to another house, or another pimp, but they don't ever send you home. Anyway, I don't believe anything the Mother says, the old whore. Can you believe it? She used to turn tricks herself, about a hundred years ago. Before she got so fat.'

I cannot imagine the Mother ever being young

or thin or ever enticing a man. I cannot imagine a time when she was not repulsive.

'It's the cold-blooded whores who end up running the houses,' says Olena. 'They're worse than the pimps. She knows what we suffer, she's done it herself. But all she cares about now is the money. A lot of money.' Olena taps off an ash. 'The world is evil, Mila, and there's no way to change it. The best you can do is stay alive.'

'And not be evil.'

'Sometimes, there's no choice. You just have to be.'

'You couldn't be evil.'

'How do you know?' She looks at me. 'How do you know what I am, or what I've done? Believe me, if I had to, I'd kill someone. I could even kill *you*.'

She stares at me, her eyes fierce in the moonlight. And for a moment – just for a moment – I think she is right. That she *could* kill me, that she is ready to do anything to stay alive.

We hear the sound of car tires rolling over gravel, and we both snap straight.

Olena immediately stubs out her precious cigarette, only half smoked. 'Who the hell is this?'

I scramble to my feet and cautiously crawl up the shallow slope of roof to peer over the edge, toward the driveway. 'I don't see any lights.'

She clambers up beside me and peeks over the edge as well. 'There,' she murmurs as a car emerges from the woods. Its headlights are off, and all we see is the yellow glow of its parking lights. It stops at the edge of the driveway, and two men step out. Seconds later, we hear the door buzzer. Even at this early hour, men have their needs. They demand satisfaction.

'Shit,' hisses Olena. 'Now they're going to wake her up. We have to get back to the room before she finds out we're gone.'

We slide back down the roof and don't even bother to snatch up our blankets, but immediately scramble onto the ledge. Olena slips through the window, into the dark attic.

The doorbell buzzes again, and we hear the Mother's voice as she unlocks the front door and greets her latest clients.

I scramble through the window after Olena, and we cross to the trap door. The ladder is still down, the blatant evidence of our location. Olena is just backing down the rungs when she suddenly stops cold.

The Mother is screaming.

Olena looks up at me through the trap door. I can see the frantic glow of her eyes in the shadows below me. We hear a thud, and the sound of splintering wood. Heavy footsteps pound up the stairs.

The Mother's screams turn to shrieks.

All at once, Olena is climbing back up the ladder, shoving me aside as she scrambles through the trap door. She reaches down through the opening, grabs the ladder, and pulls. It rises, folding, as the trap door closes.

'Back,' she whispers. 'Out on the roof!'

'What's happening?'

'Just *go*, Mila!'

We run back to the window. I am the first one through, but I'm in such a rush that my foot slides across the ledge. I give a sob as I fall, clawing in panic at the windowsill.

Olena's hand closes around my wrist. She hangs on to me as I dangle, terrified.

'Grab my other hand!' she whispers.

I reach for it and she pulls me up, until I am doubled over the windowsill, my heart slamming against my chest.

'Don't be so fucking clumsy!' she hisses.

I regain my footing and cling with sweating hands to the sill as I make my way along the ledge, back to the rooftop. Olena wriggles out, closes the window behind her, then clambers after me, quick as a cat.

Inside the house, the lights have come on. We can see the glow spilling through the windows below us. And we can hear running footsteps, and the crash of a door flying open. And a scream – not the Mother this time. A lone, piercing shriek that cuts off to a terrible silence.

Olena snatches up the blankets. 'Climb,' she says. 'Hurry, up the roof, where they can't see us!'

As I crawl up the asphalt shingles, toward the highest point, Olena swings her blanket, brushing off the footprints we have left on the snowy ledge. She does the same with the area where we had been sitting, obscuring all traces of our presence. Then she clambers up beside me, onto the peak above the attic window. There we perch, like shivering gargoyles.

Suddenly I remember. 'The chair,' I whisper. 'We left the chair under the trap door!'

'It's too late.'

'If they see it, they'll know we're up here.'

She grabs my hand and squeezes so hard that I think she will snap the bones. The attic light has just come on.

We cringe against the roof, not daring to move. One creak, one skitter of falling snow, and the intruder will know where we are. I feel my heart thumping against the shingles, and think that surely he can hear it through the ceiling.

The window slides open. A moment passes. What does he see, gazing out? A fragment of a footprint on the ledge? A telltale trail that Olena's frantic swipes with the blanket did not obliterate? Then the window slides shut again. I give a soft sob of relief, but Olena's fingers again dig into my hand. A warning.

He may still be there. He may still be listening.

We hear a sharp thump, followed by a scream that even closed windows cannot muffle. A shriek of such excruciating pain that I break out sweating, shaking. A man is shouting in English. *Where are they? There should be six! Six whores.*

They are looking for the missing girls.

Now the Mother sobs, pleads. Truly she does not know.

Another thud.

The Mother's scream pierces straight to my marrow. I cover my ears and press my face to the icy shingles. I cannot listen to this, but I have no choice. It does not stop. The blows, the shrieks, go on and on so long that I think they will find us here at sunrise, still clinging with frozen hands to this roof. I close my eyes, fighting nausea. *See no evil, hear no evil.* That's what I chant to myself a thousand times over, to drown out the sounds of the Mother's torment. *See no evil, hear no evil.*

When the screams finally fall silent, my hands have gone numb and my teeth are chattering from the cold. I lift my head, and feel icy tears on my face.

'They're leaving,' Olena whispers.

We hear the front door creak open, hear footsteps on the porch. From our perch on the roof, we can see them walk across the driveway. This time they are more than just indistinct silhouettes; they have left the house lights on, and by the glow spilling through the windows, we can see the two men are dressed in dark clothes. One of them pauses, and his short blond hair catches the reflection of the porch lights. He looks back at the house, his gaze lifting to the roof. For a few terrifying heartbeats I think he can see us. But the light is in his eyes, and we remain hidden in shadow.

They climb into the car and drive away.

For a long time, we do not move. The

moonlight shines down with icy radiance. The night is so still I can hear the rush of my own pulse, the chatter of my teeth. At last, Olena stirs.

'No,' I whisper. 'What if they're still out there? What if they're watching?'

'We can't stay on the roof all night. We'll freeze.'

'Wait just a little longer. Olena, please!'

But she is already easing her way down the shingles, moving back toward the attic window. I'm terrified of being left behind; I have no choice but to follow her. By the time I crawl back inside, she is already through the trap door and climbing down the ladder.

I want to scream: *Please wait for me!* but I'm too afraid to make a sound. I scramble down the ladder, too, and follow Olena into the hallway.

She has come to a standstill at the top of the stairs, gazing downward. Only when I move beside her do I see what has made her freeze in horror.

Katya lies dead on the stairs. Her blood has streamed down the steps like a dark waterfall, and she is a swimmer, diving toward the glistening pool at the bottom.

'Don't look in the bedroom,' Olena says. 'They are all dead.' Her voice is flat. Not human, but a machine's, cold and matter-of-fact. I do not know this Olena, and she scares me. She moves down the stairs, avoiding the blood, avoiding the body. As I follow her, I cannot stop staring at Katya. I see where the bullet has torn through the back of her T-shirt, the same shirt she wears every night. It has yellow daisies and the words BE HAPPY. Oh Katya, I think; now you will never be happy. At the bottom of the stairs, where a pool of blood has collected, I see the imprints of large shoes that have tracked through it on their way to the front door.

Only then do I notice that the door is ajar.

I think: *Run!* Out of the house and down the porch steps, into the woods. This is our escape, this is our chance at freedom.

But Olena does not immediately flee the house. Instead she circles right, into the dining room.

'Where are you going?' I whisper.

She does not answer me, but continues into the kitchen.

'Olena!' I plead, trailing after her. 'Let's go *now*, before—' I stop in the doorway and clap my hand over my mouth, because I think I am going to throw up. There are splatters of blood on the walls, on the refrigerator. The Mother's blood. She sits at the kitchen table, and the bloody remnants of her hands are stretched out before her. Her eyes are open, and for a moment, I think that maybe she can see us, but of course she cannot.

Olena moves past her, through the kitchen, to the back bedroom.

So desperate am I to escape that I think I should just leave now, without Olena. Leave her to whatever insane reason keeps her in this house. But she is moving with such purpose that

I follow her to the Mother's bedroom, which has always before been locked.

This is the first time I have ever seen the room, and I gape at the large bed with satin sheets, at a dresser that has a lace runner and a row of silver hairbrushes. Olena goes straight to the dresser, yanks open drawers, and rifles through the contents.

'What are you looking for?' I ask.

'We need money. We can't survive out there without it. She must keep it here somewhere.' She pulls out a woolen hat from the drawer and tosses it to me. 'Here. You'll need warm clothes.'

I'm loath to even touch the hat, because it was the Mother's, and I can see her ugly brown hairs still clinging to the wool.

Olena whisks across to the nightstand, pulls open the drawer, and finds a cell phone and a small wad of cash. 'This can't be everything,' she says. 'There has to be more.'

I only want to flee, but I know she's right; we need money. I cross to the closet, which hangs open; the killers have searched it, and several hangers have been knocked to the floor. But they were hunting for frightened girls, not money, and the shelf above has not been disturbed. I pull down a shoe box, and old photographs spill out. I see pictures of Moscow and smiling faces and a young woman whose eyes are disconcertingly familiar. And I think: Even the Mother was young once. Here is the proof.

I pull down a large tote bag. Inside is a heavy

jewelry pouch and a videotape and a dozen passports. And money. A thick bundle of American cash, tied with a rubber band.

'Olena! I found it.'

She crosses to me and glances in the bag. 'Take it all,' she says. 'We'll go through the bag later.' She throws in the cell phone as well. Then she snatches a sweater from the closet and thrusts it at me.

I don't want to put on the Mother's clothes; I can smell her scent on them, like sour yeast. I pull them on anyway, quelling my disgust. A turtleneck, a sweater, and a scarf all layered over my own blouse. We dress quickly and in silence, donning the clothes of the woman who sits dead in the next room.

At the front door we hesitate, staring out at the woods. Are the men waiting for us? Sitting in their dark car farther down the road, knowing that eventually we will show ourselves?

'Not that way,' Olena says, reading my thoughts. 'Not the road.'

We slip out, circle around to the rear of the house, and plunge into the woods.

Eighteen

Gabriel charged into the throng of reporters, his gaze fixed on the well-coiffed blond woman who was the focus of klieg lights twenty yards away. As he pushed closer, he saw that Zoe Fossey was, at that moment, talking into the camera. She spotted him and she froze, clutching the microphone to her silent lips.

'Turn it off,' said Gabriel.

'Quiet,' said the cameraman. 'We're live—'

'Turn off the fucking microphone!'

'Hey! What the hell do you think you're—'

Gabriel shoved the camera aside and yanked on electrical cords, killing the klieg lights.

'Get this man out of here!' Zoe yelled.

'Do you know what you've done?' Gabriel said. 'Do you have *any* idea?'

'I'm doing my job,' she retorted.

He advanced on her, and something she saw in his eyes made her shrink away, until she bumped up against a news van and could back away no farther.

'You may have just executed my wife.'

'Me?' She shook her head, and said with a note of defiance: 'I'm not the one holding the gun.'

'You just told them she's a cop.'

'I only report the facts.'

'Whatever the consequences?'

'It's news, isn't it?'

'You know what you are?' He moved closer, and found he could barely control the urge to throttle her. 'You're a whore. No, I take that back. You're worse than a whore. You don't just sell out yourself. You'd sell out anyone else.'

'Bob!' she yelled at her cameraman. 'Get this guy outta my face!'

'Back off, mister!' The cameraman's heavy hand landed on Gabriel's shoulder. Gabriel shook it away, his gaze still fixed on Zoe. 'If anything happens to Jane, I swear—'

'I said, back *away*!' The cameraman again grasped Gabriel by the shoulder.

Suddenly all Gabriel's fears, his despair, ignited in a blinding moment of fury. He twisted around and charged straight at the barrel chest. Heard air whoosh out of the man's lungs, and caught a glimpse of a startled face as the man staggered backward and fell to the ground, landing on a viper's nest of tangled electrical cords. In an instant, Gabriel was crouched above him, his fist raised, every muscle primed to deliver the blow. Then his vision abruptly came back into focus, and he registered the man cowering beneath him. Realized that a circle of bystanders had gathered to watch the spectacle. Everyone loved a spectacle.

Chest heaving, Gabriel rose to his feet. He saw Zoe standing a few yards away, her face alight with excitement.

'Did you get that?' she called to another cameraman. 'Shit, did *anyone* get that on tape?'

In disgust, Gabriel turned and walked away. He kept walking until he was well away from the crowd, away from the glare of klieg lights. Two blocks from the hospital, he found himself standing alone on a corner. Even on this dark street, there was no relief from the summer heat, which still radiated from sidewalks that had baked all day in the sun. His feet suddenly felt rooted to the pavement, melded there by grief, by dread.

I don't know how to save you. It's my job to keep people out of harm's way, but I cannot protect the one person I love most.

His cell phone rang. He recognized the number on the digital display, and did not answer it. It was Jane's parents. They had already called him while he was in the car, right after Zoe's newscast had aired. He'd quietly endured Angela Rizzoli's hysterical sobs, Frank's demands for action. I can't deal with them now, he thought. Maybe in five minutes, or ten. But not now.

He stood alone in the night, struggling to regain his composure. He was not a man who easily lost control, yet moments ago, he'd almost slammed his fist into a man's face. Jane would be shocked, he thought. And probably amused, too, to see her husband finally lose it. *Mr. Gray Suit*, she'd once called him in a fit of irritation because he was so unflappable, while her temper flared hot. You'd be proud of me, Jane, he thought. I've finally revealed I'm human.

But you aren't here to see it. You don't know that it's all about you.

'Gabriel?'

He straightened. Turned to see Maura, who had approached so silently that he had not even noticed she was there.

'I had to get the hell away from that circus,' he said. 'Or I swear, I would have wrung that woman's neck. It's bad enough I took it out on her cameraman.'

'So I heard.' She paused. 'Jane's parents just got here. I saw them in the parking lot.'

'They called me, right after they saw the newscast.'

'They're looking for you. You'd better go to them.'

'I can't handle them right now.'

'I'm afraid you also have another problem.'

'What?'

'Detective Korsak is here. He's none too pleased that *he* didn't get notified at all.'

'Oh, Christ. He's the last person I want to see.'

'Korsak is her friend. He's known her as long as you have. You may not get along with him, but he cares a lot about Jane.'

'Yeah, I know.' He sighed. 'I know.'

'These are all people who love her. You're not

the only one, Gabriel. Barry Frost has been hanging around here all evening. Even Detective Crowe dropped by. We're all worried sick, we're all scared for her.' She stopped. Added: 'I know I'm scared.'

He turned to look up the street, toward the hospital. 'I'm supposed to comfort them? I'm barely holding it together myself.'

'That's just it, you've taken it all on yourself. It's all been on *your* shoulders.' She touched his arm. 'Go, join her family. Her friends. You need each other right now.'

He nodded. Then, taking a deep breath, he walked back toward the hospital.

It was Vince Korsak who spotted him first. The retired Newton detective came charging toward him, and intercepted him on the sidewalk. Standing under the streetlamp, Korsak looked like a glowering troll, bullnecked and belligerent.

'How come you didn't call me?' he demanded.

'I didn't get the chance, Vince. Things have been happening so fast—'

'They said she's been in there all day.'

'Look, you're right. I should have called.'

'*Coulda, shoulda, woulda* doesn't cut it. What the hell, Dean? You think I'm not worth calling? You think I wouldn't want to know what the fuck is going on?'

'Vince, calm down.' He reached toward Korsak, who angrily batted away his hand.

'She's my *friend*, goddammit!'

'I know that. But we were trying to control

223

leaks. We didn't want the press to hear that a cop was inside.'

'You think *I'd* have leaked it? You think I'd do something that fucking stupid?'

'No, of course not.'

'Then you should've called me. You may be the one who married her, Dean. But I care about her, too!' Korsak's voice cracked. 'I care about her, too,' he repeated softly, then suddenly turned away.

I know you care. I also know you're in love with her, even if you'll never admit it. That's why we can never be friends. We both wanted her, but I'm the one who married her.

'What's happening in there?' said Korsak, voice muffled. Still not looking at him. 'Does anyone know?'

'We don't know a thing.'

'That bitch popped the secret on air half an hour ago. There's been no calls from the taker? No sounds of gun—' Korsak stopped. 'No reaction?'

'Maybe they weren't watching the TV. Maybe they haven't heard they're holding a cop. That's what I'm hoping – that they don't know.'

'When was their last contact?'

'They called around five, to set up a deal.'

'What kind of deal?'

'They want a live TV interview. In exchange, they'll release two hostages.'

'Then let's do it! What's taking so long?'

'The police were reluctant to send in any

civilians. It meant endangering a reporter and a cameraman.'

'Hey, I'll run the fucking camera if someone shows me how. And you can play reporter. They should send *us*.'

'The hostage takers asked for a specific reporter. A man named Peter Lukas.'

'You mean that guy who writes for the *Tribune*? Why him?'

'That's what we'd all like to know.'

'Well, let's get on with it, then. Get her the hell out of there before—'

Gabriel's cell phone rang and he winced, thinking that it must be Jane's parents trying yet again to talk to him. He could not put them off any longer. He reached for the phone and frowned at the digital display. It was a number he did not recognize.

'This is Gabriel Dean,' he answered.

'Agent Dean? With the FBI?'

'Who is this?'

'It's Joe. I think you know who I am.'

Gabriel froze. He saw Korsak watching him, instantly alert.

'We have things to talk about, Agent Dean.'

'How did you know—'

'Your wife here tells us you're trustworthy. That your word is your bond. We hope that's true.'

'Let me talk to her. Let me hear her voice.'

'In a minute. Once you promise.'

'What? Tell me what you want!'

'Justice. We want you to promise to do your job.'

'I don't understand.'

'We need you to bear witness. To hear what we have to say, because there's a good chance we're not going to live through this night.'

A chill sliced through Dean. *They're suicidal. Are they going to take everyone else down with them?*

'We want you to tell the world the truth,' said Joe. 'They'll listen to you. Come inside with that reporter, Agent Dean. Talk to us. When it's over, tell everyone what you've heard.'

'You're not going to die. You don't have to.'

'You think we want to? We've tried to outrun them and we can't. This is the only choice left to us.'

'Why do it this way? Why threaten innocent people?'

'No one will listen to us any other way.'

'Just walk out! Release the hostages and surrender.'

'And you'll never see us alive again. They'll come up with a logical explanation. They always do. Watch, you'll see it in the news. They'll claim we committed suicide. We'll die in prison, before we ever get to trial. And everyone will think: 'Well, that's how it goes in jail.' This is our last chance, Agent Dean, to get the world's attention. To tell them.'

'Tell them what?'

'What really happened in Ashburn.'

'Look, I don't know what you're talking about. But I'll do whatever you want if you just let my wife go.'

'She's right here. She's fine. In fact, I'll let you—'

The connection suddenly went dead.

'Joe? *Joe?*'

'What happened?' Korsak demanded. 'What'd he say?'

Gabriel ignored him; all his attention was focused on reestablishing the link. He retrieved the phone number and hit DIAL.

'. . . we're sorry. This number is currently unavailable.'

'What the hell is going on?' Korsak yelled.

'I can't get through.'

'He hung up on you?'

'No, we were cut off. Right after . . .' Gabriel stopped. Turned and looked up the street, his gaze focusing on the command trailer. They've been listening in, he thought. Someone heard everything Joe said.

'Hey!' called Korsak. 'Where you going?'

Gabriel was already running toward the trailer. He didn't bother to knock, but shoved open the door and stepped inside. Hayder and Stillman turned from the video monitors and looked at him.

Hayder said, 'We don't have time for you right now, Agent Dean.'

'I'm going into the building. I'm going to get my wife.'

'Oh, yeah.' Hayder laughed. 'I'm sure you'll be greeted with open arms.'

'Joe called me on my cell phone. They're inviting me in. They want to talk to me.'

Stillman abruptly straightened, his face registering what looked like genuine surprise. 'When did he call you? No one told us.'

'It was just a few minutes ago. Joe knows who I am. He knows Jane is my wife. I can reason with these people.'

'It's out of the question,' said Hayder.

'You were willing to send in that reporter.'

'They know you're FBI. In their minds, you're probably part of this crazy government conspiracy they're so scared of. You'd be lucky to last five minutes in there.'

'I'll risk it.'

'You'll be a prize for them,' said Stillman. 'A high-profile hostage.'

'You're the negotiator. You're the one who always talks about slowing things down. Well, these people *want* to negotiate.'

'Why with you?'

'Because they know I won't do anything to endanger Jane. I'll pull no tricks, bring in no booby traps. It'll just be me, playing by *their* rules.'

'It's too late, Dean,' said Stillman. 'We're not running this show anymore. They've already got their entry team in place.'

'What team?'

'The feds flew them in from Washington. It's some crack antiterrorist unit.'

This was exactly what Senator Conway had told Gabriel was about to happen. The time for negotiations had clearly passed.

'Boston PD's been ordered to stay on the sidelines,' said Hayder. 'Our job's just to keep the perimeters secure, while they go in.'

'When is this supposed to go down?'

'We have no idea. They're calling the shots.'

'What about that deal you made with Joe? The cameraman, the reporter? He still thinks it's going to happen.'

'It's not.'

'Who called it off?'

'The feds did. We just haven't told Joe yet.'

'He's already agreed to release two hostages.'

'And we're still hoping he does. That's at least two lives we can save.'

'If you don't hold up your end of the bargain – if you don't send in Peter Lukas – there are four hostages in there you're *not* going to save.'

'By then, I hope the entry team will be in.'

Gabriel stared at him. 'Do you *want* a massacre? Because you're going to get one! You're giving two paranoid people every reason to think their delusion is real. That you *are* out to kill them. Hell, maybe they're right!'

'Now you're the one who's sounding paranoid.'

'I think I'm the only one who's making sense.' Gabriel turned and walked out of the trailer.

He heard the negotiator call out after him: 'Agent Dean?'

Gabriel kept walking, toward the police line.

'Dean!' At last Stillman caught up with him. 'I just want you to know, I didn't agree to any assault plan. You're right, it's just asking for bloodshed.'

'Then why the hell are you allowing it?'

'As if I can stop it? Or Hayder? This is now Washington's call. We're supposed to stand back and let them take it from here.'

They heard it then – the sudden buzz through the crowd. The throng of reporters tightened, surged forward.

What is happening?

They heard a shout, saw the lobby doors swing open, and a tall African-American man in an orderly's uniform stepped out, escorted by two Tactical Ops officers. He paused, eyes blinking in the glare of dozens of klieg lights, then he was hurried off toward a waiting vehicle. Seconds later, a man in a wheelchair emerged, pushed by a Boston PD cop.

'They did it,' Stillman murmured. 'They released two people.'

But not Jane. Jane's still in there. And the assault could start any minute.

He pushed toward the police line.

'Dean,' said Stillman, grabbing his arm.

Gabriel turned to look at him. 'This could all end without a single bullet being fired. Let me go in. Let me talk to them.'

'The feds will never clear it.'

230

'Boston PD controls the perimeter. Order your men to let me through.'

'It could be a death trap.'

'My wife is in there.' His gaze locked with Stillman's. 'You know I have to do this. You know this is the best chance she'll have. The best chance *any* of them will have.'

Stillman released a breath. Wearily he nodded. 'Good luck.'

Gabriel ducked under the police tape. A Boston Tac-Ops officer moved to intercept him.

'Let him pass,' said Stillman. 'He's going into the building.'

'Sir?'

'Agent Dean is our new negotiator.'

Gabriel gave Stillman a nod of thanks. Then he turned and started walking toward the lobby doors.

Nineteen

Mila

Neither Olena nor I know where we are going.

We have never walked through these woods, and we don't know where we will emerge. I wear no stockings, and the cold quickly penetrates my thin shoes. Despite the Mother's sweater and turtleneck, I am chilled and shivering. The lights of the house have receded behind us, and glancing back, I see only the darkness of woods. On numb feet, I trudge across frozen leaves, keeping my focus on the silhouette of Olena, who walks ahead of me, carrying the tote bag. My breath is like smoke. Ice crackles beneath our shoes. I think of a war movie I once saw in school, of cold and starving German soldiers staggering through the snow to their doom on the Russian front. *Don't stop. Don't question. Just keep marching* was what those desperate soldiers must have been thinking. It's what I'm thinking now as I stumble through the woods.

Ahead of us, a light suddenly twinkles.

Olena halts, holding up her arm to make me stop. We stand as still as the trees, watching as the lights move past, and we hear the whoosh of tires on wet pavement. We push through the last tangle of brush, and our feet hit blacktop.

We have reached a road.

By now my feet are so senseless from the cold that I am clumsy and floundering as I try to keep up with her. Olena is like a robot, trudging steadily forward. We begin to see houses, but she doesn't stop. She is the general, and I'm just the dumb foot soldier, following a woman who knows no more than I do.

'We can't walk forever,' I tell her.

'We can't stay here, either.'

'Look, that house has its lights on. We could ask for help.'

'Not now.'

'How long are we supposed to keep walking? All night, all week?'

'As long as we need to.'

'Do you even know where we're going?'

She suddenly turns, the rage so apparent on her face that I freeze. 'You know what? I'm sick of you! You're nothing but a baby. A stupid, scared rabbit.'

'I just want to know where we're going.'

'All you ever do is whine and complain! Well, I've had enough. I'm done with you.' She reaches into the tote bag and pulls out the bundle of American money. She breaks the rubber band

and thrusts half the cash at me. 'Here, take it and get out of my sight. If you're so smart, go your own way.'

'Why are you doing this?' I feel hot tears in my eyes. Not because I'm afraid, but because she is my only friend. And I know that I am losing her.

'You're a drag on me, Mila. You'll slow me down. I don't want to have to watch out for you all the time. I'm *not* your fucking mother!'

'I never wanted you to be.'

'Then why don't you grow up?'

'And why don't you stop being a bitch!'

The car takes us by surprise. We are so focused on each other that we do not notice its approach. Suddenly it rounds the curve, and the headlights trap us like doomed animals. Tires screech to a stop. It is an old car, and the engine makes knocking noises as it idles.

The driver sticks his head out the window. 'You two ladies need help,' he says. It sounds more like a statement than a question, but then our situation is obvious. A freezing night. Two women stranded on a lonely road. Of course we need help.

I gape at him, silent. It is Olena who takes command, as she always does. In an instant she has transformed. Her walk, her voice, the provocative way she thrusts out her hip – this is Olena at her most seductive. She smiles and says, in throaty English: 'Our car is dead. Can you drive us?'

The man studies her. Is he just being cautious?

Somehow he realizes that something is very wrong here. I am on the edge of retreating back into the woods, before he can call the police.

When he finally answers, his voice is flat, revealing no hint that Olena's charms have affected him. 'There's a service station up the road. I need to stop there for gas anyway. I'll ask about a tow truck.'

We climb into the car. Olena sits in the front seat, I huddle in the back. I have stuffed the money she gave me into my pocket, and now it feels like a glowing lump of coal. I am still angry, still wounded by her cruelty. With this money, I can manage without her, without anyone. And I will.

The man does not talk as he drives. At first I think he is merely ignoring us, that we are of no interest to him. Then I catch a glimpse of his eyes in the rearview mirror, and I realize he's been studying me, studying both of us. In his silence, he's as alert as a cat.

The lights of the service station glow ahead, and we pull into the driveway and stop beside the pump. The man gets out to fill his tank, then he says to us: 'I'll ask about the tow truck.' He walks into the building.

Olena and I remain in the car, uncertain of our next move. Through the window, we see our driver talking to the cashier. He points to us, and the cashier picks up a phone.

'He's calling the police,' I whisper to Olena. 'We should leave. We should run *now*.' I reach for the door and am about to push it open when a black car swings into the service station and pulls up right beside our car. Two men step out, both dressed in dark clothes. One of them has white-blond hair, cut short as a brush. They look at us.

In an instant, my blood freezes in my veins.

We are trapped animals in this stranger's car, and two hunters have now surrounded us. The blond man stands right outside my door, gazing in at me, and I can only stare back through the window at the last face the Mother ever saw. The last face I will probably ever see.

Suddenly, the blond man's chin snaps up and his gaze shifts to the building. I turn and see that our driver has just stepped outside, and is walking toward the car. He has paid for the gas, and he is stuffing his wallet back in his pocket. He slows down, frowning at the two men who now flank his car.

'Can I help you gentlemen?' our driver asks.

The blond man answers. 'Sir, could we ask you a few questions?'

'Who are you?'

'I'm Special Agent Steve Ullman. Federal Bureau of Investigation.'

Our driver does not seem particularly impressed by this. He reaches into the service station bucket and picks up a squeegee. Wrings out the excess water and begins to wipe his dirty windshield. 'What do you two fellows want to talk to me about?' he asks, scraping water from the glass.

The blond man leans in closer to our driver and speaks in a muted voice. I hear the words *female fugitives* and *dangerous*.

'So why are you talking to me?' the driver says.

'This is your car, right?'

'Yeah.' Our driver suddenly laughs. 'Oh, now I get it. In case you're wondering, that's my wife and her cousin sitting in the car. They look real dangerous, don't they?'

The blond man glances at his partner. A look of surprise. They don't know what to say.

Our driver drops the squeegee back in the bucket, throwing up a splash. 'Good luck, guys,' he says, and opens his car door. As he climbs in behind the wheel, he says loudly to Olena: 'Sorry, honey. They didn't have any Advil. We'll have to try the next gas station.'

As we drive away, I glance back and see that the men are still staring after us. One of them is writing down the license number.

For a moment, no one in the car speaks. I am still too paralyzed by fear to say a word. I can only stare at the back of our driver's head. The man who has just saved our lives.

Finally he says: 'Are you going to tell me what that was all about?'

'They lied to you,' says Olena. 'We are not dangerous!'

'And they're not FBI.'

'You already know this?'

The man looks at her. 'Look, I'm not stupid. I know the real deal when I see it. And I know when I'm getting bullshitted. So how about telling me the truth?'

Olena releases a weary sigh. In a whisper she says: 'They want to kill us.'

'That much I figured out.' He shakes his head and laughs, but there is no humor in it. It's the laugh of a man who cannot believe his bad luck. 'Man, when it rains on me, it just fucking pours,' he says. 'So who are they and why do they want to kill you?'

'Because of what we have seen tonight.'

'What did you see?'

She looks out the window. 'Too much,' she murmurs. 'We have seen too much.'

For the moment he lets that answer suffice, because we have just turned off the road. Our tires bump over a dirt track that takes us deep into woods. He stops the car in front of a ramshackle house surrounded by trees. It is little more than a rough-hewn cabin, something that only a poor man would live in. But on the roof is a giant satellite dish.

'This is your home?' Olena asks.

'It's where I live,' is his odd answer.

He uses three different keys to open the front door. Standing on the porch, waiting for him to open his various locks, I notice that his windows all have bars. For a moment I hesitate to step inside because I think of the other house that we have just escaped. But these bars, I realize, are different; these are not to trap people in; they are meant to keep people out.

Inside I smell wood smoke and damp wool. He does not turn on any lights, but navigates across the dark room as though he knows every square inch of it blind. 'It gets a little musty in here when I go away for a few days,' he says. He strikes a match, and I see that he is kneeling at a hearth. The bundle of kindling and logs are already waiting to be lit, and flames soon dance to life. The glow illuminates his face, which seems even more gaunt, more somber in this shadowy room. Once, I think, it might have been a handsome face, but the eyes are now too hollow, and his lean jaw has several days' growth of dark stubble. As the fire brightens, I glance around at a small room made even smaller by tall piles of newspapers and magazines, by the dozens and dozens of news clippings he has tacked to the walls. They are everywhere, like yellowing scales, and I imagine him shut up in this lonely cabin, day after day, month after month, feverishly cutting out articles whose significance only he understands. I look around at the barred windows and remember the three locks on the front door. And I think: This is the home of a frightened man.

He goes to a cabinet and unlocks it. I am startled to see half a dozen rifles racked inside. He removes one and locks the cabinet again. At the sight of that gun in his hand, I retreat a step.

'It's okay. Nothing to be scared of,' he says,

seeing my alarmed face. 'Tonight, I'd just like to keep a gun close at hand.'

We hear a bell-like chime.

The man's head jerks up at the sound. Carrying his rifle, he moves to the window and peers out at the woods. 'Something just tripped the sensor,' he says. 'Could be just an animal. Then again . . .' He lingers at the window for a long time, his hand on his rifle. I remember the two men at the service station watching us drive away. Writing down our license number. By now, they must know who owns the car. They must know where he lives.

The man crosses to a stack of wood, picks up a fresh log, and drops it onto the fire. Then he settles into a rocking chair and sits looking at us, the rifle on his lap. Flames crackle, and sparks dance in the hearth.

'My name is Joe,' he says. 'Tell me who you are.'

I look at Olena. Neither one of us says anything. Though this strange man has saved our lives tonight, we are still afraid of him.

'Look, you made the choice. You climbed in my car.' His chair creaks as it rocks on the wooden floor. 'Now it's too late to be coy, ladies,' he says. 'The die has been cast.'

When I awaken, it is still not daylight, but the fire has burned down to mere embers. The last thing I recall, before falling asleep, were the voices of Olena and Joe, talking softly. Now, by the glow from the hearth, I can see Olena sleeping beside me on the braided rug. I am still angry at her, and have not forgiven her for the things she said. A few hours' sleep has made the inevitable clear to me. We cannot stay together forever.

The creak of the rocking chair draws my gaze; I see the faint gleam of Joe's rifle, and feel him watching me. He has probably been watching us sleep for some time.

'Wake her up,' he says to me. 'We need to leave now.'

'Why?'

'They're out there. They've been watching the house.'

'What?' I scramble to my feet, my heart suddenly thudding, and go to the window. All I see outside is the darkness of woods. Then I realize that the stars are fading, that the night will soon lift to gray.

'I think they're still parked up the road. They haven't tripped the next set of motion detectors yet,' he says. 'But we need to move now, before it gets light.' He rises, goes to a closet, and takes out a backpack. Whatever the pack contains gives a metallic clank. 'Olena,' he says, and nudges her with his boot. She stirs and looks at him. 'Time to go,' he says. 'If you want to live.'

He does not take us out the front door. Instead he pulls up floorboards, and the smell of damp earth rises from the shadows below. He backs down the ladder and calls up to us: 'Let's go, ladies.'

I hand him the Mother's tote bag, then scramble down after him. He has turned on a flashlight, and in the gloom I catch glimpses of crates stacked up against stone walls.

'In Vietnam, the villagers had tunnels under their houses, just like this one,' he says as he leads the way down a low passage. 'Mostly, it was just to store food. But sometimes, it saved their lives.' He comes to a stop, unlocks a padlock, then turns off his flashlight. He lifts up a wooden hatch above his head.

We climb out of the tunnel, into dark woods. The trees cloak us as he leads us away from the house. We do not say a word; we don't dare to. Once again, I am blindly following, always the foot soldier, never the general. But this time I trust the person leading me. Joe walks quietly, moving with the confidence of someone who knows exactly where he's going. I walk right behind him, and as dawn begins to lighten the sky, I see that he has a limp. He is dragging his left leg a little, and once, when he glances back, I see his grimace of pain. But he pushes on into the gray light of morning.

Finally, through the trees ahead, I see a tumbledown farm. As we draw closer, I can tell that no one lives here. The windows are broken, and one end of the roof has caved inward. But Joe does not go to the house; he heads instead to the barn, which appears to be at equal risk of collapse. He opens a padlock and slides the barn door open.

Inside is a car.

'Always wondered if I'd ever really need it,' he says as he slides into the driver's seat.

I climb in back. There is a blanket and pillow on the seat, and at my feet are cans of food. Enough to eat for several days.

Joe turns the ignition; the engine coughs reluctantly to life. 'Hate to leave that place behind,' he says. 'But maybe it's time to go away for a while.'

'You are doing this for us?' I ask him.

He glances at me over his shoulder. 'I'm doing this to stay out of trouble. You two ladies seem to have brought me a heaping dose of it.'

He backs the car out of the barn, and we begin to bump along the dirt road, past the ramshackle farmhouse, past a stagnant pond. Suddenly we hear a heavy *whump*. At once Joe stops the car, rolls down his window, and stares toward the woods from which we have just emerged.

Black smoke is rising above the trees, billowing up in angry columns that swirl into the brightening sky. I hear Olena give a startled cry. My hands are sweating and shaking as I think of the cabin we have just left, now in flames. And I think of burning flesh. Joe says nothing; he only stares at the smoke in shocked silence, and I wonder if he is cursing his bad luck at ever having met us.

After a moment, he releases a deep breath. 'Jesus,' he murmurs. 'Whoever these people are, they play for keeps.' He turns his attention back to the road. I know he is afraid, because I can see his hands clenching the steering wheel. I can see the white of his knuckles. 'Ladies,' he says softly, 'I think it's time to vanish.'

Twenty

Jane closed her eyes and surfed the crest of pain like a wave rider. *Please let this one be over soon. Make it stop, make it stop.* She felt sweat bloom on her face as the contraction built, gripping her so tightly that she could not moan, could not even breathe. Beyond her closed eyelids, the lights seemed to dim, all sounds muffled by the rush of her own pulse. Only vaguely did she register the disturbance in the room. A banging on the door. Joe's tense demands.

Then, suddenly, a hand closed around Jane's, its grasp warm and familiar. It can't be, she thought as the pain of the contraction eased, as her vision slowly cleared. She focused on the face gazing down at her, and she went still in wonder.

'No,' she whispered. 'No, you shouldn't be here.'

He cupped her face, pressed his lips to her forehead, her hair. 'Everything's going to be fine, sweetheart. Just fine.'

'This is the dumbest thing you've ever done.'

He smiled. 'You knew I wasn't too bright when you married me.'

'What were you thinking?'

'About you. Only about you.'

'Agent Dean,' said Joe.

Slowly, Gabriel rose to his feet. So many times before, Jane had looked at her husband and thought how blessed she was, but never as much as at this moment. He carried no weapon, held no advantage, yet as he turned to face Joe, he projected only quiet determination. 'I'm here. Now will you let my wife go?'

'After we talk. After you hear us out.'

'I'm listening.'

'You have to promise you'll follow up on what we tell you. You won't let this die with us.'

'I said I'd listen. That's all you asked. And you said you'd let these people go. You may have a death wish, but they don't.'

Olena said, 'We don't wish anyone to die.'

'Then prove it. Release these people. Then I'll sit here and listen for as long as you want me to. Hours, days. I'm at your disposal.' He stared, unflinching, at their captors.

A moment passed in silence.

Suddenly, Joe leaned toward the couch, grabbed Dr. Tam's arm, and yanked her to her feet.

'Go stand by the door, doctor,' he ordered. He turned and pointed to the pair of women on the other couch. 'You two, get up. Both of you.'

The women didn't budge; they just gaped at

Joe, as though certain this was a trick, that if they moved, there would be consequences.

'Go! Get up!'

The receptionist gave a sob and stumbled to her feet. Only then did the other woman follow her. They both edged toward the door, where Dr. Tam still stood frozen. Hours of captivity had so cowed them that they did not yet believe their ordeal was about to end. Even as Tam reached toward the door, she was watching Joe, waiting for his order to halt.

'You three can leave,' Joe said.

The instant the women had stepped out of the room, Olena slammed the door shut behind them and locked it again.

'What about my wife?' said Gabriel. 'Let her go, too.'

'I can't. Not yet.'

'Our agreement—'

'I agreed to release hostages, Agent Dean. I didn't say which ones.'

Gabriel flushed in anger. 'And you think I'm going to trust you now? You think I'd listen to a goddamn thing you say?'

Jane reached for her husband's hand, and felt tendons taut with rage. 'Just listen to him. Let him have his say.'

Gabriel released a breath. 'Okay, Joe. What do you want to tell me?'

Joe grabbed two chairs, dragged them to the center of the room, and set them down facing each other. 'Let's sit, you and me.'

'My wife is in labor. She can't stay in here much longer.'

'Olena will attend to her.' He gestured to the chairs. 'I'm going to tell you a story.'

Gabriel looked at Jane. She saw, in his eyes, both love and apprehension. *Whom do you trust?* Joe had asked her earlier. *Who'd take this bullet for you?* Staring at her husband, she thought: There will never be anyone I trust more than you.

Reluctantly, Gabriel turned his attention back to Joe, and the two men sat facing each other. It looked like a perfectly civilized summit, except for the fact that one of the men had a gun resting in his lap. Olena, now stationed on Jane's couch, held an equally lethal weapon. Just a nice little get-together with two couples. *Which pair will survive the night?*

'What did they tell you about me?' said Joe. 'What's the FBI saying?'

'A few things.'

'I'm crazy, right? A loner. Paranoid.'

'Yes.'

'You believe them?'

'I have no reason not to.'

Jane watched her husband's face. Though he spoke calmly, she could see the strain in his eyes, the tight muscles of his neck. You knew this man was insane, she thought, yet you walked in here anyway. All for me . . . She suppressed a groan as a new contraction began to build. *Keep quiet. Don't distract Gabriel; let him do what he needs to do.* She sank back on the couch, teeth gritted, suffering in silence. Kept her gaze fixed on the ceiling, on a single dark smudge on the acoustic tile. *Concentrate on your focal point. Mind over pain.* The ceiling blurred, the smudge seeming to bob in an unsteady sea of white. It made her nauseated just to look at it. She closed her eyes, like a seasick sailor woozy from rocking waves.

Only when the contraction began to ease, when the pain at last released its grip, did she open her eyes. Her gaze, once again, focused on the ceiling. Something had changed. Next to the smudge there was now a small hole, almost unnoticeable among the pores of the acoustic tile.

She glanced at Gabriel, but he was not looking at her. He was completely focused on the man sitting across from him.

Joe asked: 'Do you think I'm insane?'

Gabriel regarded him for a moment. 'I'm not a psychiatrist. I can't make that determination.'

'You walked in here expecting a crazy man to be waving a gun around, didn't you?' He leaned forward. 'That's what they told you. Be honest.'

'You really want me to be honest?'

'Absolutely.'

'They told me I'd be dealing with two terrorists. That's what I was led to believe.'

Joe sat back, his face grim. 'So that's how they're going to end it,' he said quietly. 'Of course. It's how they *would* end it. What kind of terrorists are we supposed to be?' He glanced at

Olena, then laughed. 'Oh. Chechens, probably.'

'Yes.'

'Is John Barsanti running the show?'

Gabriel frowned. 'You know him?'

'He's been tracking us since Virginia. Everywhere we go, he seems to turn up. I knew he'd show up here. He's probably just waiting to zip up our body bags.'

'You don't have to die. Hand me your weapons, and we'll all leave together. No gunfire, no blood. I give you my word.'

'Yeah, there's a guarantee.'

'You let me walk in here. Which means that, on some level, you trust me.'

'I can't afford to trust anyone.'

'Then why am I here?'

'Because I refuse to go to my grave without some hope of justice. We've tried taking this to the press. We *handed* them the fucking evidence. But no one gives a shit.' He looked at Olena. 'Show them your arm. Show them what Ballentree did to you.'

Olena tugged her sleeve above her elbow and pointed to a jagged scar.

'You see?' said Joe. 'What they put in her arm?'

'Ballentree? Are you talking about the defense contractor?'

'Latest microchip technology. A way for Ballentree to track its property. She was human cargo, brought over straight from Moscow. A little business that Ballentree operates on the side.'

Jane looked back at the ceiling. Suddenly she realized that there were other fresh holes in the acoustic tiles. She glanced at the two men, but they were still focused on each other. No one else was looking upward; no one else saw that the ceiling was now riddled with punctures.

'So this is all about a defense contractor?' said Gabriel, his voice perfectly even, revealing no hint of the skepticism he surely felt.

'Not just *any* defense contractor. We're talking about the Ballentree Company. Direct ties to the White House and Pentagon. We're talking about executives who make billions of dollars every time we go to war. Why do you think Ballentree lands almost all the big contracts? Because they *own* the White House.'

'I hate to tell you this, Joe, but this isn't exactly a new conspiracy theory. Ballentree is everyone's bogeyman these days. A lot of people are itching to bring them down.'

'But Olena can actually do it.'

Gabriel looked at the woman, his gaze dubious. 'How?'

'She knows what they did in Ashburn. She's seen what kind of people these are.'

Jane was still staring at the ceiling, trying to understand what she was now seeing. Needle-thin lines of vapor were streaming silently from above. *Gas. They are pumping gas into the room.*

She looked at her husband. Did he know this was about to happen? Did he know this was the plan? No one else seemed aware of the silent invader. No one else realized that the assault was now beginning, heralded by those fine streams of gas.

We are all breathing it in.

She tensed as she felt another contraction. Oh god, not now, she thought. Not when all hell is about to break loose. She gripped the couch cushion, waiting for the contraction to peak. The pain had her in its jaws now, and all she could do was grip the cushion and hang on. This one's going to be bad, she thought. Oh, this one's really bad.

But the pain never reached its climax. Suddenly the cushion seemed to melt away in Jane's fist. She felt herself being dragged downward, toward the sweetest of sleep. Through the gathering numbness, she heard banging, and men's shouts. Heard Gabriel's voice, muffled, calling her name from across a great distance.

The pain was almost gone now.

Something bumped up against her, and softness brushed across her face. The touch of a hand, the faintest caress on her cheek. A voice whispered, words that she did not understand, soft and urgent words that were almost lost in the banging, in the sudden crash of the door. A secret, she thought. She is telling me a secret.

Mila. Mila knows.

There was a deafening blast, and warmth splashed her face.

Gabriel, she thought. Where are you?

Twenty-one

At the sound of the first gunshots, the crowd standing in the street gave a collective gasp. Maura's heart froze to a standstill. Tactical Ops officers held the police line as fresh gunfire thudded inside. She saw looks of confusion on the officers' faces as the minutes passed, everyone waiting for word of what was happening inside. No one was moving; no one was rushing the building.

What are they all waiting for?

Police radios suddenly crackled: 'Building secure! The entry team is out, and the building is now secure! Roll medical. We need stretchers—'

Med-Q teams rushed forward, pushing through the police tape like sprinters crossing the finish line. The breaking of that yellow tape touched off chaos. Suddenly reporters and cameras surged toward the building as well, as Boston PD struggled to hold them back. A helicopter hovered overhead, blades thumping.

Through the cacophony, Maura heard Korsak

shout: 'I'm a cop, goddammit! My friend's in there! Let me through!' Korsak glanced her way and called out: 'Doc, you gotta find out if she's okay!'

Maura pushed ahead, to the police line. The cop gave her ID a harried glance, and shook his head.

'They need to take care of the living first, Dr. Isles.'

'I'm a physician. I can help.'

Her voice was almost drowned out by the chopper, which had just landed in the parking lot across the street. Distracted, the cop turned to yell at a reporter: 'Hey, you! Get back *now*.'

Maura slipped past him and ran into the building, dreading what she would find inside. Just as she turned into the hallway leading to Diagnostic Imaging, a stretcher came barreling toward her, wheeled by two EMTs, and her hand flew to her mouth to stifle a gasp. She saw the pregnant belly, the dark hair, and thought: No. Oh god, no.

Jane Rizzoli was covered in blood.

At that instant, all of Maura's medical training seemed to abandon her. Panic made her focus on the blood, and only the blood. *So much of it.* Then, as the stretcher rolled past her, she saw the chest rise and fall. Saw the hand moving.

'Jane?' called out Maura.

The EMTs were already hurrying the stretcher through the lobby. Maura had to run to catch up.

'Wait! What's her condition?'

One of the men glanced back over his shoulder. 'This one's in labor. We're moving her to Brigham.'

'But all the blood—'

'It's not hers.'

'Then whose?'

'The gal back there.' He cocked a thumb down the hallway. '*She's* not going anywhere.'

She stared after the stretcher as it rattled out the door. Then she turned and ran up the hallway, moving past EMTs and Boston PD officers, toward the heart of the crisis.

'Maura?' a voice called, oddly distant and muffled.

She spotted Gabriel struggling to sit up on a stretcher. An oxygen mask was strapped to his face, and an IV line tethered his arm to a bag of saline.

'Are you all right?'

Groaning, he lowered his head. 'Just . . . dizzy.'

The EMT said: 'It's the aftereffects of the gas. I just gave him some IV Narcan. He needs to take it easy for a while. It's like coming out of anesthesia.'

Gabriel lifted the mask. 'Jane—'

'I just saw her,' said Maura. 'She's fine. They're moving her to Brigham Hospital.'

'I can't sit here any longer.'

'What happened in there? We heard gunshots.'

Gabriel shook his head. 'I don't remember.'

'Your mask,' said the EMT. 'You need that oxygen right now.'

'They didn't have to do it this way,' said Gabriel. 'I could have talked them out of there. I could have convinced them to surrender.'

'Sir, you need to put your mask back on.'

'No,' snapped Gabriel. 'I need to be with my wife. That's what I need to do.'

'You're not ready to go.'

'Gabriel, he's right,' said Maura. 'Look at you, you can barely sit up. Lie down for a while longer. I'll drive you to Brigham Hospital myself, but not until you've had a chance to recover.'

'Just a little while,' said Gabriel, weakly settling back onto the stretcher. 'I'll be better in a while . . .'

'I'll be right back.'

She spotted the doorway to Diagnostic Imaging. As she stepped through, the first thing her eyes fixed on was the blood. It was always the blood that demanded your attention, those shocking splashes of red that shout out: Something terrible, truly terrible, has happened here. Though half a dozen men were standing around the room, and debris from the ambulance crews still lay scattered across the floor, she remained fixated on the bright evidence of death that was spattered across the walls. Then her gaze swung to the woman's body, slumped against the couch, black hair wicking blood onto the floor. Never before had she felt faint at the sight of gore, but she suddenly found herself swaying sideways, and had to catch herself on the door frame. It's the remnants of whatever gas they used in this room, she thought. It has not yet been fully ventilated.

She heard the whish of plastic, and through a fog of lightheadedness, she saw a white sheet being laid out on the floor. Saw Agent Barsanti and Captain Hayder standing by as two men wearing latex gloves rolled the bloodied corpse of Joseph Roke onto the plastic.

'What are you doing?' she said.

No one acknowledged her presence.

'Why are you moving the bodies?'

The two men who were now squatting over the corpse paused, and glanced up in Barsanti's direction.

'They're being flown to Washington,' said Barsanti.

'You don't move a thing until someone from our office examines the scene.' She looked at the two men, poised to zip up the body bag. 'Who are you? You don't work for us.'

'They're FBI,' said Barsanti.

Her head was now perfectly clear, all dizziness swept away by anger. 'Why are you taking them?'

'Our pathologists will do the autopsy.'

'I haven't released these bodies.'

'It's only a matter of paperwork, Dr. Isles.'

'Which I'm not about to sign.'

The others in the room were all watching them now. Most of the men standing around were, like Hayder, Boston PD officers.

'Dr. Isles,' said Barsanti, sighing, 'why fight this turf battle?'

She looked at Hayder. 'This death occurred in our jurisdiction. You know we have custody of these remains.'

'You sound as if you don't trust the FBI,' said Barsanti.

It's you I don't trust.

She stepped toward him. 'I never did hear a good explanation for why you're here, Agent Barsanti. What's your involvement in this?'

'These two people are suspects in a New Haven shooting. I believe you already know that. They crossed state lines.'

'It doesn't explain why you want the bodies.'

'You'll get the final autopsy reports.'

'What are you afraid I'll find?'

'You know, Dr. Isles, you're starting to sound as paranoid as these two people.' He turned to the two men standing over Roke's corpse. 'Let's pack them up.'

'You're not going to touch them,' Maura said. She pulled out her cell phone and called Abe Bristol. 'We have a death scene here, Abe.'

'Yeah, I've been watching TV. How many?'

'Two. Both of the hostage takers were killed in the takedown. The FBI's about to fly the bodies to Washington.'

'Wait a minute. First the feds shoot them, and now they want to do the autopsy? What the hell?'

'I thought you'd say that. Thanks for backing me up.' She disconnected and looked at Barsanti. 'The medical examiner's office refuses to release these two bodies. Please leave the room. After CSU finishes up here, our staff will move the remains to the morgue.'

Barsanti seemed about to argue, but she merely gave him a cold stare that told him this was not a battle she would cede.

'Captain Hayder,' she said. 'Do I need to call the governor's office on this?'

Hayder sighed. 'No, it's your jurisdiction.' He looked at Barsanti. 'It looks like the medical examiner is assuming control.'

Without another word, Barsanti and his men walked out of the room.

She followed them and stood watching as they retreated down the hallway. This death scene, she thought, will be dealt with like any other. Not by the FBI, but by Boston PD's homicide unit. She was about to make her next call, this one to Detective Moore, when she suddenly noticed the empty stretcher in the hallway. The EMT was just packing up his kit.

'Where is Agent Dean?' Maura asked. 'The man who was lying there?'

'Refused to stay. Got up and walked out.'

'You couldn't stop him from leaving?'

'Ma'am, *nothing* could stop that guy. He said he had to be with his wife.'

'How's he getting there?'

'Some bald guy's giving him a ride. A cop, I think.'

Vince Korsak, she thought.

'They're headed over to Brigham now.'

Jane could not remember how she'd arrived at this place with its bright lights and shiny surfaces and masked faces. She recalled only a fragment of a memory here and there. Men's shouts, the squeaking of gurney wheels. The flash of blue cruiser lights. And then a white ceiling scrolling above her as she was moved down a corridor into this room. Again and again she had asked about Gabriel, but no one could tell her where he was.

Or they were afraid to tell her.

'Mom, you're doing just fine,' the doctor said.

Jane blinked at the pair of blue eyes smiling down at her over a surgical mask. Everything is *not* fine, she thought. My husband should be here. I need him.

And stop calling me Mom.

'When you feel the next contraction,' the doctor said, 'I want you to push, okay? And keep pushing.'

'Someone has to call,' said Jane. 'I need to know about Gabriel.'

'We have to get your baby born first.'

'No, you need to do what *I* want, first! You need to – you need to—' She sucked in a breath as a fresh contraction came on. As her pain built to a peak, so did her rage. Why weren't these people listening to her?

'Push, Mom! You're almost there!'

'God – damn it—'

'Come on. *Push.*'

She gave a gasp as pain brutally clamped its jaws. But it was fury that made her bear down, that kept her pushing with such fierce determination that her vision began to darken. She did not hear the door whoosh open, nor did she see the man dressed in blue scrubs slip into the room. With a cry, she collapsed back against the table and lay gulping in deep breaths. Only then did she see him looking down at her, his head silhouetted against the bright lights.

'Gabriel,' she whispered.

He took her hand and stroked back her hair. 'I'm here. I'm right here.'

'I don't remember. I don't remember what happened—'

'It's not important now.'

'Yes, it is. I need to know.'

Another contraction began to build. She took a breath and gripped his hand. Clung on to it like a woman dangling over an abyss.

'Push,' the doctor said.

She curled forward, grunting, every muscle straining as sweat slid into her eyes.

'That's it,' the doctor said. 'Almost there . . .'

Come on, baby. Stop being so goddamn stubborn. Help your mama out!

She was on the edge of a scream now, her throat about to burst. Then, suddenly, she felt blood rush out between her legs. Heard angry cries, like the howling of a cat.

'We've got her!' the doctor said.

Her?

Gabriel was laughing, his voice hoarse with tears. He pressed his lips to Jane's hair. 'A girl. We've got a little girl.'

'She's a feisty one,' the doctor said. 'Look at this.'

Jane turned her head to see tiny fists waving, a face pink with anger. And dark hair – lots of dark hair, plastered in wet curls to the scalp. She watched, awestruck, as the nurse dried off the infant and wrapped it in a blanket.

'Would you like to hold her, Mom?'

Jane could not say a word; her throat had closed down. She could only stare in wonder as the bundle was placed in her arms. She looked down at a face that was swollen from crying. The baby squirmed, as though impatient to be free of its blanket. Of its mother's arms.

Are you really mine? She had imagined this would be a moment of instant familiarity, when she would stare into her newborn's eyes and recognize the soul there. But there was no sense of familiarity here, only clumsiness, as she tried to soothe the struggling bundle. All she saw, looking at her daughter, was an angry creature with puffy eyes and clenched fists. A creature who suddenly gave a scream of protest.

'You have a beautiful baby,' the nurse said. 'She looks just like you.'

Twenty-two

Jane awakened to sunlight streaming through her hospital window. She looked at Gabriel, who slept on the cot next to her bed. In his hair she saw flecks of gray that she'd never noticed before. He wore the same wrinkled shirt from last night, the sleeve flecked with bloodstains.

Whose blood?

As though he'd sensed her watching him, he opened his eyes and squinted at her against the sunlight.

'Good morning, Daddy,' she said.

He gave her a weary smile. 'I think Mommy needs to go back to sleep.'

'I can't.'

'This may be our last chance to sleep in for a while. Once the baby's home we're not going to be getting much rest.'

'I need to know, Gabriel. You haven't told me what happened.'

His smile faded. He sat up and rubbed his face,

suddenly looking older, and infinitely tired. 'They're dead.'

'Both of them?'

'They were shot to death during the takedown. That's what Captain Hayder told me.'

'When did you talk to him?'

'He came by last night. You were already asleep, and I didn't want to wake you.'

She lay on her back and stared at the ceiling. 'I'm trying to remember. God, why can't I remember anything?'

'I can't either, Jane. They used fentanyl gas on us. That's what Maura was told.'

She looked at him. 'So you didn't see it happen? You don't know if Hayder told you the truth?'

'I know that Joe and Olena are dead. The ME's office has custody of their bodies.'

Jane fell silent for a moment, trying to recall her last moments in that room. She remembered Gabriel and Joe, facing each other, talking. Joe wanted to tell us something, she thought. And he never got the chance to finish . . .

'Did it have to end that way?' she asked. 'Did they both have to be killed?'

He rose to his feet and crossed to the window. Looking out, he said: 'It was the one sure way to finish it.'

'We were all unconscious. Killing them wasn't necessary.'

'Clearly the takedown team thought it was.'

She stared at her husband's back. 'All those

crazy things that Joe said. None of it was true, right?'

'I don't know.'

'A microchip in Olena's arm? The FBI chasing them? Those are classic paranoid delusions.'

He didn't answer.

'Okay,' she said. 'Tell me what you're thinking.'

He turned to look at her. 'Why was John Barsanti here? I never got a good answer to that question.'

'Did you check with the Bureau?'

'All I could get out of the deputy director's office is that Barsanti is on special assignment with the Justice Department. No one would tell me anything else. And last night, when I spoke to David Silver at Senator Conway's house, he wasn't aware of any FBI involvement.'

'Well, Joe certainly didn't trust the FBI.'

'And now Joe's dead.'

She stared at him. 'You're starting to scare me. You're making me wonder . . .'

A sudden knock on the door made her jump. Heart pounding, she turned to see Angela Rizzoli poke her head into the room.

'Janie, you're up? Can we come in and visit?'

'Oh.' Jane gave a startled laugh. 'Hi, Mom.'

'She's beautiful, just beautiful! We saw her through the window.' Angela bustled into the room, carrying her old Revere Ware stockpot, and in wafted what Jane would always consider the world's best perfume: the aroma of her mother's kitchen. Trailing behind his wife, Frank

265

Rizzoli came in holding a bouquet so huge that he looked like an explorer peering through dense jungle.

'So how's my girl?' said Frank.

'I'm feeling great, Dad.'

'The kid's bawling up a storm in the nursery. Got a set of lungs on her.'

'Mikey's coming by to see you after work,' said Angela. 'Look, I brought lamb spaghetti. You don't have to tell me what hospital food's like. What'd they bring you for breakfast, anyway?' She went to the tray and lifted the cover. 'My god, look at these eggs, Frank! Like rubber! Do they *try* to make the food this bad?'

'Nothing wrong with a baby girl, no sir,' Frank said. 'Daughters are great, hey Gabe? You gotta watch 'em, though. When she turns sixteen, you be sure to keep those boys away.'

'Sixteen?' Jane snorted. 'Dad, by then the horse has left the barn.'

'What're you saying? Don't tell me that when *you* were sixteen—'

'—so what're you going to call her, hon? I can't believe you haven't chosen a name yet.'

'We're still thinking about it.'

'What's to think about? Name her after your grandma Regina.'

'She's got another grandma, you know,' said Frank.

'Who'd call a girl Ignatia?'

'It was good enough for my mom.'

Jane looked across the room at Gabriel, and

saw that his gaze had strayed back to the window. *He's still thinking about Joseph Roke. Still wondering about his death.*

There was a knock on the door, and yet another familiar head popped into the room. 'Hey, Rizzoli!' said Vince Korsak. 'You skinny again?' He stepped in, clutching the ribbons of three Mylar balloons bobbing overhead. 'How're you doing, Mrs. Rizzoli, Mr. Rizzoli? Congrats on being new grandparents!'

'Detective Korsak,' said Angela. 'Are you hungry? I brought Jane's favorite spaghetti. And we have paper plates here.'

'Well, I'm sort of on a diet, ma'am.'

'It's lamb spaghetti.'

'Ooh. You're a naughty woman, tempting a man off his diet.' Korsak wagged one fat finger at her and Angela gave a high, girlish laugh.

My god, thought Jane. *Korsak is flirting with my mom. I don't think I want to watch this.*

'Frank, can you take out those paper plates? They're in the sack.'

'It's only ten A.M. It's not even lunchtime.'

'Detective Korsak is hungry.'

'He just told you he's on a diet. Why don't you listen to him?'

There was yet another knock on the door. This time a nurse walked in, wheeling a bassinet. Rolling it over to Jane's bed, she announced: 'Time to visit with Mommy,' and lifted out the swaddled newborn. She placed it in Jane's arms.

Angela swooped in like a bird of prey. 'Ooh,

look at her, Frank! Oh god, she's so precious! Look at that little face!'

'How can I get a look? You're all over her.'

'She's got my mother's mouth—'

'Well, *that's* something to brag about.'

'Janie, you should try feeding her now. You need to get practice before your milk comes in.'

Jane looked around the room at the audience crowded around her bed. 'Ma, I'm not really comfortable with—' She paused, glancing down at the baby as it suddenly gave a howl. *Now what do I do?*

'Maybe she's got gas,' said Frank. 'Babies always get gas.'

'Or she's hungry,' Korsak suggested. He would. The baby only cried harder.

'Let me take her,' said Angela.

'Who's the mommy here?' Frank said. 'She needs the practice.'

'You don't want a baby to keep crying.'

'Maybe if you put your finger in her mouth,' said Frank. 'That's what we used to do with you, Janie. Like this—'

'Wait!' said Angela. 'Did you wash your hands, Frank?'

The sound of Gabriel's ringing cell phone was almost lost in the bedlam. Jane glanced at her husband as he answered it and saw him frown at his watch. She heard him say: 'I don't think I can make it right now. Why don't you go ahead without me?'

'Gabriel?' Jane asked. 'Who's calling?'

268

'Maura's starting the autopsy on Olena.'

'You should go in.'

'I hate to leave you.'

'No, you need to be there.' The baby was screaming even louder now, squirming as though desperate to escape its mother's arms. 'One of us should see it.'

'Are you sure you don't mind?'

'Look at all the company I've got here. *Go.*'

Gabriel bent down to kiss her. 'I'll see you later,' he murmured. 'Love you.'

'Imagine that,' said Angela, shaking her head in disapproval after Gabriel had walked out of the room. 'I can't believe it.'

'What, Mom?'

'He leaves his wife and new baby and runs off to watch some dead person get cut open?'

Jane looked down at her daughter, still howling and red-faced in her arms, and she sighed. *I only wish I could go with him.*

By the time Gabriel donned gown and shoe covers and walked into the autopsy lab, Maura had already lifted the breastbone and was reaching into the chest cavity. She and Yoshima did not exchange a word of unnecessary chatter as her scalpel sliced through vessels and ligaments, freeing the heart and lungs. She worked with silent precision, eyes revealing no emotion above the mask. If Gabriel did not already know her, he would find her efficiency chilling.

'You made it after all,' she said.

'Have I missed anything important?'

'No surprises so far.' She gazed down at Olena. 'Same room, same corpse. Strange to think this is the second time I've seen this woman dead.'

This time, thought Gabriel, she'll stay dead.

'So how is Jane doing?'

'She's fine. A little overwhelmed by visitors right now, I think.'

'And the baby?' She dropped pink lungs into a basin. Lungs that would never again fill with air or oxygenate blood.

'Beautiful. Eight pounds two ounces, ten fingers and ten toes. She looks just like Jane.'

For the first time, a smile tugged at Maura's eyes. 'What's her name?'

'For the moment, she's still "Baby Girl Rizzoli-Dean."'

'I hope *that* changes soon.'

'I don't know. I'm starting to like the sound of it.' It felt disrespectful, talking about such happy details while a dead woman lay between them. He thought of his new daughter taking her first breath, catching her first blurry look at the world, even as Olena's body was starting to cool.

'I'll drop by the hospital to see her this afternoon,' said Maura. 'Or is she already overdosed on visitors?'

'Believe me, you would be one of the truly welcome ones.'

'Detective Korsak been by yet?'

He sighed. 'Balloons and all. Good old Uncle Vince.'

'Don't knock him. Maybe he'll volunteer to babysit.'

'That's just what a baby needs. Someone to teach her the fine art of loud burping.'

Maura laughed. 'Korsak's a good man. Really, he is.'

'Except for the fact he's in love with my wife.'

Maura set down her knife and looked at him. 'Then he'd want her to be happy. And he can see that you both are.' Reaching once again for her scalpel, she added: 'You and Jane give the rest of us hope.'

The rest of us. Meaning all the lonely people in the world, he thought. Not so long ago, he was one of them.

He watched as Maura dissected the coronary arteries. How calmly she held a dead woman's heart in her hands. Her scalpel sliced open cardiac chambers, laying them bare to inspection. She probed and measured and weighed. Yet Maura Isles seemed to keep her own heart safely locked away.

His gaze dropped to the face of the woman they knew only as Olena. Hours ago, I was talking to her, he thought, and these eyes looked back at me, saw me. Now they were dull, the corneas clouded and glazed over. The blood had been washed away, and the bullet wound was a raw pink hole punched into the left temple.

'This looks like an execution,' he said.

'There are other wounds in the left flank.' She pointed to the light box. 'You can see two bullets on X-ray, up against the spine.'

'But this wound here.' He stared down at her face. 'This was a kill shot.'

'The assault team clearly wasn't taking any chances. Joseph Roke was shot in the head as well.'

'You've done his postmortem?'

'Dr. Bristol finished it an hour ago.'

'Why execute them? They were already down. We were *all* down.'

Maura looked up from the mass of lungs dripping on the cutting board. 'They could have wired themselves to detonate.'

'There were no explosives. These people weren't terrorists.'

'The rescue team wouldn't know that. Plus, there may have been a concern about the fentanyl gas they used. You know that a fentanyl derivative was also used to end the Moscow theater siege?'

'Yes.'

'In Moscow, it caused a number of fatalities. And here they were, using something similar on a pregnant hostage. They couldn't expose a fetus to its effects for too long. The takedown had to be fast and clean. That was how they justified it.'

'So they're claiming these kill shots were necessary.'

'That's what Lieutenant Stillman was told. Boston PD had no part in the planning or execution of the takedown.'

272

Turning to the light box where X-rays were hanging, he asked: 'Those are Olena's?'

'Yes.'

He moved in for a closer look. Saw a bright comma against the skull, a scattering of fragments throughout the cranial cavity.

'That's all internal ricochet,' she said.

'And this C-shaped opacity here?'

'It's a fragment caught between the scalp and the skull. Just a piece of lead that sheared off as the bullet punctured bone.'

'Do we know which member of the entry team fired this head shot?'

'Not even Hayder has a list of their names. By the time our Crime Scene Unit processed the scene, the entry team was probably on its way back to Washington, and beyond our reach. They swept up everything when they left. Weapons, cartridge evidence. They even took the knapsack that Joseph Roke brought into the building. They left us only the bodies.'

'It's how the world works now, Maura. The Pentagon's authorized to send a commando unit into any American city.'

'I'll tell you something.' She set down her scalpel and looked at him. 'This scares the hell out of me.'

The intercom buzzed. Maura glanced up as her secretary said, over the speaker: 'Dr. Isles, Agent Barsanti's on the line again. He wants to talk to you.'

'What did you tell him?'

'Not a thing.'

'Good. Just say I'll call him back.' She paused. 'When and *if* I have the time.'

'He's getting really rude, you know.'

'Then you don't have to be polite to him.' Maura looked at Yoshima. 'Let's finish up before we get interrupted again.'

She reached deep into the open belly and began resecting the abdominal organs. Out came stomach and liver and pancreas and endless loops of small intestine. Slitting open the stomach, Maura found it empty of food; only greenish secretions dripped out into the basin. 'Liver, spleen, and pancreas within normal limits,' she noted. Gabriel watched the foul-smelling offal pile up in the basin, and it disturbed him to think that in his own belly were the same glistening organs. Looking down at Olena's face, he thought: Once you cut beneath the skin, even the most beautiful woman looks like any other. A mass of organs encased in a hollow package of muscle and bone.

'All right,' Maura said, her voice muffled as she probed even deeper in the cavity. 'I can see where the other bullets tracked through. They're up against the spine here, and we've got some retroperitoneal bleeding.' The abdomen was now gutted of most of its organs, and she was peering into an almost hollow shell. 'Could you put up the abdominal and thoracic films? Let me just check the position of those other two bullets.'

Yoshima crossed to the light box, took down

the skull films, and clipped up a new set of X-rays. The ghostly shadows of heart and lungs glowed inside their bony cage of ribs. Dark pockets of gas were lined up like bumper cars inside intestinal tunnels. Against the softer haze of organs, the bullets stood out like bright chips against the column of lumbar spine.

Gabriel stared at the films for a moment, and his gaze suddenly narrowed as he remembered what Joe had told him. 'There's no view of the arms,' he said.

'Unless there's obvious trauma, we don't normally X-ray the limbs,' said Yoshima.

'Maybe you should.'

Maura glanced up. 'Why?'

Gabriel went back to the table and examined the left arm.

'Look at this scar. What do you think of it?'

Maura circled around to the corpse's left side and examined the arm. 'I see it, just above the elbow. It's well healed. I don't feel any masses.' She looked at Gabriel. 'What about it?'

'It's something that Joe told me. I know it sounds crazy.'

'What?'

'He claimed she had a microchip implanted in her arm. Right here, under the skin, to track her whereabouts.'

For a moment Maura just stared at him. Suddenly she laughed. 'That's not a very original delusion.'

'I know, I know what it sounds like.'

'It's a classic. The government-implanted microchip.'

Gabriel turned to look once again at the X-rays. 'Why do you think Barsanti is so eager to transfer these bodies? What does he think you're going to find?'

Maura fell silent for a moment, her gaze on Olena's arm.

Yoshima said, 'I can X-ray that arm right now. It will only take a few minutes.'

Maura sighed and stripped off her soiled gloves. 'It's almost certainly a waste of time, but we might as well settle the question right now.'

In the anteroom, shielded behind lead, Maura and Gabriel watched through the window as Yoshima positioned the arm on a film cassette and angled the collimator. Maura is right, thought Gabriel, this is probably a waste of time, but he needed to locate the dividing line between fear and paranoia, between truth and delusion. He saw Maura glance up at the clock on the wall, and knew she was anxious to continue cutting. The most important part of the autopsy – the head and neck dissection – had yet to be completed.

Yoshima retrieved the film cassette and disappeared into the processing room.

'Okay, he's done. Let's get back to work,' Maura said. She pulled on fresh gloves and moved back to the table. Standing at the corpse's head, hands tunneling through the tangle of black hair, she palpated the cranium. Then, with

276

one efficient slice, she cut through the scalp. He could scarcely stand to watch the mutilation of this beautiful woman. A face was little more than skin and muscle and cartilage, which easily yielded to the pathologist's knife. Maura grasped the severed edge of scalp and peeled it forward, the long hair draping like a black curtain over the face.

Yoshima re-emerged from the processing room. 'Dr. Isles?'

'X-ray's ready?'

'Yes. And there's something here.'

Maura glanced up. 'What?'

'You can see it under the skin.' He mounted the X-ray on the light box. 'This thing,' he said, pointing.

Maura crossed to the X-ray and stared in silence at the thin white strip tracing through soft tissue. Nothing natural could be that straight, that uniform.

'It's man-made,' said Gabriel. 'Do you think—'

'That's not a microchip,' said Maura.

'There *is* something there.'

'It's not metallic. It's not dense enough.'

'What are we looking at?'

'Let's find out.' Maura returned to the corpse and picked up her scalpel. Rotating the left arm, she exposed the scar. The cut she made was startlingly swift and deep, a single stroke that sliced through skin and subcutaneous fat, all the way down to muscle. This patient would never complain about an ugly incision or a severed nerve; the indignities she suffered in this room, on that table, meant nothing to senseless flesh.

Maura reached for a pair of forceps and plunged the tips into the wound. As she rooted around in freshly incised tissue, Gabriel was repelled by the brutal exploration, but he could not turn away. He heard her give a murmur of satisfaction, and suddenly her forceps re-emerged, the tips clamped around what looked like a glistening matchstick.

'I know what this is,' she said, setting the object on a specimen tray. 'This is Silastic tubing. It's simply migrated deeper than it should have after it was inserted. It's been encapsulated by scar tissue. That's why I couldn't feel it through the skin. We needed an X-ray to know it was even there.'

'What's this thing for?'

'Norplant. This tube contained a progestin that's slowly released over time, preventing ovulation.'

'A contraceptive.'

'Yes. You don't see many of these implanted anymore. The product has been discontinued in the US. Usually they're implanted six at a time, in a fanlike pattern. Whoever removed the other five missed this one.'

The intercom buzzed. 'Dr. Isles?' It was Louise again. 'You have a call.'

'Can you take a message?'

'I think you need to answer this one. It's Joan Anstead, in the governor's office.'

278

Maura's head snapped up. She looked at Gabriel, and for the first time he saw unease flicker in her eyes. She set down the scalpel, stripped off her gloves, and crossed to pick up the phone.

'This is Dr. Isles,' she said. Though Gabriel could not hear the other half of the conversation, it was clear just by Maura's body language that this was not a welcome phone call. 'Yes, I've already started it. This is in our jurisdiction. Why does the FBI think they can . . .' A long pause. Maura turned to face the wall, and her spine was now rigid. 'But I haven't completed the post-mortem. I'm about to open the cranium. If you'll just give me another half hour—' Another pause. Then, coldly: 'I understand. We'll have the remains ready for transfer in an hour.' She hung up. Took a deep breath, and turned to Yoshima. 'Pack her up. They want Joseph Roke's body as well.'

'What's going on?' Yoshima asked.

'They're being shipped to the FBI lab. They want everything – all organs and tissue specimens. Agent Barsanti will be assuming custody.'

'This has never happened before,' said Yoshima.

She yanked off her mask and reached back to untie the gown. Whipping it off, she tossed it in the soiled linens bin. 'The order comes straight from the governor's office.'

279

Twenty-three

Jane jerked awake, every muscle snapping taut. She saw darkness, heard the muted growl of a car passing on the street below, and the even rhythm of Gabriel's breathing as he slept soundly beside her. I am home, she thought. I'm lying in my own bed, in my own apartment, and we're all safe. All three of us. She took a deep breath and waited for her heart to stop pounding. The sweat-soaked nightgown slowly chilled against her skin. Eventually these nightmares will go away, she thought. These are just the fading echoes of screams.

She turned toward her husband, seeking the warmth of his body, the familiar comfort of his scent. But just as her arm was about to drape around his waist, she heard the baby crying in the other room. Oh please, not yet, she thought. It's only been three hours since I fed you. Give me another twenty minutes. Another ten minutes. Let me stay in my own bed just a little while longer. Let me shake off these bad dreams.

But the crying continued, louder now, more insistent with every fresh wail.

Jane rose and shuffled from the darkness of her bedroom, shutting the door behind her so that Gabriel would not be disturbed. She flipped on the nursery light and looked down at her red-faced and screaming daughter. Only three days old, and already you've worn me out, she thought. Lifting the baby from the crib, she felt that greedy little mouth rooting for her breast. As Jane settled into the rocking chair, pink gums clamped down like a vise on her nipple. But the offered breast was only temporary satisfaction; soon the baby was fussing again, and no matter how closely Jane cuddled her, rocked her, her daughter would not stop squirming. What am I doing wrong, she wondered, staring down at her frustrated infant. Why am I so clumsy at this? Seldom had Jane felt so inadequate, yet this three-day-old baby had reduced her to such help-lessness that, at four in the morning, she felt the sudden, desperate urge to call her mother and plead for some maternal wisdom. The sort of wisdom that was supposed to be instinctual, but had somehow skipped Jane by. Stop crying, baby, please stop crying, she thought. I'm so tired. All I want to do is go back to bed, but you won't let me. And I don't know how to make you go to sleep.

She rose from the chair and paced the room, rocking the baby as she walked. What did she want? Why was she still crying? She walked her into the kitchen and stood jiggling the baby as she stared, dazed by exhaustion, at the cluttered countertop. She thought of her life before motherhood, before Gabriel, when she would come home from work and pop open a bottle of beer and put her feet up on the couch. She loved her daughter, and she loved her husband, but she was so very tired, and she did not know when she'd be able to crawl back into bed. The night stretched ahead of her, an ordeal without end.

I can't keep this up. I need help.

She opened the kitchen cabinet and gazed at the cans of infant formula, free samples from the hospital. The baby screamed louder. She didn't know what else to do. Demoralized, she reached for a can. She poured formula into a feeding bottle and set it in a pot of hot tap water, where it sat warming, a monument to her defeat. A symbol of her utter failure as a mother.

The instant she offered the bottle, pink lips clamped down on the rubber nipple and the baby began to suck with noisy gusto. No more wailing or squirming, just happy-baby noises.

Wow. Magic from a can.

Exhausted, Jane sank into a chair. I surrender, she thought, as the bottle rapidly emptied. The can wins. Her gaze drifted down to the *Name Your Baby* book lying on the kitchen table. It was still open to the L's, where she'd last left off skimming the names for girls. Their daughter had come home from the hospital still nameless, and Jane now felt a sense of desperation as she reached for the book.

Who are you, baby? Tell me your name.

But her daughter wasn't giving away any secrets; she was too busy sucking down formula.

Laura? Laurel? Laurelia? Too soft, too sweet. This kid was none of those. She was going to be a hell-raiser.

The bottle was already half empty.

Piglet. Now there was an appropriate name.

Jane flipped to the M's. Through bleary eyes she surveyed the list, considering each possibility, then glancing down at her ferocious infant.

Mercy? Meryl? Mignon? None of the above. She turned the page, her eyes so tired now that she could barely focus. Why is this so hard? The girl needs a name, so just choose one! Her gaze slid down the page and stopped.

Mila.

She went stock-still, staring at the name. A chill snaked up her spine. She realized that she had said the name aloud.

Mila.

The room suddenly went cold, as though a ghost had just slipped through the doorway and was now hovering right behind her. She could not help a glance over her shoulder. Shivering, she rose and carried her now-sleeping daughter back to the crib. But that icy sense of dread would not leave her, and she lingered in her daughter's room, hugging herself as she rocked in the chair, trying to understand why she was shaking. Why seeing the name *Mila* had so disturbed her. As her baby slept, as the minutes ticked toward dawn, she rocked and rocked.

'Jane?'

Startled, she looked up to see Gabriel standing in the doorway. 'Why don't you come to bed?' he asked.

'I can't sleep.' She shook her head. 'I don't know what's wrong with me.'

'I think you're just tired.' He came into the room and pressed a kiss to her head. 'You need to go back to bed.'

'God, I'm so bad at this.'

'What are you talking about?'

'No one told me how hard it would be, this mommy thing. I can't even breast-feed her. Every dumb cat knows how to feed her kittens, but I'm hopeless. She just fusses and fusses.'

'She seems to be sleeping fine now.'

'That's because I gave her formula. From a *bottle*.' She gave a snort. 'I couldn't fight it anymore. She was hungry and screaming, and there's that can sitting right there. Hell, who needs a mommy when you've got Similac?'

'Oh, Jane. Is that what you're upset about?'

'It's not funny.'

'I'm not laughing.'

'But you've got that tone of voice. *This is too stupid to be believed.*'

'I think you're exhausted, that's all. How many times have you been up?'

'Twice. No, three times. Jesus, I can't even remember.'

'You should have given me a kick. I didn't know you were up.'

'It's not just the baby. It's also . . .' Jane paused. Said, quietly: 'It's the dreams.'

He pulled a chair close to hers and sat down. 'What dreams are you talking about?'

'The same one over and over. About that night, in the hospital. In my dream, I know something terrible has happened, but I can't move, I can't talk. I can feel blood on my face, I can taste it. And I'm so scared that . . .' She took a deep breath. 'I'm scared to death that it's your blood.'

'It's only been three days, Jane. You're still processing what happened.'

'I just want it to go away.'

'You need time to get past the nightmares.' He added, quietly: 'We both do.'

She looked up at his tired eyes, his unshaven face. 'You're having them, too?'

He nodded. 'Aftershocks.'

'You didn't tell me.'

'It would be surprising if we weren't having nightmares.'

'What are yours about?'

'You. The baby . . .' He stopped, and his gaze slid away. 'It's not something I really want to talk about.'

They were silent for a moment, neither one looking at the other. A few feet away, their daughter slept soundly in her crib, the only one

285

in the family untroubled by nightmares. This is what love does to you, Jane thought. It makes you afraid, not brave. It gives the world carnivorous teeth that are poised at any moment to rip away chunks of your life.

Gabriel reached out and took both her hands in his. 'Come on, sweetheart,' he said softly. 'Let's go back to bed.'

They turned off the light in the nursery and slipped into the shadows of their own bedroom. Under cool sheets he held her. Darkness lightened to gray outside their window, and the sounds of dawn drifted in. To a city girl, the roar of a garbage truck, the thump of car radios, were as familiar as a lullaby. As Boston roused itself to meet the day, Jane finally slept.

She awakened to the sound of singing. For a moment she wondered if this was yet another dream, but a far happier one, knit from long-ago memories of her childhood. She opened her eyes to see sunlight winking through the blinds. It was already two in the afternoon, and Gabriel was gone.

She rolled out of bed and shuffled barefoot into the kitchen. There she stopped, blinking at the unexpected sight of her mother, Angela, seated at the breakfast table, the baby in her arms. Angela looked up at her befuddled daughter.

'Two bottles already. This one sure knows how to eat.'

'Mom. You're here.'

'Did I wake you up? I'm sorry.'

'When did you get here?'

'A few hours ago. Gabriel said you needed to sleep in.'

Jane gave a bewildered laugh. 'He called you?'

'Who else is he supposed to call? You have another mother somewhere?'

'No, I'm just . . .' Jane sank into a chair and rubbed her eyes. 'I'm not quite awake yet. Where is he?'

'He left a little while ago. Got a call from that Detective Moore and rushed off.'

'What was the call about?'

'I don't know. Some police business. There's fresh coffee there. And you should wash your hair. You look like a cave woman. When did you eat last?'

'Dinner, I guess. Gabriel brought home Chinese.'

'Chinese? Well, that doesn't last long. Make yourself breakfast, have some coffee. I've got everything under control here.'

Yeah, Mom. You always did.

Jane didn't rise from the chair, but just sat for a moment, watching Angela hold her wide-eyed granddaughter. Saw the baby's tiny hands reach up to explore Angela's smiling face.

'How did you do it, Mom?' Jane asked.

'Just feed her. Sing to her. She likes attention is all.'

'No, I meant how did you raise three of us? I never realized how hard it must've been, having

287

three kids in five years.' She added, with a laugh: 'Especially since one of us was Frankie.'

'Ha! Your brother wasn't the hard one. *You* were.'

'Me?'

'Crying all the time. Woke up every three hours. With you, there was no such thing as *sleeping like a baby*. Frankie was still crawling around in diapers, and I was up all night walking you back and forth. Got no help from your father. You're lucky, at least Gabriel, he tries to do his part. But your dad?' Angela snorted. 'Said the smell of diapers made him gag, so he wouldn't do it. Like I had a choice. He runs off to work every morning, and there I was with you two, and Mikey on the way. Frankie with his little hands in everything. And you crying your head off.'

'Why did I cry so much?'

'Some babies are born screamers. They refuse to be ignored.'

Well, that explains it, thought Jane, looking at her baby. I got what I deserved. I got myself for a daughter.

'So how did you manage?' Jane asked again. 'Because I'm having so much trouble with this. I don't know what I'm doing.'

'You should just do what I did when I thought I was going crazy. When I couldn't stand another hour, another minute trapped in that house.'

'What did you do?'

'I picked up the phone and called my mother.'

Angela looked up at her. 'You call me, Janie. That's what I'm here for. God put mothers on this earth for a reason. Now, I'm not saying it takes a village to raise a kid.' She lowered her gaze back to the baby in her arms. 'But it sure does help to have a grandma.'

Jane watched Angela coo to the baby and thought: Oh Mom, I never realized how much I still need you. Do we ever stop needing our mothers?

Blinking away tears, she abruptly rose from her chair and turned to the counter to pour herself a cup of coffee. Stood there sipping it as she arched her back, stretching stiff muscles. For the first time in three days she felt rested, almost back to her old self. Except that everything has changed, she thought. Now I'm a mom.

'You're just the prettiest thing, aren't you, Regina?'

Jane glanced at her mother. 'We haven't really picked a name yet.'

'You have to call her something. Why not your grandmother's name?'

'It has to hit me just right, you know? If she's gonna get stuck with it for the rest of her life, I want the name to suit her.'

'Regina is a beautiful name. It means *queenly*, you know.'

'Like I want to give the kid ideas?'

'Well, what *are* you going to call her?'

Jane spotted the *Name Your Baby* book on the countertop. She refreshed her cup of coffee and sipped it as she flipped through pages, feeling a little desperate now. If I don't choose soon, she thought, it's going to be Regina by default.

Yolanthe. Yseult. Zerlena.

Oh, man. Regina was sounding better and better. The queen baby.

She set the book down. Frowned at it for a moment, then picked it up again and flipped to the M's. To the name that had caught her eye last night.

Mila.

Again she felt that cold breath whisper up her spine. I know I have heard this name before, she thought. Why does it give me such a chill? I need to remember. It's important that I remember . . .

The phone rang, startling her. She dropped the book, and it slapped onto the floor.

Angela frowned at her. 'You gonna answer that?'

Jane took a breath and picked up the receiver. It was Gabriel.

'I hope I didn't wake you.'

'No, I'm just having coffee with Mom.'

'Is it okay that I called her?'

She glanced at Angela, who was carrying the baby into the other room to change diapers. 'You're a genius. Did I tell you that?'

'I think I should call Mama Rizzoli more often.'

'I slept for eight hours straight. I can't believe what a difference that makes. My brain's actually functioning again.'

'Then maybe you're ready to deal with this.'

'What?'

'Moore called me a little while ago.'

'Yeah, I heard.'

'We're here now, at Shroeder Plaza. Jane, they got back a match on IBIS. A cartridge case with identical firing pin impressions. It was in the ATF database.'

'Which cartridge case are we talking about?'

'From Olena's hospital room. After she shot that security guard, a single cartridge case was recovered from the scene.'

'He was killed with his own weapon.'

'And we've just found out that weapon has been used before.'

'Where? When?'

'January third. A multiple shooting in Ashburn, Virginia.'

She stood clutching the receiver, pressing it so hard against her ear that she could hear the pounding of her own heartbeat. *Ashburn. Joe wanted to tell us about Ashburn.*

Angela came back into the kitchen carrying the baby, whose black hair was now fluffed up like a crown of curls. Regina, the queen baby. The name suddenly seemed to fit.

'What do we know about that multiple shooting?' Jane asked.

'Moore has the file right here.'

She looked at Angela. 'Mom, I need to leave for a while. Is that okay?'

'You go ahead. We're happy right where we are. Aren't we, Regina?' Angela bent forward and rubbed noses with the baby. 'And in a little while, we're going to take a nice little bath.'

Jane said to Gabriel: 'Give me twenty minutes. I'll be there.'

'No. Let's meet somewhere else.'

'Why?'

'We don't want to talk about it here.'

'Gabriel, what the hell is going on?'

There was a pause, and she could hear Moore's voice speaking softly in the background. Then Gabriel came back on the line.

'JP Doyle's. We'll meet you there.'

Twenty-four

She did not take the time to shower, but simply got dressed in the first clothes she pulled out of her closet – baggy maternity slacks and the T-shirt her fellow detectives had given her at the baby shower with the words MOM COP embroidered over the belly. In the car she ate two slices of buttered toast as she drove toward the neighborhood of Jamaica Plain. That last conversation with Gabriel had put her on edge, and she found herself glancing in the rearview mirror as she waited at stoplights, taking note of the cars behind her. Had she seen that green Taurus four blocks earlier? And was that the same white van she'd noticed parked across the street from her apartment?

JP Doyle's was a favorite Boston PD haunt, and on any evening, the bar was usually packed with off-duty cops. But at three P.M., only a lone woman was perched at the counter, sipping a glass of white wine as ESPN flickered on the overhead TV. Jane walked straight through the bar and headed into the adjoining dining area, where memorabilia of Boston's Irish heritage adorned the walls. Newspaper clippings about the Kennedys and Tip O'Neill and Boston's finest had hung here so long that they were now brittle with age, and the Irish flag displayed above one booth had acquired the dirty tinge of nicotine yellow. In this lull between lunch and dinner, only two booths were occupied. In one sat a middle-aged couple, clearly tourists, judging by the Boston map spread out between them. Jane walked past the couple and continued to the corner booth, where Moore and Gabriel were sitting.

She slipped in beside her husband and looked down at the file folder lying on the table. 'What do you have to show me?'

Moore didn't answer, but glanced up with an automatic smile as the waitress approached.

'Hey, Detective Rizzoli. You're all skinny again,' the waitress said.

'Not as skinny as I'd like to be.'

'I heard you had a baby girl.'

'She's keeping us up all night. This may be my only chance to eat in peace.'

The waitress laughed as she took out her order pad. 'Then let's feed you.'

'Actually, I'd just like some coffee and your apple crisp.'

'Good choice.' The waitress glanced at the men. 'How 'bout you fellas?'

'More coffee, that's all,' said Moore. 'We're

just going to sit here and watch her eat.'

They maintained their silence while their cups were refilled. Only after the waitress had delivered the apple crisp and walked away did Moore finally slide the folder across to Jane.

Inside was a sheet of digital photos. She immediately recognized them as micrographs of a spent cartridge case, showing the patterns left by the firing pin hitting the primer, and by the backward thrust of the cartridge against the breechblock.

'This is from the hospital shooting?' she asked.

Moore nodded. 'That cartridge came from the weapon that John Doe carried into Olena's room. The weapon she used to kill him. Ballistics ran it through the IBIS database, and they got back a hit, from ATF. A multiple shooting in Ashburn, Virginia.'

She turned to the next set of photos. It was another series of cartridge micrographs. 'They're a match?'

'Identical firing pin impressions. Two different cartridges found at two different death scenes. They were both ejected from the same weapon.'

'And now we have that weapon.'

'Actually, we don't.'

She looked at Moore. 'It should have been found with Olena's body. She was the last one to have it.'

'It wasn't at the takedown scene.'

'But we processed that room, didn't we?'

'There were no weapons at all left at the scene.

The federal takedown team confiscated all ballistics evidence when they left. They took the weapons, Joe's knapsack, even the cartridges. By the time Boston PD got in there, it was all gone.'

'They cleaned up a death scene? What's Boston PD going to do about this?'

'Apparently,' said Moore, 'there's not a thing we can do. The feds are calling it a matter of national security, and they don't want information leaks.'

'They don't trust Boston PD?'

'No one trusts anybody. We're not the only ones being shut out. Agent Barsanti wanted that ballistics evidence as well, and he was none too happy when he found out the special ops team took it. This has turned into federal agency versus federal agency. Boston PD's just a mouse watching two elephants battle it out.'

Jane's gaze returned to the photomicrographs. 'You said this matching cartridge came from a crime scene in Ashburn. Just before the takedown, Joseph Roke tried to tell us about something that happened in Ashburn.'

'Mr. Roke may very well have been talking about this.' Moore reached into his briefcase and pulled out another folder, which he set on the table. 'I received it this morning, from Leesburg PD. Ashburn's just a small town. It was Leesburg who worked the case.'

'It's not pleasant viewing, Jane,' said Gabriel.

His warning was unexpected. Together they had witnessed the worst the autopsy room could offer, and she'd never seen him flinch. If this case has horrified even Gabriel, she thought, do I really want to see it? She gave herself no time to consider, but simply opened the folder and confronted the first crime scene photograph. This isn't so bad, she thought. She had seen far worse. A slender brown-haired woman lay facedown on a stairway, as though she had dived from the top step. A river of her blood had streamed down, collecting in a pool at the bottom of the stairs.

'That's Jane Doe number one,' said Moore.

'You don't have ID on her?'

'We don't have ID on any of the victims in that house.'

She turned to the next photograph. It was a young blonde this time, lying on a cot, the blanket pulled up to her neck, hands still clutching the fabric, as though it might protect her. A trickle of blood oozed from the bullet wound in her forehead. A swift kill, rendered with the stunning efficiency of a single bullet.

'That's Jane Doe number two,' said Moore. At her troubled glance, he added: 'There are still others.'

Jane heard the note of caution in his voice. Once again she was on edge as she turned to the next image. Staring at the third crime scene photo, she thought: This is getting harder, but I can still deal with it. It was a view through a closet doorway, into the bloodsplattered interior. Two young women, both of them only partially clothed, sat slumped together in a tangle of arms and long hair, as though caught in a final embrace.

'Jane Does number three and number four,' said Moore.

'*None* of these women have been identified?'

'Their fingerprints aren't in any database.'

'You've got four attractive women here. And no one reported them missing?'

Moore shook his head. 'They don't match anyone on NCIC's missing persons list.' He nodded at the two victims in the closet. 'The cartridge that popped up in the IBIS match was found in that closet. Those two women were shot with the same weapon that the guard carried into Olena's hospital room.'

'And the other vics in this house? Also the same gun?'

'No. A different weapon was used on them.'

'Two guns? Two killers?'

'Yes.'

So far, none of the images had truly upset her. She reached without trepidation for the last photo, of Jane Doe number five. This time, what she saw made her rock back against the booth. Yet she could not drag her gaze from the image. She could only stare at the expression of mortal agony still etched on the victim's face. This woman was older and heavier, in her forties. Her torso was tied to a chair with loops of white cord.

'That's the fifth and final victim,' said Moore. 'The other four women were dispatched quickly.

A bullet to the head, and that was that.' He looked at the open folder. 'This one was eventually finished off with a bullet to the brain as well. But not until . . .' Moore paused. 'Not until *that* was done to her.'

'How long . . .' Jane swallowed. 'How long was she kept alive?'

'Based on the number of fractures in her hands and wrists, and the fact that all the bones were essentially pulverized, the medical examiner felt there were at least forty or fifty separate blows of the hammer. The hammerhead wasn't large. Each blow would crush only a small area. But there was not one bone, one finger, that escaped.'

Abruptly Jane closed the folder, unable to stomach the image any longer. But the damage was done, the memory now indelible.

'It would have taken at least two attackers,' said Moore. 'Someone to immobilize her while she was tied to the chair. Someone to hold her wrist to the table while *that* was being done to her.'

'There would have been screams,' she murmured. She looked up at Moore. 'Why didn't anyone hear her screaming?'

'The house is on a private dirt road, some distance from its neighbors. And remember, it was January.'

When people keep their windows shut. The victim must have realized that no one would hear her cries. That there would be no rescue. The best she could hope for was the mercy of a bullet.

'What did they want from her?' she asked.

'We don't know.'

'There must have been a reason for doing this. Something she knew.'

'We don't even know who she was. Five Jane Does. None of these victims match any missing persons report.'

'How can we not know *anything* about them?' She looked at her husband.

Gabriel shook his head. 'They're ghosts, Jane. No names, no identities.'

'What about the house?'

'It was rented out at the time to a Marguerite Fisher.'

'Who's that?'

'There's no such woman. It's a fictitious name.'

'Jesus. This is like going down a rabbit hole. Nameless victims. Renters who don't exist.'

'But we do know who owns that house,' said Gabriel. 'A company called KTE Investments.'

'Is that significant?'

'Yes. It took Leesburg PD a month to track it down. KTE is an off-the-books subsidiary of the Ballentree Company.'

Cold fingers seemed to stroke up the back of Jane's neck. 'Joseph Roke again,' she murmured. 'He talked about Ballentree. About Ashburn. What if he wasn't crazy at all?'

They all fell silent as the waitress returned with the coffeepot. 'Don't you like your apple crisp, Detective?' she asked, noting Jane's scarcely touched dessert.

'Oh, it's great. But I guess I'm not as hungry as I thought.'

'Yeah, no one seems to have an appetite,' the waitress said as she reached across to fill Gabriel's cup. 'Just a lot of coffee drinkers sitting around in here this afternoon.'

Gabriel glanced up. 'Who else?' he asked.

'Oh, that guy over . . .' The waitress paused, frowning at the empty booth nearby. She shrugged. 'Guess he didn't like the coffee,' she said, and walked away.

'Okay,' Jane said quietly. 'I'm starting to freak out, guys.'

Moore quickly swept up the folders and slid them into a large envelope. 'We should leave,' he said.

They walked out of Doyle's, emerging into the hot glare of afternoon. In the parking lot they paused beside Moore's car, scanning the street, the nearby vehicles. Here we are, two cops and an FBI agent, she thought, yet all three of us are jumpy. All three of us are reflexively scoping out the area.

'What happens now?' asked Jane.

'As far as Boston PD's concerned, it's hands off,' said Moore. 'I've been ordered not to rattle this particular cage.'

'And those files?' She glanced at the envelope Moore was carrying.

'I'm not even supposed to have these.'

'Well, I'm still on maternity leave. No one's issued *me* any orders.' She took the envelope from Moore.

'Jane,' said Gabriel.

She turned toward her Subaru. 'I'll see you at home.'

'*Jane.*'

As she climbed in behind the wheel, Gabriel swung open the passenger door and slid in beside her. 'You don't know what you're getting into,' he said.

'Do you?'

'You saw what they did to that woman's hands. That's the kind of people we're dealing with.'

She stared out the window, watching Moore step into his car and drive away. 'I thought it was over,' she said softly. 'I thought, okay, we survived, so let's get on with our lives. But it's *not* over.' She looked at him. 'I need to know why it all happened. I need to know what it means.'

'Let me do the digging. I'll find out what I can.'

'And what should I do?'

'You just got out of the hospital.'

She put her key in the ignition and started the engine, setting off a blast of hot air from the AC vent. 'I didn't have major surgery,' she said. 'I just had a baby.'

'That's reason enough for you to stay out of it.'

'But *this* is what's bothering me, Gabriel. *This* is why I can't sleep!' She sank back against the seat. 'This is why the nightmare doesn't go away.'

'It takes time.'

'I can't stop thinking about it.' She gazed, once again, at the parking lot. 'I'm starting to remember more things.'

'What things?'

'Pounding. Yelling, gunfire. And then the blood on my face . . .'

'That's the dream you told me about.'

'And I *keep* having it.'

'There would have been noises and shouting. And there *was* blood on you – Olena's blood. Nothing you remember is surprising.'

'But there's something else. I haven't told you about it, because I've been trying to remember. Just before Olena died, she tried to tell me something.'

'Tell you what?'

She looked at Gabriel. 'She said a name. Mila. She said: "Mila knows." '

'What does that mean?'

'I don't know.'

Gabriel's gaze suddenly turned toward the street. He tracked the progress of a car as it slowly cruised past, then rounded the corner, and glided out of sight.

'Why don't you go home?' he said.

'What about you?'

'I'll be there in a while.' He leaned over to kiss her. 'Love you,' he said, and climbed out.

She watched him walk to his own car, parked a few stalls away. Saw him pause as he reached in his pocket, as though trying to locate his keys. She knew her husband well enough to recognize the tension in his shoulders, to note his quick glance around the parking lot. She seldom saw him rattled, and now it made her anxious, knowing that he was on edge. He started his engine and sat waiting for her to leave first.

Only as she left the parking lot did he pull out. He trailed her for a few blocks. He's watching to see if I'm being followed, she thought. Even after he'd finally peeled away, she found herself glancing in the mirror, though she could think of no reason for anyone to follow her. What did she know, really? Nothing that Moore or anyone else in the homicide unit didn't already know. Just the memory of a whisper.

Mila. Who is Mila?

She glanced over her shoulder at Moore's envelope, which she'd tossed on the backseat. She did not look forward to examining those crime scene photos again. But I need to get beyond the horror, she thought. I need to know what happened in Ashburn.

Twenty-five

Maura Isles was up to her elbows in blood. Pausing in the anteroom, Gabriel watched through the glass partition as Maura reached into the abdomen, lifted out loops of intestine, and plopped them into a basin. He saw no distaste in her face as she dug through the mound, just the quiet concentration of a scientist probing for some detail out of the ordinary. At last she handed Yoshima the basin, and was reaching once again for her knife when she noticed Gabriel.

'I'll be another twenty minutes,' she said. 'You can come in, if you want.'

He pulled on shoe covers and a gown to protect his clothes and stepped into the lab. Though he tried to avoid looking at the body on the table, it was there between them, impossible to ignore. A woman with skeletal limbs and skin hanging like loose crepe over the jutting bones of her pelvis.

'History of anorexia nervosa. Found dead in

her apartment,' said Maura, answering his unspoken question.

'She's so young.'

'Twenty-seven. EMTs said all she had in her refrigerator was a head of lettuce and Diet Pepsi. Starvation in the land of plenty.' Maura reached into the abdomen to dissect the retroperitoneal space. Yoshima, in the meantime, had moved to the head, to incise the scalp. As always, they worked with a minimum of conversation, knowing each other's needs so well that words did not seem necessary.

'You wanted to tell me something?' said Gabriel.

Maura paused. In her hand she cupped a single kidney, like a lump of black gelatin. She and Yoshima exchanged a nervous glance. At once, Yoshima started up the Stryker saw, and the noisy whine almost covered Maura's answer.

'Not here,' she said quietly. 'Not yet.'

Yoshima pried off the skullcap.

As Maura leaned in to free the brain, she asked, in a cheerfully normal voice: 'So how is it, being a daddy?'

'Exceeds all my expectations.'

'You've settled on Regina?'

'Mama Rizzoli talked us into it.'

'Well, I think it's a nice name.' Maura lowered the brain into a bucket of formalin. 'A dignified name.'

'Jane's already shortened it to Reggie.'

'Not quite so dignified.'

Maura pulled off her gloves and looked at Yoshima. He gave a nod. 'I need some fresh air,' she said. 'Let's take a break.'

They stripped off their gowns, and she led the way out of the room, to the loading bay. Only when they'd stepped out of the building, and were standing in the parking lot, did she speak again.

'I'm sorry about the conversational runaround,' she said. 'We had a security breach. I'm not comfortable talking inside right now.'

'What happened?'

'Last night, around three A.M., Medford Fire and Rescue brought in a body from an accident scene. Normally we keep the exterior bay doors locked, and they have to call a night operator for the key code to get in. They discovered that the doors were already unlocked, and when they stepped inside, they saw that the lights were on in the autopsy lab. They mentioned it to the operator, and security came to check the building. Whoever broke in must have left in a hurry, because a desk drawer in my office was still open.'

'Your office?'

Maura nodded. 'And Dr. Bristol's computer was on. He always turns it off when he leaves at night.' She paused. 'It was open to the file on Joseph Roke's autopsy.'

'Was anything taken from the offices?'

'Not that we've determined. But we're all a little leery now of discussing anything sensitive inside the building. Someone's been in our offices. And in our lab. And we don't know what they were after.'

No wonder Maura had refused to discuss this over the phone. Even the levelheaded Dr. Isles was now spooked.

'I'm not a conspiracy theorist,' said Maura. 'But look at everything that's happened. Both bodies whisked out of our legal custody. Ballistics evidence confiscated by Washington. Who is calling the shots here?'

He stared at the parking lot, where heat shimmered like water on blacktop. 'It goes high,' he said. 'It has to.'

'Which means we can't touch them.'

He looked at her. 'It doesn't mean we won't try.'

Jane came awake in darkness, the last whispers of the dream still in her ear. Olena's voice again, murmuring to her from across the mortal divide. *Why do you keep tormenting me? Tell me what you want, Olena. Tell me who Mila is.*

But the whisper had fallen silent, and she heard only the sound of Gabriel's breathing. And then, a moment later, the indignant wail of her daughter. She climbed out of bed and let her husband continue sleeping. She was wide awake now anyway, and still haunted by the echoes of the dream.

The baby had punched her way out of the swaddling blanket and was waving pink fists, as though challenging her mother to a fight. 'Regina, Regina,' sighed Jane as she lifted her daughter out of the crib, and she suddenly realized how natural the name now felt on her lips. This girl was indeed born a Regina; it had just taken time for Jane to realize it, to stop stubbornly resisting what Angela had known all along. Much as she hated to admit it, Angela was right about a lot of things. Baby names and formula-as-savior and asking for help when you needed it. It was that last part Jane had so much trouble with: admitting that she needed help, that she didn't know what she was doing. She could work a homicide, could track a monster, but asking her to soothe this screaming bundle in her arms was like asking her to disarm a nuclear bomb. She glanced around the nursery, vainly hoping that some fairy godmother was lurking in the corner, ready to wave a wand and make Regina stop crying.

No fairy godmothers here. Just me.

Regina lasted only five minutes on the right breast, another five minutes on the left, and then it was time for the bottle. Okay, so your mom's a failure as a milk cow, Jane thought as she carried Regina into the kitchen. So pull me from the herd and shoot me. With Regina happily suckling from the bottle, Jane settled into the kitchen chair, savoring this moment of silence, however brief. She gazed down at her daughter's dark hair. Curly, just like mine, she thought. Angela had once told her, in a fit of frustration,

'Someday you'll get the daughter you deserve.' And here I am, she thought, with this noisy, insatiable little girl.

The kitchen clock flipped to three A.M.

Jane reached for the stack of folders that Detective Moore had dropped off last night. She had finished reading all the Ashburn files; now she opened a new folder, and saw that this one was not about the Ashburn slayings; it was a Boston PD file on Joseph Roke's car, the vehicle he had abandoned a few blocks from the hospital. She saw pages of Moore's notes, photos of the vehicle's interior, an AFIS report on the fingerprints, and various witness statements. While she'd been trapped in that hospital, her colleagues from the homicide unit hadn't been sitting idle. They'd been chasing down every scrap of information about the hostage takers. I was never on my own, she thought; my friends were out there, fighting for me, and here is the proof.

She glanced at the detective's signature on one of the witness reports and gave a surprised laugh. Hell, even her old nemesis Darren Crowe had been working hard to save her, and why wouldn't he? Without her in the unit, he'd have no one else to insult.

She flipped to the photographs of the vehicle's interior. Saw crumpled-up Butterfinger wrappers and empty cans of Red Bull soda pop on the floor. Lots of sugar and caffeine, just what every psychotic needed to calm down. On the backseat was a wadded-up blanket and a stained pillow and an issue of the tabloid newspaper, the *Weekly Confidential*. Melanie Griffith was on the cover. She tried to imagine Joe lying on that backseat, leafing through the tabloid, scanning the latest news of celebrities and bad girls, but she couldn't quite see it. Could he really have cared what the crazies out in Hollywood were up to? Maybe a glance at their screwed-up, coked-up lives made Joe's own life seem tolerable. The *Weekly Confidential* was harmless distraction for anxious times.

She set aside the Boston PD file and reached for the folder on the Ashburn slayings. Once again, she confronted the crime scene photos of slaughtered women. Once again, she paused over the photo of Jane Doe number five. Suddenly she could not bear to look at blood, at death, any longer. Chilled to the bone, she closed the file.

Regina was asleep.

She carried the baby back to the crib, then slipped into her own bed, but she could not stop shivering, even though the heat of Gabriel's body warmed the sheets. She needed so badly to sleep, but could not quiet the chaos in her head. Too many images were spinning through her brain. This was the first time she understood what the phrase *too tired to sleep* meant. She'd heard that people could go psychotic from lack of sleep; maybe she had already passed that threshold, pushed across the edge by nightmares, by her demanding newborn. *I need to make these dreams go away.*

Gabriel's arm came around her. 'Jane?'

'Hey,' she murmured.

'You're shaking. Are you cold?'

'A little.'

He wrapped her closer, pulling her into his warmth. 'Did Regina wake up?'

'A while ago. I've already fed her.'

'It was my turn to do it.'

'I was awake anyway.'

'Why?'

She didn't answer.

'It's the dream again. Isn't it?' he asked.

'It's like she's haunting me. She won't leave me alone. Every damn night, she keeps me from sleeping.'

'Olena's dead, Jane.'

'Then it's her ghost.'

'You don't really believe in ghosts.'

'I didn't. But now . . .'

'You've changed your mind?'

She turned on her side to look at him, and saw the faint glow of city lights in his eyes. Her beautiful Gabriel. How did she get so lucky? What did she do to deserve him? She touched his face, fingers brushing across stubble. Even after six months of marriage, it still astonished her that she shared her bed with this man.

'I just want things to go back to the way they were,' she said. 'Before any of this happened.'

He pulled her against him, and she smelled

312

soap and warm skin. Her husband's smells. 'Give it more time,' he said. 'Maybe you need to have these dreams. You're still processing what happened. Working through the trauma.'

'Or maybe I need to do something about it.'

'Do what?'

'What Olena wanted me to do.'

He sighed. 'You're talking about the ghost again.'

'She did speak to me. I didn't imagine that part. It's not a dream, it's a memory, something that really happened.' She rolled onto her back and stared up at the shadows. '"Mila knows." That's what she said. That's what I remember.'

'Mila knows what?'

She looked at Gabriel. 'I think she was talking about Ashburn.'

Twenty-six

By the time they boarded the plane to Washington-Reagan, her breasts were aching and swollen, her body yearning for the relief that only a suckling infant could provide. But Regina was not within reach; her daughter was spending the day in Angela's capable hands, and at that moment was probably being cooed at and fussed over by someone who actually knew what she was doing. Gazing out the plane's window, Jane thought: My baby's only two weeks old, and already I'm abandoning her. I'm such a bad mom. But as the city of Boston dropped away beneath their climbing aircraft, it wasn't guilt she felt, but a sudden lightness, as though she'd shed the weight of motherhood, of sleepless nights and hours of pacing back and forth. What is wrong with me, she wondered, that I'm so relieved to be away from my own child?

Bad mom.

Gabriel's hand settled on hers. 'Everything okay?'

'Yeah.'

'Don't worry about it. Your mother's so good with her.'

She nodded, and kept her gaze out the window. How did she tell her own husband that his child had a lousy mother who was thrilled to be out of the house and back in the chase? That she missed her job so much that it hurt just to watch a cop show on TV?

A few rows behind them, a baby started to cry, and Jane's breasts throbbed, heavy with milk. My body is punishing me, she thought, for leaving Regina behind.

The first thing she did after walking off the plane was to duck into the women's restroom. There she sat on a toilet, milking herself into wads of tissue paper, wondering if cows felt the same blessed relief when their udders were emptied. Such a waste, but she didn't know what else to do but squeeze it out and flush it down the toilet.

When she re-emerged, she found Gabriel waiting for her by the airport newsstand. 'Feeling better?' he asked.

'Moo.'

Leesburg Detective Eddie Wardlaw did not look particularly thrilled to see them. He was in his forties, with a sour face and eyes that didn't smile even when his lips tried to. Jane could not decide if he was tired or just irritated about their visit. Before offering any handshake, he asked to see their IDs, and spent an insulting length of time examining each one, as though certain they were fraudulent. Only then did he grudgingly shake their hands and escort them past the front desk.

'I spoke to Detective Moore this morning,' he said as he led them at a deliberate pace down the hallway.

'We told him we were flying down to see you,' said Jane.

'He said that you two were okay.' Wardlaw reached in his pocket for a set of keys, paused, and looked at them. 'I needed to have some background on you both, so I've been asking around. Just so you understand what's going on.'

'Actually, we don't,' said Jane. 'We're trying to figure out this whole business ourselves.'

'Yeah?' Wardlaw gave a grunt. 'Welcome to the club.' He unlocked the door and led them into a small conference room. On the table was a cardboard box, labeled with a case number, and containing a stack of files. Wardlaw pointed to the files. 'You can see how much we have. I couldn't copy it all. I only sent Moore what I felt comfortable sharing at the time. This thing has been screwy from the word go, and I needed to be absolutely sure of anyone who's seeing these files.'

'Look, you want to check my credentials again?' said Jane 'You're welcome to talk to anyone in my unit. They all know my record.'

'Not you, Detective. Cops I don't have a problem with. But guys from the Bureau . . .' He looked at Gabriel. 'I'm forced to be a little more cautious. Especially considering what's happened so far.'

Gabriel responded with that coolly impervious look that he could call up at an instant's notice. The same look that had once kept Jane at arm's length when they had first met. 'If you have a concern about me, Detective, let's discuss it right now, before we go any further.'

'Why are you here, Agent Dean? You people have already combed through everything we have.'

'The FBI's stepped in on this?' asked Jane.

Wardlaw looked at her. 'They demanded copies of everything. Every scrap of paper in that box. Didn't trust our crime lab, so they had to bring in their own technicians to examine the physical evidence. The feds have seen it all.' He turned back to Gabriel. 'So if you have questions about the case, why don't you just check with your pals at the Bureau?'

'Believe me, I can vouch for Agent Dean,' said Jane. 'I'm married to him.'

'Yeah, that's what Moore told me.' Wardlaw laughed and shook his head. 'Fibbie and a cop. Ask me, it's like cats marrying dogs.' He reached into the box. 'Okay, this is what you wanted. Investigation control files. Occurrence reports.' He took out folders one by one and slapped them down on the table. 'Lab and autopsy reports. Vic photos. Daily logs. News releases and press clippings . . .' He paused, as though suddenly remembering something. 'I've got another item you might find useful,' he said, and turned toward the door. 'I'll get it.'

Moments later, he came back carrying a video-cassette. 'I keep this locked in my desk,' he said. 'With all these feds pawing through this box, I thought I should store this video in a safe place.' He crossed to a closet and wheeled out a TV monitor and VCR player. 'Being this close to Washington, we get the occasional case with, well . . . political complications,' he said as he untangled the cord. 'You know, elected officials behaving badly. Few years ago, a senator's wife got killed when her Mercedes rolled over on one of our back roads. Trouble was, the man driving the car wasn't her husband. Even worse, the guy worked in the Russian embassy. You should've seen how quick the FBI showed up on that one.' He plugged in the TV, then straightened and looked at them. 'I'm having a sense of déjà vu on this case.'

'You think there are political implications?' said Gabriel.

'You're aware of who really owns the house? It took us weeks to find out.'

'A subsidiary of the Ballentree Company.'

'And *that's* the political complication. We're talking about a Goliath in Washington. White House buddy. The country's biggest defense contractor. I had no idea what I was walking into that day. Finding five women shot to death was bad enough. Add in the politics, the FBI meddling, and I'm ready for goddamn early retirement.' Wardlaw inserted the tape in the VCR, grabbed the remote, and pressed PLAY.

On the TV monitor, a view of snow-dusted trees appeared. It was a bright day, and sunshine sparkled on ice.

'Nine one one got the call around ten A.M.,' said Wardlaw. 'Male voice, refused to identify himself. Just wanted to report that something had happened in a house on Deerfield Road, and that the police should check it out. There aren't many homes on Deerfield Road, so it didn't take long for the cruiser to find out which residence was involved.'

'Where did that call come from?'

'A pay phone about thirty-five miles out of Ashburn. We were unable to get any usable fingerprints off the phone. We never did identify the caller.'

On the TV screen, half a dozen parked vehicles could now be seen. Against the background noise of men's voices, the camera's operator began to narrate: 'The date is January fourth, eleven thirty-five A.M. Residence address is number nine, Deerfield Road, town of Ashburn, Virginia. Present are Detective Ed Wardlaw and myself, Detective Byron McMahon . . .'

'My partner worked the camera,' said Wardlaw. 'That's a view of the driveway in front of the residence. As you can see, it's surrounded by woods. No neighbors nearby.'

The camera slowly panned past two waiting

ambulances. The crews stood in a huddle, their breath steaming in the icy air. The lens continued its slow rotation, coming at last to a stop on the house. It was a two-story brick home of stately proportions, but what had once been a grand residence was showing the signs of neglect. White paint was peeling off shutters and windowsills. A porch railing tilted sideways. Wrought-iron bars covered the windows, an architectural feature more appropriate to an inner-city apartment building, not a house on a quiet rural road. The camera now focused on Detective Wardlaw, who was standing on the front steps, like a grim host waiting to greet his guests. The image swayed toward the ground as Detective McMahon bent to pull on shoe covers. Then the lens was once again aimed at the front door. It followed Wardlaw into the house.

The first image it captured was the blood-smeared stairway. Jane already knew what to expect; she had seen the crime scene photos, and knew how each woman had died. Yet as the camera focused on the steps, Jane could feel her pulse quicken, her sense of dread building.

The camera paused on the first victim, lying facedown on the stairway. 'This one was shot twice,' said Wardlaw. 'Medical examiner said the first bullet hit her in the back, probably as the vic was trying to flee toward the stairs. Nicked her vena cava and exited out the abdomen. Judging by the amount of blood she lost, she was probably alive for five, ten minutes before the second bullet was fired, into her head. The way I read it, the perp brought her down with the first shot, then turned his attention to the other women. When he came back down the stairs again, he noticed that this one was still alive. So he finished her off with a kill shot.' Wardlaw looked at Jane. 'Thorough guy.'

'All that blood,' murmured Jane. 'There must have been a wealth of footwear evidence.'

'Both upstairs and down. Downstairs is where it got confusing. We saw two large sets of shoe prints, which we assume to be the two killers. But in addition there were other prints. Smaller ones, that tracked across the kitchen.'

'Law enforcement?'

'No. By the time that first cruiser arrived, it was at least six hours after the fact. The blood on that kitchen floor was pretty much dry. The smaller prints we saw were made while the blood was still wet.'

'Whose prints?'

Wardlaw looked at her. 'We still don't know.'

Now the camera moved up the stairs, and they could hear the sound of paper shoe covers rustling over the steps. In the upstairs hallway, the camera turned left, aiming through a doorway. Six cots were crammed into the bedroom, and on the floor were piles of clothing, dirty dishes, and a large bag of potato chips. The camera panned across the room, to focus on the cot where victim number two had died.

'Looks like this one never even got a chance to

run,' said Wardlaw. 'Stayed in bed and took the bullet right there, where she was lying.'

Again, the camera was on the move, circling away from the cots, turning toward a closet. Through the open doorway, the lens zoomed in on two pitiful occupants slumped together. They had crammed themselves into the very back of the closet, as though desperately trying to shrink from sight. But they had been all too visible to the killer who had opened the door, who had aimed his weapon at those bowed heads.

'One bullet each,' said Wardlaw. 'These guys were quick, accurate, and methodical. Every door was opened, every closet was searched. There was no place in that house to hide. These victims never had a chance.'

He reached for the remote and fast-forwarded. Images danced on the monitor, a manic tour of the other bedrooms, a race up a ladder, through a trap door and into an attic. Then a jittery retreat back down the hallway, down the stairs. Wardlaw hit PLAY. The journey slowed again, the camera moving at a walking pace through a dining room and into the kitchen.

'Here,' he said quietly, pressing PAUSE. 'The last victim. She had a very bad night.'

The woman sat bound by cord to a chair. The bullet had entered just above her right eyebrow, and the impact had shoved her head backward. She had died with her eyes turned heavenward; death had drained her face pale. Both her arms were extended in front of her, on the table.

The bloodied hammer still lay beside her ruined hands.

'Clearly they wanted something from her,' said Wardlaw. 'And this gal couldn't, or wouldn't, give it to them.' He looked at Jane, his eyes haunted by the ordeal that they were all imagining at that moment. The hammer blows falling again and again, crushing bone and joint. The screams echoing through that house of dead women.

He pressed PLAY, and the video mercifully moved on, leaving behind the bloodied table, the mangled flesh. Still shaken, they watched in silence as the video took them into a downstairs bedroom, then into the living room, decorated with a sagging couch and a green shag rug. Finally they were back in the foyer, at the foot of the staircase, right where they had started.

'That's what we found,' said Wardlaw. 'Five female victims, all unidentified. Two different firearms were used. We're assuming at least two killers, working together.'

And no place in that house for their prey to hide, thought Jane. She thought of the two victims cowering in the closet, breaths turning to whimpers, arms wrapped around each other as footsteps creaked closer.

'They walk in and execute five women,' said Gabriel. 'They spend maybe half an hour in the kitchen with that last one, crushing her hands with a hammer. And you have nothing on these killers? No trace evidence, no fingerprints?'

'Oh, we found a zillion fingerprints all over that house. Unidentifieds in every room. But if our perps left any, they didn't match anyone in AFIS.' Wardlaw reached for the remote and pressed STOP.

'Wait,' said Gabriel, his gaze fixed on the monitor.

'What?'

'Rewind it.'

'How far?'

'About ten seconds.'

Wardlaw frowned at him, clearly puzzled by what could have caught his eye. He handed Gabriel the remote. 'Be my guest.'

Gabriel pressed REWIND, then PLAY. The camera had backed up to the living room, and now repeated its sweep past the tired couch, the shag rug. Then it moved into the foyer and suddenly swung toward the front door. Outside, sunshine glinted off icy branches of trees. Two men stood in the yard, talking. One of them turned toward the house.

Gabriel hit PAUSE, freezing the man where he stood, his face framed in the doorway. 'It's John Barsanti,' he said.

'You know him?' Wardlaw asked.

'He turned up in Boston, too,' said Gabriel.

'Yeah, well, he seems to show up everywhere, doesn't he? We got to the house barely an hour before Barsanti and his team arrived. They tried to step right into our show, and we ended up having a tug-of-war right there, on the front porch. Till we got a call from the Justice Department, asking us to cooperate.'

'How did the FBI get wind of this case so quickly?' asked Jane.

'We never got a good answer to that question.' Wardlaw crossed to the VCR, ejected the tape, then turned to face her. 'So that's what we were dealing with. Five dead women, none of them with fingerprints on file. No one's reported them missing. They're all Jane Does.'

'Undocumented aliens,' said Gabriel.

Wardlaw nodded. 'My guess is, they were Eastern Europeans. There were a few Russian-language newspapers in the downstairs bedroom. Plus a shoe box with photos of Moscow. Considering what else we found in that house, we can make a pretty good guess as to their occupations. In the pantry, there were supplies of penicillin. Morning-after pills. And a carton full of condoms.' He picked up the file containing the autopsy reports and handed it to Gabriel. 'Check out the DNA analysis.'

Gabriel flipped directly to the lab results. 'Multiple sexual partners,' he said.

Wardlaw nodded. 'Put it all together. A bevy of young, attractive women living together under the same roof. Entertaining a number of different men. Let's just say that house was no convent.'

Twenty-seven

The private road cut through stands of oak and pine and hickory. Chips of sunlight filtered through the canopy, dappling the road. Deep among the trees, little light shone through, and in green shadows thick with underbrush, saplings struggled to grow.

'No wonder the neighbors didn't hear anything that night,' Jane said, gazing at dense woods. 'I don't even see any neighbors.'

'I think it's just ahead, through those trees.'

Another thirty yards, and the road suddenly widened, their car emerging into late afternoon sunshine. A two-story house loomed before them. Though now in disrepair, it still had good bones: a redbrick façade, a wide porch. But nothing about this house was welcoming. Certainly not the wrought-iron bars across the windows, or the NO TRESPASSING signs tacked to the posts. Knee-high weeds were already taking over the gravel driveway, the first wave of invaders, preparing the way for encroaching

326

forest. Wardlaw had told them that an attempt at renovations was abruptly abandoned two months ago, when the contractor's equipment had accidentally touched off a small fire, scorching an upstairs bedroom. The flames had left black claw marks on a window frame, and plywood still covered the broken glass. Maybe the fire was a warning, thought Jane. *This house is not friendly.*

She and Gabriel stepped out of the rental car. They had been driving with the AC on, and the heat took her by surprise. She paused in the driveway, perspiration instantly blooming on her face, and breathed in the thick and sullen air. Though she could not see the mosquitoes, she could hear them circling, and she slapped her cheek, saw fresh blood on her hand. That was all she heard, just the hum of insects. No traffic, no birdsong; even the trees were still. Her neck prickled – not from the heat, but from the sudden, instinctive urge to leave this place. To climb back in the car and lock the doors and drive away. She did not want to go in there.

'Well, let's see if Wardlaw's key still works,' said Gabriel, starting toward the porch.

Reluctantly she followed him up creaking steps, where blades of grass grew through seams between the boards. On Wardlaw's video, it had been wintertime, the driveway bare of vegetation. Now vines twisted up the railings and pollen dusted the porch like yellow snow.

At the door, Gabriel paused, frowning at what

remained of a padlock hinge that had once secured the front entrance. 'This has been here a while,' he said, pointing to the rust.

Bars on the windows. A padlock on the door. Not to guard against intruders, she thought; this lock was meant to keep people *in*.

Gabriel jiggled the key in the lock and gave the door a push. With a squeal it gave way, and the smell of old smoke wafted out; the aftermath of the contractor's fire. You can clean a house, repaint its walls, replace the drapes and the carpets and furniture, yet the stench of fire endures. He stepped inside.

After a pause, so did she. She was surprised to find bare wood floors; on the video, there had been an ugly green carpet, since removed during the cleanup. The banister leading up the stairs was handsomely carved, and the living room had ten-foot ceilings with crown molding, details that she had not noticed while watching the crime scene video. Water stains marred the ceiling, like dark clouds.

'Whoever built this place had money,' Gabriel noted.

She crossed to a window and looked through the bars at the trees. The afternoon was slipping toward evening; they did not have more than an hour before the light would fade. 'It must have been a beautiful house when it was built,' she said. But that was a long time ago. Before shag carpets and iron bars. Before bloodstains.

They walked through a living room empty of

furniture. Floral wallpaper showed the wear of passing years – smudges and peeling corners and the yellow tinge from decades of cigarette smoke. They moved through the dining room and came to a halt in the kitchen. The table and chairs were gone; all they saw was tired linoleum, the edges nicked and curling. Afternoon sun slanted in through the barred window. Here is where the older woman died, Jane thought. Sitting in the center of this room, her body tied to a chair, tender fingers exposed to the hammer's blows. Though Jane was staring at an empty kitchen, her mind superimposed the image she had seen on the video. An image that seemed to linger in the sunlit swirl of dust motes.

'Let's go upstairs,' said Gabriel.

They left the kitchen and paused at the bottom of the staircase. Looking up toward the second-floor landing, she thought: Here is where another one died, on these steps. The woman with the brown hair. Jane gripped the banister, her hand clasping carved oak, and felt her own pulse throbbing in her fingertips. She did not want to go upstairs. But that voice was once again whispering to her.

Mila knows.

There's something I'm supposed to see up there, she thought. Something the voice is guiding me toward.

Gabriel headed up the stairs. Jane followed more slowly, her gaze focused downward on the steps, her palm clammy against the railing. She came to a halt, staring at a patch of lighter wood. Crouching down to touch a recently sanded surface, she felt the hairs lift on the back of her neck. Darken the windows, spray these stairs with luminol, and the grain of this wood would surely light up a spectral green. The cleaners had tried to sand away the worst of it, but the evidence was still there, where the victim's blood had spilled. This was where she died, sprawled on these steps, this very spot Jane was touching.

Gabriel was already on the second floor, walking through the rooms.

She followed him to the upper landing. The smell of smoke was stronger here. The hallway had drab green wallpaper and a floor of dark oak. Doors hung ajar, spilling rectangles of light into the corridor. She turned into the first doorway on her right, and saw an empty room, walls marked by ghostly squares where pictures had once hung. It could be any vacant room in any vacant house, all traces of its occupants swept away. She crossed to the window, lifted the sash. The iron bars were welded in place. No escape in a fire, she thought. Even if you could climb out, it was a fifteen-foot drop onto bare gravel, with no shrubs to break the fall.

'Jane,' she heard Gabriel call.

She followed his voice, moving across the hall into another bedroom.

Gabriel was gazing into an open closet. 'Here,' he said quietly.

She moved beside him and crouched down to

touch sanded wood. She could not help mentally superimposing yet another image from the video. The two women, slender arms entwined like lovers. How long had they huddled here? The closet was not large, and the smell of fear must have soured the darkness.

Abruptly she rose to her feet. The room felt too warm, too airless; she walked into the hall, her legs numb from crouching. This is a house of horrors, she thought. If I listen hard enough, I'll hear the echoes of screams.

At the end of the hall was one last room – the room where the contractor had touched off the fire. She hesitated on its threshold, repelled by the far stronger stench of smoke in this room. Both broken windows had been covered with plywood, blocking out the afternoon light. She took the Maglite from her purse and shone it around the dim interior. Flames had scorched walls and ceiling, devouring sections all the way down to charred timber. She swung the Maglite beam around the room, past a closet missing its door. As her beam swept past, an ellipse flashed on the closet's back wall, then vanished. Frowning, she swung the Maglite back.

There it was again, that bright ellipse, briefly flickering across the back wall.

She crossed to the closet for a closer look. Saw an opening large enough to poke a finger through. Perfectly round and smooth. Someone had drilled a hole between the closet and the bedroom.

Beams groaned overhead. Startled, she glanced up as footsteps creaked across the ceiling. Gabriel was in the attic.

She went back into the hallway. Daylight was rapidly fading, dimming the house to shades of gray. 'Hey!' she called. 'Where's the trap door to get up there?'

'Look in the second bedroom.'

She saw the ladder and scrambled up the rungs. Poking her head into the space above, she saw the beam of Gabriel's Maglite slicing through the shadows.

'Anything up here?' she asked.

'A dead squirrel.'

'I mean, anything interesting?'

'Not a whole lot.'

She climbed up into the attic and almost banged her head on a low rafter. Gabriel was forced to move at a crouch, long legs crabwalking as he inspected the perimeter, his beam slowly scanning the deepest pockets of shadow.

'Stay away from this corner over here,' he warned. 'The boards are charred. I don't think the floor is safe.'

She headed to the opposite end, where a lone window admitted the last gray light of day. This one had no bars; it did not need them. She lifted open the sash and stuck her head out to see a narrow ledge and a bone-shattering drop to the ground. An escape route only for the suicidal. She pushed the window shut, and fell still, her gaze fixed on the trees.

In the woods, light briefly flickered, like a darting firefly.

'Gabriel.'

'Nice. Here's another dead squirrel.'

'There's someone out there.'

'What?'

'In the woods.'

He crossed to her side and stared out at the thickening dusk. 'Where?'

'I saw it just a minute ago.'

'Maybe it was a passing car.' He turned from the window and muttered, 'Damn. My battery's going.' He gave his flashlight a few hard raps. The beam briefly brightened, then began to fade again.

She was still staring out the window, at woods that seemed to be closing in on them. Trapping them in this house of ghosts. A chill whispered up her spine. She turned to her husband.

'I want to leave.'

'Should have changed batteries before we left home . . .'

'Now. Please.'

Suddenly he registered the anxiety in her voice. 'What is it?'

'I don't think that was a passing car.'

He turned to the window again and stood very still, his shoulders blotting out what dim light still remained. It was his silence that rattled her, a silence that only magnified the drumming of her heartbeat. 'All right,' he said quietly. 'Let's go.'

They climbed down the ladder and retreated

into the hall, past the bedroom where blood still lingered in the closet. Moved down the stairs, where sanded wood still whispered of horrors. Already, five women had died in this house, and no one had heard their screams.

No one would hear ours, either.

They pushed through the front door, onto the porch.

And froze, as powerful lights suddenly blinded their eyes. Jane raised her arm against the glare. She heard footsteps crunch on gravel, and through squinting eyes, could just make out three dark figures closing in.

Gabriel stepped in front of her, a move so swift that she was surprised to suddenly find his shoulders blocking the light.

'Right where you are,' a voice commanded.

'Can I see who I'm talking to?' said Gabriel.

'Identify yourselves.'

'If you could lower your flashlights first.'

'Your IDs.'

'Okay. Okay, I'm going to reach in my pocket,' Gabriel said, his voice calm. Reasonable. 'I'm not armed, and neither is my wife.' Slowly he withdrew his wallet and held it out. It was snatched from his hand. 'My name is Gabriel Dean. And this is my wife, Jane.'

'Detective Jane Rizzoli,' she amended. 'Boston PD.' She blinked as the flashlight suddenly shifted to her face. Though she could not see any of these men, she felt them scrutinizing her. Felt her temper rise as her fear ebbed away.

'What's Boston PD doing here?' the man asked.

'What are *you* doing here?' she retorted.

She didn't expect an answer; she didn't get one. The man handed back Gabriel's wallet, then he waved his flashlight toward a dark sedan parked behind their rental car. 'Get in. You'll have to come with us.'

'Why?' said Gabriel.

'We need to confirm your IDs.'

'We have a flight to catch, back to Boston,' said Jane.

'Cancel it.'

Twenty-eight

Jane sat alone in the interview room, staring at her own reflection and thinking: It sucks to be on the wrong side of the one-way mirror. She had been here for an hour now, every so often rising to her feet to check the door, on the off chance that it had miraculously unlocked itself. Of course they had separated her from Gabriel; that's the way it was done, the way she herself handled interrogations. But everything else about her situation was new and unfamiliar territory. The men had never identified themselves, had presented no badges, offered no names, ranks, or serial numbers. They could be the Men in Black for all she knew, protecting Earth from the scum of the universe. They had brought their prisoners into the building through an underground parking garage, so she did not even know which agency they worked for, only that this interrogation room was somewhere within the city limits of Reston.

'Hey!' Jane went to the mirror and rapped on

the glass. 'You know, you never read me my rights. Plus you took my cell phone so I can't call an attorney. Man, are you guys in trouble.'

She heard no answer.

Her breasts were starting to ache again, the cow in desperate need of milking, but no way was she going to pull up her shirt in view of that one-way mirror. She rapped again, harder. Feeling fearless now, because she knew these were government guys who were just taking their sweet time, trying to intimidate her. She knew her rights; as a cop, she'd wasted too much effort ensuring the rights of perps; she was damn well going to demand her own.

In the mirror, she confronted her own reflection. Her hair was a frizzy brown corona, her jaw a stubborn square. Take a good look, guys, she thought. Whoever you are behind that glass, you are now seeing one pissed-off cop who is getting less and less cooperative.

'Hey!' she shouted and slapped the glass.

Suddenly the door swung open, and she was surprised to see a woman step into the room. Though the woman's face was still youthful, no older than fifty, her hair had already turned a sleek silver, a startling contrast to her dark eyes. Like her male colleagues, she too was wearing a conservative suit, the attire of choice for women who must function in a man's profession.

'Detective Rizzoli,' the woman said. 'I'm sorry you had to wait so long. I got here as soon as I could. DC traffic, you know.' She held out her hand. 'I'm glad to finally meet you.'

Jane ignored the offered handshake, her gaze fixed on the woman's face. 'Should I know you?'

'Helen Glasser. Department of Justice. And yes, I agree, you have every right to be pissed off.' Again she held out her hand, a second attempt to call a truce.

This time Jane shook it, and felt a grasp as firm as any man's. 'Where's my husband?' she asked.

'He'll be joining us upstairs. I wanted a chance to make peace with you first, before we all get down to business. What happened this evening was just a misunderstanding.'

'What happened was a violation of our rights.'

Glasser gestured toward the doorway. 'Please, let's go upstairs, and we'll talk about it.'

They walked down the hall to an elevator, where Glasser inserted a coded key card and pressed the button for the top floor. One ride took them straight from the doghouse to the penthouse. The elevator slid open, and they walked into a room with large windows and a view of the city of Reston. The room was furnished with the undistinguished taste so typical of government offices. Jane saw a gray couch and armchairs grouped around a bland kilim rug, a side table with a coffee urn and a tray of cups and saucers. On one wall was the lone piece of decorative art, an abstract painting of a fuzzy orange ball. Hang that in a police station, she thought, and you could be sure some smart-ass cop would draw in a bull's-eye.

The whine of the elevator made her turn, and she saw Gabriel step out. 'Are you okay?' he asked.

'Wasn't too crazy about those electric shocks. But yeah, I'm . . .' She paused, startled to recognize the man who had just stepped off the elevator behind Gabriel. The man whose face she had just glimpsed that afternoon in the crime scene videotape.

John Barsanti tipped his head. 'Detective Rizzoli.'

Jane looked at her husband. 'Do *you* know what's going on?'

'Let's all sit down,' said Glasser. 'It's time to get a few wires uncrossed.'

Jane settled warily on the couch beside Gabriel. No one spoke as Glasser poured coffee and passed around the cups. After the treatment they'd endured earlier that evening, it was a belated gesture of civility, and Jane was not ready to surrender her well-earned anger in exchange for a mere smile and a cup of coffee. She did not take even a sip, but set the cup down in a silent rebuff to this woman's attempts at a truce.

'Do we get to ask questions?' Jane asked. 'Or will this be a one-way interrogation?'

'I wish we *could* answer all your questions. But we have an active investigation to protect,' said Glasser. 'It's no reflection on you. We've done background checks on you and Agent Dean.

You've both distinguished yourselves as fine law enforcement officers.'

'Yet you don't trust us.'

Glasser shot her a look as steely as the color of her hair. 'We can't afford to trust anyone. Not on a matter this sensitive. Agent Barsanti and I have tried our best to keep our work quiet, but every move we make has been tracked. Our computers have been quietly accessed, my office was broken into, and I'm not sure my phone is secure. Someone is tunneling into our investigation.' She set down her coffee cup. 'Now I need to know what *you're* doing here, and why you went to that house.'

'Probably for the same reason you had it under surveillance.'

'You know what happened there.'

'We've seen Detective Wardlaw's files.'

'You're a long way from home. What's your interest in the Ashburn case?'

'Why don't you answer a question for us first,' said Jane. 'Why is the Justice Department so interested in the deaths of five prostitutes?'

Glasser was silent, her expression unreadable. Calmly she took a sip from her coffee cup, as though the question had not even been asked of her. Jane could not help but feel a stab of admiration for this woman, who had yet to show even a glimpse of vulnerability. Clearly Glasser was the one in command here.

'You're aware that the victims' identities have never been established,' said Glasser.

'Yes.'

'We believe they were undocumented aliens. We're trying to find out how they got into the country. Who brought them in, and which routes they took to penetrate our borders.'

'Are you going to tell us this is all about national security?' Jane could not keep the skepticism out of her voice.

'That's only part of it. Ever since September eleventh, Americans just assume that we've tightened our borders, that we've clamped down on illegal immigration. That's hardly the case. The illicit traffic moving between Mexico and the US is still as busy as a major highway. We have miles and miles of unmonitored coastline. A Canadian border that's scarcely patrolled. And human smugglers know all the routes, all the tricks. Shipping in girls is easy. And once they've brought them here, it's not hard to put them to work.' Glasser set her cup on the coffee table. She leaned forward, her eyes like polished ebony. 'Do you know how many involuntary sex workers we have in this country? Our so-called civilized country? At least fifty thousand. I'm not talking about prostitutes. These are slaves, serving against their will. Thousands of girls brought into the US where they simply vanish. They become invisible women. Yet they're all around us, in big cities, small towns. Hidden in brothels, locked into apartments. And few people know they even exist.'

Jane remembered the bars on the windows,

341

and thought of the isolation of that house. No wonder it had made her think of a prison; *that's exactly what it was.*

'These girls are terrified of cooperating with authorities. The consequences, if they're caught by their pimps, is too horrible. And even if the girls do escape, and they do make it back to their home countries, they can still be tracked down there. They're better off dead.' She paused. 'You saw the autopsy report on victim number five. The older one.'

Jane swallowed. 'Yes.'

'What happened to her was a very clear message. *Fuck with us, and you end up like this.* We don't know what she did to make them angry, what line she stepped over. Maybe she pocketed money that wasn't hers. Maybe she was doing business on the side. Clearly, she was the matron of that house, in a position of authority, but it didn't save her. Whatever she did wrong, she paid for it. And the girls paid with her.'

'So your investigation isn't about terrorism at all,' said Gabriel.

'What would terrorism have to do with this?' Barsanti asked.

'Undocumented aliens coming in from eastern Europe. The possibility of a Chechen connection.'

'These women were brought into the country purely for commerce, and not for any other reason.'

Glasser frowned at Gabriel. 'Who mentioned terrorism to you?'

'Senator Conway did. As well as the deputy director of National Intelligence.'

'David Silver?'

'He flew up to Boston in response to the hostage crisis. That's what they believed they were dealing with at the time. A Chechen terrorist threat.'

Glasser snorted. 'David Silver is fixated on terrorists, Agent Dean. He sees them under every bridge and overpass.'

'He said the concern went all the way to the top. That's why Director Wynne sent him.'

'That's what the DNI is paid to think about. It's how he justifies his existence. For these people, it's *all terrorism, all the time.*'

'Senator Conway seemed concerned about it as well.'

'You trust the senator?'

'Shouldn't I?'

Barsanti said, 'You've had dealings with Conway, haven't you?'

'Senator Conway's on the intelligence committee. We met a number of times, about my work in Bosnia. The war crimes investigations.'

'But how well do you actually *know* him, Agent Dean?'

'You're implying that I don't.'

'He's been a senator for three terms,' said Glasser. 'To last that long, you have to make a lot of deals, a lot of compromises along the way. Be careful whom you trust. That's all we're saying. We learned that lesson a long time ago.'

'So terrorism isn't what concerns you here,' said Jane.

'My concern is fifty thousand vanished women. It's about slavery within our borders. It's about human beings abused and exploited by clients who only care about getting a good fuck.' She paused and took a deep breath. 'That's what this is all about,' she finished quietly.

'This sounds like a personal crusade for you.'

Glasser nodded. 'It has been for almost four years.'

'Then why didn't you save those women in Ashburn? You must have known what was going on in that house.'

Glasser said nothing; she didn't have to. Her stricken look confirmed what Jane had already guessed.

Jane looked at Barsanti. 'That's why you showed up at the crime scene so quickly. Practically at the same time the police did. You already knew what was going on there. You must have.'

'We'd gotten the tip only a few days before,' said Barsanti.

'And you didn't immediately step in? You didn't rescue those women?'

'We had no listening devices in place yet. No way to monitor what was really happening inside.'

'Yet you knew it was a brothel. You knew they were trapped in there.'

'There was more at stake than you realize,' said Glasser. 'Far more than just those five women. We had a larger investigation to protect, and if we stepped in too early, we would have blown our chances of secrecy.'

'And now five women are dead.'

'You think I don't *know* that?' Glasser's anguished response startled them all. Abruptly, she rose to her feet and paced over to the window, where she stood gazing out at the city lights. 'Do you know what the worst export our country ever sent to Russia was? The one thing we gave them that I wish to God had never been made? That movie, *Pretty Woman*. You know, the one with Julia Roberts. The prostitute as Cinderella. In Russia, they love that movie. The girls see it and think: If I go to America, I'll meet Richard Gere. He'll marry me, I'll be rich, and I'll live happily ever after. So even if the girl's suspicious, even if she's not sure a legitimate job's really waiting for her in the US, she figures she'll only have to turn a few tricks, and then Richard Gere will show up to rescue her. So the girl gets put on a flight, say, to Mexico City. From there, she travels by boat to San Diego. Or the traffickers drive her through a busy border crossing, and if she's blond and speaks English, she'll get waved right through. Or sometimes, they'll just walk her across. She thinks she's coming to live the life of *Pretty Woman*. Instead, she's bought and sold like a side of beef.' Glasser turned and looked at Jane. 'Do you know what a nice-looking girl can earn for a pimp?'

Jane shook her head.

'Thirty thousand dollars a week. A *week*.' Glasser's gaze turned back to the window. 'There aren't any mansions with Richard Gere waiting to marry you. You end up locked in a house or apartment, supervised by the real monsters in the business. The people who train you, enforce discipline, crush your spirit. Other women.'

'Jane Doe number five,' said Gabriel.

Glasser nodded. 'The house mother. So to speak.'

'Killed by the same people she worked for?' said Jane.

'When you swim with sharks, you're bound to get bitten.'

Or, in this case, have your hands crushed, the bones pulverized, thought Jane. Punishment for some trespass, some betrayal.

'Five women died in that house,' said Glasser. 'But there are fifty thousand other lost souls out there, trapped in the land of the free. Abused by men who just want sex and don't give a damn if the whore is sobbing. Men who never spare a thought for the human being they just used. Maybe the man goes home to the wife and kids, plays the good husband. But days or weeks later, he's back at the brothel, to fuck some girl who may be his daughter's age. And it never occurs to him, every morning when he looks in the mirror, that he's staring at a monster.' Glasser's voice had dropped to a tight whisper. She took a deep breath, and rubbed the back of her neck, as though massaging away the rage.

'Who was Olena?' Jane asked.

'Her full name? We'll probably never know it.'

Jane looked at Barsanti. 'You followed her all the way to Boston, and you never even knew her name?'

'But we knew something else about her,' said Barsanti. 'We knew she was a witness. She was in that house, in Ashburn.'

This is it, thought Jane. The link between Ashburn and Boston. 'How do you know?' she asked.

'Fingerprints. The crime scene unit collected literally dozens of unidentified prints in that house. Prints that didn't match any of the victims. Some of them may have been left by male clients. But one set of unidentifieds matched Olena's.'

'Wait a minute,' said Gabriel. 'Boston PD immediately requested an AFIS search on Olena's prints. They got back absolutely no matches. Yet you're telling me her prints were found at a crime scene in January? Why didn't AFIS gives us that information?'

Glasser and Barsanti glanced at each other. An uneasy look that only too clearly answered Gabriel's question.

'You kept her prints out of AFIS,' said Gabriel.

'That was information Boston PD could have used.'

'Other parties could have used it as well,' said Barsanti.

'Who the hell are these *others* you talk about?' cut in Jane. 'I was the one trapped in the hospital with that woman. I was the one with a gun to my head. Did you ever give a damn about the hostages?'

'Of course we did,' said Glasser. 'But we wanted *everyone* out of there alive. Including Olena.'

'Especially Olena,' said Jane. 'Since she was your witness.'

Glasser nodded. 'She saw what happened in Ashburn. That's why those two men showed up in her hospital room.'

'Who sent them?'

'We don't know.'

'You have the fingerprints on the man she shot. Who was he?'

'We don't know that, either. If he was ex-military, the Pentagon isn't telling us.'

'You're with Justice. And *you* can't get access to that information?'

Glasser crossed toward Jane and sat down in a chair, looking at her. 'Now you understand the hurdles we're facing. Agent Barsanti and I have had to handle this quietly and discreetly. We've stayed under the radar, because *they* were looking for her, too. We were hoping to find her first. And we came so close. From Baltimore to

Connecticut to Boston, Agent Barsanti has been just one step behind her.'

'How were you able to track her?' asked Gabriel.

'For a while it was easy. We just followed the trail left by Joseph Roke's credit card. His ATM withdrawals.'

Barsanti said, 'I kept reaching out to him. Voice mails on his cell phone. I even left a message with an old aunt of his in Pennsylvania. Finally Roke called me back, and I tried to talk him into coming in. But he wouldn't trust me. Then he shot that policeman in New Haven, and we lost track of them entirely. That's when I think they split up.'

'How did you know they were traveling together?'

'The night of the Ashburn slayings,' said Glasser, 'Joseph Roke bought gas at a nearby service station. He used his credit card, then asked the clerk if the station had a tow truck, because he'd picked up two women on the road who needed help with their car.'

There was a silence. Gabriel and Jane looked at each other.

'*Two* women?' said Jane.

Glasser nodded. 'The station's security camera caught a view of Roke's car while it was parked at the pump. Through the windshield, you can see there's a woman sitting in the front seat. It's Olena. That's the night their lives intersected, the night Joseph Roke got involved. The minute he invited those women into his car, into his life, he was a marked man. Five hours after that stop at the service station, his house went up in flames. That's when he surely realized he'd picked up a whole hell of a lot of trouble.'

'And the second woman? You said he picked up two women on the road.'

'We don't know anything about her. Only that she was still traveling with them as far as New Haven. That was two months ago.'

'You're talking about the cruiser video. The shooting of that police officer.'

'On the video, you can see a head pop up from Roke's backseat. Just the back of the head – we've never seen her face. Which leaves us with almost no information on her at all. Just a few strands of red hair left on the seat. For all we know, she's dead.'

'But if she's alive,' said Barsanti, 'then she's our last witness. The only one left who saw what happened in Ashburn.'

Jane said, softly: 'I can tell you her name.'

Glasser frowned at her. 'What?'

'That's the dream.' Jane looked at Gabriel. 'That's what Olena says to me.'

'She's been having a nightmare,' said Gabriel. 'About the takedown.'

'And what happens in the dream?' Glasser asked, her gaze riveted on Jane.

Jane swallowed. 'I hear men pounding on the door, breaking into the room. And she leans over me. To tell me something.'

'Olena does?'

'Yes. She says: "Mila knows." That's all she tells me. "Mila knows." '

Glasser stared at her. 'Mila *knows*? Present tense?' She looked at Barsanti. 'Our witness is still alive.'

Twenty-nine

'I'm surprised you're here, Dr. Isles,' said Peter Lukas. 'Since I haven't been able to reach you on the phone.' He gave her a quick handshake, a greeting that was justifiably cool and business-like; Maura had not been returning his calls. He led her through the *Boston Tribune* lobby to the security desk, where the guard handed Maura an orange visitor's badge.

'You'll have to return that when you leave, ma'am,' the guard said.

'And you'd better,' added Lukas, 'or this man will hunt you down like a dog.'

'Warning noted,' said Maura, clipping the badge to her blouse. 'You have better security here than the Pentagon.'

'You have any idea how many people a newspaper pisses off every day?' He pressed the elevator call button and glanced at her unsmiling face. 'Uh-oh. I think you must be one of them. Is that why you haven't called me back?'

'A number of people were unhappy with that column you wrote about me.'

'Unhappy with you or with me?'

'With me.'

'Did I misquote you? Misrepresent you?'

She hesitated. Admitted, 'No.'

'Then why are you annoyed with me? Because you clearly are.'

She looked at him. 'I spoke too frankly with you. I shouldn't have.'

'Well, I enjoyed interviewing a woman who speaks frankly,' he said. 'It was a nice change.'

'Do you know how many calls I got? About my theory of Christ's resurrection?'

'Oh. That.'

'From as far away as Florida. People upset by my blasphemy.'

'You only spoke your mind.'

'When you have a public job like mine, it's sometimes a dangerous thing to do.'

'It goes with the territory, Dr. Isles. You're a public figure, and if you say something interesting, it gets into print. At least you *had* something interesting to say, unlike most people I interview.'

The elevator door opened, and they stepped in. Alone together, she was acutely aware that he was watching her. That he was standing uncomfortably close.

'So why have you been calling me?' she asked. 'Are you trying to get me into more trouble?'

'I wanted to know about the autopsies on Joe and Olena. You never released a report.'

'I never completed the postmortem. The bodies were transferred to the FBI labs.'

'But your office did have temporary custody. I can't believe you'd just let bodies sit in your cold room without performing some kind of examination. It wouldn't be in your character.'

'What, exactly, is my character?' She looked at him.

'Curious. Exacting.' He smiled. 'Tenacious.'

'Like you?'

'Tenacity is getting me absolutely nowhere with you. And here I thought we could be friends. Not that I was expecting any special favors.'

'What do you expect from me?'

'Dinner? Dancing? Cocktails, at the very least?'

'Are you serious?'

He answered her question with a sheepish shrug. 'No harm in trying.'

The elevator opened and they stepped out.

'She died of gunshot wounds to the flank and the head,' said Maura. 'I think that's what you wanted to know.'

'How many wounds? How many different shooters?'

'You want all the gory details?'

'I want to be accurate. That means going directly to the source, even if I have to make a nuisance of myself.'

They walked into the newsroom, past reporters tapping at keyboards, to a desk where every horizontal square inch was covered with files and Post-it notes. Not a single photo of a kid or a woman or even a dog was displayed here. This space was purely for work, although she wondered how much work anyone could actually do, surrounded by such clutter.

He commandeered an extra chair from his neighbor's desk and rolled it over for Maura to sit in. It gave a noisy squeak as she settled into it.

'So you won't return my calls,' he said, sitting down as well. 'But you *do* come by to see me at work. Does this qualify as a mixed message?'

'This case has gotten complicated.'

'And now you need something from me.'

'We're all trying to understand what happened that night. And why it happened.'

'If you had any questions for me, all you had to do was pick up the phone.' He pinned her with a look. 'I would have returned *your* calls, Dr. Isles.'

They fell silent. At other desks, phones rang and keyboards clacked, but Maura and Lukas just looked at each other, the air between them spiked with both irritation and something else, something she didn't want to acknowledge. A strong whiff of mutual attraction. *Or am I just imagining it?*

'I'm sorry,' he finally said. 'I'm being a jerk. I mean, you *are* here. Even if it's for your own purposes.'

'You have to understand my position, too,' she said. 'As a public official, I get calls all the time from reporters. Some of them – many of them – don't care about victims' privacy or grieving families or whether investigations are at risk. I've learned to be cautious and watch what I say. Because I've been burned too many times by reporters who swear that my comments will stay off the record.'

'So that's what kept you from calling? Professional discretion?'

'Yes.'

'There's no other reason you didn't call me back?'

'What other reason would there be?'

'I don't know. I thought maybe you didn't like me.' His gaze was so intent, she had trouble keeping eye contact. He made her that uncomfortable.

'I don't dislike you, Mr. Lukas.'

'Ouch. Now I fully appreciate what it means to be damned with faint praise.'

'I thought reporters had thicker skin.'

'We all want to be liked, especially by people we admire.' He leaned closer. 'And by the way, it's not Mr. Lukas. It's Peter.'

Another silence, because she didn't know if this was flirtation or manipulation. For this man, it might amount to the same thing.

'That went over like a lead balloon,' he said.

'It's nice to be flattered, but I'd rather you just be straightforward.'

'I thought I *was* being straightforward.'

'You want information from me. I want the

same from you. I just didn't want to talk about it over the phone.'

He gave a nod of understanding. 'Okay. So this is just a simple transaction.'

'What I need to know is—'

'We're getting right to business? I can't even offer you a cup of coffee first?' He rose from the chair and crossed toward the community coffeepot.

Glancing at the carafe, she saw only tar-black dregs, and said quickly, 'None for me, thank you.'

He poured a cup for himself and sat back down. 'So what's with the reluctance to discuss this over the phone?'

'Things have been . . . happening.'

'Things? Are you telling me you don't even trust your own telephone?'

'As I told you, the case is complicated.'

'Federal intervention. Confiscated ballistics evidence. FBI in a tug-of-war with the Pentagon. A hostage taker who still remains unidentified.' He laughed. 'Yeah, I'd say it's gotten *very* complicated.'

'You know all this.'

'That's why they call us reporters.'

'Who have you been talking to?'

'Do you really think I'm going to answer that question? Let's just say I have friends in law enforcement. And I have theories.'

'About what?'

'Joseph Roke and Olena. And what that hostage taking was really all about.'

'No one really knows that answer.'

'But I know what law enforcement is thinking. I know what *their* theories are.' He set down his coffee cup. 'John Barsanti spent about three hours with me, did you know that? Picking and probing, trying to find out why I was the only reporter Joseph Roke wanted to talk to. Funny thing about interrogations. The person being interrogated can glean a lot of information just by the questions they ask you. I know that two months ago, Olena and Joe were together in New Haven, where he killed a cop. Maybe they were lovers, maybe just fellow delusionals, but after an incident like that, they'd want to split up. At least, they would if they were smart, and I don't think these were dumb people. But they must have had a way to stay in contact. A way to regroup if they needed to. And they chose Boston as the place to meet.'

'Why Boston?'

His gaze was so direct she could not avoid it. 'You're looking at the reason.'

'You?'

'I'm not being egotistical here. I'm just telling you what Barsanti seems to think. That Joe and Olena somehow identified me as their crusading hero. That they came to Boston to see me.'

'And that leads to the question I came here to ask.' She leaned toward him. 'Why you? They didn't pick your name out of a hat. Joe may have been mentally unstable, but he was intelligent. An obsessive reader of newspapers and magazines. Something you wrote must have caught his eye.'

'I know the answer to that one. Barsanti essentially spilled the beans when he asked about a column I wrote back in early June. About the Ballentree Company.'

They both fell silent as another reporter walked past, on her way to the coffeepot. While they waited for her to pour her cup, their gazes remained locked on each other. Only when the woman was once again out of earshot did Maura say: 'Show me the column.'

'It'll be on LexisNexis. Let me call it up.' He swiveled around to his computer and called up the LexisNexis news search engine, typed in his name, and hit search.

The screen filled with entries.

'Let me find the right date,' he said, scrolling down the page.

'This is everything you've ever written?'

'Yeah, probably going all the way back to my Bigfoot days.'

'Excuse me?'

'When I got out of journalism school, I had a ton of student loans to pay off. Took every writing gig I could get, including an assignment to cover a Bigfoot convention out in California.' He looked at her. 'I admit it, I was a news whore. But I had bills to pay.'

'And now you're respectable?'

'Well, I wouldn't go *that* far . . .' He paused, clicked on an entry. 'Okay, here's the column,' he said and rose to his feet, offering her his chair. 'That's what I wrote back in June, about Ballentree.'

She settled into his just-vacated seat and focused on the text now glowing on the screen.

War is Profit: Business Booming for Ballentree
While the US economy sags, there's one sector that's still raking in big profits. Mega defense contractor Ballentree is reeling in new deals like fish from their private trout pond . . .

'Needless to say,' said Lukas, 'Ballentree was none too happy about that piece. But I'm not the only one who's writing these things. The same criticism has been leveled by other reporters.'

'Yet Joe chose you.'

'Maybe it was the timing. Maybe he just happened to pick up a *Tribune* that day, and there was my column about big bad Ballentree.'

'Can I look at what else you've written?'

'Be my guest.'

She returned to the list of his articles on the LexisNexis page.

'You're prolific.'

'I've been writing for over twenty years, covering everything from gang warfare to gay marriage.'

'And Bigfoot.'

'Don't remind me.'

She scrolled down the first and second pages of entries, then moved onto the third page. There she paused. 'These articles were filed from Washington.'

'I think I told you. I was the *Tribune*'s Washington correspondent. Only lasted for two years there.'

'Why?'

'I hated DC. And I admit, I'm a born Yankee. Call me a masochist, but I missed the winters up here, so I moved back to Boston in February.'

'What was your beat in DC?'

'Everything. Features. Politics, crime beat.' He paused. 'A cynic might say there's no difference between the last two. I'd as soon cover a good juicy murder than chase after some blow-dried senator all day.'

She glanced back over her shoulder at him. 'Have you ever dealt with Senator Conway?'

'Of course. He's one of our senators. 'He paused. 'Why do you ask about Conway?' When she didn't answer, he leaned closer, his hands grasping the back of her chair. 'Dr. Isles,' he said, his voice suddenly quiet, whispering into her hair. 'You want to tell me what you're thinking?'

Her gaze was fixed on the screen. 'I'm just trying to make some connections here.'

'Are you getting the tingle?'

'What?'

'That's what I call it when I suddenly know I'm onto something interesting. Also known as ESP or Spidey sense. Tell me why Senator Conway makes you sit up and take notice.'

'He's on the intelligence committee.'

'I interviewed him back in November or December. The article's there somewhere.'

She scanned down the headlines, about Congressional hearings and terrorism alerts and a Massachusetts congressman arrested for drunk driving, and found the article about Senator Conway. Then her gaze strayed to a different headline, dated January 15.

Reston Man Found Dead Aboard Yacht. Businessman Missing Since January 2nd.

It was the date that she focused on. January 2nd. She clicked on the entry and the page filled with text. Only a moment before, Lukas had talked about *the tingle*. She was feeling it now.

She turned to look at him. 'Tell me about Charles Desmond.'

'What do you want to know about him?'

'Everything.'

Thirty

Who are you, Mila? Where are you?

Somewhere, there had to be a trace of her. Jane poured herself a fresh cup of coffee, then sat down at her kitchen table and surveyed all the files she had collected in the days since coming home from the hospital. Here were autopsy and Boston PD crime lab reports, Leesburg PD files on the Ashburn massacre, Moore's files on Joseph Roke and Olena. She had already combed these files several times, searching for a trace of Mila, the woman whose face no one knew. The only physical evidence that Mila had ever existed had come from the interior of Joseph Roke's car: several human head hairs, found on the backseat, which matched neither Roke's nor Olena's.

Jane took a sip of coffee, and reached once again for the file on Joseph Roke's abandoned car. She had learned to work around Regina's nap times, and now that her daughter was finally asleep, she wasted no time plunging back into the search for Mila. She scanned the list of items found in the vehicle, reviewing again the pathetic collection of his worldly possessions. There'd been a duffel bag full of dirty clothes and stolen towels from Motel Six. There'd been a bag of moldy bread and a jar of Skippy peanut butter and a dozen cans of Vienna sausages. The diet of a man who had no chance to cook. A man on the run.

She turned to the trace evidence reports and focused on the hair and fiber findings. It had been an extraordinarily filthy car, both the front and the back seats yielding up a large variety of fibers, both natural and man-made, as well as numerous hair strands. It was the hairs on the backseat that interested her, and she lingered over the report.

Human. A02/B00/C02 (7 cm)/D42

Scalp hair. Slightly curved, shaft is seven centimeters, pigment is medium red.

So far, this is all we know about you, thought Jane. You have short red hair.

She turned to the photographs of the car. She had seen these before, but once again, she studied the empty Red Bull soda cans and crumpled candy wrappers, the wadded-up blanket and dirty pillow. Her gaze paused on the tabloid newspaper lying on the backseat.

The *Weekly Confidential*.

Again, she was struck by how incongruous that newspaper was, in a man's car. Could Joe really have cared about what was troubling Melanie Griffith, or whose out-of-town husband was enjoying lap dances? The *Confidential* was a woman's tabloid; women *did* care about the woes of film stars.

She left the kitchen and peeked into her daughter's room. Regina was still asleep – one of those rare moments that would all too soon be over. Quietly she closed the nursery door, then slipped out of the apartment and headed up the hall to her neighbor's.

It took a few moments for Mrs. O'Brien to answer her door, but she was clearly delighted to have a visitor. Any visitor.

'I'm sorry to bother you,' said Jane.

'Come in, come in!'

'I can't stay. I left Regina in her crib, and—'

'How is she? I heard her crying again last night.'

'I'm sorry about that. She's not a good sleeper.'

Mrs. O'Brien leaned close and whispered. 'Brandy.'

'Excuse me?'

'On a pacifier. I did it with both my boys, and they slept like angels.'

Jane knew the woman's two sons. *Angels* was not a word that still applied to them. 'Mrs. O'Brien,' she said, before she had to listen to any more bad-mother tips, 'you subscribe to the *Weekly Confidential*, don't you?'

'I just got this week's issue. "Pampered Hollywood pets!" Did you know some hotels have special rooms just for your dog?'

'Do you still have any issues from last month?

365

I'm looking for the one with Melanie Griffith on the cover.'

'I know just the one you're talking about.' Mrs. O'Brien waved her into the apartment. Jane followed her into the living room and stared in amazement at tottering stacks of magazines piled on every horizontal surface. There had to be a decade's worth of *People* and *Entertainment Weekly* and *US* magazines.

Mrs. O'Brien went straight to the appropriate pile, rifled through the stack of *Confidentials*, and pulled out the issue with Melanie Griffith. 'Oh yes, I remember, this was a *good* one,' she said. ' "Plastic Surgery Disasters!" If you ever think about getting a face-lift, you'd better read this issue. It'll make you forget the whole thing.'

'Do you mind if I borrow it?'

'You'll bring it back, though?'

'Yes, of course. It's just for a day or two.'

'Because I *do* want it back. I like to reread them.'

She probably remembered every detail, too.

Back at her own kitchen table, Jane looked at the tabloid's issue date: July 20th. It had gone on sale only a week before Olena was pulled from Hingham Bay. She opened the *Confidential* and began to read. Found herself enjoying it even as she thought: God, this is trash, but it's *fun* trash. I had no idea *he* was gay, or that *she* hasn't had sex in four years. And what the hell was this craze about colonics, anyway? She paused to ogle the plastic surgery disasters, then moved on, past the fashion emergencies and 'I Saw Angels' and 'Courageous Cat Saves Family.' Had Joseph Roke lingered over the same gossip, the same celebrity fashions? Had he studied the faces disfigured by plastic surgeons and thought: *Not for me. I'll grow old gracefully?*

No, of course not. Joseph Roke wasn't a man who'd read this.

Then how did it end up in his car?

She turned to the classified ads on the last two pages. Here were columns of advertisements for psychic services and alternative healers and business opportunities at home. Did anyone actually answer these? Did anyone really think you could make 'up to $250 a day at home stuffing envelopes'? Halfway down the page, she came to the personal ads, and her gaze suddenly froze on a two-line ad. On four familiar words.

The Die Is Cast.

Beneath it was a time and date and a telephone number with a 617 area code. Boston.

The phrase could be just a coincidence, she thought. It could be two lovers arranging a furtive meeting. Or a drug pickup. Most likely it had nothing at all to do with Olena and Joe and Mila.

Heart thumping, she picked up the kitchen telephone and dialed the number in the ad. It rang. Three times, four times, five times. No answering machine picked up, and no voice came on the line. It just kept ringing until she lost count. *Maybe it's the phone of a dead woman.*

'Hello?' a man said.

She froze, her hand already poised to hang up. She snapped the receiver back to her ear.

'Is anyone there?' the man said, sounding impatient.

'Hello?' Jane said. 'Who is this?'

'Well, who's *this*? You're the one calling.'

'I'm sorry. I, uh, was given this number, but I didn't get a name.'

'Well, there's no name on this line,' the man said. 'It's a public pay phone.'

'Where are you?'

'Faneuil Hall. I was just walking by when I heard it ringing. So if you're looking for someone in particular, I can't help you. Bye.' He hung up.

She stared down again at the ad. At those four words.

The Die Is Cast.

Once again, she reached for the phone and dialed.

'*Weekly Confidential*,' a woman answered. 'Classifieds.'

'Hello,' said Jane. 'I'd like to place an ad.'

'You should have talked to me first,' said Gabriel. 'I can't believe you just did this on your own.'

'There was no time to call you,' said Jane. 'Their deadline for ads was five P.M. today. I had to make a decision right then and there.'

'You don't know who's going to respond. And now your cell phone number will be in print.'

'The worst that can happen is I'll get a few crank calls, that's all.'

'Or you get sucked into something a lot more dangerous than we realize.' Gabriel tossed the tabloid down on the kitchen table. 'We have to set this up through Moore. Boston PD can screen and monitor the calls. This needs to be thought out first.' He looked at her. 'Cancel it, Jane.'

'I can't. I told you, it's too late.'

'Jesus. I run over to the field office for two hours, and come home to find my wife's playing *dialing for danger* in our kitchen.'

'Gabriel, it's only a two-line ad in the personals. Either someone calls me back, or no one takes the bait.'

'What if someone does?'

'Then I'll let Moore handle it.'

'You'll *let* him?' Gabriel gave a laugh. 'This is his job, not yours. You're on maternity leave, remember?'

As if to emphasize the point, a loud wail suddenly erupted from the nursery. Jane went to retrieve her daughter, and found Regina had, as usual, kicked her way free of the blanket and was flailing her fists, outraged that her demands were not being instantly met. No one's happy with me today, thought Jane as she lifted Regina from the crib. She directed the baby's hungry mouth to her breast and winced as little gums clamped down. I'm trying to be a good mom, she thought, I really am, but I'm tired of smelling like sour milk and talcum powder. I'm tired of being tired.

I used to chase bad guys, you know.

She carried her baby into the kitchen and stood rocking from leg to leg, trying to keep Regina content, even as her own temper was about to combust.

'Even if I could, I wouldn't cancel the ad anyway,' she said defiantly. She watched as Gabriel crossed to the phone. 'Who are you calling?'

'Moore. He takes over from here.'

'It's my cell phone. My idea.'

'It's not your investigation.'

'I'm not saying I need to run the show. I gave them a specific time and date. How about we all sit together that night and wait to see who calls? You, me, and Moore. I just want to *be* there when it rings.'

'You need to back off on this, Jane.'

'I'm already part of this.'

'You have Regina. You're a mother.'

'But I'm not dead. Are you listening to me? I'm. Not. *Dead*.'

Her words seemed to hang in the air, her fury still reverberating like a clash of cymbals. Regina suddenly stopped suckling and opened her eyes to stare at her mother in astonishment. The refrigerator gave a rattle and went still.

'I never said you were,' Gabriel said quietly.

'But I might as well be, the way you talk. *Oh, you have Regina. You have a more important job now. You need to stay home and make milk and let your brain rot.* I'm a cop, and I need to go back to work. I *miss* it. I miss having my

370

goddamn beeper go off.' She took a breath and sat down at the kitchen table, her breath escaping in a sob of frustration. 'I'm a cop,' she whispered.

He sat down across from her. 'I know you are.'

'I don't think you do.' She wiped a hand across her face. 'You don't get who I am at all. You think you married someone else. Mrs. Perfect Mommy.'

'I know exactly who I married.'

'Reality's a bitch, ain't it? And so am I.'

'Well.' He nodded. 'Sometimes.'

'It's not like I didn't warn you.' She rose to her feet. Regina was still strangely quiet, still staring at Jane as though Mommy had suddenly become interesting enough to watch. 'You know who I am, and it's always been take it or leave it.' She started out of the kitchen.

'Jane.'

'Regina needs her diaper changed.'

'Damn it, you're running away from a fight.'

She turned back to him. 'I don't run from fights.'

'Then sit down with me. Because I'm not running from you, and I don't plan to.'

For a moment she just looked at him. And she thought: This is so hard. Being married is so hard and scary, and he's right about my wanting to run. All I really want to do is retreat to a place where no one can hurt me.

She pulled out the chair and sat down.

'Things *have* changed, you know,' he said. 'It's

not like before, when we didn't have Regina.'

She said nothing, still angry that he'd agreed she was a bitch. Even if it was true.

'Now if something happens to you, you're not the only one who gets hurt. You have a daughter. You have other people to think about.'

'I signed up for motherhood, not prison.'

'Are you saying you're sorry we had her?'

She looked down at Regina. Her daughter was staring up, wide-eyed, as though she understood every word being said. 'No, of course not. It's just . . .' She shook her head. 'I'm more than just her mother. I'm *me*, too. But I'm losing myself, Gabriel. Every day, I feel like I'm disappearing a little more. Like the Cheshire Cat in Wonderland. Every day it seems harder and harder to remember who I was. Then you come home and get ticked off at me for placing that ad. Which, you have to admit, is a *brilliant* idea. And I think: Okay, now I'm really lost. Even my own husband has forgotten who I am.'

He leaned forward, his gaze burning a hole in her. 'Do you know what it was like for me, when you were trapped in that hospital? Do you have any idea? You think you're so tough. You strap on a weapon and suddenly you're Wonder Woman. But if you get hurt, you're not the only one who bleeds, Jane. I do, too. Do you *ever* think of me?'

She said nothing.

He laughed, but it came out the sound of a wounded animal. 'Yeah, I'm a pain in the ass,

372

always trying to protect you from yourself. Someone has to do it, because you are your own worst enemy. You never stop trying to prove yourself. You're still Frankie Rizzoli's despised little sister. A *girl*. You're still not good enough for the boys to play with, and you never will be.'

She just stared back at him, resenting how well he knew her. Resenting the accuracy of his arrows, which had so cruelly hit their mark.

'Jane.' He reached across the table. Before she could pull away, his hand was on hers, holding on with no intention of releasing her. 'You don't need to prove yourself to me, or Frankie, or anyone else. I know it's hard for you right now, but you'll be back at work before you know it. So give the adrenaline a rest. Give *me* a rest. Let me enjoy just having my wife and daughter safe at home for a while.'

He still held her hand captive on the table. She looked down at their hands and thought: This man never wavers. No matter how hard I push against him, he is always right there for me. Whether I deserve him or not. Slowly their fingers linked in a silent armistice.

The phone rang.

Regina gave a wail.

'Well.' Gabriel sighed. 'That moment of peace didn't last long.' Shaking his head, he rose to answer the call. Jane was just carrying Regina out of the kitchen when she heard him say: 'You're right. Let's not talk about this on the phone.'

Instantly she was alert, turning to search his face for the reason his voice had suddenly dropped. But he was facing the wall, and she focused instead on the knotted muscles of his neck.

'We'll be waiting for you,' he said, and hung up.

'Who was that?'

'Maura. She's on her way over.'

Thirty-one

Maura did not show up at their apartment alone. Standing beside her in the hallway was an attractive man with dark hair and a trim beard. 'This is Peter Lukas,' she said.

Jane shot Maura an incredulous look. 'You brought a reporter?'

'We need him, Jane.'

'Since when do we ever need reporters?'

Lukas gave a cheery wave. 'Nice to meet you, too, Detective Rizzoli, Agent Dean. Can we come in?'

'No, let's not talk in here,' said Gabriel, as he and Jane, carrying Regina, stepped out into the hallway.

'Where are we going?' asked Lukas.

'Follow me.'

Gabriel led the way up two flights of stairs, and they emerged on the apartment rooftop. Here, the building's tenants had established an exuberant garden of potted plants, but the heat of a city summer and the baking surface of asphalt tiles was starting to wilt this oasis. Tomato plants drooped in their pots, and morning glory vines, their leaves scorched brown by the heat, clung like withering fingers to a trellis. Jane set Regina in her infant seat under the shade of the umbrella table, and the baby promptly dozed off, her cheeks a rosy pink. From this vantage point, they could see other rooftop gardens, other welcome patches of green in the concrete landscape.

Lukas placed a folder beside the sleeping baby. 'Dr. Isles thought you'd be interested in seeing this.'

Gabriel opened the folder. It contained a news clipping, with a photo of a man's smiling face and the headline: *Reston Man Found Dead Aboard Yacht. Businessman Missing Since January 2nd.*

'Who was Charles Desmond?' asked Gabriel.

'A man very few people really knew,' said Lukas. 'Which, in and of itself, was what intrigued me about him. It's the reason I focused on this story. Even though the medical examiner conveniently ruled it a suicide.'

'You question that ruling?'

'There's no way to prove it wasn't suicide. Desmond was found in the bathroom on his motor yacht, which he kept moored at a marina on the Potomac River. He died in the tub, with both his wrists slashed, and left a suicide note in the stateroom. By the time they found him, he'd been dead for about ten days. The medical examiner's office never released any photos, but, as you can imagine, it must have been quite a pleasant postmortem.'

Jane grimaced. 'I'd rather not imagine it.'

'The note he left wasn't particularly revelatory. *I'm depressed, life sucks, can't stand to live another day.* Desmond was known to be a heavy drinker, and he'd been divorced for five years. So it made sense that he'd be depressed. All sounds like a pretty convincing case for suicide, right?'

'Why don't you sound convinced?'

'I got that tingle. A reporter's sixth sense that there was something else going on, something that might lead to a bigger story. Here's this rich guy with a yacht, missing for ten days before someone thinks to go looking for him. The only reason they could pinpoint the date he went missing was the fact his car was found in the marina parking lot with January second stamped on the entry ticket. His neighbors said he traveled abroad so often, they weren't alarmed when they didn't see him for a week.'

'Traveled abroad?' said Jane. 'Why?'

'No one could tell me.'

'Or they wouldn't tell you?'

Lukas smiled. 'You've got a suspicious mind, Detective. So do I. It made me more and more curious about Desmond. Made me wonder if there was more to the story. You know, that's the way the Watergate story got started. A routine burglary case blows up into something much, much bigger.'

'What was big about this story?'

'Who the guy was. Charles Desmond.'

Jane looked at the photo of Desmond's face. He wore a pleasant smile, a neatly knotted tie. It was the sort of photo that might appear in any corporate report. The company executive, projecting competence.

'The more questions I asked about him, the more interesting stuff started to turn up. Charles Desmond never went to college. He served twenty years in the army, most of it working for military intelligence. Five years after he leaves the army, he owns a nice yacht and a big house in Reston. So now you have to ask the obvious question: What did he do to amass that huge bank account?'

'Your article here says that he worked for a company called Pyramid Services,' said Jane. 'What's that?'

'That's what I wondered. Took me a while to dig it up, but a few days later I learned that Pyramid Services is a subsidiary of guess which company?'

'Don't tell me,' said Jane. 'Ballentree.'

'You got it, Detective.'

Jane looked at Gabriel. 'That name just keeps popping up, doesn't it?'

'And look at the date he went missing,' said Maura. 'That's what caught my eye. January second.'

'The day before the Ashburn massacre.'

'An interesting coincidence, don't you think?'

Gabriel said, 'Tell us more about Pyramid.'

Lukas nodded. 'It's the transportation and security arm of Ballentree, part of the range of services they provide in war zones. Whatever our defense needs abroad – bodyguards, transport escorts, private police forces – Ballentree can do it for you. They'll go to work in parts of the world where there are no functioning governments.'

'War profiteers,' said Jane.

'Well, why not? There's a lot of money to be made in war. During the Kosovo conflict, Ballentree's private soldiers protected construction crews. They're now manning private police forces in Kabul and Baghdad and towns all around the Caspian Sea. All paid for by the US taxpayer. That's how Charles Desmond financed his yacht.'

'I'm working for the wrong damn police force,' said Jane. 'Maybe I should sign up for Kabul, and I could have a yacht, too.'

'You don't want to work for these people, Jane,' said Maura. 'Not when you hear what's involved.'

'You mean the fact they work in combat zones?'

'No,' said Lukas. 'The fact they're tied in with some pretty unsavory partners. Anytime you deal in a war zone, you're also making deals with the local mafia. It's merely practical to form partnerships, so local thugs end up working with companies like Ballentree. There's a black market trade in every commodity – drugs, arms, booze, women. Every war is an opportunity, a new market, and everyone wants in on the booty. That's why there's so much competition for defense contracts. Not just for the contracts themselves, but for the chance at the black market business that comes with it. Ballentree landed more deals last year than any other defense contractor.' He paused. 'Partly because Charles Desmond was so damn good at his job.'

'Which was?'

'He was their deal maker. A man with friends in the Pentagon, and probably friends in other places as well.'

'For all the good it did him,' said Jane, looking down at the photo of Desmond. A man whose corpse had lain undiscovered for ten days. A man so mysterious to his neighbors that no one had thought to immediately report him missing.

'The question is,' said Lukas, 'why did he have to die? Did those friends in the Pentagon turn on him? Or did someone else?'

For a moment, no one spoke. The heat made the rooftop shimmer like water, and from the street below rose the smell of exhaust, the rumble of traffic. Jane suddenly noticed that Regina was awake, and her eyes were fixed on Jane's face. *It's eerie, how much intelligence I see in my daughter's eyes.* From where she sat, Jane could see a woman sunning herself on another rooftop, her bikini top untied, her bare back glistening with oil. She saw a man standing on a balcony, talking on his cell phone, and a girl seated near a window, practicing her violin. Overhead, the white streak of a contrail marked the passage of a jet. How many people can see us? she wondered. How many cameras or satellites, at this moment, are trained on our rooftop? Boston had become a city of eyes.

'I'm sure this has crossed everyone's mind,' said Maura. 'Charles Desmond once worked in military intelligence. The man Olena shot in her hospital room was almost certainly ex-military, yet his prints have been scrubbed from the files. My office security has been breached. Are we all thinking about spooks here? Maybe even the Company?'

'Ballentree and the CIA have always gone hand in hand,' said Lukas. 'Not that it should surprise anyone. They work in the same countries, employ the same kind of guys. Trade on the same info.' He looked at Gabriel. 'And nowadays, they even pop up here, on home territory. Declare a terrorist threat, and the US government can justify any action, any expenditure. Untold funds get channeled into off-the-books programs. That's how people like Desmond end up with yachts.'

'Or end up dead,' said Jane.

The sun had shifted, its glare now slanting under the umbrella, onto Jane's shoulder. Sweat trickled down her breast. It's too hot for you up here, baby, she thought, looking down at Regina's pink face.

It's too hot for all of us.

Thirty-two

Detective Moore looked up at the clock as the time closed in on eight P.M. The last time Jane had sat in the homicide unit's conference room, she'd been nine months pregnant, weary and irritable and more than ready for maternity leave. Now she was back in the same room, with the same colleagues, but everything was different. The room felt charged, the tension winding tighter with each passing minute. She and Gabriel sat facing Moore; Detectives Frost and Crowe sat near the head of the table. At their center was the object of their attention: Jane's cell phone, connected to a speaker system. 'We're getting close,' Moore said. 'Are you still comfortable with this? We can have Frost take the calls.'

'No, I have to do it,' Jane said. 'If a man answers, it could scare her off.'

Crowe gave a shrug. 'If this mystery girl calls at all.'

'Since you seem to think this is such a big

waste of time,' snapped Jane, 'you don't have to hang around.'

'Oh, I'll stay just to see what happens.'

'We wouldn't want to bore you.'

'Three minutes, guys,' interjected Frost. Trying, as usual, to play peacemaker between Jane and Crowe.

'She may not even have seen the ad,' said Crowe.

'The issue's been on the stands for five days,' said Moore. 'She's had a chance to see it. If she doesn't call, then it's because she's chosen not to.'

Or she's dead, thought Jane. Something that surely crossed all their minds, though no one said it.

Jane's cell phone rang, and everyone's gaze instantly swung to her. The caller ID showed a number from Fort Lauderdale. This was merely a phone call, yet Jane's heart was pounding with a kick as powerful as fear.

She took a deep breath and looked at Moore, who nodded. 'Hello?' she answered.

A man's voice drawled over the speaker. 'So what's this all s'posed to be about, huh?' In the background was laughter, the sounds of people enjoying a jolly good joke.

'Who are you?' Jane asked.

'We're all just wondering here. What's it s'posed to mean? "The die is cast"?'

'You're calling to ask me that?'

'Yeah. This some kinda game? We s'posed to guess?'

383

'I don't have time to talk to you now. I'm waiting for another call.'

'Hey. Hey, lady! We're calling long distance, goddammit.'

Jane hung up and looked at Moore. 'What a jerk.'

'If that's your typical *Confidential* reader,' said Crowe, 'this is gonna be one hell of a fun night.'

'We're probably going to get a few more of those,' warned Moore.

The phone rang. This call was from Providence.

A fresh jolt of adrenaline had Jane's pulse racing once again. 'Hello?'

'Hi,' a female voice said brightly. 'I saw your ad in the *Confidential*, and I'm doing a research paper on personal ads. I wanted to know if yours is for the purpose of romance, or is this a commercial enterprise?'

'Neither,' snapped Jane, and disconnected. 'God, what is it with people?'

At 8:05, the phone again rang. A Newark caller, asking: 'Is this some kind of contest? Do I get a prize for calling?'

At 8:07: 'I just wanted to find out if someone would really answer this number.'

At 8:15: 'Are you, like, a spy or something?'

By 8:30, the calls finally stopped. For twenty minutes, they stared at a silent phone.

'I think that's it,' said Crowe, rising to his feet and stretching. 'I'd call that a *valuable* use of our evening.'

'Wait,' said Frost. 'We're coming up on central time.'

'What?'

'Rizzoli's ad didn't specify which time zone. It's almost eight P.M. in Kansas City.'

'He's right,' said Moore. 'Let's all sit tight here.'

'All time zones? We'll be here till midnight,' said Crowe.

'Even longer,' pointed out Frost. 'If you include Hawaii.'

Crowe snorted. 'Maybe we should bring in some pizza.'

In the end, they did. During the lull between ten and eleven P.M., Frost stepped out and returned with two large pepperonis from Domino's. They popped open cans of soda and passed around napkins and sat watching the silent phone. Though Jane had been away from her job for over a month, tonight it was almost as if she had never left. She was sitting around the same table, with the same tired cops, and as usual, Darren Crowe was annoying the hell out of her. Except for the fact Gabriel had joined the team, nothing had changed. I've missed it, she thought. Crowe and all. I've missed being part of the hunt.

The ringing phone caught her with a slice of pizza halfway to her mouth. She grabbed a napkin to wipe the grease from her fingers and glanced up at the clock. Eleven P.M. sharp. The caller ID display showed a Boston number. This call was three hours too late.

'Hello?' she answered.

Her greeting was met with silence.

'Hello?' Jane said again.

'Who are you?' It was a female voice, barely a whisper.

Startled, Jane looked at Gabriel and saw that he'd registered the same detail. *The caller has an accent.*

'I'm a friend,' said Jane.

'I don't know you.'

'Olena told me about you.'

'Olena is dead.'

It's her. Jane glanced around the table and saw stunned faces. Even Crowe had rocked forward, his face tense with anticipation.

'Mila,' said Jane. 'Tell me where we can meet. Please, I need to talk to you. I promise, it will be perfectly safe. Anywhere you want.' She heard the click of the receiver hanging up. '*Shit.*' Jane looked at Moore. 'We need her location!'

'You got it yet?' he asked Frost.

Frost hung up the conference room phone. 'West End. It's a pay phone.'

'On our way,' said Crowe, already out of his chair and headed toward the door.

'By the time you get there, she'll be long gone,' said Gabriel.

Moore said, 'A patrol car could be there in five minutes.'

Jane shook her head. 'No uniforms. She sees one, she'll know it's a setup. And I'll lose any chance of connecting with her again.'

'So what are you saying we should do?' said Crowe, pausing in the doorway.

'Give her a chance to think about it. She has my number. She knows how to reach me.'

'But she doesn't know who you are,' said Moore.

'And that's got to scare her. She's just playing it safe.'

'Look, she might never call back,' said Crowe. 'This could be our one and only chance to bring her in. Let's do it now.'

'He's right,' said Moore, looking at Jane. 'It could be our only chance.'

After a moment, Jane nodded. 'All right. Go.'

Frost and Crowe left the room. As the minutes passed, Jane stared at the silent phone, thinking: Maybe I should have gone with them. I should be the one out there, looking for her. She pictured Frost and Crowe navigating the warren of streets in the West End, searching for a woman whose face they didn't know.

Moore's cell phone rang and he snapped it up. Just by his expression, Jane could tell that the news was not good. He hung up and shook his head.

'She wasn't there?' said Jane.

'They've called in CSU to dust the pay phone for prints.' He saw the bitter disappointment in her face. 'Look, at least we now know she's real. She's alive.'

'For the moment,' said Jane.

*　*　*

Even cops needed to shop for milk and diapers.

Jane stood in the grocery store aisle, Regina snug against her chest in a baby sling, and wearily surveyed the cans of infant formula on the shelves, studying the nutritional contents of every brand. They all offered one hundred percent of a baby's daily needs from A to zinc. Any one of these would be perfectly adequate, she thought, so why am I feeling guilty? Regina *likes* formula. And I need to clip on my beeper and get back to work. I need to get off the couch and stop watching those reruns of *Cops*.

I need to get out of this grocery store.

She grabbed two six-packs of Similac, moved down another aisle for the Pampers, and headed to the cashier.

Outside, the parking lot was so hot she broke into a sweat just loading the groceries into her trunk. The seats could sear flesh; before strapping Regina into her infant seat, Jane paused with the doors open to air out the car. Grocery carts rattled by, pushed by perspiring shoppers. A horn honked, and a man yelled: 'Hey, watch where you're going, asshole!' None of these people wanted to be in the city right now. They all wanted to be at the beach holding ice cream cones, not trapped elbow to elbow with other cranky Bostonians.

Regina began to cry, her dark curls sweaty against her pink face. Yet another cranky Bostonian. She kept screaming as Jane leaned into the backseat and buckled her in, was still screaming blocks later as Jane inched through traffic, the AC going full blast. She hit another red light and thought: Lord, get me through this afternoon.

Her cell phone rang.

She could have just let it continue ringing, but she ended up fishing it out of her purse and saw on the display a local number that she did not recognize.

'Hello?' she answered.

Through Regina's angry wails, she could barely hear the question: 'Who are you?' The voice was soft and instantly familiar.

Jane's muscles all snapped taut. 'Mila? Don't hang up! Please don't hang up. Talk to me!'

'You are police.'

The traffic light turned green, and behind her, a car honked. 'Yes,' she admitted. 'I'm a policewoman. I'm only trying to help you.'

'How do you know my name?'

'I was with Olena when . . .'

'When the police killed her?'

The car behind Jane's blasted its horn again, an unrelenting demand that she get the hell out of its way. *Asshole*. She goosed the accelerator and drove through the intersection, the cell phone still pressed to her ear.

'Mila,' she said. 'Olena told me about you. It was the last thing she said – that I should find you.'

'Last night, you sent policemen to catch me.'

'I didn't send—'

389

'Two men. I saw them.'

'They're my friends, Mila. We're all trying to protect you. It's dangerous for you to be out there on your own.'

'You do not know how dangerous.'

'Yes I do!' She paused. 'I know why you're running, why you're scared. You were in that house when your friends were shot to death. Weren't you, Mila? You saw it happen.'

'I'm the only one left.'

'You could testify in court.'

'They will kill me first.'

'Who?'

There was silence. Please don't hang up again, she thought. Stay on the line. She spotted an open space at the curb and abruptly pulled over. Sat with the phone pressed to her ear, waiting for the woman to speak. In the backseat Regina kept crying and crying, angrier by the minute that her mother dared ignore her.

'Mila?'

'What baby is crying?'

'It's my baby. She's in the car with me.'

'But you said you are police.'

'Yes, I am. I *told* you I am. My name is Jane Rizzoli. I'm a detective. You can confirm that, Mila. Call the Boston Police Department and ask them about me. I was with Olena when she died. I was trapped in that building with her.' She paused. 'I couldn't save her.'

Another silence passed. The AC was still going full blast, and Regina was still crying, determined to make gray hairs pop out on her mother's brow.

'Public gardens,' said Mila.

'What?'

'Tonight. Nine o'clock. You wait by the pond.'

'Will you be there? Hello?'

No one was on the line.

Thirty-three

The weapon felt heavy and strangely unfamiliar on Jane's hip. Once an old friend, it had sat locked up and ignored in a drawer these past few weeks. Only reluctantly had she loaded it and snapped it into her holster. Though she'd always regarded her weapon with the healthy respect due any object that could blast a hole in a man's chest, never before had she hesitated to reach for it. This must be what motherhood does to you, she thought. I look at a gun now, and all I can think of is Regina. How one twitch of a finger, one wayward bullet, could take her from me.

'It doesn't have to be you,' said Gabriel.

They were sitting in Gabriel's parked Volvo on Newbury Street, where fashionable shops were preparing to close for the night. The Saturday restaurant crowd still lingered in the neighborhood, well-dressed couples strolling past, happily sated with dinner and wine. Unlike Jane, who'd been too nervous to eat more than a few bites of the pot roast her mother had brought to their apartment.

'They can send in another female cop,' said Gabriel. 'You can just sit this one out.'

'Mila knows my voice. She knows my name. I have to do it.'

'You've been out of the game for a month.'

'And it's time for me to get back in.' She looked at her watch. 'Four minutes,' she said into her comm unit. 'Is everyone ready?'

Over the earpiece, she heard Moore say: 'We're in place. Frost is at Beacon and Huntington. I'm in front of the Four Seasons.'

'And I'll be behind you,' said Gabriel.

'Okay.' She stepped out of the car and tugged down the light jacket she was wearing, so it would cover the bulge of her weapon. Walking up Newbury Street, heading west, she brushed past Saturday night tourists. People who did not need guns on their belts. At Arlington Street she paused to wait for traffic. Across the street were the public gardens, and to her left was Beacon Street, where Frost was posted, but she did not glance his way. Nor did she hazard a look over her shoulder, to confirm that Gabriel was behind her. She knew he was.

She crossed Arlington and strolled into the public gardens.

Newbury Street had been bustling, but here there were few tourists. A couple sat on a bench by the pond, arms wrapped around each other, heedless of anyone outside their own fevered universe. A man was hunched over a trash bin, picking out aluminum cans and dropping them into his clanking sack. Sprawled on the lawn, shadowed by trees from the glow of streetlights, a circle of kids took turns strumming a guitar. Jane paused at the pond's edge and scanned the shadows. *Is she here? Is she already watching me?*

No one approached her.

She made a slow circuit around the pond. During the day there would be swan boats gliding in the water, and families eating ice cream, and musicians pounding on bongo drums. But tonight the water was still, a black hole reflecting not even a shimmer of city lights. She continued to the north end of the pond and paused, listening to traffic along Beacon Street. Through the bushes she saw the silhouette of a man loitering beneath a tree. Barry Frost. She turned and continued her circle around the pond, and finally came to a halt beneath a streetlamp.

Here I am, Mila. Take a good long look at me. You can see that I'm alone.

After a moment, she settled onto a bench, feeling like the star of a one-woman stage play, with the lamplight shining down on her head. She felt eyes watching her, violating her privacy.

Something rattled behind her, and she jerked around, automatically reaching for her weapon. Her hand froze on the holster when she saw it was only the scruffy man with the trash bag of clanking aluminum cans. Heart pounding, she again settled back against the bench. A breeze blew through the park, rippling the pond, raking its surface with sequins of reflected light. The man with the cans dragged his bag to a trash receptacle beside her bench and began to poke through the rubbish. He took his time excavating treasure, each find announced by a cymbal's clash of aluminum. Would the man never go away? In frustration, she rose to her feet to escape him.

Her cell phone rang.

She thrust a hand in her pocket and snapped up the phone. 'Hello? *Hello?*'

Silence.

'I'm here,' she said. 'I'm sitting by the pond, where you told me to wait. Mila?'

She heard only the throb of her own heartbeat. The connection was dead.

She spun around and scanned the park, spotting only the same people she'd seen before. The couple necking on the bench, the kids with the guitar. And the man with the sack of cans. He was motionless, hunched over the trash receptacle, as though eyeing some minute jewel in the mound of newspapers and food wrappings.

He's been listening.

'Hey,' Jane said.

The man instantly straightened. He began to walk away, the sack of cans clanking behind him.

She started after him. 'I want to talk to you!'

The man did not look back, but kept walking.

Faster now, knowing that he was being pursued. She sprinted after him, and caught up just as he stepped onto the sidewalk. Grabbing the back of his windbreaker she yanked him around. Beneath the glare of the streetlight, they stared at each other. She saw sunken eyes and an unkempt beard streaked with gray. Smelled breath soured by alcohol and rotting teeth.

He batted away her hand. 'What're you doing? What the hell, lady?'

'Rizzoli?' Moore's voice barked over her earpiece. 'You need backup?'

'No. No, I'm okay.'

'Who ya talking to?' the bum said.

Angrily, she waved him off. 'Go. Just get out of here.'

'Who do you think you are, ordering me around?'

'Just *leave*.'

'Yeah, yeah.' He gave a snort and walked away, dragging his cans behind him. 'Park's full of crazy people these days . . .'

She turned, and suddenly realized that she was surrounded. Gabriel, Moore, and Frost had all moved within yards of her position, to form a protective circle around her. 'Oh man,' she sighed. 'Did I ask for help?'

'We didn't know what was going on,' said Gabriel.

'Now we've blown it.' She looked around the park, and it seemed emptier than ever. The couple on the bench was walking away; only the kids with the guitar remained, laughing in the shadows. 'If Mila's been watching, she knows it's a setup. There's no way she'll come near me.'

'It's nine forty-five,' said Frost. 'What do you think?'

Moore shook his head. 'Let's wrap it up. Nothing's going to happen tonight.'

'I was doing fine,' said Jane. 'I didn't need the cavalry.'

Gabriel pulled into his parking space behind their apartment building and shut off the engine. 'We didn't know what was happening. We saw you running after that man, and then it looked like he was taking a swing at you.'

'He was just trying to get away.'

'I didn't know that. All I thought was—' He stopped and looked at her. 'I just reacted. That's all.'

'We've probably lost her, you know.'

'Then we've lost her.'

'You sound like you don't even care.'

'You know what I care about? That you don't get hurt. That's more important than anything else.' He got out of the car; so did she.

'Do you happen to remember what I do for a living?' she asked.

'I'm trying not to.'

'Suddenly my job is not okay.'

He shut his car door and met her gaze over the roof. 'I admit it. I'm having trouble right now, dealing with it.'

'You're asking me to quit?'

'If I thought I could get away with it.'

'What am I supposed to do instead?'

'Here's a novel idea. You could stay home with Regina.'

'When did you go all retro on me? I can't believe you're saying this.'

He sighed and shook his head. 'I can't believe I'm saying it, either.'

'You knew who I was when you married me, Gabriel.' She turned and walked into the building, and was already climbing to the second floor when she heard him say, from the bottom of the stairs: 'But maybe I didn't know who *I* was.'

She glanced back at him. 'What does that mean?'

'You and Regina are all I have.' Slowly he came up the stairs, until they were face-to-face on the landing. 'I never had to worry about anyone else before, about what I could lose. I didn't know it would scare me so much. Now I've got this big exposed Achilles heel, and all I can think about is how to protect it.'

'You can't protect it,' she said. 'It's just something you have to live with. It's what happens when you have a family.'

'It's too much to lose.'

Their apartment door suddenly opened, and Angela poked her head into the hallway. 'I thought I heard you two out here.'

Jane turned. 'Hi, Mom.'

398

'I just put her down for the night, so keep your voices quiet.'

'How was she?'

'Exactly like you were at her age.'

'That bad, huh?' Stepping into the apartment, Jane was taken aback by how neat everything looked. The dishes were washed and put away, the countertops wiped clean. A lace doily graced the dining table. When had she ever owned a lace doily?

'You two had a fight, didn't you?' said Angela. 'I can tell just by looking at you.'

'We had a disappointing night, that's all.' Jane took off her jacket and hung it in the closet. When she turned back to look at her mother, she saw that Angela's gaze had focused on Jane's weapon.

'You're going to lock that thing up, aren't you?'

'I always do.'

'Because babies and guns—'

'Okay, okay.' Jane took off her weapon and slid it into a drawer. 'You know, she's not even a month old.'

'She's precocious, just like you were.' Angela looked at Gabriel. 'Did I ever tell you what Jane did when she was three?'

'Mom, he doesn't want to hear that story.'

'Yes I do,' said Gabriel.

Jane sighed. 'It involves a cigarette lighter and the living room curtains. And the Revere Fire Department.'

'Oh, that,' said Angela. 'I forgot all about *that* story.'

'Mrs. Rizzoli, why don't you tell me about it while I drive you home?' said Gabriel, reaching into the closet to retrieve Angela's sweater.

In the other room, Regina suddenly let out a howl to announce that she was not, in fact, down for the night. Jane went into the nursery and lifted her daughter out of the crib. When she came back into the living room, Gabriel and her mother had already left the apartment. Rocking Regina in one arm, she stood at the kitchen sink, running warm water into a pan to heat the milk bottle. The apartment's front door buzzer sounded.

'Janie?' Angela's voice crackled over the speaker. 'Can you let me back in? I forgot my glasses.'

'Come on up, Mom.' Jane pressed the lock release and was waiting at the door to hand over the glasses when her mother came up the stairs.

'Can't read without these,' said Angela. She paused to give her fussing granddaughter one last kiss. 'Better go. He's got the car running.'

'Bye, Mom.'

Jane went back into the kitchen, where the pan was now overflowing. She set the bottle in hot water, and as the formula warmed, she paced the room with her crying daughter.

The apartment door buzzed again.

Oh, Ma. What'd you forget this time? she wondered, and pressed the lock release.

By now the bottle was warm. She slipped the nipple into Regina's mouth, but her daughter simply batted it away, as though in disgust. What do you want, baby? she thought in frustration as she carried her daughter back into the living room. If you could just tell me what you want!

She opened the door to greet her mother.

It was not Angela standing there.

Thirty-four

Without a word, the girl slipped right past Jane, into the apartment, and locked the door. She scurried across to the windows and yanked the Venetian blinds shut, one after the other in quick succession, as Jane watched in astonishment.

'What do you think you're doing?'

The intruder spun around to face her, and pressed her finger to her lips. She was small, more a child than a woman, her thin frame almost lost in the bulky sweatshirt. The hands that poked out the faded sleeves had bones that looked as delicate as a bird's, and the bulging tote bag she carried seemed to drag down her frail shoulder. Her red hair was cut in a wildly uneven fringe, as though she herself had wielded the scissors, hacking blindly. Her eyes were pale, an unearthly shade of gray, transparent as glass. It was a hungry, feral face, with jutting cheekbones and a gaze that darted around the room in a search for hidden traps.

'Mila?' said Jane.

Again the girl's finger snapped up to her lips. The look she gave Jane needed no interpretation. *Be quiet. Be afraid.*

Even Regina seemed to understand. The baby suddenly went still, her eyes wide and alert as she lay quietly in Jane's arms.

'You're safe here,' Jane said.

'No place is safe.'

'Let me call my friends. We'll get you police protection right now.'

Mila shook her head.

'I know these men. I work with them.' Jane reached for the telephone.

The girl shot forward and slammed her hand down on the receiver. '*No police.*'

Jane stared into the girl's eyes, which were now burning with panic. 'Okay,' she murmured, backing away from the phone. 'I'm police, too. Why do you trust me?'

Mila's gaze dropped to Regina. And Jane thought: This is why she's risked this visit. She knows I'm a mother. Somehow that makes all the difference.

'I know why you're running,' said Jane. 'I know about Ashburn.'

Mila went to the couch and sank onto the cushions. Suddenly she seemed even smaller, wilting by the moment beneath Jane's gaze. Her shoulders crumpled forward. Her head drooped into her hands, as though she was too exhausted to hold it up any longer. 'I am so tired,' she whispered.

Jane moved closer until she was standing just above the bowed head, looking down at the raggedly cut hair. 'You saw the killers. Help us identify them.'

Mila looked up with hollow, haunted eyes. 'I will not live long enough.'

Jane dropped to a crouch, until their eyes were level. Regina too was staring at Mila, fascinated by this exotic new creature. 'Why are you here, Mila? What do you want me to do?'

Mila reached into the dirty tote bag she had carried in, and rummaged through wadded-up clothes and candy bars and crumpled tissues. She pulled out a videotape and held it out to Jane.

'What is this?'

'I am afraid to keep it anymore. I give it to you. You tell them there are no more. This is the last copy.'

'Where did you get it?'

'Just *take* it!' She held it at arm's length, as though it was poisonous, and she wanted to keep it as far away as possible. She breathed a sigh of relief when Jane finally took it from her.

Jane set Regina in her infant carrier, then crossed to the TV. She slipped the cassette into the VCR, and pressed PLAY on the remote control.

An image appeared on the screen. She saw a brass bed, a chair, heavy drapes covering a window. Off camera, footsteps creaked closer, and a woman giggled. A door clunked shut, and now a man and woman came into view. The woman had a sleek mane of blond hair, and her low-cut blouse revealed bountiful cleavage. The man was dressed in a polo shirt and khaki slacks.

'Oh yeah,' the man sighed as the woman unbuttoned her blouse. She wriggled out of her skirt, peeled down her underwear. She gave the man a playful shove onto the bed, and he flopped back, utterly passive, as she unbuckled his pants, pulled them down over his hips. Bending over him, she took his erect penis into her mouth.

It's just a porno tape, thought Jane. Why am I watching this?

'Not this one,' Mila said, and took the remote control from Jane's hand. She pressed FAST-FORWARD.

The blonde's head jerked back and forth, performing a blow job with manic efficiency. The screen went blank. Now another couple jittered into view. At her first glimpse of the woman's long black hair, Jane was stunned. It was Olena.

Clothing magically melted away. Nude bodies tumbled onto the bed, writhing in FAST-FORWARD on the mattress. I have seen this bedroom before, Jane suddenly realized, remembering the closet with the hole drilled through the wall. That's how this videotape was filmed – with a camera mounted in that closet. She realized, too, who the blond woman in the first clip was. She'd been Jane Doe number two in Detective Wardlaw's crime scene video, the woman who had died in her cot, cowering beneath a blanket.

All the women in this video are now dead.

Once again, the screen went blank.

'Here,' Mila said softly. She pressed STOP, then PLAY.

It was the same bed, the same room, but with different sheets this time: a floral pattern with mismatched pillowcases. An older man walked into view, balding with wire-rimmed glasses, dressed in a white button-down shirt and a red tie. He pulled off the tie and tossed it on the chair, then unbuttoned his shirt to reveal a pale belly, sagging with middle-age spread. Though he stood facing the camera, he did not seem aware of its presence, and he peeled off his shirt with an utter lack of self-consciousness, revealing to the camera an unflattering slouch. Suddenly he straightened, his attention swinging to something the camera could not yet see. It was a girl. Her cries preceded her, shrill protests in what sounded like Russian. She did not want to come into the room. Her sobs were cut off by a sharp slap, and a woman's stern command. Then the girl stumbled into view as though shoved, and she sprawled on the floor at the man's feet. The door slammed shut, followed by the clack of footsteps moving away.

The man looked down at the girl. Already an erection bulged in his gray trousers. 'Get up,' he said.

The girl did not move.

Again: 'Get up.' He gave her a nudge with his foot.

At last the girl raised her head. Slowly, as

though exhausted just by the pull of gravity, she struggled to her feet, blond hair disheveled.

Against her will, Jane was drawn closer to the TV. She was too appalled to look away, even as her rage mounted. The girl was not yet even a teenager. She was wearing a pink cropped blouse and a short denim skirt that exposed painfully thin legs. Her cheek still bore the angry red imprint of the woman's slap. Fading bruises on her bare arms told of other blows, other cruelties. Though the man towered over her, this frail girl now faced him with quiet defiance.

'Take off the blouse.'

The girl just looked at him.

'What, are you stupid? Don't you understand English?'

The girl's spine snapped straight, and her chin jutted up. *Yes, she does understand. And she's telling you to fuck off, asshole.*

The man stepped toward her, grabbed her blouse with both hands, and ripped it open, releasing a hail of loose buttons. The girl sucked in a startled breath and slapped him, sending his glasses flying. They clattered onto the floor. For a few seconds the man just stared at her in surprise. Then a look of such fury contorted his face that Jane flinched away from the TV, knowing what would happen next.

The blow landed on the girl's jaw, the impact so powerful that it seemed to lift her right off her feet. She slammed to the floor. He grabbed her around the waist, dragged her toward the bed, and threw her down on the mattress. With a few sharp tugs, he pulled off her skirt, then unbuckled his trousers.

Though the blow had temporarily stunned her, the girl was not finished fighting back. All at once she seemed to spring back to life, screaming, fists beating against him. He trapped her wrists and climbed on top of her, pinning her to the mattress. In his haste to maneuver himself between her thighs, he lost his grip on her right hand. She clawed at his face, and her nails scraped skin. He jerked back and touched his cheek where she had scratched him. Stared, disbelieving, at his fingers. At the blood she had drawn.

'You cunt. You little *cunt*.'

He slammed his fist into her temple. The thud made Jane flinch. Nausea soured her throat.

'I paid for you, goddammit!'

The girl shoved at his chest, but she was weaker now. Her left eye was swelling, and blood trickled from her lip, yet she continued to fight. Her struggles only seemed to excite him. Too feeble to resist, she could not stop the inevitable. As he thrust into her, she gave a scream.

'Shut up.'

She did not stop screaming.

'Shut up!' He hit her again. And again. Finally he clapped his hand over her mouth to stifle her cries as he repeatedly rammed into her. He did not seem to notice that she finally stopped screaming, or that she had fallen perfectly still. The only noise now was the rhythmic creak of the bed, and the animal grunts from his throat. He gave a final moan and his back arched in a spasm of release. Then, with a sigh, he collapsed onto the girl.

For a moment he lay breathing heavily, his body flaccid with exhaustion. Slowly, he seemed to register that something was not right. He looked down at her.

She was motionless.

He gave her a shake. 'Hey.' He patted her cheek, and a note of worry slipped into his voice. 'Wake up. Goddammit, you wake *up*.'

The girl did not move.

He rolled off the bed and stood staring down at her for a moment. He pressed his fingers to her neck to check her pulse. Every muscle in his body seemed to go taut. Backing away from the bed, his breathing accelerated in panic.

'Oh, Jesus,' he whispered.

He glanced around, as though the solution to his dilemma lay somewhere in the room. Frantic now, he snatched up his clothes and began to dress, hands shaking as he fumbled with buckles and buttons. He dropped to his knees to retrieve his glasses, which had slid under the bed, and slipped them on. One last time, he looked at the girl and confirmed his worst fears.

Shaking his head, he backed away, out of the camera's range. A door squealed open, swung shut, and footsteps hurried away. An eternity passed, the camera still focused on the bed with its lifeless occupant.

Different footsteps approached, and there was a knock on the door, a voice calling out in Russian. Jane recognized the woman who stepped into the room. It was the house mother, who had died while tied to a kitchen chair.

I know what happens to you. What they will do to your hands. I know you will die screaming.

The woman moved to the bed and gave the girl a shake. Barked out a command. The girl did not respond. The woman stepped back, her hand covering her mouth. Then, abruptly, she turned and stared directly at the camera.

She knows it's there. She knows it is filming.

At once she moved straight toward it, and there was the sound of the closet door swinging open. Then the screen went blank.

Mila turned off the VCR.

Jane could not speak. She sank onto the couch and sat in numb silence. Regina was silent as well, as though aware that this was not the time to fuss. That at this moment, her mother was too shaken to attend to her. Gabriel, she thought. I need you here. She glanced at the telephone and realized that he had left his cell phone on the table, and she had no way to reach him in his car.

'He is an important man,' Mila said.

Jane turned to look at her. 'What?'

'Joe says the man must be high in your government.' Mila pointed to the TV.

'Joe saw this tape?'

Mila nodded. 'He gave me a copy when I left. So we would all have one, in case . . .' She

410

stopped. 'In case we never see each other again,' she said softly.

'Where does it come from? Where did you get this video?'

'The Mother keeps it in her room. We didn't know. We only wanted the money.'

This is the reason for the massacre, thought Jane; this is why the women in that house were killed. Because they knew what happened in that room. And this videotape is the proof.

'Who is he?' Mila asked.

Jane stared at the blank TV. 'I don't know. But I know someone who might.' She crossed to the telephone.

Mila stared at her in alarm. 'No police!'

'I'm not calling the police. I'm going to ask a friend to come here. A reporter. He knows people in Washington. He's lived there. He'll know who that man is.' She flipped through the phone book until she found the listing for Peter Lukas. His address was in Milton, just south of Boston. As she dialed, she could feel Mila watching her, clearly not ready to trust her. If I make one false move, Jane thought, this girl will run. I have to be careful not to scare her.

'Hello?' said Peter Lukas.

'Could you come over right now?'

'Detective Rizzoli? What's going on?'

'I can't talk about it on the phone.'

'This sounds serious.'

'It could be your Pulitzer Prize, Lukas.' She stopped.

Someone was ringing her apartment buzzer.

Mila shot Jane a look of sheer panic. Snatching up her tote bag, she made a dash toward the windows.

'Wait. Mila, don't—'

'Rizzoli?' said Lukas. 'What's happening over there?'

'Hold on. I'll call you right back,' said Jane, and hung up.

Mila was darting from window to window, desperately searching for the fire escape.

'It's okay!' said Jane. 'Calm down.'

'They know I am here!'

'We don't even know who's at the door. Let's just find out.' She pressed the intercom button. 'Yes?'

'Detective Rizzoli, it's John Barsanti. Can I come up?'

Mila's reaction was instantaneous. She went sprinting toward the bedrooms, looking for an escape route.

'Wait!' Jane called, following her up the hall. 'You can trust this man!'

Already, the girl was lifting up the bedroom window.

'You can't leave.'

Again, they heard the apartment buzzer. It sent Mila scrambling through the window, onto the fire escape. If she leaves, I'll never see her again, thought Jane. *The girl has survived this long on sheer instinct. Maybe I should listen to her.*

She grabbed Mila's wrist. 'I'll come with you,

okay? We'll go together. Just don't leave without me!'

'Hurry,' Mila whispered.

Jane turned. 'The baby.'

Mila followed her back into the living room and kept a nervous eye on the door as Jane ejected the videotape and threw it into the diaper bag. Then she unlocked the gun drawer, took out her weapon, and slipped it into the diaper bag as well. *Just in case.*

The buzzer sounded again.

Jane swept Regina into her arms. 'Let's go.'

Mila scrambled down the fire escape ladder, quick as a monkey. Once, Jane would have been just as quick, just as reckless. But now she was forced to take care with every step, because she was holding Regina. *Poor baby, I have no choice now,* she thought. *I have to drag you along on this adventure.* At last she dropped to the alley, and led the way to her parked Subaru. As she unlocked the car door, she could still hear, through the open apartment window, Barsanti's persistent buzzing.

Driving west on Tremont Street, she kept her eye on the rearview mirror, but she saw no sign of pursuit, no headlights dogging them. *Now to find a secure location where Mila won't freak out,* she thought. *Where she won't see police uniforms. Above all, some place I can keep Regina perfectly safe.*

'Where do we go?' Mila asked.

'I'm thinking, I'm thinking.' She glanced down

at her cell phone, but now she did not dare call her mother. She did not dare call anyone.

Abruptly she turned south, onto Columbus Avenue. 'I know a safe place,' she said.

Thirty-five

Peter Lukas stared in silence as the brutal assault played out on his TV screen. When the tape at last ended, he did not move. Even after Jane turned off the VCR, Lukas sat frozen, his gaze fixed on the screen, as though he could still see the girl's battered body, the bloodstained sheets. The room had gone silent. Regina dozed on the couch; Mila stood near the windows, glancing out at the road.

'Mila never learned the girl's name,' said Jane. 'There's a good chance the body's buried some-where in the woods behind the house. It's a lonely spot, with a lot of places to dispose of a corpse. God knows how many other girls might be buried back there.'

Lukas dropped his head. 'I feel like throwing up.'

'You and me both.'

'Why would anyone videotape something like that?'

'This man clearly didn't realize he *was* caught

on film. The camera was mounted in a closet, where the clients couldn't see it. Maybe it was just another source of revenue. Sell the girls for sex, videotape the acts, then offer the tapes on the pornography market. Every which way you turn, there's money to be made. This brothel was just another one of their subsidiaries, after all.' She paused, and added drily: 'Ballentree seems to believe in diversification.'

'But this is a snuff film! Ballentree could never get away with selling this.'

'No, this was too explosive. The house mother definitely knew it was. She hid it in the tote bag. Mila says they carried around that bag for months without knowing what was on the video. Then Joe finally played it on a motel room VCR.' Jane looked at the TV. 'Now we know why those women in Ashburn were killed. Why Charles Desmond was killed. Because they knew this client; they could ID him. They all had to die.'

'So this is all about covering up a rape and murder.'

She nodded. 'Suddenly Joe realizes he's holding dynamite. What to do with the evidence? He didn't know who to trust. And who would listen to a guy who's already been labeled a paranoid kook? That must be what he sent you. A copy of this tape.'

'Only I never received it.'

'And by then they'd split up, to avoid capture. But each of them took a copy. Olena was caught before she could bring hers to the *Tribune*. Joe's was probably swept up after the hospital take-down.' She pointed to the TV. 'This is the last copy.'

Lukas turned to Mila, who'd been hanging back in a far corner of the room, like a skittish animal afraid to come any closer. 'Have you yourself seen this man in the video, Mila? He came to the house?'

'The boat,' she said, and gave a visible shudder. 'I saw him at a party, on the boat.'

Lukas looked at Jane. 'You think she means Charles Desmond's yacht?'

'I think this is how Ballentree did business,' said Jane. 'Desmond's world was a boys' club. Defense contracts, Pentagon players. Whenever there are big boys playing with a lot of money, you can bet sex comes into it. A way to close the deal.' She ejected the videocassette and turned to face Lukas. 'Do you know who this man is? The one on the video?'

Lukas swallowed hard. 'I'm sorry. I'm just having a hard time believing that tape is real.'

'The man's got to be a major player. Look at everything he's managed to do, the resources he's been able to call up, to track down this video-tape.' She stood before Lukas. 'Who is he?'

'You don't recognize him?'

'Should I?'

'Not unless you were watching last month's confirmation hearings. He's Carleton Wynne. Our new director of National Intelligence.'

She released a sharp breath and sank into a

chair facing him. 'Jesus. You're talking about the guy in charge of every intelligence agency in the country.'

Lukas nodded. 'The FBI. CIA. Military Intelligence. Fifteen agencies in all, including branches of Homeland Security and the Department of Justice. This is someone who can pull strings from the inside. The reason you don't recognize Wynne is that he's not a very public man. He's one of those guys in the gray suits. He left the CIA two years ago, to head up the Pentagon's new Strategic Support Branch. After the last intelligence director was forced to resign, the White House nominated Wynne to replace him. He's just been confirmed.'

'Please,' interjected Mila. 'I need to use the bathroom.'

'It's down the hall,' murmured Lukas, not even glancing up as Mila slipped out of the living room. His gaze stayed on Jane. 'This is not an easy man to bring down,' he said.

'With this videotape, you could bring down King Kong.'

'Director Wynne has a whole network of contacts in the Pentagon and the Company. This is the *President's* hand-picked man.'

'Now he's mine. And I'm taking him down.'

The doorbell rang. Jane looked up, startled.

'Relax,' said Lukas, rising to his feet. 'It's probably just my neighbor. I promised I'd feed his cat for the weekend.'

Despite that reassurance, Jane sat on the edge

of her chair, listening, as Lukas answered the front door. His greeting was a casual: 'Hey, come on in.'

'Everything under control?' the other man said.

'Yeah, we were just watching a video.'

That's the moment she should have understood that something was not right, but Lukas's relaxed tone of voice had disarmed her, had lulled her into feeling safe in this house, in his company. The visitor walked into the room. He had cropped blond hair and powerfully muscled arms. Even when Jane saw the gun he was holding, she did not fully accept what had just happened. Slowly she rose to her feet, her heart pounding in her throat. She turned to Lukas, and her shattered look of betrayal evoked in him merely a shrug. A look of *sorry, but that's how it goes.*

The blond man took in the room at a glance, and his gaze focused on Regina, who slept soundly among the couch cushions. At once he turned his weapon on the baby, and Jane felt a stab of panic, sharp as a knife to the heart. 'Not a word,' he said to Jane. He knew just how to control her, just how to find a mother's most vulnerable spot. 'Where's the whore?' he asked Lukas.

'The bathroom. I'll get her.'

It's too late to warn Mila, thought Jane. Even if I screamed, she would have no chance to escape.

'So you're the cop I heard about,' the blond man said.

The cop. The whore. Did he even know the names of the two women he was about to kill?

'My name is Jane Rizzoli,' she said.

'Wrong place, wrong time, Detective.' He did know her name. Of course; a professional would have to know. He also knew enough to keep a respectful distance from her, far enough away to react to any move she might make. Even without his gun, he was not a man she could easily tackle. His stance, the quietly efficient way he had taken control, told her that, unarmed, she did not have a chance against this man.

But armed . . .

She glanced at the floor. Where the hell had she left the diaper bag? Was it behind the couch? She didn't see it.

'Mila?' Lukas was calling through the bathroom door. 'Are you all right in there?'

Regina suddenly gave a start and let out a jittery cry, as though aware that something was wrong. That her mother was in trouble.

'Let me pick her up,' said Jane.

'She's fine right where she is.'

'If you don't let me pick her up, she'll start screaming. And she knows how to scream.'

'Mila?' Lukas was rapping on the bathroom door now. 'Unlock this, will you? Mila!'

Regina, as predicted, began to howl. Jane looked at the man, and he finally gave a nod. She gathered the baby into her arms, but her embrace seemed to hold no comfort for Regina. *She can feel my heart pounding. She can feel my fear.*

There was banging in the hallway, then a crash as Lukas broke through the door. Seconds later he came running back into the living room, his face flushed. 'She's gone.'

'What?'

'The bathroom window's open. She must have crawled out.'

The blond man reacted with a mere shrug. 'Then we'll find her another day. The video is what he really wants.'

'We have it.'

'You're sure it's the last copy?'

'It's the last.'

Jane stared at Lukas. 'You already knew about the videotape.'

'Do you have any idea how much unsolicited junk a reporter gets in the mail?' said Lukas. 'How many conspiracy theorists and paranoid nuts there are out there, desperate for the public to believe them? I wrote that one column about Ballentree, and suddenly I'm the new best friend for all the Joseph Rokes in this country. All the weirdos. They think if they tell me about their little delusions, I'll take the story from there. I'll be their Woodward and Bernstein.'

'That's how it *should* work. That's what journalists are supposed to do.'

'You know any rich reporters? Once you get past the rare superstars, how many names do you remember? The reality is, the public doesn't give a shit about the truth. Oh, maybe there'd be a flutter of interest for a few weeks. A few front-page stories above the fold. *Director of National Intelligence charged with murder.* The White House would express the appropriate amount of horror, Carleton Wynne would plead guilty, and then this would go the way of every other scandal in Washington. In a few months, the public would forget about it. And I'd go back to writing my column, paying my mortgage, and driving the same beat-up Toyota.' He shook his head. 'As soon as I saw the videotape Olena left me, I knew it was worth a lot more than just a Pulitzer. I knew who'd pay me for it.'

'That video Joe sent you. You *did* receive it.'

'Almost threw it away, too. Then I thought, what the hell, let's see what's on it. I recognized Carleton Wynne right away. Until I picked up the phone and called him, he didn't even know the tape existed. He thought he was just chasing down a couple of whores. Suddenly this got much, much more serious. And more expensive.'

'He was actually willing to deal with you?'

'Wouldn't you be? Knowing what this tape could do to you? Knowing there are other copies floating around out there?'

'Do you really think Wynne is going to let you live? Now that you've given him Joe and Olena? There's nothing else he needs from you.'

The blond man cut in: 'I'll need a shovel.'

But Lukas was still looking at Jane. 'I'm not stupid,' he said. 'And Wynne knows that.'

422

'The shovel?' the blond man repeated.

'There's one in the garage,' said Lukas.

'Get it for me.'

As Lukas walked toward the garage, Jane called out: 'You're a moron if you think you're going to live long enough to enjoy any payoff.' Regina had fallen silent in her arms, stilled by her mother's rage. 'You've seen how these people play the game. You know how Charles Desmond died. They're going to find you in *your* bathtub with *your* wrists slit. Or they'll force a bottle of phenobarb tablets down your throat and dump you in the bay, like they did to Olena. Or maybe this guy will just put a bullet in your head, nice and simple.'

Lukas came back into the house, carrying a spade. He handed it to the blond man.

'How deep do those woods go, in back of the house?' the man asked.

'It's part of Blue Hills Reservation. They go back at least a mile.'

'We'll need to walk her in far enough.'

'Look, I don't want anything to do with that. That's what he pays you for.'

'Then you'll have to take care of her car.'

'Wait.' Lukas reached behind the couch and came up holding the diaper bag. He handed it to the other man. 'I don't want any trace of her in my house.'

Give it to me, thought Jane. Give me my goddamn bag.

Instead, the blond man slung it over his

shoulder and said: 'Let's take a walk in the woods, Detective.'

Jane turned to give Lukas her parting shot. 'You'll get yours. You're a dead man.'

Outside, a half-moon glowed in a starry sky. Holding Regina, Jane stumbled through underbrush and saplings, her path faintly lit by the beam of the gunman's flashlight. He was careful to follow at a distance, giving her no chance to strike out at him. She could not have, in any event, not with Regina in her arms. Regina, who had known only a few short weeks of life.

'My baby can't hurt you,' Jane said. 'She's not even a month old.'

The man said nothing. The only sound was their footfalls in the woods. The snap of twigs, the rustle of leaves. So much noise, but no one was around to listen. *If a woman falls in the forest, but no one hears her . . .*

'You could just take her,' said Jane. 'Leave her where someone will find her.'

'She's not my problem.'

'She's just a *baby*!' Jane's voice suddenly broke. She paused there among the trees, clutching her daughter to her chest as tears flooded her throat. Regina gave a soft coo, as though to comfort her, and Jane pressed her face to her daughter's head and inhaled the sweetness of her hair, felt the heat of her velvety cheeks. How could I bring you into this? she thought. There is no worse mistake a mother can make. And now you'll die with me.

'Keep walking,' he said.

I've fought back before and survived, she thought. I can do it again. I *have* to do it again, *for you*.

'Or do you just want me to finish it here?' he said.

She took a deep breath, inhaling the scent of trees and damp leaves. She thought of the human remains she had examined in Stony Brook Reservation a summer ago. How vines had snaked through the orbital fossae, hugging the skull in greedy tendrils. How the hands and feet were missing, gnawed off and carried away by scavengers. She felt her own pulse, bounding in her fingers, and thought of how small and fragile were the bones in a human hand. How easily they are scattered across a forest floor.

She began to walk again, deeper into the woods. Keep your head, she thought. Panic, and you lose all chance to surprise him. All chance to save Regina. Her senses sharpened. She could feel the blood pumping through her calves, could almost feel every molecule of air that brushed against her face. You only come alive, she thought, just as you're about to die.

'I think this is far enough,' the man said.

They were standing in a small clearing. Trees encircled them, a dark ring of silent witnesses. The stars were cold glitters. None of this will change when I'm gone, she thought. The stars don't care. The trees don't care.

He threw the shovel at her feet. 'Start digging.'

'What about my baby?'

'Put her down and start digging.'

'The ground's so hard.'

'Like that matters now?' He tossed the diaper bag at her feet. 'Let her lie down on that.'

Jane knelt, her heart now thumping so wildly she thought it would slam through her ribs. I have one chance, she thought. Reach in the bag, grab the weapon. Turn and squeeze off the round before he knows what's happening. No mercy, just blow out his brains.

'Poor baby,' she murmured as she crouched over the bag. As she quietly slipped her hand inside. 'Mommy has to put you down now . . .' Her hand brushed across her wallet, a baby bottle, diapers. *My gun. Where is my goddamn gun?*

'Just set the baby down.'

It's not here. Her breath whooshed out of her in a sob. *Of course he took it. He's not stupid. I'm a cop; he knew I'd be carrying.*

'Dig.'

She bent down to give Regina a kiss, a caress, then laid her on the ground with the diaper bag as a cushion. She picked up the shovel and slowly rose to her feet. Her legs felt drained of all energy, all hope. He was standing too far away for her to swing at him with the shovel. Even if she threw it, it would stun him only for a few seconds. Not enough time to pick up Regina and run.

She looked down at the ground. Under the

426

light of the half-moon, she saw a scattering of leaves on moss. Her bed for eternity. *Gabriel will never find us here. He will never know.*

She planted the spade in the soil, and felt the first tears trickle down her cheek as she began to dig.

Thirty-six

The door to his apartment was ajar.

Gabriel paused in the hallway, instincts prickling with alarm. He heard voices talking inside, and the sound of footsteps pacing across the floor. He gave the door a push and stepped in. 'What are you doing here?'

John Barsanti turned from the window to face him. His first question took Gabriel aback. 'Do you know where your wife is, Agent Dean?'

'Isn't she here?' His gaze swung to the second visitor, who'd just emerged from the baby's room. It was Helen Glasser from the Justice Department, her silver hair pulled back in a tight ponytail, starkly emphasizing the worried lines of her face.

'The bedroom window's wide open,' she said.

'How did you two get in here?'

'Your building super let us in,' said Glasser. 'We couldn't wait any longer.'

'Where's Jane?'

'That's what we'd like to know.'

'She should be here.'

'How long have you been gone? When did you last see your wife?'

He stared at Glasser, unnerved by the urgency in her voice. 'I've been gone about an hour. I drove her mother home.'

'Has Jane called you since you left?'

'No.' He started toward the telephone.

'She doesn't answer her cell, Agent Dean,' said Glasser. 'We've already tried reaching her. We *need* to reach her.'

He turned to look at them. 'What the hell is going on?'

Glasser asked, quietly: 'Is she with Mila right now?'

'The girl never showed up at the . . .' He paused. 'You already knew that. You were watching the park, too.'

'That girl is our last witness,' said Glasser. 'If she's with your wife, we need to know.'

'Jane and the baby were alone here when I left.'

'Then where are they now?'

'I don't know.'

'You understand, Agent Dean, that if Mila is with her, Jane is in a very dangerous situation.'

'My wife knows how to take care of herself. She wouldn't walk into anything without making damn sure she's prepared.' He crossed to the drawer where Jane usually stored her weapon and found the drawer unlocked. He yanked it open and stared at the empty holster.

She took her gun.

'Agent Dean?'

Gabriel slammed the drawer shut and went into the bedroom. As Glasser had reported, the window was wide open. Now he was scared. He walked back into the living room and felt Glasser's gaze searching his face, reading his fear.

'Where would she go?' Glasser said.

'She'd call *me*, that's what she'd do.'

'Not if she thought her phone was tapped.'

'Then she'd go to the police. She'd drive straight to Schroeder Plaza.'

'We've already called Boston PD. She's not there.'

'We need to find that girl,' said Barsanti. 'We need her alive.'

'Let me try her cell phone one more time. Maybe this is nothing at all. Maybe she just ran out to the store to buy milk.' *Right. And she took her gun with her.* He picked up the receiver and was about to punch in the first number when he suddenly frowned, his gaze on the keypad. A long shot, he thought. But just maybe . . .

He pressed redial.

After three rings, a man answered. 'Hello?'

Gabriel paused, trying to place the voice. Knowing he had heard it before. Then he remembered. 'Is this . . . Peter Lukas?'

'Yes.'

'It's Gabriel Dean. Would Jane happen to be there?'

There was a long silence. A strange silence. 'No. Why?'

'Your number's on our redial. She must have called you.'

'Oh, that.' Lukas gave a laugh. 'She wanted all my notes on the Ballentree story. I told her I'd dig them up.'

'When was that?'

'Let me think. It was about an hour ago.'

'And that was it? She didn't say anything else?'

'No. Why?'

'I'll keep calling around, then. Thanks.' He hung up and stood staring down at the phone. Thinking about that silence when Lukas had not immediately answered his question. *Something is very wrong.*

'Agent Dean?' said Glasser.

He turned and looked at her. 'What do you know about Peter Lukas?'

The hole was now knee-deep.

Jane scooped up another spadeful of dirt and heaved it onto the growing mound of soil. Her tears had stopped, to be replaced by sweat. She worked in silence. The only sounds were the scraping of the shovel and the clatter of pebbles. Regina was quiet, too, as though she understood that there was no longer any point in making a fuss. That her fate, like that of her mother's, had already been decided.

No it hasn't. Goddammit, nothing has been decided.

Jane rammed the spade into stony soil, and though her back ached and her arms were quivering, she felt the heat of rage flood her muscles like the most potent of fuel. You won't hurt my baby, she thought. I will rip off your head first. She heaved the soil onto the mound, her aches and fatigue unimportant now, her mind focused on what she had to do next. The killer was only a silhouette standing at the edge of the trees. Though she could not see his face, she knew he must be watching her. But she'd been digging for nearly an hour, her efforts stymied by the rocky soil, and his attention would be flagging. What resistance, after all, could an exhausted woman mount against an armed man? She had nothing working in her favor.

Only surprise. And a mother's rage.

His first shot would be rushed. He'd go for the torso first, not the head. No matter what, just keep moving, she thought, keep charging. A bullet takes time to kill, and even a falling body has momentum.

She bent to scrape up another load of dirt, her spade deep in the hole's shadow, hidden from the beam of his flashlight. He could not see her muscles tense, or her foot brace itself against the edge of the hole. He did not hear her intake of breath as her hands clamped around the shovel handle. She crouched, limbs coiled tight.

This is for you, my darling baby. All for you.

Lifting the spade into the air, she flung the soil at the man's face. He stumbled backward, grunting in surprise, as she sprang out of the hole. As she charged headfirst, straight at his abdomen.

They both went down, branches snapping under the weight of their bodies. She lunged for his weapon, her hands closing around his wrist, and suddenly realized he was no longer holding it, that it had been knocked from his grasp when they'd fallen.

The gun. Find the gun!

She twisted away and clawed through underbrush, scrabbling for the weapon.

The blow knocked her sideways. She landed on her back, breathless from the impact. At first she felt no pain, only the numb shock that the battle was so quickly over. Her face began to sting, and then the real pain shrieked its way into her skull. She saw that he was standing above her, his head blotting out the stars. She heard Regina screaming, the final wails of her short life. *Poor baby. You'll never know how much I loved you.*

'Get in the hole,' he said. 'It's deep enough now.'

'Not my baby,' she whispered. 'She's so small—'

'Get in, bitch.'

His kick thudded into her ribs and she rolled onto her side, unable to scream because it hurt so much just to breathe.

'Move,' he commanded.

Slowly she struggled to her knees and crawled to Regina. Felt something warm and wet trickling from her nose. Gathering the baby into her arms, she pressed her lips to soft wisps of hair and rocked back and forth, her blood dripping onto her baby's head. *Mommy has you. Mommy will never let you go.*

'It's time,' he said.

Thirty-seven

Gabriel stared into Jane's parked Subaru, and his heart gave a sickening lurch. Her cell phone was on the dashboard, and the baby seat was buckled into the back. He turned, aiming his flashlight directly at Peter Lukas's face.

'Where is she?'

Lukas's gaze flitted to Barsanti and Glasser, who were standing a few feet away, watching the confrontation in silence.

'This is her car,' said Gabriel. 'Where is she?'

Lukas raised his hand to shield his eyes against the glare of the flashlight. 'She must have knocked on my door while I was in the shower. I didn't even notice that her car was parked out here.'

'First she calls you, then she comes to your house. Why?'

'I don't know—'

'Why?' Gabriel repeated.

'She's *your* wife. Don't you know?'

Gabriel went for the man's throat so quickly

that Lukas didn't have time to react. He stumbled backward against Barsanti's car, his head slamming onto the hood. Gasping for air, he clawed at Gabriel's hands but could not free himself, could only flail helplessly, his back pinned against the car.

'Dean,' said Barsanti. 'Dean!'

Gabriel released Lukas and backed away, breathing hard, trying not to give in to panic. But it was already there, gripping his throat as surely as he had gripped Lukas, who was now down on his knees, coughing and wheezing. Gabriel turned to the house. Ran up the steps and banged through the front door. Moving at a blur now, he ran from room to room, opening doors, checking closets. Only when he came back into the living room did he spot what he had missed on the first pass: Jane's car keys, lying on the carpet behind the couch. He stared down at them, panic freezing into dread. You were in this house, he thought. You and Regina . . .

Distant gunshots made his head snap up.

He ran out of the house, onto the porch.

'It came from the woods,' said Barsanti.

They all froze at the crack of a third gunshot.

All at once, Gabriel was running, heedless of whipping branches and saplings as he plunged into the woods. His flashlight beam danced crazily across a forest floor strewn with dead leaves and fallen birches. Which way, which way? Was he going in the right direction?

A tangle of vines caught his ankle and he

436

pitched forward, landing on his knees. He rose back to his feet, chest heaving, as he caught his breath.

'Jane?' he shouted. His voice broke, her name fading to a whisper. 'Jane . . .'

Help me find you. Show me the way.

He stood listening, trees looming all around him like the bars of a prison. Beyond the beam of his flashlight was a night so thick it might be solid, unbreachable.

From the distance came the snap of a twig.

He spun around, but could see nothing beyond his flashlight's glow. He shut off the light and stared, heart thudding, as he strained to make out anything at all in the darkness. Only then did he see the twinkling, so faint it might merely be fireflies dancing among the trees. Another snap of a twig. The light was moving in his direction.

He drew his weapon. Held it pointed toward the ground as he watched the light grow brighter. He could not see who was wielding the other flashlight, but he could hear the approaching footfalls, the rustle of leaves, only a few yards away now.

He raised his weapon. Switched on the flashlight.

Caught in the beam of Gabriel's light, the figure shrank like a terrified animal, eyes squinting against the glare. He stared at the pale face, the spiky red hair. Just a girl, he thought. Just a scared, skinny girl.

'Mila?' he said.

Then he saw the other figure emerge from the shadows right behind the girl. Even before he saw her face, he recognized the walk, the silhouette of unruly curls.

He dropped the flashlight and ran toward his wife and daughter, arms already open and hungry to hold them. She leaned against him, shaking, her arms wrapped around Regina, just as his arms were wrapped around her. A hug within a hug, their whole family contained in the universe of his embrace.

'I heard gunshots,' he said. 'I thought—'

'It was Mila,' Jane whispered.

'What?'

'She took my gun. She followed us . . .' Jane suddenly stiffened and looked up at him. 'Where's Peter Lukas?'

'Barsanti's watching him. He's not going anywhere.'

Jane released a shuddering breath and turned to face the woods. 'There'll be scavengers showing up for the body. We need to get CSU out here.'

'Whose body?'

'I'll show you.'

Gabriel stood at the edge of the trees, staying out of the way of the detectives and the crime scene unit, his gaze fixed on the open hole that would have been the grave of his wife and daughter. Police tape had been strung around the site, and battery-powered lights glared down on the man's body. Maura Isles, who'd been crouching over the corpse, now rose to her feet and turned to Detectives Moore and Crowe.

'I see three entry wounds,' she said. 'Two in the chest, one in the forehead.'

'That's what we heard,' said Gabriel. 'Three shots.'

Maura looked at him. 'How long an interval between them?'

Gabriel thought about it, and felt once again the echoes of panic. He remembered his plunge into the woods, and how, with every step, his sense of dread had mounted. 'There were two in quick succession,' he said. 'The third shot was about five, ten seconds after that.'

Maura was silent as her gaze swung back to the corpse. She stared down at the man's blond hair, the powerful shoulders. A SIG Sauer lay near his right hand.

'Well,' said Crowe, 'I'd call this a pretty obvious case of self-defense.'

No one said anything, not about the powder burns on the face, or the delay between the second and third shots. But they all knew.

Gabriel turned and walked back toward the house.

The driveway was now crammed with vehicles. He paused there, temporarily blinded by the flashing blue lights of cruisers. Then he spotted Helen Glasser helping the girl into the front passenger seat of her car.

'Where are you taking her?' he asked.

Glasser turned to him, her hair reflecting the cruiser lights like blue foil. 'Somewhere safe.'

'Is there any such place for her?'

'Believe me, I'll find one.' Glasser paused by the driver's door and glanced back toward the house. 'The videotape changes everything, you know. And we can turn Lukas around. He has no choice now, he'll cooperate with us. So you see, it doesn't all rest with the girl. She's important, but she's not the only weapon we have.'

'Even so, will it be enough to bring down Carleton Wynne?'

'No one's above the law, Agent Dean.' Glasser looked at him, her eyes reflecting steel. 'No one.' She slid in behind the wheel.

'Wait,' called out Gabriel. 'I need to speak to the girl.'

'And we need to leave.'

'It'll only take a minute.' Gabriel circled to the passenger side, opened the door, and peered in at Mila. She was hugging herself, shrinking against the seat as though afraid of his intentions. Just a kid, he thought, yet she's tougher than all of us. Given half a chance, she'll survive anything.

'Mila,' he said gently.

She gazed back with eyes that did not trust him; perhaps she would never again trust a man, and why should she? *She has seen the worst we have to offer.*

'I want to thank you,' he said. 'Thank you for giving me back my family.'

There it was – just the wisp of a smile. It was more than he'd expected.

He closed the door, and gave a nod to Glasser. 'Take him down,' he called out.

'That's why they pay me the big bucks,' she said with a laugh, and she drove away, followed by a Boston PD escort.

Gabriel climbed the steps into the house. Inside he found Barry Frost conferring with Barsanti as members of the FBI's Evidence Response Team carried out Lukas's computer and boxes of his files. This was clearly a federal case now, and Boston PD would be ceding control of the investigation to the Bureau. Even so, thought Gabriel, how far can they take it? Then Barsanti looked at him, and Gabriel saw in his eyes the same steel he'd seen in Glasser's. And he noticed that Barsanti was clutching the video-tape. Guarding it, as though he held the Holy Grail itself.

'Where's Jane?' he asked Frost.

'She's in the kitchen. The baby got hungry.'

He found his wife sitting with her back to the doorway; she did not see him walk into the room. He paused behind her, watching as she cradled Regina to her breast, humming tune-lessly. Jane never could carry a tune, he thought with a smile. Regina didn't seem to mind; she lay quiet in her mother's newly confident arms. Love is the part that comes naturally, thought Gabriel. It's everything else that takes time. That we have to learn.

He placed his hands on Jane's shoulders and bent down to kiss her hair. She looked up at him, her eyes glowing.

'Let's go home,' she said.

Thirty-eight

Mila

The woman has been kind to me. As our car bumps along the dirt road, she takes my hand and squeezes it. I feel safe with her, even though I know she will not always be here to hold my hand; there are so many other girls to think of, other girls who are still lost in the dark corners of this country. But for now she is here with me. She is my protector, and I lean into her, hoping she will put her arm around me. But she is distracted, her gaze focused instead on the desert outside our car. A strand of her hair has fallen onto my sleeve and glitters there like a silver thread. I pluck it up and slip it into my pocket. It may be the only souvenir I will ever have to remember her by when our time together ends.

The car rolls to a stop.

'Mila,' she says, giving me a nudge. 'Are we getting close? Does this area look right?'

I lift my head from her shoulder and stare out

the window. We have stopped beside a dry riverbed, where trees grow stunted, tormented. Beyond are brown hills studded with boulders. 'I don't know,' I tell her.

'Does it look like the place?'

'Yes, but . . .' I keep staring, forcing myself to remember what I have tried so hard to forget.

One of the men in the front seat looks back at us. 'That's where they found the trail, on the other side of that riverbed,' he says. 'They caught a group of girls coming through here last week. Maybe she should get out and take a look. See if she recognizes anything down there.'

'Come, Mila.' The woman opens the door and gets out, but I do not move. She reaches into the car. 'It's the only way we can do this,' she says softly. 'You need to help us find the spot.' She holds out her hand. Reluctantly, I take it.

One of the men leads us through the tangle of scrub brush and trees, down a narrow trail and into the dry riverbed. There he stops and looks at me. He and the woman are both watching me, waiting for my reaction. I stare at the bank, at an old shoe lying dry and cracked in the heat. A memory shimmers, then snaps into focus. I turn and look at the opposite bank, which is cluttered with plastic bottles, and I see a scrap of blue tarp dangling from a branch.

Another memory locks in place.

This is where he hit me. This is where Anja stood, her foot bleeding in her open-toed shoe.

Without a word, I turn and climb back up the

riverbank. My heart is racing, and dread clamps its fingers around my throat, but I have no choice now. I see her ghost, flitting just ahead of me. A wisp of windblown hair. A sad, backward glance.

'Mila?' the woman calls.

I keep moving, pushing my way through the bushes, until I reach the dirt road. Here, I think. This is where the vans were parked. This is where the men waited for us. The memories are clicking faster now, like terrible flashes from a nightmare. The men, leering as we undress. The girl shrieking as she is shoved up against the van. And Anja. I see Anja, lying motionless on her back as the man who has just raped her zips up his pants.

Anja stirs, staggers to her feet like a newborn calf. So pale, so thin, just a shadow of a girl.

I follow her, the ghost of Anja. The desert is strewn with sharp rocks. Thorny weeds push up from the dirt, and Anja is running across them, stumbling on bloody feet. Sobbing, reaching toward what she thinks is freedom.

'Mila?'

I hear Anja's panicked gasps, see the blond hair streaming loose around her shoulders. Empty desert stretches before her. If she can just run fast enough, far enough . . .

The gunshot cracks.

I see her pitch forward, the breath knocked out of her, and her blood spills onto warm sand. Yet she rises to her knees and crawls now across thorns, across stones that cut like shards of glass.

The second gunshot thunders.

Anja collapses, white skin against brown sand. Is this where she fell? Or was it over there? I am circling now, frantic to find the spot. *Where are you, Anja, where?*

'Mila, talk to us.'

I suddenly halt, my gaze fixed on the ground. The woman is saying something to me; I scarcely hear her. I can only stare at what lies at my feet.

The woman says, gently, 'Come away, Mila. Don't look.'

But I cannot move. I stand frozen as the two men crouch down. As one of them pulls on gloves and brushes away sand to reveal leathery ribs and the brown dome of a skull.

'It appears to be a female,' he says.

For a moment no one speaks. A hot wind swirls dust at our faces, and I blink against the sting. When I open my eyes again, I see more of Anja peeking out from the sand. The curve of her hip bone, the brown shaft of her thigh. The desert has decided to give her up, and now she is re-emerging from the earth.

Those who vanish sometimes come back to us.

'Come, Mila. Let's go.'

I look up at the woman. She stands so straight, unassailable. Her silver hair gleams like a warrior's helmet. She puts her arm around me, and together, we walk back to the car.

'It's time, Mila,' the woman says quietly. 'Time to tell me everything.'

We sit at a table, in a room with no windows.

I look down at the pad of paper in front of her. It is blank, waiting for the mark of her pen. Waiting for the words that I have been afraid to say.

'I have told you everything.'

'I don't think you have.'

'Every question you ask, I answer.'

'Yes, you've helped us a great deal. You've given us what we needed. Carleton Wynne *is* going to jail. He *is* going to pay. The whole world now knows what he did, and we thank you for that.'

'I do not know what more you want from me.'

'I want what's locked up in there.' She reaches across the table and touches my heart. 'I want to know the things you're afraid to tell me. It will help me understand their operation, help me fight these people. It will help me save more girls, just like you. You *have* to, Mila.'

I blink back tears. 'Or you will send me back.'

'No. *No.*' She leans closer, her gaze emphatic. 'This is your home now, if you want to stay. You won't be deported, I give you my word.'

'Even if . . .' I stop. I can no longer look her in the eye. Shame floods my face and I stare down at the table.

'Nothing that happened to you is your fault. Whatever those men did to you – whatever they made you do – they forced on you. It was done to your body. It has nothing to do with your soul. Your soul, Mila, is still pure.'

I cannot bear to meet her gaze. I continue to

stare down, watching my own tears drip onto the table, and feel as if my heart is bleeding, that every tear is another part of me, draining away.

'Why are you afraid to look at me?' she asks gently.

'I am ashamed,' I whisper. 'All the things you wish me to tell you . . .'

'Would it help if I wasn't here in the room? If I didn't watch you?'

I still do not look at her.

She releases a sigh. 'All right, Mila, here's what I'm going to do.' She places a tape recorder on the table. 'I'm going to turn this on and leave the room. Then you can say whatever you want to. Whatever you remember. Say it all in Russian if that makes it easier. Any thoughts, any memories. Everything that's happened to you. You're not talking to a person, you're just talking to a machine. It can't hurt you.'

She rises to her feet, presses the RECORD button, and walks out of the room.

I stare at the red light glowing on the machine. The tape is slowly spinning, waiting for my first words. Waiting for my pain. I take a deep breath, close my eyes. And I begin to speak.

My name is Mila, and this is my journey.

THE END

Acknowledgements

My deepest thanks for my guiding light and literary agent Meg Ruley, to Jane Berkey and Don Cleary of the Jane Rotrosen Agency, to Linda Marrow and Gina Centrello at Ballantine Books, and to Selina Walker at Transworld. You all made it happen.

DON'T MISS THE NEW RIZZOLI & ISLES THRILLER BY TESS GERRITSEN

Detective Jane Rizzoli and **Forensic Pathologist Maura Isles** are investigating the gruesome murder of a nurse, whilst also protecting a young student from a stalker. But immersed in their day jobs, will they lose sight of something sinister happening much closer to home?

OUT NOW IN PAPERBACK, EBOOK AND AUDIO

One

Amy

I should have worn my boots, she thought as she stepped out of Snell Library and saw the fresh layer of sleet and slush covering the campus. When she'd left for school that morning it had been a balmy forty-nine degrees, one in a string of springlike days that made her believe winter was finally over, and she had come to campus wearing blue jeans and a hoodie and brand-new pink flats made of buttery leather. But while she'd been inside all day working on her laptop, outside, winter had come roaring back. Now it was dark, and with this frigid wind sweeping across the courtyard, the pavement would soon be as slick as an ice rink.

With a sigh, she zipped up her hoodie and hauled her backpack, heavy with books and her laptop, onto her shoulders. *There's no way around it. Here we go.* Gingerly she descended the library stairs and landed ankle-deep in slush. Her feet now wet and stinging, she forged ahead down the path between Haydn Hall and Blackman Auditorium. Well, these new shoes were ruined. Stupid, stupid.

That's what she got for not checking the forecast this morning. For forgetting that March in Boston could break a girl's heart.

She reached Eli Hall and suddenly stopped. Turned. Were those footsteps she'd heard behind her? For a moment she stared at the alley that cut between the two buildings but all she saw was the deserted walkway, glistening beneath the lamplight. Darkness and bad weather had emptied out the campus and she heard no footsteps now, just the rattle of falling sleet and the distant *whish* of cars traveling down Huntington Avenue.

She hugged her hoodie tighter and kept walking.

The campus quadrangle was slick and gleaming with a crust of ice and her sadly inadequate shoes crunched through the rime into puddles, splashing her jeans with ice water. She could no longer feel her toes.

This was all Prof. Harthoorn's fault. He was the reason she'd spent all day in the library, the reason she wasn't at home right now, eating dinner with her parents. But here she was, toes numb with impending frostbite, all because her senior thesis – the thirty-two-page paper she'd been working on for months – was *incomplete*, he'd said. *Inadequate*, he'd said, because she hadn't addressed the pivotal event in Artemisia Gentileschi's life, the life-changing trauma that imbued her paintings with such violent and visceral power: being raped.

As if women were formless lumps of clay, needing to be pummeled and abused to be shaped into something greater. As if what Artemisia needed to become an artist was a good old-fashioned sexual assault.

She felt more and more angry about Harthoorn's comments as she walked across the quad, splashing through slush. What did a dried-up old man like him know about women and all the wearying and infuriating annoyances they had to tolerate? All the helpful advice foisted on them by men with their *I know better* voices.

She reached the crosswalk and stopped at the pedestrian light, which had just turned red. Of course it was red; nothing today had gone her way. Cars rolled past, tires spraying up water. Sleet clattered on her backpack, and she thought about her laptop and whether it was getting wet and she'd lose all the work she'd put in this afternoon. Yes, that would perfectly cap off her day. It's what she deserved for not checking the forecast. For not bringing an umbrella. For wearing these stupid shoes.

The light was still red. Was it broken? Should she ignore it and just make a dash across the street?

She was so focused on the light that she wasn't aware of the man standing behind her. Then something about him caught her attention. Perhaps it was the rustle of his nylon jacket, or the odor of alcohol drifting on his breath. All at once she knew someone was there and she turned to look at him.

He was so bundled up against the cold, with a scarf wrapped up to his chin and a wool cap pulled down to his eyebrows, that all she could really see of his face were his eyes. He didn't avoid her gaze but looked straight back at her with a stare so piercing that she felt violated, as if that stare was vacuuming out her deepest secrets. He made no move toward her but his gaze was enough to make her uneasy.

She glanced across Huntington Avenue, at the businesses across the street. The taco shop was open, its windows brightly lit, and she could see half a dozen customers inside. A safe place, with people to turn to if she needed help. She could duck in there to get warm, and maybe call an Uber to take her home.

The light turned green at last.

She stepped too quickly off the curb and the sole of her leather flat instantly skidded across the ice-slicked road. Arms flywheeling, she fought to stay upright but the backpack threw her off-balance and down she went, her rump splashing down into slush. Soaked and shaken, she staggered back to her feet.

She never saw the headlights hurtling toward her.

Two

Angela

Two Months Later

If you see something, say something. We've all heard that advice so many times that whenever we find a suspicious package where it shouldn't be, or notice a stranger lurking in the neighborhood, we automatically pay attention. Certainly I do, especially since my daughter, Jane, is a cop, and my boyfriend, Vince, is a retired cop. I've heard all their horror stories and if I see something, you bet I'm going to say something. So it's only second nature for me to keep an eye on my own neighborhood.

I live in the city of Revere, which strictly speaking isn't in the city of Boston proper, but is more like Boston's more affordable cousin to the north. Mine is a street of modest single-family homes tucked in side by side. *Starter homes* was what Frank (soon to be my ex-husband) called them when we moved here forty years ago, except that we never moved on to anything bigger. Neither did

Agnes Kaminsky who still lives next door, or Glen Druckmeyer who died in the house across the street, which made it the opposite of a starter home for him. As the years went by, I watched families move in, then move out. The house to my right is once again vacant and for sale, waiting for the next family to cycle through. To my left lives Agnes, who used to be my best friend until I started dating Vince Korsak, which scandalized Agnes because my divorce isn't final yet, and this made me a scarlet woman in her eyes. Even though Frank was the one who walked out of our marriage to be with another woman. A blonde. What really turned Agnes against me is the fact I *enjoy* myself so much now that Frank's gone. I *enjoy* having a new man in my life and kissing him in my own backyard. What does Agnes think I'm supposed to do now that my husband's left me? Drape myself in virtuous black and keep my legs crossed until everything down there dries up? She and I hardly talk anymore, but we don't need to. I already know what she's up to next door. The same things she's always done: smoking her Virginia Slims, watching QVC, and overcooking her vegetables.

But that's not for me to judge.

Across the street, starting at the corner, is the blue house owned by Larry and Lorelei Leopold, who've lived here for the past twenty or so years. Larry teaches English at the local high school, and while I can't say we're close, we do play Scrabble together every Thursday night so I'm well acquainted with the breadth of Larry's vocabulary. Next to the Leopolds is the house where Glen Druckmeyer died, which used to be for rent. And next door to that, in the house directly across the street from me, lives Jonas, a sixty-two-year-old bachelor and former Navy SEAL who moved here six years ago. Lorelei recently invited Jonas to the Scrabble nights at my house, which should've been a group decision, but Jonas turned out to be an excellent addition. He always brings a bottle of Ecco Domani cabernet, he has a good vocabulary, and he doesn't try to sneak in foreign words, which shouldn't be allowed. Scrabble is, after all, an American game. I have to admit, he's also a fine-looking fellow. Unfortunately he knows it, and he likes to mow his front lawn while shirtless, his chest puffed out, his biceps bulging. Naturally, I can't help but watch him and he knows it. When he sees me at my window, he makes a point of waving to me, which makes Agnes Kaminsky think something's going on between us, which isn't true. I'm just everyone's friendly neighbor, and if someone moves onto our street, I'm always the first at their door with a smile and zucchini bread. People appreciate that. They invite me into their homes, introduce their children, tell me where they're from and what they do for a living. They ask me to recommend a plumber or a dentist. We exchange phone numbers and promises to get together soon. That's how it's been with all my neighbors.

Until the Greens moved in.

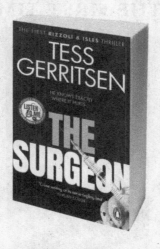

dead good

Looking for more gripping must-reads?

Head over to Dead Good —
the home of killer crime books,
TV and film.

Whether you're on the hunt for an intriguing
mystery, an action-packed thriller
or a creepy psychological drama,
we're here to keep you in the loop.

Get recommendations and reviews from
crime fans, grab discounted books at bargain
prices and enter exclusive giveaways
for the chance to read brand-new releases
before they hit the shelves.

Sign up for the free newsletter:
www.deadgoodbooks.co.uk/newsletter